THE FOSSIL

JOSHUA T. CALVERT

DEDICATION AND ACKNOWLEDGMENTS

This book is dedicated to my life partner, Ellada Azoidou. Not only has she supported my literary efforts from day one with her fantastic cover art, but for so many years she has supported anything and everything I have taken it into my head to do. She has been my Greek guardian angel, and I have only ever known her to be the most helpful, most understanding, and most of all, the toughest person I have ever encountered along this journey called Life.

When I think of covering her with the words of gratitude I have for her in my heart, I feel like a jeweler presented with a flawless gemstone—what possible material could there be in which to set such natural perfection, this jewel that outshines everything around it?

We have already sat together in an Iranian prison, been nearly kidnapped in Kyrgyzstan, camped out with Uzbeki smugglers, and suffered through tropical fever together in a Vietnamese hospital with the world falling down around us—literally! When I think of these things, I am blown away by what can bring two people closer together in this world. And that world is a beautiful place, for it has produced you, and it has been kind enough to make you able to put up with this tiresome old dog, for which he will be forever thankful. At the risk of sounding overly, Hellenically, romantic—you are my ambrosia. Nourished by you, I shall never hunger.

Though I never dared to write a dedication for any of my previous novels, this one was long overdue. Without you, I would never have had the courage to put my stories out into this world. They are not my books, but *ours*, σε αγαπάω!

PROLOGUE

TRANSCRIPTION OF THE CLOSED-DOOR UN HEARING DC-4-88
ON THE OPERATION RED HOPE DISASTER, NEW YORK,
FEBRUARY 4TH, 2040. SOURCE: UNITED NATIONS ARCHIVES.

Abbreviations used in the transcription: SG – Secretary-General, HS – Head of State, SE – Special Envoy, S – Subject

SG Mombatu: Dr. Amorosa, you are the sole survivor of the *Mars One* explosion. Can you explain why that is?

S Amorosa: Sir, I think the answer to your question has already been reported on every newsfeed in the world, and has been dissected down to the finest details since then.

SG Mombatu: Dr. Amorosa, if I could offer you a word of advice, it would be to take this hearing seriously and simply answer our questions. Otherwise this will turn into a very long and unpleasant session for you.

S Amorosa: Very well, sir. During re-entry, we got an error message from EDI. Apparently some of the foam sealant had expanded and caused a hairline crack in the heat shield of *Mars One*. That eventually allowed plasma to penetrate the aluminum cover of the right valve control, and that ultimately caused the destruction of the ship. Right before the explosion, when it was clear we weren't going to make it, Commander Vlachenko ordered me to check the cargo covers.

HS Phelps: But you survived, Doctor Amorosa. How do you explain that?

S Amorosa: I can't, sir. I can't.

HS Greulich: What's the first thing you remember after the crash, Doctor?

S Amorosa: I was in the water, and I saw the surface getting farther away from me, so I tried to swim up to it.

HS Phelps: Did you also see any part of 'The Object?'

S Amorosa: I am not sure I recall.

HS Phelps: What's that supposed to mean, you're 'not sure?'

S Amorosa: Sir, Mr. President, I was fighting for my life, and I didn't understand where I was or what I was seeing. I saw a lot of debris, a lot of wreckage, fire on the surface of the water, and I could hardly breathe because my suit had been damaged.

HS Phelps: So you would say it's possible that The Object was not destroyed at all, as is assumed?

S Amorosa: With all due respect, sir, since my return from Mars, I don't even know what I would say is possible.

HS Greulich: Ms. Amorosa, would you please tell again about what you found?

S Amorosa: Mr. Chancellor, I...

HS Greulich: Listen, Ms. Amorosa. You were a member of the first manned mission to Mars, and I'm sure I don't have to tell you the preparations and the financial commitments from the international community that were required to make this mission happen. Now, you were on that mission. So you'll just have to excuse us if you have to answer a few questions more than once. We're not interested in the media, or your future tell-all book—what we're interested in are the facts that we are asking you about right here. Do you understand?

S Amorosa: Yes, sir. It was in the fourth week after our landing at the Olympus Zero outpost. We were still sorting through what equipment and supplies had been used up in the previous unmanned missions, and getting the kilopower nuclear reactor—that had been brought two years earlier on the MMR—up and running. Dr. Marks and I were assigned to look for the entrance to the lava tunnels that had been seen on the satellite images.

SG Mombatu: And you found them.

S Amorosa: Yes, Mr. Secretary-General. We did find an entrance where we thought we would. It was an elongated depression in the regolith, curving slightly to the northeast, that led us into one of the bigger caves. It was about sixty meters below the surface, and we saw that even at that depth the radiation values were already minimal because of the basalt layer above us.

SG Mombatu: Did you make the decision to move your outpost there immediately?

S Amorosa: Yes, sir. Commander Vlachenko ordered us to start moving things right away, because the next sandstorm was only two weeks away, according to the forecasts.

HS Phelps: Did you make that decision on your own?

S Amorosa: No, sir. There was a short discussion, at which time Vlachenko suggested that Dr. Marks and I check the other tunnels that led further down off the main cave.

SG Mombatu: Didn't you think that was dangerous?

S Amorosa: No, sir. I thought it would be a good idea to know what the other tunnels around our future base looked like. It was entirely possible that there were old lava caverns underneath our cave, which might then collapse in an earthquake.

SG Mombatu: And did you find any such caverns?

S Amorosa: No, sir.

SG Mombatu: Instead, you found The Object. Tell us about it.

S Amorosa: We were about three hundred meters beneath the landing zone when we came upon a tapering tunnel.

The Fossil

The basalt on the walls was ancient, and the temperature was significantly lower. That's where we saw the light.

SG Mombatu: You saw a light? What kind of light?

S Amorosa: I... I don't know, Mr. Secretary-General. Further down the tunnel we just saw... a light.

SG Mombatu: An artificial light? Sunlight from the surface coming through a crevice?

S Amorosa: No, there was no contact with the surface and no power source. There was nothing down there. And it wasn't a light that gave off any heat. It was just there, floating in the darkness, shining.

HS Phelps: You'll understand if that's all rather difficult to believe, doctor.

S Amorosa: I do. I don't know how I'm supposed to believe it either, sir. I'm a scientist.

HS Phelps: Just continue, please.

S Amorosa: At first we just froze, then we stared in amazement, but finally our curiosity won out and we moved towards the light, but when we got to where we had seen it, it was gone. It was just us and our flashlights.

SE Nikitu: But you weren't alone, am I right?

S Amorosa: No, sir, we were not. That's where we found The

2

AGATHA DEVENWORTH, 2042

Agatha eyed the cardboard box on her desk as if it were a wicker basket with a snake inside. She didn't dare take off the lid, knowing that if she did the snake could spring out and kill her with its deadly venom.

And that venom had a name: Grief.

She leaned back into her office chair and sighed, tuning out the background noise of the open-plan office as she always did. Then, with a series of precise, deliberate movements, she rotated the box towards herself.

The side now facing her, written in black felt-tip pen, read, 'Jaydon R. Hawthorne.' The writing looked hasty and scribbled, and that stirred something inside her that felt like rage.

"Agent Devenworth."

She looked up, into the scowling face of Director Miller. It was lean and chiseled, with a short-cut gray beard and short gray hair to match, with undertones of black like a resistance movement fighting against the advancing years.

Agatha looked him in the face and raised an eyebrow, as she always did.

"I'm really sorry about your partner," Miller said. His cold blue eyes actually seemed to contain some genuine sympathy, which they hardly ever did.

"What's the *but*?"

"But... you really have to turn in this box downstairs, so Hawthorne's wife can pick up his things."

"I'll do it in a sec."

"Take all the time you need, Devenworth, but please do it today."

"Why the sudden hurry?" she asked. "My two-week suspension, that *you* gave me, only starts today, right?"

He tilted his head down slightly at her. "I gave you two weeks of vacation, with pay, to recover from your last assignment," he said.

"That's a nice way of putting it. We made a bad judgment call, we screwed up a mission, and you don't like it. Not that I blame you."

Agatha stared at the box and Hawthorne's name written there, as if that would bring him back or make her see his face as it really looked. Details were rapidly fading from her memory, and it scared her. Of course, she could picture his face, but she didn't trust her recollection of the details. How deep was that line between his nose and mouth, really? How many wrinkles did he have on his forehead?

"It's not like that," the director answered, his voice taking on a definitive tone. "You're the sharpest tool in my shed, Devenworth. Let me tell you something. At the end of the year I'm going to tell Washington that I'm recommending you for the position of deputy director." It wasn't particularly ceremonious or emphatic—it was still Jenning Miller, after all, and he despised nothing so much as sentiment.

Since taking over the Field Agents Division, she had been sent out to a string of executive leadership seminars, which she had completed, albeit only grudgingly, because she hated time-wasting even more than she hated small talk. But she had actually found a few of these seminars not a complete waste of time. One thing she had learned was that there were some people who were so top-heavy they could have passed for robots, and that was the best way to handle them—like robots. Director Miller was one of those people, and she should know, since she also learned to recognize the robot in herself.

"Thanks for the *flowers*," she said coolly. "But I'm sure you didn't come to my desk to butter me up."

"Direct, as always," Miller replied. "I'm sending you back into the field."

"Oh?" Agatha put down the box of Hawthorne's things and fixed her gaze on her boss.

"Don't look at me like that."

"I'm giving you my intrigued look."

Miller snorted. "I'm sending you on a mission against the Sons of Terra."

Agatha narrowed her eyes to slits, and now the look she focused on her superior was one of hypnotic command. *You will not turn away until you tell me what I want to hear.*

"You have my attention."

"I don't need your attention. I give the orders and you follow them, remember?" When she didn't answer, he snorted again and shook his head. "Yeah, I'm sending you after the Sons of Terra. And I'm doing it because I know you, and I know that you're going to approach this mission using your head, and go by the book, like always, and leave the... this Hawthorne thing..."

Agatha cut him off. "He's dead," she said flatly. "You don't have to pretend for my sake."

"You're getting a new partner."

"No!" she protested immediately, but his gaze was already hardening.

"Yes, you are. I've already made my decision, and the fact of the matter is it wasn't my decision at all. This order comes directly from Homeland Security. The Secretary made a deal with Europe that we do some agent exchanges to get our activities better connected and build trust."

She sank into her chair in genuine disbelief. "You've got to be kidding. Now we're going to be letting foreign agents run around with us?"

"No, we're not only letting them run around with us, we're also letting them carry. Your partner's going to have the authority of a junior investigator."

"But he doesn't even know the law!"

"I never said anything about a *him*."

"No, you didn't. He still doesn't know our laws," she said, unmoved.

"He does. He studied European and American law in Brussels and Los Angeles. They did their homework when they picked their candidates for the exchange program. But even still, this agreement only goes for Sons of Terra investigations, because of the global nature of the threat."

"I see."

"I want to see you in the conference room in five minutes for the briefing," Miller ordered. "Your new partner is already there."

She could tell by the sudden deeper tone his voice took on that she had pissed him off. Others in the office probably wouldn't have noticed, because they only saw the utterly-impenetrable mask everybody called 'The Face.' But she had known him a long time, and knew him well enough to notice the little things.

The Fossil

"Do I have a choice? My last partner was forced on me, too—and we all know how that worked out," she grumbled.

"I'm going to pretend you didn't say that. Did it ever occur to you that you might be hurting Hawthorne with a statement like that?" Her boss was annoyed now, and made a dismissive gesture in her direction when she did not respond. Finally, he turned his heels and disappeared among the cubes.

No, because you can't hurt a dead man, she answered in her mind—but knew as soon as she thought it that it wasn't true. It only hurt her, and it hurt a lot. Hawthorne had been a good man and an even better agent, and for her, it was saying something that she was even thinking that. She would never have thought that about anyone else in the agency in a million years.

But besides that, her two years working with him had proved everything she had ever feared about working with a partner—letting yourself feel, and then having to grieve. Grieving was something she had never learned how to do, and she hated unfamiliar territory, where she wasn't in control of everything down to the last detail. This was territory where a partner just did not belong, and after her last experience in that department, no matter how well they understood each other, no matter how well they had clicked, she would still be worried about the partner on every new mission. When she worried, she couldn't think clearly. When she gave in to her innate pragmatism, there was nothing to build a fruitful partnership on.

She could see a silver lining in the director's latest order, though. Despite her recent failure—the only one in her career—he was entrusting her with a new case, and a big-league case at that. She had always had the Sons of Terra in her sights, and if one thing was for sure, she was the only one in the division who could make any move against them a success. But she could never say that, because the minute she did, she would have another misconduct complaint on her desk. Not that it bothered her when anybody in the division complained about her 'communication style'—obviously anybody who had time to send out complaints didn't have enough real work to do—but whenever someone went to the director, it was always trouble.

Never do that again, blah blah blah. Okay I won't, blah blah blah... A complete waste of time.

What was not a waste of time was the Sons of Terra, an army of nutjobs with the resources of a small Western state and the fanaticism of genuine terrorists—three attributes that didn't usually come in one package and that had confounded the whole world, to say nothing of Agatha herself, for two years now.

So, after taking a deep breath, she got up from her chair and, taking one last look at the box of Hawthorne's things, stepped out of her cube and moved off towards the glass-walled conference room.

The other agents she passed on the way greeted her with uncertain looks from their cubicles. She only nodded back in silence. Approaching the conference room, she could already see her new partner through the glass. He was sitting at the long wooden conference table, wearing a brown leather jacket and jeans, leaning back in his chair casually with his cowboy boots up on the table.

Great. A douchebag.

The first thing she did as she came through the door was to press the button next to the light switch. It darkened the glass of the walls. It was evidently just her and the European for now.

"So, you must be Special Agent Agatha Devenworth," he

began. His accent was German and his grin was broad. He had short, curly hair, a striking face with three-day stubble that managed to look sloppy and well-groomed at the same time. He was the kind of man that lots of women would find extremely attractive, a fact that of which he seemed to be all too aware.

"If you're always this sharp, we'll have this case solved in no time," she replied, walking over to him and extending a courtesy handshake.

"Pano Hofer, Europol," he said, rising, and his jaws stopped working on his chewing gum long enough for him to make his grin even broader. "Your file said you're forty-one. Now why is HR lying about a thing like that?"

"Wow, flattery. How imaginative." Agatha sat down in one of the chairs next to him and folded her hands in the lap of her dark blue pantsuit.

"You having a lousy day?" he asked, still grinning as he sat back down, folded his hands across his stomach, and put his feet back up on the table, one crossed over the other at the ankles.

"You might say that."

"I understand. Are you married?"

Agatha, irritated by the question, raised an eyebrow at him. "Why do you ask? If I say no, are you going to think I'm damaged somehow?"

"No..."

"Or maybe for a single woman, you open up your can of boiler-plate pickup lines you collected from the," she paused and scribed a set of air quotes, *"Handbook for the Handsome Man with a Complex about Women?"*

"You really think you got me all figured out after less than a minute, don't you?" Hofer asked. His friendly smile hadn't flickered for an instant, and she couldn't decide whether she thought he was an idiot or a very cool customer.

"Yes."

Her new partner unfolded his hands and, with a wink, invited her to continue.

"You have a German accent—Southern German, probably. But you're wearing 'exclusive' Italian brands—Gucci and Versace, if I'm seeing rightly. Your cowboy boots aren't American-made—the heels are too short. They're not the kind of thing you wear in Germany—I've been there often enough to know that you don't make a lot of friends there by being extravagant. So I'm thinking German-speaking Italy, South Tyrol or Trentino. You like to stand out and project confidence because you come from a poor family without a lot of social standing. Your mother lived on welfare and was stretched too thin raising the children, your father walked out on the family, maybe you never even knew him. You had to grow up faster than was good for you, and you never had anybody there to serve as a corrective or positive role model." Agatha pointed to his boots on the table.

Hofer's eyes narrowed, giving him a more serious expression, and his mouth twitched. Now it was not a relaxed grin, but a frozen smile as Agatha continued.

"Then, you had a brief phase of trouble with the law, because in your rebellious years you wanted to rise up as the savior of your mother and siblings, which you tried to achieve on the street with questionable methods. Your eyes betray a certain depth that the painstakingly-constructed mask you call a face tries to hide. I can imagine that your mother died young, and it devastated you and woke you up to the need to turn your life around. You studied law, because you had something to prove to yourself, but as the child of a single mother from a bad neighborhood you never got your foot in the door in the academic world, because you never felt like you belonged and you always felt inferior. So you did the next best thing that you could succeed at, and joined the police, where you can live your dream of bettering yourself without having to live in fear that someone will recognize what you really are: an upstart, living in fear that one day someone won't be taken in by the name-brand jacket and the self-confident grin and will see that the only thing that makes you feel like you used to is falling asleep in front of the VR football with a bottle of beer and a bag of potato chips. So? Was I close enough?"

Agatha looked him straight in the eye. Hofer opened his mouth to say something, but nothing came out. The door to the conference room opened for a moment, and then was closed again with a grating noise.

Director Miller and his staff had come in. Miller went to the head of the table, with his deputy Warren Shapiro taking the chair to his left. The other two were Miller's secretaries, Betty Johnson and Liza Degeunes, who took seats opposite Pano and Agatha and immediately rolled out their holo displays.

Miller was the only one who did not sit down right away. Instead, he furrowed his brow and looked over Hofer first, and then Agatha. His gaze finally stuck on Agatha and hardened. "You were insufferable again, weren't you?" he asked.

"I only answered a question," Agatha replied and raised her hands innocently.

Hofer, who had taken his feet off the table as soon as the door started opening, had recovered his smile and even winked at her before turning to the director. "That's right," he said. "I just asked her something, and she gave me an answer."

"She's like this with everyone," Miller replied, with

something of an apologetic tone. He shot his cuffs and squared his shoulders, and then finally sat down. With a wave of his hand he activated the holotank running the length of the tabletop.

"That's disappointing. I thought she was giving me special treatment," Hofer said with a broader smile.

"Listen, whatever you get up to on your own time is none of my business," Miller said impatiently. "Right now I've got the Secretary breathing down my neck, and right after this meeting I'm flying straight to Washington. Unfortunately, in my position I'm not allowed to say what I really think of this whole agent exchange thing, so let's just get down to it, shall we? Before I sprout any more gray hairs."

When the director had determined that no one dared interject anything further, he gave a satisfied nod.

"Director Miller. Authorization for the Ron Jackson case," he commanded, and the fluorescent green holofield between the table and the ceiling activated, displaying an image of a man with mid-length brown hair. His eyes looked gentle and good-natured, and the slightly oversized glasses gave him something of an absent-minded professor look.

"Access granted," the system assistant purred.

"Who is this?" Agatha asked.

"This is Doctor-Doctor-Doctor Ron Jackson," Miller explained. "Three PhDs: archaeology, anthropology, and philology."

"Wait a sec, I know that name from somewhere." Agatha leaned forward, looking like she was trying to recall something. "That's the... conspiracy theorist who disappeared?"

"Something like that. *Time* magazine once called him the Canadian Erich von Däniken, because he was a modern-day adherent of the 'ancient astronauts theory.'"

"Was?" asked Hofer. His English was astonishingly good,

although Agatha thought he had a slightly snobbish British accent mixed in with his German one.

"He's been listed as missing for over twenty years," Agatha said, without ever taking her eyes off the scientist's hologram as it slowly revolved clockwise.

"You're familiar with the case?"

"I read an article about it once. In high school, when I was doing a presentation on pseudoscience."

"In high school? That was over 20 years ago," Hofer said. "You're not seriously telling me you still remember it?"

"I never forget anything." Agatha shrugged her shoulders as if this was the most normal thing in the world.

"Okay then, different question, since it looks like you have a knowledge advantage here, what exactly is 'ancient astronauts theory?'"

"I was just getting to that," Miller cut in. He made a few different gestures. The hologram was replaced by several panels of ancient paintings, archaeological finds, a long wall, and a device that looked like a wheel encrusted with shells.

"The 'ancient astronauts theory' is a catch-all term for any pseudoscience that propounds the hypothesis that somewhere back in history, extraterrestrials visited Earth and influenced the civilizations of the time. They explain things like the building of the pyramids with the blunt argument that aliens must have done it. I've given both of you access to all the NSA's files on the subject, and Europol has done the same. So please get up to speed on this shit."

"What could this Ron Jackson have to do with our case? That logo on the wall right behind me says 'CTD.' As in, 'Counter-Terrorist Directive.' It doesn't seem to me like some nutjob who hasn't been seen in decades could be a member of the Sons of Terra, which only appeared two years ago." Agatha had her full attention focused on her boss, and was unfazed by his snort.

"I need you to find Ron Jackson," Miller answered straightforwardly, returning her piercing gaze.

"You can't be serious," Hofer blurted. His ever-present grin had vanished in an instant.

"Yes, I'm serious, and if you prefer keeping your ass in that chair for longer than five minutes to sitting on the next flight back to Bolzano, I recommend you zip it and listen," Miller growled, and with a raised finger he motioned for Agatha to keep quiet too.

"Now I know what you're going to say," he went on. "We're not private detectives, we're not cops, we don't do missing-persons cases, blah, blah, blah. Shut up and listen. Two days ago, Jackson's wife died. He had no children and no other family to inherit anything, so everything went to the state. Now, guess what the civil servants who went through his things found? An unfinished manuscript, by Jackson, that begins with the sentence, 'We are not the rulers of this planet.'" Miller made a sweeping gesture with his arm again, and the images of the archaeological artifacts disappeared. With a wave of his hand, the table changed to an extended display film with a text reading, in scrolling text: 'FBI evidence. Top Secret.'

"That's the slogan of the Sons of Terra," Agatha said.

"Right. The FBI's initial investigation says that this manuscript never saw the light of day. Now, I don't believe in coincidences, and neither does the Secretary of Homeland Security. So I'm putting you two on the case. Find the connection between this crazy pseudo-scientist and the Sons of Terra," the director ordered, ending the holoprojection by clenching his open hand into a fist.

"This is a disciplinary transfer," Agatha grumbled.

The Fossil

"Your other option is to start your two weeks' leave right now," Miller shot back, and when she remained silent, his lips flattened into a tight smile. "Thought so. Take all the time you need, put whatever it costs on the expense account, but just find me a connection that I can wave in front of the Secretary without her laughing me out of her office."

With that, Miller and his entourage stood up and left the conference room, leaving Agatha and Hofer alone again.

"Well, that's just great," Hofer muttered with a sigh.

"So, what did *you* do to end up in the doghouse?" Agatha asked.

3

RON JACKSON, 2018

The first time Ron Jackson saw Pyramid Mountain with his own eyes, it was snowless. Just experiencing this sight in front of him—not on a satellite picture, a video or a photo, like umpteen times before—was incredible.

Nothing could have prepared him for how overwhelming it was to actually see it. A mountain of stone jutting nearly three thousand meters up from the eternal Antarctic ice, its shape a perfect pyramid. It was his business to be fascinated by every pyramid that he came across, but this one really was the top of the heap. Compared to this megalithic mammoth, the 140-meter pyramid of Cheops seemed downright puny.

"So, do you still believe that this thing was built?" Peter Gould asked Ron, shouting over the rotors of the helicopter as they stepped out. He pulled his hood tighter around his face against the blowing snow.

Ron waited until the helicopter had taken off and the students from McMurdo Station had headed out towards the excavation with the supply crates. "Yes, I do," he confirmed, cupping his heavy gloves together before blowing into them, as if that might make one bit of difference in the Antarctic cold.

"See the entrance over there?" Ron pointed towards a rectangular opening where the darkness of the mountain met the unchanging whiteness of the snow that stretched as far as the eye could see in every direction.

In response, Gould gave him a curious look that might have meant either, 'of course I see it' or 'what the hell are you talking about?'

"This excavation has already cost the Human Foundation sixteen million dollars, and it only started two weeks ago! What does that tell you?"

"That there's someone out there just as crazy as you, but with a lot more money?" Gould guessed, earning a resigned sigh from Jackson.

"Why did you come out here with me, anyway?"

Gould shrugged. "Just to make sure that Mr. Karlhammer's money is being spent properly." In the cold, his face was taking on a red glow, like he had drunk too much wine—which Ron also considered a possibility.

"You mean, you're my babysitter," Jackson said with a sigh, his shoulders tightening.

"I'm not your enemy, Dr. Jackson, trust me on this."

"Why should I? It seems you want to laugh at my theories, just like everyone else."

"Because I'm a pragmatist. If you're wrong, Doctor, the Human Foundation is finished. It's that simple. So, I'm clinging to the infinitesimal chance that you might actually be right and when it's all said and done, we're all going to be rich," Gould said, hustling to keep up with Jackson, who was stomping off through the snow towards the entrance to the mountain. As he did, he clutched his briefcase close to his chest, looking around nervously as if the ice might suddenly come to life and swallow it.

"Get rich? Get rich! That's all anyone ever wants is to get rich," Ron grumbled disappointedly, and his words flew away on the wind like dead leaves. *But what for?* he added in his thoughts. *Then you're rich, and you while away your precious time on this earth in luxury, without having given one useful thing to the world.*

"What? I didn't understand what you said," Gould gasped, already out of breath from running the few meters in the cold to catch up. He didn't belong here, at the end of the world, the most hostile place on earth.

But Ron could say the same for himself, as he was all too aware. He had always hated the cold, and was much more at home in Syria, Egypt, or Mesopotamia. Sure, maybe you had mosquitoes and scorpions, but at least there was no risk of your chisel freezing to your hand.

"Never mind," Jackson replied, and didn't speak again as he walked the last hundred meters to the entrance.

The opening of the passage was about the size of a standard door, and had been roughly hewn out of the mountain. After about a meter, the passage became a perfectly round cylinder that had been drilled to slope at a downward angle, deep into the heart of the pyramid. As they entered, a metal carriage came up, drawn on two sealed steel cables, and stopped in front of them.

The faint, chill daylight that came through the entrance with them disappeared after only a few meters, swallowed by the blackness below. Ron thought he could barely make out the light of the excavation site at the bottom, but couldn't be sure he wasn't imagining it.

"That's where we're supposed to go? Down there?" Gould asked, swallowing hard.

Ron nodded. "Yes, that's where we're supposed to go." He wasn't particularly wild about the idea of jumping into this electric cable car and plunging deep into the darkness under a mountain—no, a *pyramid*. But that's where his research was, and the most promising project he'd ever headed. He couldn't just let all those late-night discussions with Luther go to waste. At least, to Ron they were discussions. To Luther, they were probably fights—they had always been very different people, and that was never going to change. And another thing that was never going to change was that their two very different geniuses were locked forever in a deadly embrace. Luther was a brilliant businessman, and just as idealistic and visionary as Ron, although he never would have admitted it.

He recalled their last conversation in Zell am See, in Luther's obscenely expensive chalet, as they looked out at the lake through the breathtaking glass façade. To this day, when he closed his eyes, he could still smell the 18-year-old single malt they had been drinking. "We can't give up, Ron," Luther had said. "We can't give up looking for answers where no one would ever think to find them."

That had been exactly what Ron had needed to hear, after having become accustomed to a never-ending stream of malice and ridicule from the scientific world through the years. When they had called him a Stargate type, he had taken it as a badge of honor, especially as he had always been a big fan of the series. His doctorates in archaeology, anthropology, and linguistics changed nothing. Anyone who thought outside the narrow boundaries of current research paradigms was quickly marginalized, and for one simple reason: all the greats—Einstein, Newton, Darwin, Schrödinger, and so many more—had all not only been scientists but visionaries, each enduring ridicule from their peers, to varying degrees, until the field was ready to recognize their genius.

Ron Jackson did not see himself as a scientist on that level—no, it would never have occurred to him to name himself in such illustrious company—but he did see himself as, like them, a visionary so committed to his cause that he could endure all the scorn and derision that his peers, whose recognition he so desperately desired, could dish out. He had to, because he knew that momentous breakthroughs could only come from breaking down walls. And walls could only be broken down with blood, sweat, and tears.

"Hey—you OK?" Gould had mistaken Ron's hesitation for fear.

"Fine," Ron said, and sat down in the small electric carriage. It was something like a sled, not quite three meters long, and he had to slide over on the cold metal, studded with numerous eyelets and hooks for the safety straps, to make room for Gould, who settled in behind him with some trepidation. "Try to relax. Don't worry, it's a short trip."

The control box was attached to a retractable crank. Ron pulled it into position and pushed the button marked with the down arrow. A moment later the carriage shuddered to life and descended into the darkness, just fast enough to cause a light airflow around them, making the cold feel a touch frostier.

As they neared the light of the excavation site at the end of the narrow tunnel, the smells of ancient dust and musty stone intensified. These were smells that Ron was more familiar with than those of his own home, having spent most of the last ten years on excavation sites in Egypt, Mesopotamia, and Central America. It amazed him that the same smell could arise even here, in the ancient ice, which could only have preserved everything in a frozen state all this time.

"How you can do this job, I'll never know," Gould said from behind him, and Ron thought he could actually feel a little warmth at the back of his neck. But it vanished so quickly that he decided he must have imagined it.

"How you can crunch numbers day and night, when they don't even really mean anything, I'll never know," Ron countered.

"But they do mean something. They mean a lot of jobs, and I'm sure I don't have to remind you that the Human Foundation, which you cofounded, is a nonprofit organization. Of course what I do means something."

Ron heard an insulted snort behind him.

"You're right, of course. I didn't mean to offend you. It's just, when everyone thinks you're a crackpot and they shake their heads the minute you turn around, and even the employees in your own organization are laughing at you behind your back the whole time, it's a bit much sometimes," he sighed, sinking into his seat a little.

"Listen. I really want to believe you, and I think Mr. Karlhammer does too, otherwise he wouldn't be so busy holding fundraisers and chasing after celebrities."

"Oh, he just does that all the time, because that's his *thing*."

"That's why you complement each other so well."

"We did once, maybe," Ron replied, and was glad that Gould didn't press any further.

A few seconds later, their sled reached the end of the short, horizontal runout zone. In a space about the size of a small church nave a dozen or so people were waiting for them, looking like a Michelin Man party in their down jackets and thermal pants, their faces framed by tightly pulled, fur-lined hoods. Apart from Professor Patchuvi and his assistant Dr. Ross, the entire team was made up of students, reminding Ron how far removed from everything their work here was—and he wasn't even thinking of the jaw-dropping distance to the nearest human settlement.

"Mr. Jackson, what a pleasure to finally see you here!" said Patchuvi, stepping forward to help Ron out of the sled. He was a short Indian man with ocher skin and twinkling eyes. Ron had once thought he had a few screws loose, but he simply oozed enthusiasm and adventurousness.

"Thank you, Mr. Patchuvi. And please call me Ron."

"Of course, Ron. And please call me Mitra. My assistant, James." The professor pointed to the tall American with the long nose, whom Ron had met once briefly at a conference in Alexandria.

"Nice to see you again," he said, also shaking his hand.

Gould struggled his way out of the sled, looking a little peeved that no one had helped him out of it because all the attention was on the other man. Meanwhile, Ron surmised from the uncomfortable silence that it was time to say something.

"Thank you all for being here. The work of an archaeologist is tedious—it means poor pay, never leads to fame, and you're generally either laughed at for spending your days bashing at rocks, or you're unemployed. Now you all work for me and Luther, so at least you're employed—but that might just make the ridicule part that much more painful. No one believes me, and that means no one believes you. That's why I want to tell you how much I appreciate that you've all taken time out of your semesters and your research groups to come down here and poke around in the cold for evidence to support my theories.

"No, it goes beyond just appreciation. I feel truly

honored. I am indebted to each and every one of you. Everyone, please call me Ron, and feel free to ask me any questions at any time. We are doing something truly pioneering here, and can't afford to waste any energy on hierarchical hurdles, which I have never put much stock in anyway. There's nothing special about me, I'm just the loudest monkey in the circus."

A murmur of laughter ensued, and Ron knew that while he might not have broken the ice—if that was even possible here at the coldest place on earth—at least everyone had relaxed a little. That would have to do for a start.

He felt good expressing what their presence and their confidence meant to him. After all these years of unsuccessful attempts to prove his theories, maybe that was what had made him fly out here and pick up a chisel and a brush.

Ron looked up to see that the team was still gathered, looking at him expectantly. He frowned. "Ah, let's get right back to work, shall we?"

"All right, you heard the man," Patchuvi called out a little too loudly, and clapped his gloved hands together, which made a 'whoomp-whoomp' sound like two smacking oven mitts. "Everybody get back to work!"

When the students had disappeared into the various passageways that branched off from the ice-walled cavern, Patchuvi turned to Jackson and Gould. "So, you'd obviously like an update."

"Certainly," Ron said, nodding keenly, at the same time that Gould was making a sour face in apparent preparation for an onslaught of boredom.

"All right. This here is the first space that we opened up, after we had identified it on the plots from the reflection seismics. It was immediately clear after we drilled the shaft that this was a planned and precisely laid out tunnel system.

Right now we're clearing the ice from many of the passages, and we're constantly finding new chambers as we go."

Ron felt a tingling of excitement rise in his guts. This was, perhaps, the sensation he had been waiting for, but he couldn't let himself get carried away. He was all too familiar with being on the edge of what he thought was a breakthrough, and then being disappointed. "What about the boys in magnetics back home? Have they learned anything yet?"

"Yes. Using the data from our scans, they created extremely clear computer models." Patchuvi paused, seeming to enjoy drawing out the moment.

Ron scraped his feet across the floor impatiently. "Well? Let's have it!"

"We detected elevated iridium concentrations in the rock walls," the professor announced with a sweeping gesture, finishing with a broad grin and revealing teeth that looked a little too white.

"That's... that's..." Ron was speechless, and instead of finishing his sentence he walked over to the wall on their right and placed his gloved hands on the thin layer of ice covering the stone.

Gould spoke up. "Um, excuse me, Mr. Patchuvi," he said, shaking a clearly confused head. "Can you explain to me what just happened?"

"*Professor* Patchuvi," he corrected, and his grin degenerated into a scowl as soon as he turned to look at the financial man.

"Pardon me. *Professor*," said Gould sardonically, rolling his eyes. "Would you please, pretty please, with sugar and a cherry on top, explain what in the hell you were just talking about? Maybe try pretending that you're talking to a first-year student, or that this is your first time teaching?"

Patchuvi was about to launch into a tirade, but Ron beat him to the punch. "Have you ever heard of the iridium anomaly, Mr. Gould?"

"No."

"The impact event that probably ended the Cretaceous period and began the Paleogene around sixty-six million years ago."

"Impact...?" the accountant asked thoughtfully. "That was the comet, right?"

"Meteorite."

"Right."

"Anyway, the sedimentary rock of the Cretaceous-Paleogene boundary had elevated concentrations of the element iridium, and other platinum group metals, which is how we know today where the line between the Cretaceous and the Paleogene is. This unusually high density of these specific elements is unique in the entire history of the planet, and had to have been brought to Earth in these meteorites," Ron explained patiently, although he was itching to run through the passageways and see everything all at once.

"OK, so, this place is ancient?"

"You don't seem to understand, Mr. Gould. This place is not only over sixty million years old, but it was built."

"Built? By who? At that time weren't there only... well, what? Dinosaurs on the planet?"

"No, they died out at the end of the Cretaceous period... from the impact." Ron shook his head and pointed, one by one, to several of the passageways that led away from this chamber in a star-shaped pattern. From within them came the yellow light of the hanging spotlights powered by the cables lining the walls and leading down another passageway, and the rhythmic humming of diesel generators off in the distance.

"So..." Gould paused, and his brow furrowed. "That means that, after the dinosaurs, someone was here, and that someone built this?"

Ron allowed a smile to creep over his face, even though what he really wanted to do was leap for joy. "Yes, Mr. Gould, that is exactly what it means," he said, containing his excitement.

"So you were right," Gould whispered. "You old dog, you were right!"

"Not entirely... not yet. Even if the height of the passageways is approximately correct, we still don't have the definitive proof that I was really, actually right."

"So you're saying that people made this place, long before the *Homo habilis* that we know ever walked in Africa —what, over two million years ago?"

"Yes, Mr. Gould. That is exactly what I'm saying." Ron looked up at the roof and put both his hands over his half-frozen lips. *I'm so close,* he thought. He felt tears welling in his eyes.

4

FILIO AMOROSA, 2042

Filio patted Oscar's head and scratched him behind the ears. "It's all right, boy," she explained to the golden retriever, reassuringly. "You don't have to go down there with me."

Oscar stopped his panting to smack his lips, then looked at her expectantly with what might have been a smile.

She sighed and reached into the pocket of her overalls. The dog's eyes followed her every move.

"But just don't tell daddy, OK?" She threw a treat into the air, and he deftly snatched it between his jaws. Then it was gone, as quickly as it had appeared.

"Now get out of here, I have to concentrate!" Filio waved the dog away, and he trundled off through the door, onto the bridge of the *Ocean's Bitch*.

Sighing, she turned back to the display film in front of her, which was stretched across an entire wall. She put on her data glasses. The satellite image of the Indian Ocean was updated every half-hour. It showed a nearly cloudless view of the deep turquoise sea surrounding an archipelago —the Maldives. She had been working on the scrapper ship *Ocean's Bitch* for two years. Right now they were holding position forty nautical miles east of the main island of Malé, just as she had advised.

"And?" Romain asked, suddenly appearing in the doorway to the bridge. The captain was a handsome Frenchman in his early forties, wiry like a professional diver but with a Casanova smile. From behind him, Oscar slipped through the doorway, trotted over to Filio, and nuzzled the pocket of her overalls, the pocket containing the dog treats.

Romain raised an eyebrow, and she rolled her eyes. "You traitor!" she scolded Oscar, shooing him away.

"He doesn't know friend from enemy when there's food at stake," the Frenchman laughed in his silky accent as he came in. He stood next to her to survey the vast display. "And? Are you satisfied?"

"I need some more time for the calculations."

"Haven't you been calculating this super-equation of yours for over a year?"

"Yes, because it's complicated. You, Thomas, Jane, Alberto, none of you understand, because you're divers and you don't have advanced degrees in mathematics," she explained, zooming out the satellite image until they were looking at nearly the entire Indian Ocean, with India to the north, Africa to the west, and Australia to the east.

"Drawing mode," she commanded, and with an outstretched finger she circled a large area in the middle of the ocean. "Now, this is the area where, for just about two years now, some eight hundred registered scrapper ships just like ours have been searching for the wreckage of *Mars One*. Eight hundred! That sounds like a lot, but it's not. When the shuttle exploded and largely burned up in reentry, the parts were spread out over such a wide area that not even God could show us where to find them all. Statistically, just searching around blind like we're doing wouldn't pay off in a thousand years."

"I get it," the captain sighed, in an attempt to shut her up, but Filio was getting excited—maybe because of the exhaustion that had plagued her for so long, or perhaps she was starting to crack under the constant tension.

"Now, the fact that I can make any kind of model at all about the probable location of the tail section is only because of two things: one, there are parts of this ocean that are relatively unaffected by deep currents; and two, I know pretty much everything about *Mars One* that there is to know." She was getting worked up now, and zoomed the view back to their current position.

Smiling at her, Romain put an arm over her shoulder. "Take as much time as you need."

Filio smiled back, pleased with his encouraging response, but his eyes couldn't hide the fact that he cared, too. They still had enough funding to keep at it for a few months, but then that was that. Since their backer, Francis Montgomery, had retired a while ago, taking his money with him, the future hadn't looked quite as adventurous as it had at the beginning of their search.

She still remembered so well the almost euphoric craze that had erupted when *Mars One* had crashed, as macabre as that sounds. Everyone wanted to know what this mysterious mission had been about, and how they could earn money off it. The ten million dollars that the space agencies NASA, ESA, and Roskosmos had put up for whoever found the black box had been raised to twenty million after a few months, much to the annoyance of the treasure hunting community around the world. Especially because there was a further million on the table for every piece of wreckage larger than twenty centimeters square.

That, of course, only set the rumor mill into overdrive and set off a feeding frenzy among treasure hunters everywhere. Before long the Indian Ocean was teeming with scrappers, as the fortune-hunters from the four corners of the earth came to be known. Then, when legendary treasure hunter and diver Workai Dalam found the black box and actually got the twenty million dollars, things started to go really crazy.

But even that was not what, in the end, brought the whole world swarming to this corner of South Asia. That happened when the space agencies quintupled the reward for every piece of the craft recovered. That not only brought on more greed, and more investors, who took any available captain under their financial wings, eager to equip them for years at a time in exchange for splitting the finder's fees—but it also set rumors swirling. What had they learned from the black box that made them want the rest of the wreckage that badly?

Filio knew, of course. They wanted The Object.

"I think I'll be ready soon," she finally said, staring thoughtfully at the long trailing clouds drifting gently over the endless blue of the ocean on the display.

"And I," Romain said, "believe in you." He smiled, exposing a row of white teeth. "But today, you should take a break and come below with me. Thomas made zucchini ragout."

"All right. You go ahead, I'm right behind you," she assured him, but after Romain had left the meeting room her gaze remained on the display. She closed her eyes, and images of the crash flashed before her. Unreal impressions of burning wreckage in the water, a flash of light, her in her pressure seat seeing hot flames dancing across the glass of the cockpit. Then a vague recollection of unbuckling herself, falling, and going to the hold.

She was now holding herself up, elbows locked and hands firmly planted on the table in front of the display, gasping for air as if she had just run a marathon. The more involved she got with returning to *Mars One*, the more often the crash came to her in her dreams, and the harder it hit her. She simply had to know what had happened on Mars. Why did her friends, everyone on the team have to die on the mission? Why couldn't she remember anything?

The grief, and the trauma, that was one thing, but knowing that you had been part of a disaster that no one could explain—least of all yourself—that was something else. She simply could *not* remember, and as time passed her few impressions of her time on the red planet faded ever faster. She thought about her preparation for the mission, several years ago now. No physical injuries had been found, so there must be a psychological reason for her brain to shut down. But she couldn't really imagine that, either. Her whole life, Filio had always had a healthy psyche—otherwise she would never have been selected for mankind's first manned mission to Mars. Now she was the sole survivor of a historic disaster, but there was nothing she could do to close the book on it.

Not nothing, she corrected herself in her thoughts. *I can find The Object. I have to find The Object.*

But she also knew that she couldn't let her obsession run away with her. Like Workai Dalam, who turned around right after the most significant find in his career, the black box, and jumped right back into the game. In interviews from that time, he had been so confident that he knew exactly where the big prize was to be found, he had all the other treasure hunters out there shitting themselves. But then he just disappeared, never to be seen again—boat went down, it seems, in a massive storm east of Seychelles. At least, the wreckage of his boat seemed to confirm this. The fact that his body was never found surprised no one, given the currents in that area.

But his legend lived on, and he became something of a patron saint of the scrappers. Most boats had his picture somewhere, his face like a talisman that reminded the adventurers and fortune-seekers that the treasure really was out there and that sometimes, you really could do the impossible. A picture of him was hanging on the bridge of the *Ocean's Bitch* right now. Filio never thought it strange that scrappers tended to be superstitious. Realistically, ninety-nine percent of them would end up spending a lot of time in a lot of dangerous places, and find absolutely nothing.

Filio looked, one last time, over her scribbled calculations across the countless scraps of paper on the table in front of her. Then she left the meeting room.

The *Ocean's Bitch* was an old ship, launched at the end of the nineties—nearly fifty years ago now. She was probably one of the last vessels still on diesel engines, which right now were roaring away down in an engine room that always reeked of oil and grease. She was like a floating museum, from a time when humanity was still blind to the amount of CO_2 being pumped into the atmosphere. The only reason she could even be sailed at all was that the old lady was registered in Mauritius—after the energy transitions most nations went through, the island had repositioned itself as the last refuge of the climate sinner, those who had not scrapped their soot-spewing garbage-slingers for financial or sentimental reasons. Sometimes she felt guilty for never chartering any of the newer, electric-drive ships, but at this

The Fossil

point, this crew and the *Bitch* had grown on her to the point where she hardly ever thought about it.

She glanced at the three Human Foundation bracelets she was wearing on her bare right arm. 'With open arms. Living a Shared Future,' one read. The others bore only the blue image of planet Earth and the logo of the Human Foundation. She didn't wear these bracelets out of pride and principles, or as a symbol of hope, or because she supported the Human Foundation's myriad efforts to save the world by purchasing her monthly lottery tickets, although that was a nice side effect..

No, Filio wore the bracelets as a symbol of hope for herself. She played in the Foundation's most expensive lottery, a game called Space Dream, where the winner would get a ticket to Mars. Not the next mission, but the third, which was slated for 2044. She would rather have been on *Mars Two*, but beggars can't be choosers. Of course, she was too good at math to really let herself hope, but she had to try everything, literally *everything*, to get back to the Red Planet and find out what had happened to her and her team. She simply had to know why her life had been destroyed.

Filio came down the stairs into the lounge, which adjoined the galley, and saw Jane and Alberto talking in the small sitting area. Thomas and Romain were in the galley, grabbing aluminum bowls for the table and preparing to serve the crew from the steaming pot of ragout.

"Hey, Filio," Jane called to her. She was sitting directly under the old oil painting of the HMS *Terror* and the HMS *Erebus*, depicted in a stormy polar sea beneath low-hanging clouds. "Can you explain to this thick-skulled Spaniard that the movie *Moon* is not realistic?"

"What?"

"You know, *Moon*, it's like thirty years old, this kind of one-man show by Duncan Jones," explained the blonde. "This guy, he's alone on the moon, and he finds out he's a clone that keeps getting thrown away and replaced by a new version of himself."

"Oh, yeah, I remember. Good movie," Filio said, nodding.

"Yeah, but it was totally unrealistic, wasn't it?" Jane insisted, looking at her expectantly with those bright eyes of hers.

"Oh, yeah. When the guy leaves the base, he's clearly moving like he's in the low gravity of the Moon," Filio began, sitting down and straightening her place at the table. "But while he's in the base, he's moving around just like he's on Earth, with a full G."

"Ha!" Jane exclaimed triumphantly, flipping Thomas off with twin birds for further emphasis.

The Spaniard smiled in surrender, and gave her an amused wink. "Well," he shot back with a grin, "at least I know enough not to swim at a triggerfish coming out of a crevice."

Jane's expression suddenly turned sour.

"It's still a great movie, Alberto," Filio said. "If you had to fill every science fiction movie with total realism, the audience would be asleep in ten minutes. Space is a pretty boring place."

"Was it boring on the way to Mars?" Thomas asked. He had just pulled up a chair after parking the ragout in the middle of the table.

Filio kept her facial expression controlled, pretending that this question did not jolt her to the core. If she were to be honest, she would have to answer, *I don't remember.* But she wasn't going to admit that. Telling the truth had already caused her trouble in the past—namely, being discredited in front of the entire space exploration community, and being expelled from ESA and the Mars project—all in all, it had cost her everything she once lived for.

"The flight is not boring because there's always something to do. Four months pass by pretty quickly when you have to stay on top of the mountains of data that the satellites we shot into Mars orbit were sending back. When you're in a hostile environment, tens of millions of kilometers from any kind of help, you want to be as prepared as you can be. Anyone who was bored was obviously on the wrong mission."

"That's exactly why I love diving," Romain interjected with an understanding wink. Filio flashed a grateful smile. "Underwater is a place that's as alien as the infinite universe up there—but unlike out in space, there are strange life forms all around you."

"And a scoop of ragout on top," Thomas rumbled in his German basso profundo. He grinned from behind his epic mustache and, with a stocky arm, delivered load after load of the crew's dinner from a massive aluminum ladle.

"Mmm," Alberto hummed, expressing his appreciation as he swallowed his first bite, "delicious."

"Thanks. Ah, the original Rheinland recipe!"

"If you try to claim ragout for your country again, I will have to declare war on you, in the name of France," Romain laughed.

"Well, we've seen how that turns out," Thomas shot back, and the two men clicked their beer cans together in a toast.

Filio enjoyed every evening with this odd troop of divers and sailors who had bet their whole lives on finding the score of the century out here. These were people who chose risk over the idea of a life spent at a desk from 9 to 5 making someone else rich.

"Hey, Captain," Jane called across the table, jolting Filio back into the here and now with her sudden volume. "When does our astronaut get to take the wheel?"

"She's getting there," Romain said, smiling kindly in Filio's direction.

"Yeah, so why do you spend your nights listening to this frog-eater tell you how to steer this old rust-bucket, anyway?" Jane asked Filio, tearing off a piece of baguette and stuffing it in her mouth. "I mean, you two obviously aren't fucking."

Filio decided to pretend she hadn't heard that last part.

"It's just that after being wrapped up in my calculations all day, I have to do something practical or I'll go nuts," she lied. "Besides, I'm considering getting my offshore license one of these days, so I'm happy to get anything out of this that I can."

"Well, you're ambitious, I'll say that," Jane replied. "I guess you'd have to be. Otherwise you wouldn't be the astronaut who beat out several thousand other candidates."

The rest of the evening flew by, and before she knew it she was helping Thomas clean up the kitchen. Not long after that she was back at her calculations. She felt like she was on the verge of a breakthrough, like she was finally about to nail down all these formulas that she had been developing all this time. It was like there was a key, right in front of her, that would open all the doors to the solution, and all she had to do was turn it. She just hadn't found it yet.

Late that night, as she nodded off in front of her calculations yet again, a blinking light jolted her awake. It was her hand terminal, lying somewhere in the impenetrable jumble of paper that had turned the meeting room into the very picture of chaos.

Through a yawn she reached for it reflexively, blinking to drive the stubborn sleepiness from her eyes. She had to blink again before she could see the screen halfway clearly.

It was a new e-mail.

"Read new e-mail," she commanded while yawning, but received only a buzz in reply. When the yawn ended, she repeated the command more recognizably.

"Incoming e-mail from certified sender Human Foundation, Human Resources, Head Office. To: Doctor Filio Amorosa. Subject: Open position. Message: Dear Doctor Amorosa, I would like to take this opportunity to bring the attached job opening to your attention, and I would very much like to hear your thoughts about it. We have, in fact, created this position specifically with you in mind, and I think you will find we have been extremely accommodating with regards to your salary needs. The Human Foundation is not only dedicated to the interests of our planet, but also very much to the interests of its personnel..."

"Stop reading," Filio cut off the digital assistant, shaking her head. "Delete e-mail."

A gentle tone told her that the command had been carried out, and she slid the terminal away again, across the jumble of papers. They just didn't get it. No one got it. Filio wasn't at all interested in money, or a job. The only thing that mattered to her was what had happened to her and the mission on Mars, and on the return trip.

The Human Foundation only wanted to get her in their pocket because they hoped she could give them information about the Mars mission and what had been behind it. Like all the other big players on Earth, they just wanted to know what had happened—but she didn't know that herself.

What she did know, however, was that the Human Foundation didn't have a space program, and it didn't finance or support one apart from the astronaut lottery—which it used to fund its own projects—with a portion of the lottery money also going to NASA. Their main goal was to save this planet, and in fact they considered space travel counterproductive to that goal, as their fearless leader Luther Karlhammer emphasized in every one of his TV appearances. Looking at the stars, he said, only distracted from the things that had to be done here and now, in the real world, our only home world, to save it.

In fact, she largely agreed with the charismatic South African, but they needed alternatives, and those would be found out in space, mankind's final frontier. But if she was being honest, she didn't even care about that either. The one and only thing that mattered to her was finding out what that thing was, The Object that had blown her life apart, leaving behind only logs and sensor data. By going to the Human Foundation, she would be locking herself in a gilded cage, and giving up her last chance, however small, to shed light on that darkness.

No, thank you.

5

AGATHA DEVENWORTH, 2042

Three days later, Agatha and Pano were in a basement in the National Archives in New York, combing through file folders full of handwritten documents, and scrolling through digital records on their display films.

Agatha sat at an old, dusty desk crammed between damp-proofed plastic file boxes, breezing through the various digital files. Pano sat behind her on an office chair that had seen better days. His cowboy boots were up on a box, and he was leafing through paper file after paper file, his boredom apparent. Whenever he finished one, he slammed it down pointedly on the growing stack of brown folders behind him.

"If I read too many more of these, I'm going to start believing this shit myself," he muttered. When Agatha didn't respond, he just kept on talking. "Did you know that in Bolivia, there's an ancient megalithic temple complex called Puma Punku? There's a wall of stones there, each weighing over a hundred tons, and they're stacked so precisely that most of the joins, you wouldn't even be able to get a sheet of paper into. At the beginning of this millennium, scientists studying it had to conclude that they couldn't even build this structure with the modern tools of their time. So, how could the Maya have possibly done it?"

"Inca," Agatha corrected him.

"Them, too. Whatever. Have you ever seen what this wall looks like? I really can't imagine how the Inca could have ever built anything like it without advanced technology."

"Look, just because we can't imagine something doesn't mean it's proof that aliens did it, or that there was some lost civilization more advanced than we are today. Not by a long shot," Agatha countered, not even looking away from the file on her display film. "Sooner or later, the scientists always figure out how they did it, and then all the nutjobs feel pretty stupid, I guess."

"But there's more!" Pano grabbed one of the files he had put in the stack behind him and leafed through it quickly. "Here. The Antikythera mechanism. Around 1900, an object was recovered from a Greek shipwreck. Now, the shipwreck was dated to about 70 BC. The device was cast metal, with gears and dials, and it worked like an astronomical clock, but it was way more precise than anything up into the Late Modern era. It's sometimes referred to as the miracle machine."

He put the file aside and picked up another one. "Then there's the Palenque sarcophagus. Look at this. This was found in the burial chamber of King Pakal in Mexico. Now, see, the lid of the sarcophagus has these strange drawings, that obviously show the king sitting in a rocket and working some controls. But this carving was made in the seventh century. How do you explain that?"

Another file.

"Here, see, the Paluxy River footprints! In a riverbed in Texas, they found human-like footprints that were over a hundred million years old. Paleo-SETI theorists see this as proof that humans and dinosaurs existed at the same time, or else there had to have been a humanoid alien culture there then."

He flung that file onto the stack, and a new one found its way into his hand.

"So, next up. The boreholes at Abusir. In Egypt, near Giza, you've got these stone slabs made from diorite, one of the hardest rocks in the world. Now, they found these slabs with high-precision drill holes, real core drill work. These couldn't possibly have been made by the Egyptians. Even today you would need all kinds of modern drill bits to make holes like these."

"You don't really believe all this idiocy, do you?" Agatha asked, turning to him for the first time. Her expression made it absolutely clear that there was only one right answer.

"Yeah, well, but there's more. The Voynich manuscript, painstakingly written out in a completely unknown and unique language, which has still not been deciphered to this day. What we do know is that it's not based on any language system known in human history, and it's full of images of strange plants and constellations. It's at Yale, where they're still studying it because there's just so many things they don't..." He trailed off when Agatha's only response was a raised eyebrow.

Pano closed the file with a sigh. "Okay, fine, so what have you got?"

"Here, I've got the lending data archives," she replied. "There were two waves of checking out papers and books on paleo-SETI and ancient astronauts. Guess when."

"2040?"

"Yes. And in 2018, and then back in the 1960s when Erich von Däniken's stuff was popular."

"Hang on, it was 2018 when Ron Jackson disappeared, right?" Pano asked, leaning over to hold his hand terminal towards Agatha. She made a tossing gesture with her hand, and his terminal beeped, informing him that he had received a file.

"Hmm... His last confirmed location was the McMurdo Station in Antarctica... That was in May 2018. The borrowing began in June 2018. Proof?"

"A data point," she corrected him. "Another data point is that around that time, thirty percent of the material borrowed was reported stolen. But it was never traced."

"In the Internet Age? Why would someone even bother to steal something from the National Archive?" Pano asked. "That doesn't make sense."

"Maybe they were files or books that hadn't been put online yet. I mean, we're talking 2018 here," she suggested.

"Maybe. But that's not really why we're here, am I right?"

"You are. We're looking for something else, and I think I've found it. Rachel Jackson, our Doctor-Doctor-Doctor's late wife, borrowed a book about pyramids in May 2018—a bunch of specific pyramids found in Egypt by a well-known Egyptologist named Angela Micol. Now we know that these were hidden pyramids, even bigger than Giza, but not as well-preserved. At the time, that was still controversial."

"So that's what we've been looking for?" Pano asked, looking around the dusty basement. "If that's all, we could have called."

"If you want to know the truth, always get your information yourself. Otherwise it's like building a house out of guesswork—if one piece doesn't hold up like you thought it would, your whole case is going to come crashing down."

"Fine, then. So what are you thinking? His wife wanted

to finish his manuscript?" he asked, not sounding very convinced.

"I don't know," Agatha conceded, and abruptly stood up. "What it does tell me is that she wasn't as uninterested in her husband's work as the NSA thinks. And that, in turn, means they have very little data on what she *was* interested in. And that's pretty unusual these days, wouldn't you say?"

"Hmm. That's true. So she's trying to hide the fact that she was researching in his field, but she goes and checks stuff out from the National Archive on that exact subject?" Pano's interest was getting piqued now, and he stood up too.

"Exactly. The NSA's AI tracking is mainly tuned into terrorism and threat-related keywords, and generally focuses on the internet. I don't think they've extended the uncontrolled data dragnet all the way to the National Archive," Agatha said, smoothing her perfectly fitting pantsuit. "We should check out her house."

"But surely the FBI's already been there and messed it all up?"

"They mess everything up, but after the manuscript was found, Homeland Security ordered every agency to leave everything untouched and not let anyone in or out," she explained, grabbing her dark jacket, with CTD in large letters across the back, from where she had hung it on the chair. "Let's go."

They left the basement and soon they were in their CTD fleet Tesla 6 heading north along the Hudson River. From the viaduct over West Street, they had a good view beyond the floodwalls, all the way to the Upper Hudson Bay. A giant container ship with four tall Flettner rotors, like oversized watchtowers, was just pushing out of the bay, making a beeline towards the Atlantic.

Traffic was light, and Agatha looked out of the window

while the Tesla's self-driving mode steered her and her new partner unerringly towards her goal.

The day was unusually bright for early fall, and there were even some patchy sunbeams breaking through the thick gray cloud cover here and there. Where they did, they revealed the heavy drone traffic above the street level—countless taxi drones, and maybe even more package-delivery drones, like a swarm of flying ants feeding the city's insatiable hunger for the newest and the latest, the products of your dreams.

Pano, in the bucket seat next to her, dropped his *New York Times* into his lap and looked up at them, too. "Hard to imagine, isn't it," he said. "Barely 15 years ago, you would have looked up and seen not one thing flying around up there."

"I know. It's amazing how fast the world is changing."

"You mean, how fast the Human Foundation is changing the world."

"Yeah." She tore her gaze away from the hundreds of black dots zipping around above them and disappearing between the Manhattan skyscrapers.

"Do you think Karlhammer is behind the attacks on the members of the Senate and Congress?" the Italian asked her, pointing to the portrait of the impeccably coiffured man himself above his editorial in today's NYT. In the photo he was wearing a T-shirt that said, 'Save the Planet, Save Yourself,' and a comfy-looking, casual jacket. It was a look that could have been Silicon Valley Executive, or Street Person on a good hair day.

"It's hard to imagine anyone being so stupid. And to be honest, I don't really get a terrorist vibe from Mr. Self-Proclaimed Savior of the Planet," Agatha answered. She gestured vaguely behind her, where the rotor ship was setting off. "What his foundation has done for the Earth speaks for itself."

"But the floodwalls are still there," countered Pano.

"Well, he can't fix everything we screwed up in human history all at once, can he?" she countered.

"Man, you really are a groupie, aren't you?"

"No, I'm not. Can we just keep focused on the case? The sooner we've wrapped this up, the sooner we can get back to doing something useful, right?" Agatha stared the European defiantly in the face until he finally smiled and stuck his nose back into his newspaper.

The drive to Long Island took a little less than an hour. The Jackson house was one of the charming suburban colonials dotting Connetquot Avenue near Connetquot River State Park Preserve. The car stopped in front of number 22, with its white wooden paneling and its well-maintained shingle roof.

The front lawn was entirely cordoned off with yellow 'CRIME SCENE' tape. Two FBI-jacketed agents stood there waiting for them. One of them, an older man whose hair was already graying and whose belly extended farther than his belt, waved to them as they got out. "Hey, there you are!" he called.

"There you have it," Pano said. "If you needed any more proof that we've been put out to pasture, you're looking at it." He didn't even bother to lower his voice. As he said it, they closed their car doors.

Agatha walked around the sleek vehicle with its federal plates. She introduced herself and her new partner. "I'm Special Agent Devenworth, this is Capitano Hofer."

The two FBI men looked concerned for a moment before their smiles returned. They were probably relieved that they could finally go home—but that wasn't going to happen just yet.

"Agent Malone," the heavyset man said by way of introducing himself. He pointed to his younger colleague with his perfect haircut and the classic dark glasses. "This is Agent Juarez. Knock yourselves out." He pointed to the tape-cordoned property, starting to turn as if to go. Agatha stopped him with a raised hand.

"Not so fast, Malone. Were you here when the property was cordoned off and forensics arrived?" Agatha asked.

"Yes. That was only this morning. The lady died the day before yesterday, in the evening, was found last night, and we got the call from the police this morning when they noted that her husband was on the national missing persons list. So we came here, looked over everything, and found the manuscript," Malone said, scratching his gut. He seemed in a hurry to get somewhere.

Agatha inwardly raised an eyebrow, thinking, *'somewhere' is probably a donut shop.* Outwardly, she gestured to the door on the front porch. "Come with me. I might have a couple of questions for you."

The older officer grimaced, but nodded and motioned for the other man to accompany her.

Pano raised the crime scene tape so they could stoop under it, and together they walked to the porch.

Agatha noted a dog leash on the ground to her right. She turned to Malone. "A dog? Where is it now?"

"We found him behind the house with a smashed skull."

"What?" Pano asked.

"Behind the house." Malone pointed to the wall at his left.

"Well, where is he now?"

"No idea. The police took him and I expect they disposed of him," the FBI agent shrugged.

"Did you take any fingerprints? Was there an autopsy?" At Pano's question, Malone suddenly bristled, and his complexion turned from its former washed-out yellow to a deepening red.

"Listen, who the hell are you anyway, coming down here and giving orders?" he spat back. "*Capitano*? What the hell kind of name is that? And what's with that accent? I'm not answering anything until you identify yourself, pal!"

"Just what I needed, a walking, talking stomach ulcer," Agatha muttered, attracting a fuming glare from the agent. It seemed Malone wanted to say something but thought better of it, and just gnashed his teeth instead. "He's with me, and he's from Europol and he's been assigned to this investigation. This case is now a Homeland Security matter. You got anything to say about it, tell it to CTD Director Miller."

She held out her hand terminal to him with a 'what-do-I-care?' look. When he just stared at it, she shrugged. "Didn't think so. Now... answer *Capitano* Hofer's question."

"There was one usable fingerprint on the dog collar, but they didn't get any hits in the database. The neighbors didn't see or hear anything either, so that makes Mrs. Jackson the only suspect. But whaddya gonna do, prosecute a dead woman for cruelty to a dead animal? I didn't think so. So we just had the poor mutt taken away." Malone's voice was still trembling.

"Send the photos to my terminal." Agatha held her device out and waited until the agent had pulled out his and made the file-sending gesture, and hers had chirped in confirmation. "Thanks. Let's go in. Hofer? Since you're the charming one on this team, why don't you go talk to the neighbors? Maybe our dedicated colleagues might have missed something."

Malone grunted. Pano looked at Agatha briefly, smiled obligingly, and even made the slightest hint of a curtsy before disappearing around the side of the house.

It was dim inside the house because the officers had closed the blinds, evidently to keep out the neighbors' prying eyes.

Agatha pointed vaguely towards the windows in the large living room. "Could you please open those for me?"

Malone at first seemed hesitant to do so, but then gave a sign to Juarez and they flipped the switches on the walls to raise the blinds. The entire floor was a single space, except for the kitchen which was a separate room.

Daylight flooded in as Agatha strode into the living room, where the pale corpse of Mrs. Jackson lay on the sofa —lying stretched out with eyes open and hands contorted. The instructions had been not to move or remove the body, and no one had.

Agatha called up the forensics report on her terminal and scrolled down. "Interesting. A fingerprint on the right cheek, no match in the databases."

How can anyone in this day and age have fingerprints that aren't in any database? she wondered as she scanned what the forensic file had to say about the likelihood of scanning errors or contamination. *This is just the typical legalese somebody would write when they don't have an explanation but don't want to push through all the paperwork that a special case would require.*

Agatha moved to the display foil that was still stretched across the umbrella holder of the wooden secretary. It still displayed the document that had alerted the FBI to the plan in the first place. She breezed through the anthropology mumbo-jumbo until she got to the sentence, "We are not the rulers of this planet." The next sentence read, "Rather, we are the inheritors of this planet, and we should treat it accordingly."

Doesn't really sound like someone cobbling bombs together, she thought as she turned off the display foil with a gesture. It turned a barely glossy black.

"Agent Juarez?" Agatha called to the young Latino agent, who was in the adjoining dining room and had just finished rolling up the blind on the last window. "Could you move a little to your left and shine your flashlight in my direction?"

"Yes, ma'am," he answered. He reached for his flashlight and did what she had asked.

"Interesting."

"You found something?" Juarez asked, surprised.

"Maybe, maybe not," she replied, peering at a single, small greasy spot in the center of the display. It was about the size of a fingertip. "Agent Juarez, could you explain to me how someone would write text on a display film today?"

"Is this a serious question?"

"I only ask serious questions."

"Well, you dictate the text, and it gets saved on the hand terminal, and it appears on the display," he said, annoyed by the question, and moved next to her. "Or you could use the virtual keyboard on an AR headset."

"When was the last time someone used the touch function on a display film to enter input?"

"No clue... A hundred years ago?"

"Do you have your biometric scanner with you?" she asked, studying the spot more closely.

"Um..."

"Never mind. If you would, just go out to my car and

you'll find a silver case in the trunk. Would you please bring it in?"

"Of course." Still acting a little irritated, Juarez walked out of the house.

Agatha looked around, but didn't see anything else that caught her attention, so she read further in the forensic report. "No other fingerprints in the apartment that didn't belong to Rachel Jackson, but an unknown fingerprint on the dog collar and one on her face. Hmm."

When Juarez came back in, she pointed to the display and he opened the case, removing the small biometric scanner from it and using it to illuminate the display

"Let me guess," she said. "A print, but no match in our databases?"

"Um, yeah," he replied, without looking up from the device, and scanning the display again.

"Show me."

The agent handed her the device and she held it next to her hand terminal. It took a moment for the machines to exchange their authentication codes, and then the scanned image of the fingerprint appeared on her terminal. She compared it to the other two unknown prints and could see at a glance that they were identical.

"Well, look at that."

"You got something?"

"Yes," she said simply, and when Juarez figured out that she wasn't going to say anything else, he turned and left the living room, shaking his head.

"Who are you?" Agatha murmured to the image of the fingerprint on her terminal. Her eyes narrowed.

"Devenworth?" said a voice behind her. It was Pano, who had just come inside.

"Hmm?"

"The neighbors didn't see anything. Said they didn't hear the dog and they didn't see anyone unusual," he informed her, and his face revealed how much he thought of this story —as little as she did.

"We'll take them all down to the Bureau and have them questioned. There was obviously someone here. I found a third fingerprint, identical to the one on the dog collar and the one on Mrs. Jackson's cheek." Agatha pointed to the body and the display on the secretary. "Right there."

"There, where the text would have been displayed. Well, that's quite a coincidence." Pano pursed his lips and crossed his powerful arms over his chest.

"Apparently someone really wanted us to see this particular line of text."

"And investigate," Pano added.

"Well," she said, "it worked. Whoever you are, you've got my attention."

6

RON JACKSON, 2018

"Jackson, wait," Gould called, chasing after Ron with quick steps that echoed off the smooth walls. As always, he was still carrying his briefcase, although he was clutching it to his chest now, like a shield, and looking around frantically as if the ghosts of this place might descend upon him at any time.

"What is it you want, Mr. Gould?" Patchuvi asked with a roll of his eyes. He made no secret of what he thought of the bean-counter's presence.

"Jackson!" Gould repeated, ignoring the other man.

Ron stopped in front of a passageway leading west and spun around with barely concealed impatience. "Yes, what is it?"

"Can you please explain to me what all this means?"

"What it means is that in the early Paleozoic Era, there were creatures here who built this pyramid, or at least whatever is under it," the archaeologist quietly explained.

"But who would build anything in the Antarctic?"

"In the first chronostratigraphic phase, Antarctica as we

know it did not yet exist," Patchuvi interjected in a demeaning tone, a mocking expression on his face.

Gould didn't miss the snark. "I'm no rock-basher, Professor," he retorted, visibly annoyed, poking the professor in the chest, his index finger leaving a crater in the thick down jacket. "You want to be an asshole to me all the time? Fine! That's certainly going to be very helpful for my assessment."

"Aha, so you're here to audit us, is that right?" Patchuvi countered, his eyes narrowing and the corners of his mouth twitching in imagined triumph.

"Well, I'm not here to be treated like some dim first-grader, you got that? Oh, I know your kind—all you nerds who used to get beat up in school—why don't you go back in time to where you picked up this piss-poor attitude?" Gould bristled at the other man, leaving no doubt that he planned to have the last word in this conversation.

Sighing, Ron said, "Could we all just please calm down? We are about to take the last big step that is going to shore up all our theories, and all our work, with evidence that no one's going to be able to refute. Now, let's don't throw everything away for all of us by getting caught up in petty squabbles. Mr. Gould, I'm really trying to answer as many of your questions as possible, but please try to stay with us and don't keep interrupting. As I'm sure you can understand, I want to get familiar with this installation as quickly as possible. And you, Mitra, please don't make life harder on him than it already is down here. Luther's the one who sent him down here, he certainly didn't come voluntarily."

Patchuvi sighed and nodded reluctantly. Gould nodded too, and turned to Ron with an expectant look.

"To answer your question," he said, striking his gloved hand on the ice-coated wall where they stood, "chronostratigraphy is a method of classifying different types of rock by their age. The Paleocene was the period between about sixty-six million years B.C. and fifty-six million years B.C. If you want to be precise, we mean 'before now,' because we really date it as MYA, which stands for 'million years ago.' So anyway, in the Paleocene, you've got three *ages*: the lowest is the Danian; then you've got the middle one, the Selandian; and on top the Thanetian. What we're standing in was made in the Danian, which means within a few million years after the meteorite that killed the dinosaurs struck the Earth. At that time, there was no Arctic, and no frozen poles. At the beginning of the Danian, what is now South America, Australia, and Antarctica were all still a single continent, and its climate was, by and large, hot and humid. The only places on Earth you could call temperate were the North Pole and the South Pole—in other words, where we're standing right now."

"So you're saying, right here, it was a gentle climate... like Europe?" Gould asked, visibly astonished, and looked around like he was trying to rein in his imagination but failing.

"That's what I'm saying. Now, if you had been standing in Europe in the Danian, on the other hand, it would have been hot like Cambodia is today... maybe even a little hotter."

Gould nodded, beginning to understand. "So that's why you always focused on Antarctica in your research?"

"Right. At that time it was the most habitable place on Earth." Ron gestured to the passage behind him, where a power cable hung like a garland along the right wall. The yellow glow of the floodlights hanging from it at widely-spaced intervals occasionally flickered, as if they were in a bunker that was being bombed from high above. "Let's go."

Not waiting for Gould's response, Ron headed off down

the passage. Through his glove, the rock at either side and above him felt as smooth as linoleum as he dragged his hand over it. But when he brushed off the thin coating of ice covering it, the surface of the rock looked strangely rough. As his every breath left his lips, it formed a great cloud that quickly froze the instant it came into contact with the wall.

When they reached the largest room that Patchuvi's students had yet discovered, Ron was stunned. It was a vast chamber, more or less the size of a football field, but oval in shape. There were a dozen floodlights illuminating the ceiling, and countless smaller lights hung around the walls, but it was still not enough to drive away the millions of years of darkness from this place. He felt like he was in another dimension. It was as if he had stepped through a time portal and emerged inside a bubble made of pure darkness and tranquility.

An oppressive silence reigned here, so total and so thick that he thought he could have touched it if he had only been able to reach out far enough, until the noise of a small group of students working on the other side of the chamber pierced the silence. They were sounds that were all too familiar to him. The clanking of hammer and chisel, and the whirring of drills and high-frequency equipment, echoed around the perfectly formed cavern.

"What are they working on?" Ron asked.

"They're analyzing the composition of the structural material," explained Patchuvi. "We're doing that in all the chambers."

"What have they found so far?"

"Nothing yet. They're only just starting the analysis of the sediment layers."

"Are there any, actually?" Ron asked, looking over at the

distant shadows of the students busily working on the walls in the dim lamplight.

"What do you mean?"

"Well, it's clear that these are wall constructions, made according to a plan. They don't look like they've been affected by sediment deposits," Ron said. He took two steps to his left, produced a pen from his jacket pocket and began using it to scratch ice off the wall.

Patchuvi shook his head resolutely. "Something so old would not still exist in its original form."

"Have you ever looked at this? Does this wall at all resemble anything you've ever seen in Egypt or Mesopotamia?"

"No, but those places are not as cold and dry as here."

"What are the two of you going on about?" Gould interrupted, and he raised his case defensively as the two archaeologists turned to look at him.

"See, ancient stone structures are normally compressed by the layers of sediment on top of them. They lose their original shape through tectonic and seismic activity, from the pressure of the changing Earth's surface, as I said, and before that, of course through corrasion," Ron explained, tapping his pen against the grayish wall.

"Corrosion?"

"*Corrasion*," Patchuvi corrected, rolling his eyes and sighing. "Wearing caused by wind and weather. It's unusual, I grant you, but so is this place. I don't believe that there has ever been any kind of excavation at either one of the poles, so we have no reference values. According to everything that we know, the landscape here has remained virtually unchanged all these millions of years because there has been no dust to be blown on the wind." Patchuvi folded his hands in front of his mouth and blew into his puffy polar mittens, but the moment it left his mouth, the air that he blew was as cold as the environment.

"We'll see," Ron said thoughtfully. "We will see. Now, show me the rest of the installation and please send a map to my tablet, would you?"

"Of course."

The walk-through of the excavation site took several more hours, because they kept stopping. Ron began to think that they shouldn't really call it an excavation anymore, but rather a discovery, because in fact they were not excavating anything—it was all already exposed, and there were no layers of dirt, stone, or dust to be removed as there would be at any archaeological site in Europe, Asia, or Africa. While it all looked long-abandoned, and certainly not maintained in any way, at the same time it gave the impression that it had only been mothballed. Because no creatures lived in these tunnels, there was no moisture, and because the cold had blanketed the whole place in an impenetrable layer of death, there was no need for any maintenance. But he was still astonished, even after everything he had seen in his career, that this place could have remained so unchanged for millions upon millions of years.

As far as he could tell, the chambers and passageways made up quite an extensive complex. The map that had been sent to Ron's tablet had been made by laser scanning, and it showed how vast the entire complex was. Eighty passageways, two hundred and thirteen rooms, chambers and caves—it was truly incredible. Since the survey had actually been done by drone, there were vast sections that the team had not yet reached. One thing was clear, however, and that was that there were no objects or fossils anywhere. It was all empty and virtually sterile, and something about that kept nagging in Ron's mind. It was almost like a house that had been thoroughly inspected, packed up, and vacated —by someone.

"The high iridium concentration, where exactly did you measure it?" Ron asked when they paused in one elongated room that looked just as smooth and featureless as all the others they had seen.

"In the sedimentary rock layers lower down in the mountain," Patchuvi replied.

"You mean pyramid?" Gould blurted. He had remained impressively quiet over the past few hours but couldn't keep up the discipline any longer.

"The pyramid and the mountain are one and the same."

"I don't understand. Didn't you tell me, Mr. Jackson, that nature abhors symmetry?"

"That's right," Ron nodded. "And this pyramid isn't perfectly symmetrical, if you actually measure it. But it seems like in this case nature, by sheer coincidence, came pretty close."

"But I saw you on CNN when you said that you don't believe in coincidence."

Ron smiled. "That's right, and I don't. But I don't have any other explanation, either. The data doesn't support the idea that this mountain is artificial, because the rock strata clearly identify the different epochs. The one at the bottom has the iridium anomaly, so that means the early Paleozoic. The one above it does not, which means that that rock was deposited there over millions of years. That makes the symmetrical shape very hard to explain."

"But maybe there was a pyramid built here over 60 million years ago, and then it grew by some natural process? Could that be possible?" Gould mused with lips so cold that they were turning blue.

"At this point, I have to consider that anything is possible. What's going to be important now is to find out how old the rock in these walls is. When can we expect the first results?" Ron asked, turning to Patchuvi, who had just taken a sip from a steaming thermos. He passed it to Ron, who grunted his thanks before taking his own sip.

"We sent the first samples from the walls of the passageways and chambers to Vienna a week ago," the professor said, wiping his nose with the back of his hand. "We should have the results first thing tomorrow."

"Why Vienna?" Gould asked.

"The university there is the location of the particle accelerator that performs the accelerator mass spectrometry for us, which is what we need to do to date materials like this."

"Oh."

"You thought we could do that here?" Patchuvi snorted, once more belittling the accountant. "No, every time we need to do that we need a helicopter to pick up a few crates of samples. That's why this entire operation is very, very, time-intensive, Mr. Gould."

"Then I'll be very much looking forward to seeing those results tomorrow," Ron said, passing the thermos to the accountant, who smiled with a grateful nod while the professor raised a disapproving eyebrow.

Ron didn't particularly care for Peter Gould, whom he considered basically a small-minded bean-counter, a desk jockey with no vision, but that didn't make him a bad person. He didn't believe that there were any bad people. Just people you had a lot in common with and with whom you could get along, and those with whom you didn't, and couldn't. That's just the way things were, and it shouldn't have to cause problems between himself and Gould—which was why he found Patchuvi's overt hostility more irksome than Gould just being Gould.

"You know, at this point I could really use some shuteye," the financial man announced, visibly stifling a yawn, as he handed the thermos back to Patchuvi.

Ron would have preferred to keep marching on, to see the next room and the next passageway, although fully aware that there was going to be nothing new to see. But there was still the tiny chance that he would find something that the drones and the students had missed. That was, after all, why he had come.

"All right then, let's go back to the expedition area," Ron said before Patchuvi could say anything. He'd thought he had seen the glimmer of a contrarian response developing on the professor's face. Before that point, they had walked through a second cavern, the same size as the first. This was where the students had taken the latest samples. But this 'expedition cavern,' as it was apparently being called, was much better illuminated, and there were six tents here, each looking like half a balloon stuck to the smooth cavern floor and glowing with a whitish light from within. They were connected by tent tunnels, and their number was an indication of how many experts from various fields were due to arrive in the coming days and weeks to expand the work going on here. The Human Foundation was staking everything on this, that much was clear. Luther had kept his word, and that gave Ron hope for himself, the future of his foundation, and Luther's state of mind.

Each of the tents was the size of a small house, but they still looked small in this vast chamber. In the middle of the tent cluster were four blocks of shielded generators, from which thick cables snaked off to each tent. One thing was for sure, he would have to sleep with earplugs. But being that the alternative was freezing to death, he didn't want to complain.

Looking at this otherworldly human settlement now, and realizing that it must have cost titanic sums of money to transport all this, plus all the diesel fuel to run it, to this remote, icy darkness at the edge of the world, Ron suddenly found it entirely reasonable that Luther had forced him to take Gould with him. It might really be that cutting a few costs here and there could keep the exhibition running long enough to find some answers.

Patchuvi gave him a very brief tour of the little tent city. The entrance tent served as a changing room. It had about thirty lockers, two of which had been prepared for Ron and Gould. Here they exchanged their thick thermal suits for jeans and turtleneck sweaters with the Human Foundation logo, and walked through the gleaming white light of the first tent tunnel into the second tent. The dome of the tent was also lined with a kind of grayish-white, inflatable insulation material, which looked like spray-on polyurethane foam but was slightly translucent. It wasn't warm here, but nothing like as cold as it was outside. For Ron, it was like a chilly autumn day, and he kept crossing his arms to keep warm. It seemed he would have to get used to being constantly cold, although he probably should have expected that.

This tent was a workroom with six long tables, where students were sorting rock samples into various plastic crates, and then labeling the crates. When Ron walked in, all eyes fixated on him and most of the students gave him an awestruck nod. It made him feel uncomfortable, and he could only muster a brief wave before signaling to Patchuvi to bustle him on.

"That was the dining room, and also our workroom. We don't have all that much space, so at mealtimes we clear the work area, wipe it down, and set up the chairs," Patchuvi explained.

Ron and Gould nodded and followed the professor through a storage room and then the washroom with three showers, three chemical toilets, and three washbasins. The whole washroom was filled with a penetrating and unpleasant smell of solvent. Ron didn't want to think about what it would smell like when the expedition reached its full complement of personnel.

Next were the two sleeping tents, with ten triple-bunkbeds, most of which were still unoccupied. In the rearmost sleeping tent, only two beds were taken, one by Patchuvi and one by his assistant James, who had left the tour earlier to take care of other duties.

"I'll sleep in the tent with the students," Ron announced.

Patchuvi looked at him incredulously. "Are you serious?"

"Yeah. I don't want us to end up with two classes of people here, or for them to always be looking at me with that look like I could just point my finger and explain the universe to them. That will be over as soon as they hear me snore, and wake up in the same room with me every morning. That's always how it goes," he explained, and strode off back to the other tent where nearly half of the beds were occupied. There, he took a free bottom bunk, tossed his backpack under it, and took off his shoes. He crawled under the blanket, still with all his clothes on, to warm up.

Gould stayed in the other tent with Patchuvi, and that was fine with Ron. He was still thinking about whether to get up and go to the washroom to maintain some modicum of hygiene when he fell asleep.

7

FILIO AMOROSA, 2042

In the morning someone awakened her by gently shaking her shoulder.

"Hey, little one. Time to go," Alberto said in his familiar Spanish accent.

Filio nodded dreamily and glanced at her diver's watch. It said 7:30. *Three hours of sleep*, she thought, shaking her head in exhausted disbelief. If she kept this up, soon she wouldn't even be able to remember her own name.

Her limbs stiff, she rolled out of her bunk and pulled her earplugs out. Despite the constant drone of the engines, with the earplugs she could at least get some halfway decent sleep—when she finally got to sleep, that was. Passing the mess hall on her way to the rear deck, she grabbed a banana and, without stopping, peeled it and robotically stuffed it into her mouth.

The deck behind the bulky superstructure of the *Ocean's Bitch* was a long, flat space, fully roofed over, with racks down the middle for all the oxygen tanks and diving equipment.

Romain and Jane were already there, taking their BCD

vests down from their hooks, gathering their masks and wetsuits, and collecting their tools into crates.

As they had agreed, Thomas was staying on the bridge and would be taking the watch. Alberto was standing by the air tanks and waved to Filio when she came in.

"Well, *you* look like you're ready to roll," he said.

"Thanks a lot," she sneered back.

"Seriously, little one, you really need to get more sleep. I know how you give it your all—we all do, and we all appreciate it." He spoke almost pleadingly, and his soft, clean-shaven face looked genuinely concerned. "But you really don't have to prove anything to us, Filio. We all know that you're an irreplaceable member of our little family of dreamers and weirdos, and all of us would go through fire for you. Just like you would for us. You can sit out this dive, you know. Really. You won't miss anything."

But I know if I miss something once, then I'll have missed it all, she thought to herself. But what she said out loud was, "It's all right, I'll be fine."

"Heads up, people," Thomas's voice suddenly erupted from the speaker beneath the deck's cover. "We've got a visitor—two clicks north by northeast."

Alberto's face fell, and Filio also saw his body tighten. Everyone ran to the starboard side, where Romain and Jane leaned over the railing and looked forward.

"Oh, *putain*," the captain cursed, and angrily reached for a hanging line.

"Who is it?" Filio asked, taking the Frenchman's binoculars. Leaning over the railing, she put them to her eyes and scanned the horizon.

It didn't take her long to spot the other ship, heading straight for their position.

"It's the *Gloucester*," she growled, and handed the binoculars off to Alberto.

"Ah, shit! *Les goddams*, they follow us to every dive spot we approach," Romain seethed, and his French accent got stronger, as it always did when he got angry. "And we've never even found anything yet. What the hell are they expecting?"

"They must have followed us out of Malé when we refueled," Filio guessed. She wasn't getting angry, probably because she was simply too tired to. But the *Gloucester* was going to be a problem if they found something here, because then it would be a race. The idea that the crew of the other scrapper could come along and snatch their prize right out of their hands—and achieve that without having done anything other than chasing around after them—was pretty hard to swallow.

"So what do we do?" Alberto asked after returning the binoculars to Romain. "Go down anyway?"

"Of course. We get down there as fast as we can, so if there is anything, we get it before they do," Romain answered, clenching his fists.

"Or, we could try a different approach," Filio suggested, and all eyes turned to her. "We can sail away and come back here by night. If the weather report is right, it's going to be cloudy tonight. That means no light. If we shut everything down, they'll lose us."

"But that also means diving in the dark, with just our dive lights—and they could still find us by radar, or they might just hold this position," Jane cautioned.

"We have to at least get out of their radar range once. We could pretend we're heading back into Malé for fuel."

"Jane's right. If they decide to stay here and see why we wanted to get down here, we're screwed."

Romain shook his head. "We're going down."

Filio wanted to say something back, but she could see that the Frenchman had decided. Whenever he got that look on his face, there was no changing his mind.

Romain pushed the talk button next to the speaker and asked, "How much time do we have?"

Thomas's voice sounded tinny through the old loudspeaker. "If they keep their speed, their course is going to intersect our position in about 15 minutes."

"Intersect!" Filio shouted suddenly, and a hot, shivering feeling sprouted from the top of her head and ran down to the soles of her feet. "Wait!"

"What?" Romain, Jane, and Alberto asked, all at the same time, looking at her like she was a ghost.

"I have to get to my calculations!" she shouted, and ran to the stairs without another word.

"Hey! We've got to get down there," Romain yelled after her, angry, but she paid no attention, and she had disappeared into the ship before he could take another breath.

Gasping, Filio reached her desk and began frantically rummaging through the hundreds of sheets of paper covered in equations, geometric diagrams, and notes. She let out a frustrated hiss when half of them fell to the floor, but she quickly managed to find the scrap she was looking for. The key had not been some piece of the puzzle she was missing, but a mistake in the calculation of two intersections—an error so clear to her now that she would have liked nothing better than to grab herself by the collar and beat herself silly.

"What's going on?" she heard Romain asking frantically from behind her, his voice trembling with rage.

"Just go without me, if you guys don't want to wait," she shot back, adding a sigh. "I'm sorry, I'm just really exhausted and stressed. And I think I just nailed my calculation of the probable location of the *Mars One* tailpiece! I just have to put in one last number."

"But what if you're wrong and we lose this claim?" Romain called back, still angry and panting from running after her.

"I know I'm asking a lot. But *please* just trust me," she begged him, then put a hand on his arms which were now crossed over his chest. Their eyes locked for what felt like an eternity, during which time she could see the deep affection he had for her, and which always triggered feelings of guilt because she could never reciprocate it.

"OK then," he sighed, finally yielding. "I just hope you're right. In two months, the money to pay the crew will be gone, and that includes you. And that would break my heart."

"Well, I'm not going to let that happen," she promised him, even though she knew she might not be able to keep that promise. Even if her calculations were correct, the target area was still extensive. The search had gone from finding a grain of sand in the universe to merely finding a needle in a haystack—something that at least offered a spark of hope.

"I'll tell the others and change course," Romain said after one more long look.

"Yeah. We still have to shake these guys, too."

"Leave that to me," Romain assured her with a mischievous grin. "*Les goddams* won't know what hit them."

"Make sure they *do* know what hit them," she said, laughing.

"See, I don't even get your language." With that, he turned on his heel and headed for the bridge, shooing

Oscar, who had appeared in the doorway with a confused look on his face.

Filio didn't waste any time, spreading her notes out on the floor. Her system was entirely logical in her own head, but would have looked like an incomprehensible mess to anyone else. She did sometimes wonder whether she had gone crazy. If she had been watching someone else doing what she was doing—clearly obsessed, losing sleep and scribbling notes on hundreds of scraps of paper—she would have called in the funny farm crew without a second thought.

But for her there was no way back, only forward, as always when there was something she wanted—and what could possibly be a stronger motivation than learning why her comrades, her friends, her family had been fated to die up there, high in the Earth's atmosphere, all those years ago?

She stopped, exhaled deeply, and scanned the scraps with her eyes. As always, she unerringly zoomed in on the spot she wanted. Amazingly, it was barely five minutes before the error was corrected and the key was in her hand.

She was exploding with excitement as she ran to the bridge, clutching a sheet of paper on which she had scribbled a bunch of coordinates. Romain was there, at the wheel now, with Thomas keeping an eye on the *Gloucester* through a pair of binoculars. She could tell by the roar of the diesel engines that they were already running hard. The *Ocean's Bitch* was plowing through the gentle swells like an old tractor, spray whipped up by her prow sweeping over the foredeck and crashing against the windows of the bridge.

"I've got it!" she shouted, waving the piece of paper in Romain's face.

The captain's eyes didn't move, but his brow furrowed

and he bellowed his reply over the roar of the engines. "What the hell are you talking about?"

"I know where we need to be looking!"

"Are you sure you're right?" he asked skeptically. He seemed nervous. Something in his eyes seemed to tell her, *you'd better be right.*

"I'm absolutely, positively, sure," she answered, her excitement barely containable.

A cautiously optimistic smile flashed on Romain's face, and he gestured to the large, slightly inclined control display at the helmsman's station. "Put the coordinates in there and let's roll."

"We've still got English on our ass," Thomas growled, pointing out the window to the starboard.

"Not for long," Romain said, his grin turning slightly evil. He reached for the radio microphone in the mounting above his head and pulled it down to his mouth. "This is Captain Romain Alhy of the *Ocean's Bitch*, calling the Coast Guard."

At first the only answer was static and noise, but after a few seconds a lilting voice drawled in English: "This is *Okamalé*, receiving you."

Romain spoke loudly and clearly into the radio. "*Okamalé*, we want to report a possible case of illegal drug trafficking and possible smuggling activities."

Filio and Thomas both stared at him, jaws dropping in unison.

"We saw the *Gloucester*, call sign One-Two-Two-Eff-Ten, loading white packages off a Zodiac. It might be nothing, but we know that you guys don't want to take any chances. We just want to do our part. We appreciate everything you do, from the bottom of our hearts."

"Thank you for the tip, *Ocean's Bitch*, we'll take it from

here. If you spot any other potentially illegal activities being carried out, do not hesitate to contact us again. *Okamalé* out."

Romain returned the microphone to the mounting, still grinning.

Thomas was apoplectic. "Do you know... what you've done?" he stammered.

"Yeah. Got rid of our shadow."

"You've made us a target for every scrapper on the seven seas! When the Gloucester gets through with the Coast Guard, they're going to tell the whole bloody world. You're breaking every code there is out here, and there's no place you'll ever be able to refuel again, the captains will see to that," Thomas admonished. His face was turning red from the agitation. "This is... a catastrophe," was all he could think of to conclude.

"*Non, mon ami*, I am only playing roulette, and putting all the stakes on one number."

"What number?"

"Filio."

Filio was nervously shifting her weight from one foot to the other and trying to look stoic.

"But what if she's wrong?"

"She's not."

"But why are you suddenly so sure now?"

"You know why—because she has to be right! It's not like we have much choice. The money is almost gone. Okay, I wasn't going to tell you like this, but Montgomery decided not to continue the funding. That means in two months we're high and dry. In fact, if we don't find anything now, on this trip, we don't even have enough money for diesel and it's all over. So we're betting it all on Filio, and if we do and she's right and we find something, I can't have our shadow

The Fossil

back there coming up behind us and taking it out from under us."

Thomas opened his mouth to answer, but closed it again before he said anything. Filio thought it made him look like a fish.

"Anyway, we've got time now. These Muslim states don't mess around when it comes to anything to do with drugs. They're gonna get hauled into port, and they're gonna take that ship apart, and what scrapper doesn't have a few joints on board somewhere?" Romain explained. Thomas gave a final grunt and headed towards the door.

"I'll go tell the others."

When the German had disappeared from the bridge, Romain looked at Filio and smiled.

Filio raised her chin and nodded to him. "Thanks," was all she said.

"You've earned it, little one."

"Do you really have to keep calling me that?" Filio groaned, rolling her eyes. "Just because I'm a midget?"

"Yes."

They both laughed hard and couldn't stop. All the pressure that had amassed to this point fell away.

"Hey, don't forget NASA is saving a lot of money with you," chuckled Romain at last, as the laughter trailed off. He made some corrections at the wheel while Filio checked the coordinates she had entered.

"ESA," she corrected him, focusing on her coordinates.

"Whatever. Them too. Smaller spacesuits, lower takeoff weight, space-saving designs."

She snorted and turned back to look at him. "I haven't been described that sweetly since my poetry album in the third grade."

"Are these the coordinates?" Romain asked, changing

the subject and focusing on his screen above the wheel. On it, an area of about thirty square nautical miles south of the last atoll of the Maldives was shaded in red.

"Yes, those are the coordinates," Filio whispered, staring at the image, spellbound. It was a surreal moment, seeing her goal and her deepest desires concentrated into this single spot on a map. It could have all been so simple, if she could have just seen it like this sooner. Two years of hard work, countless setbacks, and gnawing, ever-present self-doubt, were suddenly melting away into these thirty square miles of sea.

I can't believe it.

"We'll have that mapped out with the sonar in no time," Romain said triumphantly, grinning from ear to ear. "You know, there's something liberating about burning your bridges. From here on out, there's only one way to go, and that's forward. You either go through the wall, or you smash yourself into it. It's all or nothing. But what else for the *Ocean's Bitch*, right?"

"Well, that's the way it is now," Filio murmured as she quickly calculated the time they would need to reach the area shaded on the map. Eight hours. Eight hours stood between her and the chance of getting her old life back, or at least finding some meaning to her past and her future.

8

INTERLUDE, 2042

Senator Bob Brown sat on the back seat of a GMC EFalcon as it whisked him through the light midafternoon traffic heading to the capitol. The electric SUVs in the Senate car fleet were spacious, so he and his wife Barbara had plenty of space to comfortably go over his notes for his upcoming speeches.

In the thirty years he had been in Congress, he had still never taken to writing his speeches on a hand terminal. He wrote them all out on paper. Naturally, a lot of people, especially Democrats, of course, called him a Luddite, opposed to progress, for that reason—but that was not the only reason.

"So *now* what's eating you?" Barbara asked, looking up from one of the sheets in front of her.

"I'm thinking about the political fallout this speech is going to cause," he admitted, collecting the pages spread out between them and shuffling them together. "Don't look at me like that, Barb."

His wife had now pulled her old-fashioned reading glasses down to the tip of her nose to peer at him over the top of the frames. This was the look she always put on when she wanted to show him that she had something to say.

"Why not? Because you know I'm right? Then I guess we don't need to talk about it."

"It's not as simple as that. Even in my own party, only a handful of senators and congressmen are willing to speak out against the Human Foundation. And only a few of those would support a bill to strip it of its nonprofit status," he explained. Looking ahead between his driver and his bodyguard, he could see the Capitol Building gradually growing larger.

"But your argument is so solid that no one could really reject it, or almost no one," she reassured him, leaning forward to place a petite hand on his forearm. "And besides, you're the best speaker I know."

"Thanks, Barb."

"That's what I'm here for, darling. Now, let's just go over the middle part again, okay? And this time, make your voice a little deeper when you get to the market penetration part, to give that point more weight."

"Yes, yes, that's good." Senator Brown cleared his throat, took the third page from the barely organized stack of paper and began to read.

"Each of you benefits in some way from the Human Foundation. Remember the Clean Ocean Project? It's been out there for twenty years, quietly sucking up and disposing of the plastic in our oceans. And it's been so successful, with 90% of plastic waste gone, that it would be easy to forget about the problem! Well, that was a Human Foundation project. Then there are the incredible breakthroughs in the treatment of cancer and autoimmune diseases—these, too, an achievement of the Human Foundation.

"But there's more—much more. Reduction of CO_2 levels

in the atmosphere with Breathing Earth One, the algae CO_2 filtration carpet in the Pacific, and its companion installation Breathing Earth Two in the Atlantic—again, a project of the Human Foundation. I could go on, of course, with the endless list of revolutionary technologies that we owe to the foundation—the Hypertrack, the revival of airship travel that took so many vehicles off our roads, the continuing advancements in electromobility. And I will be the first to acknowledge that without the Human Foundation, we would never have landed on Mars three years ago.

"But, my esteemed colleagues of the Senate, there is a *but*. With most, if not all, of our advancements of recent decades coming to us from the Human Foundation, we must remember that ultimately, the Human Foundation is a single person: Luther Karlhammer. I ask you, my fellow senators, when, in the history of this great country, have we ever allowed a single company to take hold of half of all the markets that power our economy? The answer, my colleagues, is never! And amazingly, the Human Foundation is not even a company, but a nonprofit organization. Luther Karlhammer lives in his palace in Cape Town, much less like an altruist than an emperor. His foundation's facilities are guarded by the most dangerous private armies that money can buy—something the foundation can easily afford. I ask you, Senators, does that sound like a charitable foundation to you?"

"Good, and right there you pause briefly," Barbara interrupted him gently, and smiled as he nodded.

"Obviously not. Over my more than thirty years in this house, I have earned the reputation of being a fiscal conservative, but I am also pragmatic, and proud of that. I am very much aware that over half of the world population participates in the Human Foundation's lottery system. I am very much aware that we cannot break them up or bring them down, nor do I wish to do any such thing. But what I am calling for today, with every possible urgency, is that we in the United States must reclassify the Human Foundation as a for-profit business. We must rally the full strength of the Internal Revenue Service behind us, and give to the Human Foundation all the rights and obligations of a corporate structure in which all Americans have the right to participate... We... uh..." he trailed off, looking first at Barbara and then over his shoulder and out the window.

"What?"

"Where did all the cars go?"

He was still wondering why all the traffic around them had completely disappeared when the two kilograms of plastic explosives that had been wrapped around the titanium plate protecting the battery of the GMC E-Falcon exploded.

The vehicle and all its occupants went up in a giant fireball barely eight hundred meters from the Capitol Building.

9

AGATHA DEVENWORTH, 2042

Director Miller had assigned Agatha and Pano an office that they could clear out and use. Now they were sitting in that office, staring at the television, transfixed. The images of the assassination of the very popular Senator Bob Brown and his wife Barbara were on a permanent loop on every channel. There was footage showing the explosion from different angles, then the screaming passersby running away in panic and the first public safety officers and firefighters arriving on the scene and trying to extinguish the flames of the wreck.

The news anchor, a blonde with makeup meticulously applied to make her look like every other female news anchor, was superimposed on the screen, and next to her ran a video clip of a man talking straight into the camera. Behind him, the flag of the Sons of Terra hung on a wall—the stylized alien face, one eye black and the other identifiable as the Earth.

"Why are they still out there taking responsibility, anyway?" Pano asked, shaking his head. "Everyone knows it was them."

"They live for these videos."

"But why? 'Oh hey, did you hear Luther Karlhammer and the Human Foundation's most influential critic was blown up today? Yeah, that was us.' It's like putting up a sign that says the ocean is blue and the sun is yellow."

"They want attention, and they get it. Every time that flag appears on the news, more people know about them."

"Wonderful. Obviously they're so hell-bent on hitting the Human Foundation as hard as they can that even Senator Brown wasn't too sensitive a target for them," Pano turned off the video display and turned his chair to face Agatha. She turned slowly to look at him, as if she was still seeing images on the black screen. "So what do you think?"

"I think you're right," Agatha said. "It's clear the Sons of Terra want to bring down the Human Foundation in the U.S. by making it look like they're doing it a favor. I'm sure you realize that the murder of the Human Foundation's most famous antagonist is going to set off one of the biggest investigations of recent decades. And it's going to be highly political. And if it doesn't produce the right results or if any mistakes are made, heads are going to roll—"

"—and that means the first thing to do is to get bogged down and wrapped up in the craziest, most harebrained connections to anything and everything, like way back with the Unabomber," Pano finished her line of thought, ending with a contemptuous snort. "The possibility that they've got it backwards, and that the Sons of Terra are actually gunning for the Human Foundation, will be the very last thing they consider, because no one's going to stick their neck out when the Secretary and the President are breathing down their necks."

"That's always how it goes," Agatha said apathetically, with a shrug of her shoulders. "They need the bad guy, and if they don't get him fast, they'll take whatever scapegoat they can get their hands on to save their own political skins."

"So what are we going to do about it?"

"Nothing," she replied resolutely. "Our assignment is to discover whatever Ron Jackson's connection to the Sons of Terra was."

"But it's all connected!" he protested, staring at her like she had just started speaking Swahili. "You can see that, can't you?"

"Maybe so. It seems likely enough that someone planted this document in his house to substantiate a link between Jackson and the Human Foundation, and from there to the Sons of Terra. I don't believe in coincidence, and since the bomb happened not even half a day later, I'm going to assume that somebody wants to raise the stakes on this case until we have no choice but to end up at that conclusion. But that doesn't mean that if we start coming up with a bigger picture than the small one Director Miller was looking for, he'll just let us off the leash."

Pano looked at her for a moment and then smiled. "But once you smell smoke, you're not going to let that stop you, are you?"

"That's right," Agatha admitted, and reached for her hand terminal on the file-laden table behind her. "Call Agent Mitchell Fanning, Level Three."

She waited for a second and then put the terminal to her ear. "Hi, Fanning. I need the footage from all the traffic and surveillance cameras within a hundred-meter radius of the site of the attack sent to my terminal. Yeah, everything you have. Of course. Yes. The release code is four, three, two, two, two, one, seven. Good. Thanks."

Agatha put the terminal back down, seemingly satisfied.

"Miller probably shouldn't have said that we could use *all* the resources of the whole department."

Pano grinned. "He probably only said that because he knew we wouldn't need them."

"Yeah. Until those files arrive, we should go over our results so far one more time," she suggested, and picked up her hand terminal again. "Okay, so the examination and autopsy report are now complete, and they give the cause of death as acute heart failure resulting from scarring of the heart valve tissue. It seems that Rachel Jackson had been aware of this but had refused surgery for it. No signs of external trauma. Results of blood tests are normal, except for slightly elevated bilirubin, which would be consistent with a mild viral or bacterial infection. No residues of toxins or other foreign substances. So clearly whoever left the strange fingerprints didn't kill her."

"We also have the reports from the neighbors' questioning," Pano took over, pointing to his own hand terminal. His looked different from Agatha's, more like a flexible, rectangular shard of glass. "They all said they didn't see or hear anyone, and the polygraph says they weren't lying. Three of them were even outside in their own gardens at the time the dog died, and still didn't notice anything. But lie detectors don't lie, so we let them go."

Agatha thought for a moment. "Hmm... the one thing that ties this whole case together is the Sons of Terra. Forget for the moment whether they're working for or against the Human Foundation. Jackson's manuscript and Brown's assassination both have some connection with them, so let's start there."

"Makes sense so far. So... where do we start?"

"With the images."

Pano seemed confused. "What images?"

The Fossil

"From the assassination. The first thing they're going to focus on is the explosive and the device—what mixture, what detonator, how complex? Then they are going to trim down the circle of possible suspects to the people who could have pulled it off. Then, they're going to identify and question all the eyewitnesses," Agatha explained, looking at her hand terminal when it beeped. She made a swiping gesture across its screen, towards the television. It blinked on, showing a black GMC E-Falcon SUV from a slightly elevated angle. After a few seconds, it exploded and the video stopped.

"The camera images are here. There were eight cameras total that had the attack and the area in view. We're going through them now," she said. When Pano held up a finger she looked at him with a raised eyebrow.

"What exactly are we looking for?" he asked, and pointed to the frozen image on the TV.

"A spotter."

"A spotter? Isn't that what Islamists used to use, like, fifty years ago? I don't think that—"

"Why not?" Agatha interrupted him, more curious than irate.

"Because any self-respecting terrorist organization has software applications that can tell whether a television recording is real. They're the same software that the multimedia broadcasters use. The job is successful when the images make it onto the TV news."

"You're thinking like a normal person," Agatha said, and kept talking when she saw Pano's look of astonishment. "But the Sons of Terra are not normal people. They are fanatics and nutjobs who are convinced that an all-powerful alien has taken over our world, and is controlling their fate. And they don't believe anything unless one of their fanatics has seen it with his own eyes and confirmed it. Their philosophy is that all media, all of it, has been infiltrated by *The Enemy,* as they call the alien, just like most governments have been. They haven't said much about the Human Foundation yet, but even a nutjob can see that at this point Karlhammer's had a decisive influence on the fate of our species—maybe even controls it entirely. So it's only logical for the foundation to be a target, too. I guarantee you there was a spotter on the scene of this attack, the real old-fashioned analog kind. And they wouldn't have been too concerned about it, because they know that these days every agency runs their prosecutions by algorithms. Profilers are extinct, and lateral thinkers are undesirable."

"Yeah, I guess we both know that first-hand," Pano agreed, and nodded. "All right, then. What are we looking for exactly?"

"A person who doesn't turn when it happens—someone who either doesn't react with surprise, fear, or panic like everyone else, or who is pretending to react like everyone else," Agatha explained, swiping the files towards his hand terminal. The familiar triad tone confirmed that they had been received. "So put on your data glasses and get started."

"I love it when you do the boss thing," Pano remarked with a smirk and a wink.

Agatha rolled her eyes and put on her glasses. After the device had paired with her hand terminal, multiple videos appeared before her eyes, all of them running simultaneously and overlaid into a single virtual reality view. Now and then, she gestured to stop one, zoom in or out of another, enlarge a section, or move one camera view beside another to compare them. She focused on groups of bystanders, going through one face after another, paying attention to the expressions in the eyes, mouth, and facial coloration. It was complex and tedious work, and it demanded that she watch each video countless times in search of any irregular pattern of behavior in any of the bystanders in her virtual view.

After a while, an object that didn't belong in the virtual environment floated in front of her eyes. It was a cup, and it smelled like coffee. She turned off the glasses and took the steaming cup from Pano's hand with a grateful nod.

"Got anything yet?" Pano asked, and she shook her head.

"Me neither," he admitted, taking a thick file off of his desk chair. "So I read Ron Jackson's file for a while."

Agatha suppressed the urge to call him out for not doing what he was told, deciding to listen to him instead.

"Jackson knew Karlhammer. He first met him in 2010, and was even Chairman of the Human Foundation when he disappeared in 2018. Did you know that?"

"Yes. I skimmed through the file on the way to his house. 'Chairman' with no operational authority—probably just a goodwill gesture by Karlhammer, who had—by that point—long since taken the reins. Today, hardly anyone remembers that the two of them established the foundation together."

"So it would seem. Do you know from where Jackson disappeared?"

"In Cape Town."

"That's right. In the harbor there, to be precise. Now, why do people disappear?"

"Statistically, eighty percent because they want to disappear," Agatha said, and narrowed her eyes to show him that she was in no mood for a game of twenty questions.

"Exactly. So, the last time Jackson's seen is in the harbor of the city that is home to the headquarters of the most powerful organization in the world," Pano continued, waving a piece of paper from the file.

"But at that time it's still just an unremarkable foundation headed by two guys everyone thinks are nutjobs and utopians. In those days, the only places their names came up were in the pseudoscientific rags," Agatha countered, and waved him away when Pano tried to hand her the piece of paper.

"Sure. But according to the file, they already had anonymous donors by that time. And exactly one year after Jackson's disappearance, Karlhammer set three major environmental innovations into motion at the same time—the algae, the plastic collectors and the Flettner rotors," he explained flatly, and turned the page.

"Flettner rotors are an old theory," she objected.

"That may be, but he made them so efficient both financially and performance-wise that they became really viable, and the shipping companies lined up to buy them from him. That's when they started to turn their backs on diesel, en masse."

"What are you getting at?"

"Jackson disappears, and suddenly the Human Foundation takes off. There has to be a connection."

"Jackson knew a lot of people who thought he was a nutjob," Agatha argued. "His disappearance could have boosted the Foundation's credibility."

"Maybe. But he was just a little fish, a fringe figure like Von Däniken, and basically forgotten today."

"Maybe all the ridicule of the scientific community finally got to him, and he disappeared when he realized he would never be able to prove his wild theories."

"I don't think so. No, I think he was convinced of his work. Just listen to any recording of any lecture he ever gave."

She leaned back with her cup of coffee. "What doesn't fit," she acknowledged, "is the fact that he left a wife behind.

Who would do that? They'd known each other since high school."

"She agreed to call off the search for him after only six months. She never reopened the case, and she never hired a private investigator. In my experience, that's quite unusual. If the love of your life just disappears off the face of the earth, it's going to take you a lot longer than six months to come to terms with it." Pano shook his head firmly, disagreeing.

"All right, so what's your conclusion?" Agatha asked. "That she knew about it ahead of time? Why would she have accepted that? Much more likely that he would have popped up again at some point, and certainly when that did not happen she would have continued his research—but she didn't."

Agatha snatched the file out of his hand and closed it. "This case was already a fringe thing at the time and very little was done with it. But now, the only possible witness, Rachel Jackson, is dead. So, what does all that say to you?"

"I think Karlhammer's involved in some way. He's what binds it all together. He knew Rachel and Jackson, he was close to Jackson no matter how rocky the relationship was between the two guys, and Jackson disappeared right under Karlhammer's nose, in Karlhammer's hometown, in broad daylight. I'm telling you, he's the connection." Pano seemed sure, and he snatched the file back from her like a child defiantly reclaiming a toy that had been taken away from him.

"Well, what are you suggesting? That we question Karlhammer? That's going to be difficult. He's out of our jurisdiction."

A mysterious smile spread across Pano's face. "Suppose we flew out to South Africa and started poking around in the harbor in Cape Town. Do you think that might stir anything up?" he asked.

"Assuming Karlhammer did actually have something to do with it," she speculated.

Her new partner shrugged. "Of course, if we had all the answers at the start, there'd be nothing to investigate."

Agatha was about to say something but was interrupted by a beep from her hand terminal. It was a text message from Director Miller. "Hmm," she murmured as she read it.

"What is it?" Pano asked.

"We are cordially invited to keep our grubby little hands off this case," Agatha told him, translating Miller's message somewhat freely on the fly. "It seems he'll be handling the investigation of the attack on Brown himself."

"Oh? What does that mean?"

"That means we are going to South Africa, because he'll be happy to get rid of us. I'm the last person he wants to see getting caught up with his agents in a politically charged case," she declared. She recalled Miller offering her the deputy director position at CTD not so long ago. This certainly put a different spin on it, she thought, tilting her head.

But Pano was all smiles. "Great!" he said. "I love to travel."

Agatha gave him a penetrating look. "Well, you've never traveled with me."

Pano's face fell, and the look he gave her was one of genuine antipathy.

"Joke," she said as she picked up her jacket from the back of her chair.

10

RON JACKSON, 2018

"Dr. Jackson! Dr. Jackson!" Someone was shaking his shoulder, and as he woke the residual memories of his dream of being trapped, naked, and helpless, in an endless sheet of eternal ice, melted away.

It still took some effort to open his eyes. When he did, he was looking into the face of an over-excited student, a girl with unwashed blonde hair and rosy cheeks. Her eyes were frantic and her gaze was going everywhere.

"What... what is it?" he managed to ask through a yawn so big it made his jaw crack.

"Sir, you have to get up!" the young woman demanded, jumping up and down.

"I thought I told all of you to call me Ron," he said groggily, shaking his head. "What time is it?"

"Time?" For a moment, she didn't seem to understand the question. So deep underground, there was no natural light at all, and the light was dimmed in the sleeping quarters. But even on the surface there were only a few hours of daylight anyway, apart from the question of whether time zones had any meaning in Antarctica.

Finally she looked at her watch and told him, "It's 9:30."

Ron tried to figure out how long he had slept, but the only thing he knew was that he had arrived by helicopter at noon on the day before. He hadn't looked at a clock since then.

He reluctantly stuck his legs out from under the blanket and was shivering before they got to his shoes.

"All right, all right. What is it?"

"We got an e-mail from Vienna. They've sent the results of the tests on the samples we sent them!" the student squealed. At this point it seemed she had genuine difficulty staying on the floor.

"Oh," he said, and got up so quickly that he banged his head on the bottom edge of the bunk above. "Ouch!"

"Careful, Doctor!"

"Never mind," he said, even as he rubbed the sore spot on the back of his head. "Just take me to wherever it is we read the e-mails. Man, it's cold."

"Last night the generator went out for an hour, because the fuel level gauge was malfunctioning and nobody knew it," she explained as they hurried past empty bunks into the tunnel, and then made a right turn into the work area. James Ross and Mitra Patchuvi were already there, along with two students whose beards were so full and wild that nobody but the Human Foundation would ever have hired them. They were crowded around two open laptops and seemed to be engaged in an animated discussion.

"Well, what have we got?" asked Ron, trying not to get too close, because he hadn't brushed his teeth yet and was pretty sure his breath smelled worse than an ox's.

"The results are here," Patchuvi said. He looked up at Ron only briefly, and the glimpse of the exhaustion on his face didn't bode well. The corners of his mouth were pointing down.

"And?" Ron's excited anticipation suddenly turned into seething impatience.

"The results raise new questions. The rocks in the samples turn out not to be rock at all, but a composite material permeated with rock. The analysis of some of the fragments identified talc, mica, graphite, and aluminum hydroxide, among other components."

"Those are all reinforcement additives for compound materials," Ron observed with some irritation.

"Correct. Some of the fragments seem to be made up of a basic structure of carbon and aramid, others look like they're made of something resembling carbon nanotubes. The rest are normal rock, nothing worth mentioning." Patchuvi waved a hand dismissively and sighed.

"The problem is the dating," James interjected. His British voice sounded nasal, as if he had a cold, and his red, watery eyes corroborated that theory.

"What was the result there?" Ron asked, trying to stay as calm as possible, because everyone seemed on edge.

"Most of the samples are around two million years old."

"Two million?" Stunned, Ron forced his way through the others to peer at the laptops. He hastily ran through the accelerator mass spectrometry report from Vienna. His shoulders sank when he reached the end.

Parts of the pyramid structure of the mountain dated from the Paleozoic, over sixty million years ago, but the walls were barely two million years old. How could that be? How could a construction at a deeper stratum be so much younger?

He took a step back from the laptop and was still for a

moment. Then he remembered he had to conserve precious body heat, and crossed his arms over his chest. "Two million years ago, this continent was already glaciated. Everything around here was buried under a sheet of ice."

"Correct," Patchuvi replied.

"So who could have come here at that time and built walls made out of composite material that we could still find traces of today? And how can the whole structure be so smooth even though much of it is fossilized?"

"Well, one thing we do know is that these walls weren't built in the Paleozoic," said Ross.

Which, roughly translated, means, "Your theory about the Builders is obviously wrong," Ron thought.

"This expedition is not over yet," he answered firmly. All eyes were on him now and he saw the confusion in their eyes, as well as the exhaustion and disappointment. They didn't believe him. This was nothing short of a disaster, but Ron refused to accept it. They had bet everything on the next card. It was supposed to be an ace, but it had come up as a joker in a game that didn't have wildcards.

"All right, look," he said, turning to his two colleagues and the students. "The next supply helicopter is only due in a week. We're only going to need, what, one whole day to pack up everything here? I want to use every one of those other days, that's six of them, to find out more. We've got a few samples of, what... the walls?"

"Walls and ceilings," said one of the students, the one who had been scratching his wiry beard incessantly.

"All right then. We keep going with the floors, and knock on the walls looking for cavities. I've already been doing this myself and found a few," Ron said in an effort to sound confident, not for the others but for himself.

The Fossil

"But Doctor," said a voice behind him. It was the student who had shaken him out of bed, looking at him with an expression that was as exhausted as it was helpless. "There's no way to send new samples to Vienna and get the results back in less than a week."

"Do we have an X-ray fluorescence machine here?"

"Sure we do," she told him.

"So we can do X-ray fluorescence analyses to hunt down other high concentrations of iridium. That should do to start with. All we have to do is find one room, one wall, one piece of floor, anything that's not of natural origin, and as sure as the sun rises, we'll have more money pouring in to keep this expedition going."

Ron clapped his hands together and continued, "Mitra, get me a list of all team members and where they are assigned right now. James, I need to know all the tools and analytical equipment we've got available. You," he said, turning to the blonde student with the stringy hair and the friendly face, "would you please go get me my tablet with the map of the complex excavated so far? I need you to find a way to project it on that screen over there." He pointed to the only television, a large flat-screen display mounted on a rolling stand.

The three nodded and scurried off diligently, either infected by his enthusiasm, or because the alternative was too painful to contemplate. He looked at the two other students briefly, before asking them with a little trepidation, "Do we have a muon detector here?"

"Yes, Doctor," answered one of them, nodding as if he was clearly pleased with himself.

Ron gave a long, drawn-out sigh. "That's good. That's very good. Would you go get it, please?"

"Yes, sir." Evidently the two didn't know which of them he had spoken to, because they both headed off towards the changing room and the exit.

"What's going on here?" a voice asked, and Ron started. He hadn't even been aware that he had been staring at the laptop on the right for some time. It was Gould. He came shuffling into the work area with a cup of coffee in his hand and a thick scarf around his neck, trying to stifle a yawn.

"We got the results." Ron said it straight. He would have preferred to lie, because he was worried that Gould might pull the plug right then and there. One call on the satellite phone to Luther would do the trick. But Ron wasn't the type to do that, and never wanted to be.

"And?"

"A few samples of the walls and roofs contain traces of composite materials that can be traced back to the early Pleistocene."

"Wait, that was the one right before our current era, right? The one where man first appeared?"

"Right."

Gould nodded with a smile and raised his steaming coffee mug in a kind of toast, as if they had just shared some sort of moment. Clearly, he didn't understand the significance of the data.

"That means that my theory has, most likely, been proven wrong," Ron clarified.

Gould remained unperturbed. "But you don't believe it yourself."

"What?"

"That your theory's wrong."

"No, I don't," Ron admitted. "But based on the available data for this place, it would appear that I still haven't found the evidence."

"You're not seeing the elephant in the room, are you?" Gould asked with a shake of his head.

"What elephant?"

"Well, whatever we just found, it's goddamn crazy! Two million years ago, there were people, or somebody here, and they built this!" Gould shook his coffee cup in small circles in his hand as he said it, as if to make it more meaningful, and his short black hair had been finely styled, looking as if he had already spent an hour in the bathroom this morning. "We're not talking about a couple of stone blocks here, you know. These are modern construction compounds. Isn't that big enough for you?"

"Yeah, no, but—"

"No, it's not, is it? Because you are so focused on your theory of the First Mankind, the Builders, the Lords of the Earth, those we must be the inheritors of—that this might still be our salvation. But this right here, *this* is nothing short of explosive! You're looking at the proof that there are traces of technology from long before our furthest ancestors discovered fire or the wheel. You should be incredibly thankful for what's being uncovered here."

"Yes, well, I am," Ron said, as he worked through all this in his head. His thoughts were racing so fast that he could hardly follow them. "But it wasn't *them*."

"Who? The Builders?" Gould asked, frowning. "Look, whoever it was has been completely and totally off the scientific radar. Until today. Sure, Von Däniken hypothesized all kinds of aliens who built the pyramids or whatever, but nobody took him seriously. But we've got rock-solid evidence for something that can't possibly exist!"

"If the data proves to be correct once it's verified," Ron cautioned.

"Yeah. That's how it works." Gould shrugged and took a sip of coffee.

"We still have a week before the supply helicopter arrives. Until then, let's keep looking for anything we can find," Ron said.

"Right," the accountant said, agreeing—to his own surprise—with Ron. "So could you explain to me what you think would be a meaningful use of this time? You look like either you have a plan, or you're going into a manic phase. And I hope it's the former."

"All right then. I'm, uh... ah, there she is!" Ron pointed to the blonde student who had just walked back in, carrying his black tablet in one hand and a rolled-up cable in the other.

"So?" asked Gould.

"Wait just a minute." The student plugged one end of the cable into the tablet and then moved to the large-screen monitor, her upper body disappearing behind it. She quickly reappeared and made a thumbs-up gesture.

"What's your name, anyway?" Ron asked her.

"Dana," she answered, and flashed a quick, almost shy smile when their eyes met.

"Thank you, Dana," Ron said, returning a friendly look. He grabbed a remote control from in front of the notebooks and switched the monitor on. Suddenly the screen showed a two-dimensional map of the chamber and the entire complex as they had mapped it so far. It looked like an extremely complicated blueprint.

He walked around the table and stood next to it, gesturing to Dana and Gould. "So, we're here, if I'm not mistaken." He pointed to one of the two large caverns, which looked like oversized eggs on the map. He looked at Dana for confirmation, and she nodded.

"Right, so here we are." He went on pointing to different rooms, leaving tiny grease stains where his finger touched the screen. "Now, we've taken rock samples from all these. And if we've found rocks with elevated iridium concentrations above us, that may be the case below us as well. That would indicate either that this subterranean complex was dug in, or that there are still constructions below these that are much older. We can check that very quickly, because we have an X-ray fluorescence machine, and both hydrochloric acid and sodium chlorate."

"Is that supposed to tell me something? If so, I'm going to need a little help."

"Iridium dissolves in hydrochloric acid and sodium chlorate, and can be detected by tiny crystals that form during the chemical reaction."

"Sounds kind of like wishful thinking, don't you think?" Gould asked skeptically between sips of his coffee.

"No, it's just chemistry."

"I didn't mean that part."

"Perhaps," Ron admitted with a sigh and a shrug. "But it's something we have to check out. Archaeology is full of cases where digging under a lost city reveals even older buildings from even earlier times."

"But you said yourself that down here sediment moves and shifts much less than on other continents."

"That's true, but we can't rule it out," Dana intervened, and looked at Ron with wide-open eyes like a pet waiting for a reward.

"It can't be ruled out," he echoed, and turned back to look at the screen. "More importantly, however, will be the muon detector. I just can't imagine that this entire complex is absolutely free of any artifacts. Even after so many millions of years, in this cold and dry climate, there must be something to find. It's colder than minus ninety degrees down here. It's so cold that all of us have to come back here every hour to warm up and replace the internal heating elements in our clothes. Now, we're going to search for spaces beneath us, and we're going to start with the two large caverns. There has to be something preserved here somewhere."

"Why are we starting there?" Gould asked, not dismissively but genuinely curious.

"The Builders always left the most important artifacts in the largest rooms, or in hidden areas off of those rooms. Think of the Great Pyramid of Cheops, or the ancient necropolis of Abusir."

"What kind of important artifacts are you talking about?"

"Later." Ron silenced Gould with a wave as Patchuvi walked into the tent dome. He was breathing heavily, and as soon as he stopped, he fell to his knees, exhausted.

"What is it? You didn't have to run here that fast."

"I... I... my God." Patchuvi took a deep breath and raised his head. "I just spoke to one of the students who took the morning call. He just came back down from the surface and was waving the satellite phone so frantically that I stopped."

"What did he say?" Ron asked, alarmed. Luther had surely received a copy of the results from Vienna—was he turning off the money right now, to cut his losses?

"We're getting a visit."

"A visit?"

"Yes!"

"From...?" Gould asked impatiently. "Mr. Karlhammer?"

"No! Elsa at McMurdo Station sent a message that an expedition ship docked yesterday. Twenty people, with their own snowcats and a heap of provisions. They didn't identify themselves, and immediately headed off straight in our direction," explained Patchuvi, pursing his lips.

"Is it our new crew arriving ahead of schedule?" Ron asked, irritated.

"No. Elsa thought the same thing and called Mr. Karlhammer's office. It's not our people. They definitely would have identified themselves."

"Who could it be?" Gould asked.

Patchuvi shrugged.

"It could be anyone," Ron responded. "There are evangelical groups in the USA who see me as the Canadian devil, because I call the Creation story into question and I've gotten a lot of attention for it. But it could be competing excavation teams that intercepted the data from Vienna, although if that's the case they got here pretty fast. It could be national governments that want to grab a piece of the pie. There are no territorial claims here because, due to the Antarctic Treaty of 1959, everything between sixty- and ninety-degrees latitude South has to be accessible to all nations."

Ron paused and looked thoughtfully at the wall calendar tacked up on a metal cabinet next to the monitor. "The journey by ship from Hobart to McMurdo Station takes over a week. Anybody coming to us without an announcement had been on the way for a while, and knows that there's something to see here, despite our best efforts to keep this whole thing as secret as possible."

"But what are we going to do now?" Patchuvi asked.

Ron noticed that Patchuvi, Dana, and Gould were all looking at him in total helplessness, as if the answer might appear on his face in glowing letters at any moment. *Who do these people think I am, anyway?* "I'm going to go upstairs and talk to Luther myself. Maybe he can put out a few feelers and get some information. Don't worry."

Their faces told him that they were going to worry anyway, and he could hardly blame them, because he was worried himself. Research teams typically announced themselves. They always did.

11

FILIO AMOROSA, 2042

The time it took to travel to the search area that she had calculated for the location of the stern of *Mars One*, Filio spent in the meeting room, for the most part staring at the map and feverishly running over her calculations in her head. She was painfully aware that while she had identified a fundamental error in her calculations, and felt that this one factor was indeed the missing piece of the puzzle, there might well be a few other mistakes. If not *dozens*. Ever since her release from the hospital after the crash, she hadn't been able to think as fast or focus as intently as before. The clarity in her head that had enabled her to win speed math competitions, debates, and chess matches as a teenager was gone. She did mourn the fact that those days were never coming back, but crying for them would accomplish nothing.

No, Filio would rather focus on her future and her goal. She was sure that when she finally understood what had happened, she would find her clarity and peace of mind. And to do that, she had to go back to Mars. Whenever she thought about it, she felt the rage welling up within her. Rage at ESA who had fired her simply because she hadn't been able to give the answers that they were looking for. Rage at NASA, for ignoring her applications, probably a quid pro quo for her old chums at ESA.

Could these people really be so dumb that they were going to turn their backs on her experience, knowledge, and enthusiasm? She was the only person alive who had been to Mars and come back. That alone should have been enough to make her the most valuable astronaut on the planet—at least to anyone who could think at all rationally. Evidently, that did not include the directors of the world's two largest space agencies at this point. It was simply tragic, seeing how politics and bureaucracy had taken control of humanity and crowded out reason.

Filio had a stack of reports certifying to her—and to anybody who cared to look—that she was neither mentally ill nor suffering from any stress disorder or physical condition of any kind. But nobody wanted to hear that. They only saw her as the survivor of the *Mars One* disaster, who had mysteriously lost all memory of the incident, and was therefore unfit for duty. It was not the result of any disease or condition, and she had passed every psychoanalysis and intelligence test they could throw at her. She had even agreed to repeat everything she had been able to tell them under a lie detector, but they had only graciously thanked her for her service and sent her on her way.

It was enough to drive her mad. But she never even thought of giving up. Ever since her childhood in the suburbs of Hamburg, she'd had to fight for everything she wanted. First for her place in a good high school, then fighting her way off the street to escape the life of crime and drug addiction that had befallen her parents. Then for a place in foster care so she didn't have to stay in the home where she had been beaten. And later, her fight for scholarships to the University of Barcelona, Oxford, and then Yale. She had faced unfair treatment and bureaucratic hurdles each step of the way, and all of them she had overcome with her sheer determination. Every single fight had made her stronger. And now she only needed to focus that iron will and determination again, which came as naturally to her as breathing.

When Romain came in, she smiled and looked at her diving watch. "It's almost time."

"*Oui*," the captain replied. He was already wearing his Sharkskin, which accentuated his wiry muscles. "You're absolutely as sure as you can be, right?"

"Yes," she said, mustering a convincing tone and looking him straight in the face. "The tailpiece has to be somewhere here. It would've sunk fast, because it was the largest single piece of the wreckage. And the seafloor of this area is very nutrient-poor, which means very little influence from currents. The flow data from here, and from the areas around here, have all gone into my calculations."

"And the tailpiece is really what we want?" asked Romain. His eyes had been glowing ever since they headed south. It was the sparkle of hope that had almost disappeared from her excitable friend over the past weeks and months.

"Yes," she said definitively. "That's where all the cargo was, so that's where the most parts are—and that means the biggest bounty." *And that's where the thing I'm looking for is. The thing I need,* she thought to herself.

"Perfect," Romain said gleefully, and put a hand on her shoulder to pull her towards him. "I want to thank you. For everything."

Filio could see that he wasn't just saying it to be nice. Even through his euphoria at the thought of bringing his two-year grind as a scrapper to a successful end, she could see in his eyes how important it was to him for her to understand. A pang of guilt shot through her when she realized that she could never be completely honest with him. Filio simply had no interest in the money. Money wasn't going to get her what she was looking for. She needed something much more valuable, and had to focus on that and only that. If there was anything in her power that would shower her friend with the riches that the crew sought, then she would do it. But she was going to keep her eyes on her own prize.

"Don't mention it. You guys, you're my family," she answered with genuine affection.

Romain smiled, and they turned and looked pensively at the large display, which was showing a bird's-eye view of the area of the ocean they were approaching.

"We've been out here for so long, I can't even imagine what it would be like to actually find something," the Frenchman muttered, taking a deep breath and blowing it out, cheeks puffed. "For two years, we've been sailing back and forth in an area of the sea half the size of the moon, leaving no stone unturned, making dive after dive, and still finding nothing. Tussling with other scrappers, motherfuckers who lord it over us that they found a screw and turned it into a pile of cash. You know, not a single month has gone by without somebody calling us the unluckiest adventurers since the crash.

"All around us, we've got those new super-container ships with their Flettner rotors, that don't blow any exhaust into the atmosphere. And the airports are full of suborbital planes that can take you anywhere on earth within three hours. Meanwhile, we're trundling around the sea in an old piece-of-shit barge. It's like the future passed us by, Filio.

"You know what we are? We're relics. Relics of a time

The Fossil

when there were real wonders and discoveries out there, when the ocean hadn't yet been completely mapped out, when there were still new species of animal to be discovered. But maybe, in a few hours, it's all going to pay off so big that we can put all the past behind us. It's just... so hard to get my head around."

"Yeah, but right now, we've still got nothing," she reminded him gently.

"*Oui*, I know. But I've decided to choose optimism, because all the other options take too much effort."

"What are you going to do with the money?" Filio asked, curious.

"If ESA really paid out big? I'll buy a chalet in Nice and set up my ex-wife and her children there."

"That's pretty... patronizing."

"We just weren't a good match. But I have great respect for my ex-wife. And besides, we both love our children, and I want them to do all right. Children only do well if their mothers are doing well, so I make sure of that. When you love your children, you'll do anything for them, even if it means swallowing some pride," he explained, turning his face from the display to look her in the eyes. "You don't have any kids, do you?"

She shook her head. "No. I've always lived for my work. The only thing I ever wanted was to get into the astronaut program for the Mars Mission, and I worked over a hundred hours a week to get there. That left no time for a partner, let alone for children, and now it's too late."

"You regret it?"

"Sometimes, yeah."

"So what are you going to do with the money?" he asked suddenly. Caught off guard by the turnabout, Filio pursed her lips in thought. She could hardly tell him that she wasn't interested in the money.

After a while, she said, "I'm going to buy into the Human Foundation."

"But it's not a company, it's a foundation," Romain reminded her.

"Maybe, but you know how it is. If I say I'm interested in putting a million dollars behind a certain project, they're going to find me a position on that project. That's how the foundation business works."

"But the Human Foundation is already the most valuable company in the world, without even being a real company. They made over seven hundred *billion* dollars last year, and it's all tax-free, because it's a nonprofit foundation. It's just unimaginable," he countered. "What do you think they care about a million dollars?"

"Let's just say I'm willing to try my luck." She shook her right arm a little, so that her Human Foundation lottery ribbons shook merrily.

"You know, I—"

"Hey, you guys." An announcement from Thomas on the ship's speakers interrupted them. Because they were right behind the bridge, Filio heard him both from the speakers and through the door. "You really ought to see this."

She and Romain exchanged looks and pushed Oscar aside. The dog had parked himself on Filio's feet and was happily panting away, and now he followed them to the bridge.

"What is it?" they asked in unison as they came into the sun-drenched bridge.

"I thought you'd want to see this," Thomas said, and he pointed ahead out the window.

When Filio put her hand over her eyes to block the

reflections from the endless blue ocean, she could make out something like a carpet swimming in the distance. "Is that...?"

"Yeah," Thomas exclaimed, grinning from ear to ear.

Filio didn't wait, but snatched the binoculars off the diver's chest and ran out the side door of the bridge onto the deck next to it. Through the binoculars, she could see it as if it was right next to them. A massive structure, the size of a football stadium only much flatter, was forging its way across the endless expanse of blue, undeterred by the waves. Out of a semicircular bulge in the middle, a series of long struts jutted forward from it, like the teeth of some nightmarishly large comb. Between each strut, a mountain of plastic waste churned. Atop the bulge was a box-shaped structure with a forest of antennas and a large radar dish pointed upwards. Through the binoculars, she could easily see the Human Foundation logo in several places. Behind the top of the bulge she had just managed to see a drone ship docking—a distended cube with four giant Flettner rotors protruding from its bow and stern.

"Is that..."

"That's a sweeper," Filio answered Romain's question before he finished it, handing him the binoculars. "Those things are filtering the plastic out of the oceans, millions of tons per year. It's not just picking up the plastic in those gill-like projections, it's scooping it up in nets below the surface. It's got a row of keels, forty meters deep, that suck the garbage down and slow down the wake vortex to stop the interchange between surface water and deep water. That right there is a masterpiece of human ingenuity, and there's only twenty of them.

"The plastic gets sucked in both above and below the water, and it goes into that bulge there, where it gets broken down into hydrogen and CO_2. The hydrogen goes into its own fuel cells, so it provides its own clean energy. And it feeds the carbon dioxide to algae, which it also grows in that bulge and then scatters around with drone ships, like that thing that just docked. The algae produce oxygen, and they multiply in the seas, so they keep filtering CO_2 out of the atmosphere and converting it into oxygen. It's really pretty genius. A German architecture student named Marcella Hansch designed this system thirty years ago. It was originally called *Pacific Garbage Screening*. Really genius."

"That it is," Romain agreed, and nodded with fascination. "It's amazing that I've never seen one in all this time."

"Your chances of running into one are pretty small, given how much ocean there is. But they're having a tremendous impact. They've already reduced the mass of microplastics, all that stuff that's making us and the animal world sick, by seventy percent from what it was forty years ago. And the Human Foundation keeps building more sweepers."

"OK, I'm sold," Romain said, smiling, and handed her back the binoculars. "When I get my money, I'm going to buy as many Karlhammer lottery tickets as I can get."

"That's a smart decision. If it hadn't been for the brave young people who pushed projects like this, we'd be a lot worse off today than you'd think, looking at our big cities behind their floodwalls. Try to imagine, when Hansch designed this system, there was a garbage patch twice the size of France floating around in the Pacific, between North America and Asia. That was 2018!"

"And now?"

"Now it's gone. Collected, processed, and turned into algae and clean energy," she said, pointing in the direction of the sweeper. At this distance, to the naked eye it looked like it might be a giant sponge.

"I don't mean to break up this conversation," Thomas interrupted from the doorway behind them, "but we're going to be at the search area in less than half an hour. You'd better start getting ready." The old sea-lion's voice, usually so measured and unflappable, was tense with excitement—another thing that reinforced Filio's feeling that this was really it. They were nearing the end, and soon they would be finding out whether it was a good end or a bad one.

Romain's steely gaze told her that he was thinking the same, and after a moment he turned and walked down the stairs towards the aft deck.

Filio dashed through the bridge and the meeting room, and continued down through the crew area to the quarters. One of the luxuries of having a small crew on a big old ship was that they each had their own private quarters—something that would have been unthinkable on most other scrapper ships. An excited Oscar, tail wagging, followed her to her bunk, where she grabbed her hand terminal. After scrolling through some files, she found the image she was looking for and with a gesture, she tossed it onto the screen above her little table. Even though she did the same thing every night before she fell asleep, she studied the objects in the image one more time and then, with a deep sigh, pushed Oscar out of her way.

"Sorry, old buddy, but I've got to go now, and find what been looking for all this time," she explained to the dog with a pat behind his ears. Oscar acknowledged the attention with a satisfied rumble and closed his eyes. "This is my first and last chance. Wish me luck."

With that she ran to the stern of the *Ocean's Bitch*. Jane, Alberto, and Romain were already there under the awning, putting together their crates of diving equipment. Their every movement was practiced and precise, honed by decades of training, but their faces betrayed the tension under which they were operating, doing what they always did.

"So how are we doing this?" she asked, after packing her own crate with her mask, fins, weight belt, dive computer, and toolkit.

"You and Jane are buddies, like always," Romain instructed. The silky voice he usually used on her had been replaced by a professional, almost clipped tone. This was definitely new. Even under the tensest encounters they had ever had, with competing scrappers around contested claims, he had never gone full boss mode like this. "I'll be going down with Alberto. We'll take the jets. My charts say it's no deeper than a hundred and forty meters there, and there's a long reef. Pay attention to your equipment and keep eye contact. We stay four the whole time. Nobody leaves the group, right?"

They all turned and nodded, entirely focused.

"Filio, you take the balloons. Jane, you take the transport hooks and the metal detector. Alberto and I will take the spare tanks with the heliox."

Romain clapped his hands together, and French began spewing out of his mouth, Filio took it as her cue to go grab her wetsuit. Because they expected that they might be staying down deep for an extended period, she had chosen a thick full-body suit with shoes and hood. She walked around the dive departure platform along the stern, past the white water being churned up by the screws, stretching beyond them like a road towards the horizon.

When she reached her spot, just behind the central aisle where the suits were hung and the heliox tanks were arranged in their wooden crates, she looked back at the others for a moment. They all looked busy with their own things and weren't looking at her. She stooped before an aluminum crate and opened it, quickly removing six transport hooks and throwing them into her crate before moving to the other side.

Because they were going by the book, she needed nearly twenty minutes to lay out all her equipment except the hooks in front of her, run down the list, test everything, and pack it in the crate again. Thirty minutes after that, she had suited up, strapped on her BCD, fastened the weights around her hips, put on her harness, and checked all the buckles. Finally, before putting on her hood, she nestled the transducer net onto her scalp and checked the Velcro fastener under her chin. At last she was satisfied.

Within five minutes, Thomas's voice boomed from the old speakers: "All right, I've already got something on the sonar that's worth a look! We'll be directly over it in two minutes."

"Here we go, folks! Buddy check!" Romain shouted. "Come on, we're not going to let the routine slide on the zillionth time through. If this is the day we've been waiting for, we're going to make sure that we did everything right. I'm not having any accidents or 'one of those days' today, all right?"

Here we go, Filio thought nervously. *Here we go and it's all or nothing.*

12

FILIO AMOROSA, 2042

Her dive computer read precisely 11:40 when they were all standing on the flat departure grid, giving each other the OK sign. Because of the depth, the *Ocean's Bitch* couldn't anchor, so Thomas had to turn off the engine briefly to avoid danger from the screws, and would only be able to hold its position after they dived.

Romain jumped first, followed by Alberto, Jane, and finally Filio.

Filio pressed one hand against her face mask, the other against her belt, and took a big step forward. The moment she entered the water, for that familiar two seconds her world was made of white bubbles against the blue background, until she broke through the surface again, carried by her inflated BCD. She checked her mask one more time and then gave the OK sign to the others, who like her were bobbing up and down like buoys on the gently swelling surface.

Romain gestured with his thumb pointed downward. She vented her BCD and exhaled slowly, immediately slipping like a stone into the depths, the small bubbles from her mouthpiece rising to where the belly of the *Ocean's Bitch* waited like a mighty shadow.

Filio took a quick look around, then down into the dark blue of the deep, and finally to her friends and companions, these final adventurers of the last frontier. Romain was already a few meters below her, with Jane and Alberto a few above. Their colorful armpieces and the toolkits and transport bags wrapped with marking tape made them all look utterly alien to this world of absolute silence and tranquility. Every two meters or so of her descent she equalized the pressure by blowing into her closed nose and moving her jaws.

A glance at her dive computer told her she was already fifty meters down, so she slowed her rate of sinking a little by increasing the amount of air she kept in her lungs as she breathed. Her momentum decreased, and her descent into the darkness became more controlled.

At seventy meters she switched on the lighting system on her harness. Six lights began to glow, illuminating the void of floating particles and plankton all around her. Reflections, and a small school of silvery fish hurrying away from the lights and off into the distance, reduced her visibility.

Floating around her, the others also lit up like Christmas trees. When her gaze crossed Romain's, he made the OK sign and she returned it. Jane and Alberto also raised their hands with spread fingers and then formed an O with thumb and index finger.

Everything okay, Filio thought. If the rest of the dive goes like this, this might be the best day of her lost life.

It took several more minutes to reach the bottom. Here and there she saw large stones, each about the size of a small truck, on which large mussels and sea plants, mostly brown and yellowish, had established themselves. A small pack of

The Fossil

barracudas whizzed past. Smaller fish could be seen nibbling toothlessly at the plants that had taken over the rocks. A little further on, Filio made out a shark, possibly a tiger, but it was too shy and disappeared too fast for her to identify it for sure.

Apart from that there was not much to look at, at this depth—certainly nothing like the coral reefs and shipwrecks favored by tourists.

And that's a good thing, she thought, letting herself focus on the meditative sound of her own breathing. Each breath sounded hollow in her head. Romain kept checking the display on his forearm. After passing one of the rocks, he corrected their diving direction towards a large sandbar with a few isolated clumps of sea plants growing out of it. A ray suddenly swished away from her into the dimness ahead of her, which was like the twilight of a summer evening, and she watched a cloud of sand settle down in the place it had been hiding.

"We're almost there," the computer-generated Romain-voice said in her right ear. It sounded artificial, which it was, but still enough like Romain to know that it was him.

How far? she thought, and beneath her hood, the transducer net stretched across her head translated her scanned brainwaves into spoken words that were transmitted to the others.

"Forty meters. Thomas? Everything OK up there?" asked Romain.

"Everything's OK, boss," Thomas reported from the boat after a slight delay. "No unwanted guests on the radar. Guess the *Gloucester* is still having their date with Customs."

Transducer systems were still not capable of synthesizing evil laughter, but if theirs could have, she was sure she would be hearing a lot of it now.

"What are you getting off the signature of the sonar contact?" asked Filio.

"Looks good. The shape doesn't suggest a rock or anything natural. Oh, *putain*, if this is the stern section, then I'm just going to... I don't know what."

"Well, how would you feel about recovering the damn thing?" Jane proposed.

"Good idea," Alberto remarked, giving the OK sign.

"All right, folks, concentrate, we're coming into visual range." Romain again. "I've got six objects. One large and multiple small. First we distribute the lightsticks to light up the area so we can work, OK?"

"Got it." After a few more hollow breaths Filio saw her goal, and her heart leapt.

The beam from Romain's flashlight had passed across a grayish object, and Filio had seen it so quickly that at first she wasn't sure she had really seen anything at all. But then the circle of brightness suddenly moved back, and she was staring at the tail section of the *Mars One* reentry capsule. It was a ring-shaped section at least five meters across, overgrown with algae, and with eight drive nacelles that looked like firebowls. An impressive school of fish was swarming out of them at that moment.

A bull shark appeared in the light, tracing a slow circle around the module, his rough skin gleaming dimly and his predator eyes seemingly looking in all directions at once.

"I must be going crazy, you guys!" Jane exclaimed. "Dammit, I must be going crazy! It's the goddamn jackpot!"

"*Putain, putain*, oh la, I can't believe it," Romain said. The strangely emotionless voice of the computer somehow didn't fit with what Filio imagined he must have been sounding like.

"Hey, dad, I found this, can I keep it?" Alberto asked.

Romain gave him the OK sign. "When we get this up top, I'll make a call, and you can buy anything you want."

"Great, I've got a list already," Alberto quipped. "It's not that long, I only had two years to let my imagination run away with me."

"All right, folks, let's not get cocky," Romain said, reining him in and making a circular motion with an outstretched index finger. In the deep water, it looked strangely slowed down, almost as if he were out in space. "Unload your gear, and distribute the lightsticks."

"I'll start here," Filio said immediately, dropping the bags with the balloons and taking out one of the two lightsticks she had brought with her. It was a pole, about a meter long. Twisting the upper third of it would turn that section into a powerful light source that was particularly strong in the red-orange spectrum, to help you see better in deep water conditions.

Due to the refraction at this depth, the eye perceived colors very differently down here. Her navy-blue wetsuit didn't look blue, it appeared basically pale and colorless.

Romain studied his display while the two others swam away in different directions, staking a lightstick into the sand of the bottom every ten meters. In five minutes, they had illuminated an area about fifty meters in diameter around the wreck of the stern section of the *Mars One* module with a light equivalent to five meters below the surface at midday.

"And there was light," Romain said ceremoniously. "Filio?"

"Captain?"

"It's only right that you go in first," he said, and waved for her to go. Jane and Alberto had already swum back, and now the group was floating in a loose circle, the endless stream of their air bubbles floating away into the semi-darkness above them.

"I'm honored," she replied. "I'm really... I'm overwhelmed."

"I believe it," Jane said, gently laying a hand on her shoulder. "I can only imagine what this must be like for you."

Filio could hardly feel it through her thick suit. "Well, if you don't mind, I'd like to go inside and... you can..."

"We'll give you a minute. Of course we will," Romain replied immediately, and Alberto nodded in slow motion. "We've all waited two years for this moment, so we can wait another minute to give the woman who made it possible a chance to put herself together. This thing here," Romain said, pointing to the grayish piece of wreckage in front of them, "I don't think it is going anywhere."

"Thank you," Filio said with genuine emotion. She took one last deep breath from her tank and then, finally, with a few gentle flips of her fins, entered what was left of *Mars One*.

The module tubular shaped, with a diameter of about five meters—its exact width was five meters and twenty centimeters, as she well knew. Its smooth eight-meter length contained two sections of the ship and ended in ragged edges, like the tattered leg of an old pair of cut-off jeans, where the extreme forces of re-entry had blown the hull open. After two years down here, every crack and opening had been occupied by some variety of algae, seaweed, or crustacean, and the entire module was now teeming with them.

A cold shiver ran through her as she moved as far into the section as she could and looked into what was once the crew compartment, now wide open, where the six pressure seats had been configured in a circle.

The pressure seats where my friends died, she thought grimly. One of the seats was still there. It had been torn halfway off its floor moorings, and it was in tatters, but for her there was no mistaking it. The wall leading to the transport section was a muddy brown. It had probably been blackened by the explosion and then gradually lightened over time by the salt and the water movement.

The door to it was open, but just by a crack. The gap was wide enough for Filio to work her small crowbar into and heave right. The bulkhead moved aside surprisingly easy, and then she was looking into the darkness of the transport section, the light from her harness flooding in.

Open crates, shredded wall netting, and burst wall panels were everywhere. Here and there, a small fish or shrimp darted, but there was almost no sand and very few floating particles.

One minute, you've got one minute.

She hurriedly slipped into the five-meter-deep hold, scaring a fish away, and began searching the crates. She disregarded four with barely a glance, and started getting nervous, until she spotted a darker box about the size of a carry-on suitcase. It was metal, and much more challenging to move.

Filio dragged it out so that it was in front of her and she could see the locking clasps. When she did, she breathed a sigh of relief. The vacuum seal was still intact. Its contents had been spared from the effects of the saltwater.

"Filio?" Romain's computer-generated voice asked in her ear. "Are you okay?"

"Yes," she answered quickly, looking around. The transport section suddenly seemed small. Struggling, she dragged the box behind her through the bulkhead. She had just managed to rub off the waterlogged label with a thumb, so the words 'Sample Material' could no longer be deciphered, even with a scanner program.

"I'm coming out now."

For an instant, her heart jumped into her throat when she saw the others lined up in front of the stern section.

"Can somebody help me?"

"What's that?" It was Alberto who asked the question.

"It's my personal locker, with the things I lost back then," she lied. Luckily for Filio, her friends were as supportive and understanding as ever, and didn't ask any questions. Romain came over and helped her carry the box the five meters to her equipment, where they put it down.

"Thanks. Really, for everything," she said emotionally, and she exhaled deeply. Then she leaned back slowly until she was sitting in the sand, and stayed there for a moment. "Go on, get in there. There are so many parts, you're all multimillionaires now."

Filio winced inwardly, realizing she had said *you're*.

"Take all the time you need," Romain said. She could see through his wide diving mask that he was looking at her with compassion. "Just come in when you're ready. We'll start looking around, dreaming of champagne, count our money and start the recovery, *oui*?"

"That sounds like a great idea!"

Romain gave her the OK sign and swam to the others. Five seconds later, they were all inside.

Filio looked around again quickly. The bull shark was gone. She turned, took four of the balloons she had carried, and brought them to the box. Using the hooks she had secretly taken, she attached the balloon lines to the four corners of the box. Then she ran a long line on a winch through an eyelet on the bottom. She looked back at the others.

Through the connection, she heard the others laughing, joking, telling each other what they were going to do with their money. With a last, mournful look at the remains of *Mars One*, she swam to the relay unit that connected them to Thomas on the surface. It was a watertight plastic ball that contained all the hardware. It had a simple on-off switch at the bottom. She sighed deeply before she flipped it, and then cut the cable with her knife. Then she swam back to the box and, using her dive computer, activated the oxygen tubes on the short ropes below the balloons. In an instant, they shot their oxygen reservoirs into the balloons, inflating them. The box took off at lightning speed. The rope on the bottom rolled out longer and longer from the winch in her hand as the box rose.

Filio was crying as she swam towards the surface. She performed a controlled emergency swimming ascent. This meant unbuckling her weight belt and pushing the button to completely inflate her BCD. She shot upwards like a rocket. She had to watch the depth reading of her dive computer closely. At fifteen meters she stopped abruptly and forced herself to slow to a climb of a maximum of ten meters per minute. It wouldn't help anything to get the bends right now. If she did, it all would have been for nothing.

Everything in her was screaming *hurry, get there faster*, but she succeeded in talking herself into keeping her cool.

The others are probably still trying to figure out what's wrong with the communications. You've got a lot more time before they realize you're gone and not swimming around somewhere down there. They can't come to the surface any faster than you, and that gives you enough of a head start.

At a depth of three meters, she stopped and held her position for three minutes for decompression. Looking up, she could see the outline of the box in the water, with the balloons bobbing on the light swell. It seemed to her like the surface of the water was a crumpled sheet of aluminum foil, and the broken sunbeams made the plankton sparkle.

"Hey, Thomas!" she called through the net. "Can you hear me?"

"Filio? What's going on, little one? I lost the connection."

"Yeah, we had a problem with the relay unit. I've already brought a piece up! Romain said you should come down," she explained, without taking her eyes off her dive computer. Two more minutes.

"Okay, got it, I'll get ready. I've got you on the sensor and I'll be right there, don't move."

I won't, she thought, and felt the sting of tears welling in her eyes.

In her whole life she had hardly ever felt so terrible as right now. Betraying her friends, her family, hurt her so badly that she suddenly realized she might just be trading one trauma for another.

It wasn't long before she heard the muffled drone of the ship's screws and saw the mysterious shadow of the *Ocean's Bitch* approaching. It stopped about ten meters away, and Filio began a slow, controlled swim upwards.

When she completely reinflated her BCD, her head broke the surface of the water and she took off her mask. She had to turn once to spot the stern of *Bitch* on the endless watery horizon. Thomas had just appeared there, already in his wetsuit, and she heard the engines gurgling and saw the pumps belching out some burbles of liquid into the sea.

Filio grabbed two of the balloon lines, lay rolled to her back and struggled hard to move herself and the box towards the ship. When she got to it she took one fin off, then the other, and handed them to a worried-looking Thomas. The adrenaline pumping in her veins told her to scream at him, make him hurry, but she forced herself to be quiet. She had to act like everything was okay.

She had the strange feeling that the betrayal was written all over her face, and it was sheer force of will that kept her from saying or doing something that would have blown the whole thing.

He took the heliox tank from her too, and then he grabbed the balloon cords and pulled, immediately letting out a groan.

"Shit, that thing's heavy! What the hell is it?"

"That's a million dollars," she replied with false euphoria, and Thomas's face brightened.

"Oh yeah, baby!"

Filio climbed up and over the short ladder onto the deck, tore open the Velcro fasteners of her harness and the BCD, and threw them both aside. She then helped Thomas with the box. It took all their strength to get it on board and slide it to safety.

"I'll just finish getting my stuff together," said Thomas. Filio hesitated for a moment, then she pushed him over the side, into the water. He screamed in surprise and swung his arms about wildly as he disappeared into the rolling waves. She took a step to the ladder and pulled it up, ensuring he could not climb back aboard although he was just beneath her.

When he came back to the surface, snorting, he stared at her in shock.

"If this is some kind of joke, Little One, I don't think this is the..." Thomas began to say, but stopped when he saw her crying. "Filio? What is it? What are you doing?"

"I'm so very sorry, Thomas. I love all of you. I'm really doing this. I just hope that someday you'll understand. I'm leaving a GPS buoy and a life raft here, and I'll make sure you get picked up. Down there is everything you've all been dreaming of, and what I've been dreaming of." She cast a glance back at the case behind her. "Please tell the others I'm so, so sorry. And don't worry. You're rich."

"Filio, you don't have to do this," Thomas exclaimed, pleading, but she had already turned and was running to the bridge.

"Filio!" his desperate calls followed her, but she continued to run, sobbing, forcing herself to ignore him, even though every fiber of her being was screaming, telling her to turn around and bring him back aboard. "FILIO! FILIOOO..."

13

AGATHA DEVENWORTH, 2042

Their supersonic jet took off from JFK's Runway 2 and then headed out over the Atlantic, turning southeast before accelerating to Mach 2.

Agatha hadn't been able to push through a flight on one of the private jets of the CTD fleet for herself and Pano, but she did get first-class tickets so they could work on the way.

Her new partner, whom she hadn't found to be as terrible as expected—although she really did think he was far too distracted—began flipping through the in-flight magazine immediately after takeoff, and only stopped when she threw a scorching unimpressed look in his direction.

"What?" he asked.

"Our flight time is six hours. That's enough time to run through just enough information to not be arriving completely blind."

Pano sighed and put the magazine back in the window pocket. "Fine. So what do we need to know?"

"We should go over our databanks for any other relevant missing persons reported around the same time as Jackson's disappearance. Then we look for overlaps in the key data like age, profession, personal connections, location of the incident, all that stuff. We've got a high-speed connection up here, so why don't you stick to Europol's data and I'll see what Homeland Security has," she suggested.

Pano nodded. "Right."

Agatha put on her data glasses and connected them to her terminal. Before her eyes floating windows appeared, one of which was the access to the Homeland Security databanks. To log in, she had to hold her finger in front of the DNA reader of her hand terminal and use the camera to scan her right eye. That would tell the AI whether something was wrong, like if she was under excessive stress or could potentially have been kidnapped. Once the authorization was granted, she found herself in Homeland Security's online library, displayed as a virtual space with endless rows of virtual bookshelves and, in front of them all, a virtual desk. She gestured with two fingers to call up the desktop and looked at the input field on it.

"Missing persons entries, time frame, June to September 2018, United States and Canada," she instructed quietly, and the shelves began moving. After a while they stopped and several files jumped out and landed on the desktop. "Filter by profession: archaeology, anthropology, philology, by known adherents of Pre-Astronautics, Human Foundation members, Human Foundation lottery participants, flights to Cape Town during the period indicated."

This reduced the selection of files considerably.

"Hmm. Remove all results that do not meet at least three of the criteria."

Once again, the pile became smaller. Now there were only four files left.

"Aha." With a concise gesture she opened the first file. She was now looking at a young woman, a college student with the serious look of a bad passport photo. "Elisabeth Shaw," she read. "Student of anthropology and philology, studied at the University of Toronto under... none other than Ron Jackson. Well, *that's* not a coincidence. Flew to Cape Town in June 2018 and was never seen again. That was two months before Jackson."

Agatha put the file in her terminal's buffer and looked at the next three. They were all junior academics from serious universities: Yale, Stanford, and UCLA. She looked through the files and discovered that each of them was affiliated with a department in one of Jackson's three fields and had disappeared in either June or July. When she cross-referenced with the travel data from the TSA, the connection was unmistakable. They had all flown to Cape Town and had never checked in again, anywhere.

She checked the time tracker on her AR display. It had taken her exactly one hour to find all this out. It was frightening to be confronted with how poorly things were arranged when there was no public or financial interest behind them. Even with the funding of 2018, as limited as it was by today's standards, investigators would have had to look for cross-connections to other cases.

Unless someone had actively tried to prevent that, she thought.

"And? What have you got?" she asked Pano, who had extended the comfortable recliner seat and was now lying back with his own data glasses on, making pushing, pulling, and typing gestures in the air. It took a moment, but then he took the glasses off, raised the seat back a little, and bit down on his lower lip.

"I got a college student from Munich, Dana Pickert, who was reported missing in June. She took a flight to Cape Town and then never checked in again, anywhere. She was a master's student in archaeology. And the same story with students from Stockholm and Paris, and two from Madrid. Those last two studied anthropology and computer science—a strange combination."

"Let me guess," Agatha said. "In all of them, the investigation ended fairly quickly because, although the South African police seemed to be cooperating, they found nothing."

Pano put his hands up. "Obviously someone didn't want to go too deep. Not that it would have been difficult to bury these cases anyway, since they didn't grab any public attention, and students disappear often enough to go 'find the meaning of life' in Asia or Africa, or join a commune, question reality, or whatever."

"Amazing. It's like you have a sixth sense for this kind of thing," Agatha replied, confirming his assumptions.

Pano grinned. "Wow, thanks. Hey, are you trying to hit on me or something?" he teased.

When she grunted and shuddered in response, he batted his eyes endearingly. "You know, you're pretty sexy when you're annoyed," he concluded.

"Do you have a mother complex?"

"You tell me. You're the expert in reading people."

"I'm going to be reading you your rights in a minute."

"Fine, then," he said, making an obsequious gesture, followed by a sigh. "Sooner or later, you're going to realize that my charm and your raw sexual energy were made for each other."

When he saw the seething look she shot at him, he laughed so loudly that some of the other passengers looked in their direction.

Agatha didn't want to reward Pano with the hint of a smile that almost crossed her lips, but neither did she want to reinforce his image of her as a bitch. "Maybe we should make an appointment with Luther Karlhammer," she suggested stoically.

"Well, it's worth a try."

Agatha searched Homeland Security files for the phone number of Karlhammer's secretary, and then held her hand terminal to her ear. It rang three times before it was answered by a cheerful voice with a South African accent. "Luther Karlhammer's office, this is Melbou speaking!"

"Hello. This is Special Agent Agatha Devenworth, Counter-Terrorist Directive, Homeland Security. I'd like to speak to your boss, please."

"I'm sorry, madam, but Mr. Karlhammer is currently away from home."

"Could you connect me to his mobile? It's important." Of course, Agatha knew she had no authority in South Africa. She wouldn't even have been granted permission to carry a gun in the country if Miller hadn't called the right ministerial official and pulled some strings.

"I must apologize again, Madam Devenworth. Mr. Karlhammer unfortunately cannot be reached on his mobile," the secretary with the angelic voice replied, her cheerfulness never wavering.

"How long will he be away from home?"

"I'm afraid I really can't say. It has already been a week. I could put you through to the acting director, Mr. Eugens."

"That won't be necessary at the moment. Please save my number and ask Mr. Karlhammer to call me back as soon as he's available, all right?" Agatha asked.

"Of course."

"Thank you."

She hung up, and dropped her hand terminal into her lap.

"He can't even be reached by mobile," she sighed.

"Typical dodge tactics. I bet if that Secretary of yours had called, he'd suddenly—magically—be available," Pano said.

"Probably so. Whatever the case, he knows about us now and is probably doing some homework. And that means he knows we're coming, and that if he makes a move, we're ready for it and might be able to pin it down."

"Clever... or stupid."

"What?"

"That's either very clever of you or very dumb," Pano repeated. "If he is involved in the assassination, then we're poking around in his backyard with no authority and no backup."

"You can't crack a case without taking a few risks," she countered.

Pano sighed, defeated, and his gaze wandered to the window, which was nearly the size of a television. "Says you," he said, staring absently out the window.

Agatha unbuckled her seatbelt and leaned over towards the window. To their left, she saw, was the coast of the Western Sahara. A thin strip of yellow-white sand was still visible, probably a couple of kilometers wide, but the ground beyond it was strangely darkened in color as far as the eye could see. "That's the Desertec solar farm, isn't it?"

"Yeah. I knew it was gigantic, but wow. That thing is powering all of Europe *and* Africa—can you imagine?"

"Well, it's funded and maintained by the Human Foundation, so, yeah," she replied. "It's not the only miracle they've accomplished." It was a tacit admission that it was a truly impressive sight. "Are you an Earthling?"

"I beg your pardon?" Pano asked in surprise. She held

eye contact with him as she leaned back and refastened her seat belt.

"You heard me. Are you an Earthling?"

For a moment the European just looked at her penetratingly, as if he was trying to look straight into her soul, but then he lifted his arm and raised his sleeve to expose his right wrist to her. On it was a blue elastic band with the stylized *HF* of the Human Foundation logo, like two hands shaking in front of the earth.

"Which lottery?" she asked simply.

"Gene therapy. For my sister," he replied, and his ever-present grin lost a trace of its sincerity as his eyes betrayed a sadness.

"What's wrong with her?" She wondered too late whether this line of questioning might be a social no-no.

"She has a rare form of leukemia, so rare it hasn't really been researched yet. The whole world is celebrating that we're finally beating cancer, thanks to the breakthroughs of Human Foundation-funded research, but there are still very rare types of cancer for which there is essentially no hope because the number of cases is so small. My sister is one of those cases. She participates in the monthly lottery program for high-end gene therapies, and I participate to increase her chances."

"And what about you? No incurable conditions?"

"No. I've been deaf in one ear since birth. Please, no dumb jokes—I've heard them all. That's why I wear a hearing aid." He pushed his hair back and turned farther toward her to reveal his left ear. Agatha had to look twice before she could see the tiny telltale thread.

"Huh. That's unusual. You know there are good implants and surgical procedures that can help, right?"

"But they are very expensive, and I prefer to spend the

money I have left on the lottery that might save the planet—and my sister along the way. My hearing aid doesn't bother me because I've never known life without it, so I don't get too worked up about it. And hey, I'm probably one of the last ten people in the world who still has one of these antiques in his ear."

He was silent for a moment, and when Agatha didn't respond, he asked her, "So what's wrong with you?"

"I don't do the lotteries."

"Why not? I think it's a good system. Anyone can buy a monthly ticket for a fixed amount, and you might win a new leg, a job at the Human Foundation, funding for the studies you've always dreamed of doing, or a million other prizes, and all the money goes into the Foundation and their world-saving projects," Pano explained, getting more and more excited about it as he spoke.

Agatha tried to read from his face whether he was being serious or sarcastic, but couldn't tell.

"I understand the system, and I think it's good. For thirty years, the Human Foundation has been taking on our world's problems virtually singlehandedly, while our politicians just cozy up to lobbies right under the watchful eye of the authorities. That's why I donate thirty percent of my salary to the Foundation."

"What? Thirty percent?" His eyes popped in surprise. "Seriously?"

"Yes," she said simply.

"Don't you have any hobbies? Family? Friends you do stuff with?"

"No. I'm married to my job. Happily, I should add. And they're on the hook for paying me the big bucks for that job. But since I don't need it, I'd rather see it going into something that will help all people," she explained.

"I don't know whether I find that extremely sad, or extremely admirable," Pano confessed, looking her up and down with an intense stare as if he was revising his image of her.

She didn't like it.

"All right, so how do we start?" she asked to change the subject. "I think I should note that, if it comes down to it, I will bring down the Human Foundation just like anyone else who breaks the law, whatever it takes."

"But of course," he replied quickly. "I've already informed my contacts in Brussels, and they've spoken with the State Security Agency in Cape Town. They're going to pick us up at the airport, and we've been promised the full support of the authorities."

"They've got their fingers deep in Luther Karlhammer's... pockets. He's not only the richest person in the world, but he's also South African, and he's the biggest employer in this country. They're not going to... you know what... in the well where the money comes from."

"They're not going to 'you know what?' Are you being serious right now? You can't just say 'piss' when that's what you mean?" Pano asked, grinning.

"I just don't like to swear," she answered with a shrug.

"Cute."

"I don't think so."

"Maybe you're right."

"OK, so how is this going to go down?" she asked.

"We are going to be met by a liaison officer, who's going to take us to our hotel—"

"—which is definitely already bugged," she interjected.

"Well, of course. What did you expect? But at least we know it, and they must know that we know it. Come on, just admit it. If the situation was reversed, we'd be bugging them," Pano said with a long, drawn-out sigh. "Sometimes I hate this whole world."

"I don't."

"How come?"

"Because it's a world that's predictable, that functions by certain rules and with a certain logic, and I know how it works."

"It seems to me that's just how you see the world and evaluate it," he speculated. When Agatha frowned in response, he smiled.

"Whatever," she said. "I still want to go through these files a little before we land." She reached for her data glasses. "Did you know that Peter Gould, who was the chief financial officer of the Human Foundation, was also reported missing in 2018?"

"No, I didn't know that. This gets more exciting by the minute. When was that?"

"In December. That's a good while after Jackson. But he had no family or, evidently, friends who missed him. It was only reported later, when somebody in his bowling league asked the police about him because he stopped showing up."

"How sad," Pano said. "But why would a financial boffin disappear with Jackson?"

"I don't know. But we're going to find out, because I'm not giving up until we do."

"Have you really never left a case unsolved?"

"Never," she said with finality. "Never."

14

THE OBSERVER, 2042

The man in the black suit stood up from his seat in first class on Delta flight 4777 and slowly moved towards the rear of the plane. It had been less than two minutes since the pilot's announcement that they were about to start their descent into Cape Town. His path was blocked by a heavyset woman who was in the middle of rearranging her luggage in the overhead bin above her seat.

"Excuse me," he said politely, putting on a friendly smile. "Could I just get by, please?"

"Why?" she responded brusquely, looking at him like a hawk sizing up its prey. "There's bathrooms in the front too, you know." The woman waved a chubby arm in the direction of the two restrooms next to the cockpit door, where two flight attendants were busy stowing the drink carts back into their compartments.

"I beg your pardon, but they're both occupied," he explained.

"Then just hold it until I'm finished here."

The man in the black suit sighed and tapped her again.

"What?" She turned to look at him, annoyed.

The moment their eyes met, he instructed her in a low voice: "Please return to your seat, order a bottle of vodka, open it, and drink it straight down."

The woman's eyes were locked with his, and her eyelids twitched slightly with tension. Then she stopped what she was doing, closed the bin, and sat back down.

The man in the black suit continued down the aisle, casting a sideways glance at the two agents, Devenworth and Hofer, as he passed. They both had their data glasses on and were manipulating invisible symbols and controls. He brushed Agatha's jacket for just an instant, to all appearances by accident and without her noticing, and went on without pausing until he reached the rear bathrooms. There he went into the one on the left, and came out five minutes later.

Instead of returning to his assigned seat, he sat in an open seat across the aisle. He could see Devenworth and Hofer, who had stowed their data glasses and fastened their seatbelts.

15

RON JACKSON, 2018

"Are the cameras in place?" Ron asked. Ross nodded emphatically. They were standing together in the work tent, with two students who were rewiring some circuit boards.

"When those two are up and running, everything will be online and can be accessed. But we can't send a video feed to Vienna. We don't have the bandwidth," Patchuvi's assistant reminded him of the real problem that he hadn't solved yet.

Now that there was an unknown expedition on their way to them, Ron had thought it prudent to install cameras and record everything. His telephone call with Luther three days ago hadn't produced any answers. He had been as surprised to hear about them as Ron had.

And even worse, all the searches for hidden spaces and unusual iridium concentrations had turned up nothing. They had just three or four days until the strangers arrived, and with every passing hour the knot of worry in his stomach grew heavier and heavier.

"Right. I'm taking my tablet. If anything happens, message me."

"Where are you going?" James asked.

"To Cavern One. I just wanted to check for myself whether there isn't anything to find there. Tell Dana we're taking the muon detector down there," Ron said.

Patchuvi's assistant nodded.

"Thanks," Ron said as he turned and hurried off through the inflated tube between the work tent and the locker-filled changing room to force himself into his heated thermal clothes. Honeycomb rubber mats had been placed over the floor plates, but somehow the floor still managed to be muddy. The fine ice crystals that formed quickly all over clothes and shoes the moment anyone went out melted quickly when that person came in, and the residue mixed with the dirt and dust of the nearly twenty people working here. Ron took great pains to not let his socks touch the floor when he squeezed his feet into his boots. He then passed through the 'airlock,' as they called the short passage that had an auto-closing door at either end. This helped keep as much of the heat inside as possible.

As always, the wall of cold hit him like a slap in the face, and he nearly staggered. His face began to burn almost immediately as the warm air from the tent condensed upon his exposed skin, where it instantly turned into ice crystals.

"I hate this cold," he grumbled as he hustled off toward Cavern One. He circled the living quarters, the glowing bubbles that looked to him like something out of a turn of the century science-fiction movie, and hustled into corridor 13, which passed through a somewhat sloping, shaft-like room leading directly into the cavern. He didn't see anyone on the way, because half of the students in the western quadrant were off taking soil samples, and the other half were in the work module analyzing them for iridium.

The moment he entered Cavern One, a cold shiver—unrelated to the temperature—ran down his spine. It was

The Fossil

pitch black, and he had to use a small flashlight to find the rotary switch that the team had hung on the wall. It was hanging on a loop of wire below the thick power cables.

He found it and turned the switch, and the light suddenly drove the darkness from the vast cavern with its perfectly carved-out walls. The room was more than a hundred meters long and fifty meters wide. With its high ceiling peaking in a grooved vertex, it almost seemed like he might be inside an upside-down ship's hull.

Ron first looked at the many islands of yellow light. They continually flickered as if fighting to reach an equilibrium with the darkness.

"What's the secret you're hiding from me?" he whispered, and watched the long cloud of his freezing breath for a moment before setting about adjusting the six upward-pointing construction spotlights along the walls, one by one. He tilted the LED spotlights downwards and set them for half an hour so that they illuminated as much of the dark floor as possible.

"What are you doing?"

Ron was so startled by the sudden voice that his whole body compressed like a giant spring. He spun around and saw Gould standing behind him, sipping from a thermos he held in his thickly bundled hands. Under the thick fur-ringed hood his face looked plump, although Ron knew the financial man was ascetically thin to the point of fault.

"Jesus, man, I almost had a heart attack," gasped Ron.

"Didn't mean to... I'm sorry. What are you doing?" Gould asked again.

"I want to search the floor. In a lot of burial chambers you've got hollow spaces or secret rooms and passages under the floor."

"You think that this is a burial chamber?"

"Of course I do," said Ron, wrinkling his brow. "What else?"

"No idea," Gould said with a sour tone. "Well, great."

"There's almost always burial chambers. Almost all cultures place a major significance on death and the remains of important personages. And pyramids are basically always that. Why should this one be any different?"

"You're the expert. So how are you going to do it?" Gould asked. When Ron raised an eyebrow and gave him a puzzled look, he added, "The searching, I mean."

"Oh, the same way I did with the smaller rooms. I left the drone in here yesterday." He gestured to the small case near one of the spotlights. "If I set the lights properly, I can send the drone up and scan from above with the HD camera. That's the best way to identify patterns that you can't see from close up. It's a good thing the ceiling is so high in here. I should be able to get high enough to get a total picture."

"I see. Hang on, I'll get the case." Gould picked up the aluminum suitcase and put it in front of Ron, who knelt down and opened it.

The bulky thermal clothes restricted Ron's movements so much that he felt like an astronaut. "Thank you," he said. He removed the four-rotored drone from the form-fitting foam in the case and began mounting the camera on it.

"Don't you think that we've already proven the ancient astronauts' theory? By discovering a structure over two million years old that could only have been built by humans with modern materials?" asked Gould, as he watched Ron attentively.

"'Ancient astronauts?'" Ron asked quizzically, almost offended. "I'm no fan of that stuff!" He shook his head in frustration as he screwed the camera mounting to the underside of the drone, holding all of it between his thickly gloved fingers like an uncooperative crab.

"No?"

"No! That's what I've been trying to make everyone understand the whole time! 'Ancient astronauts' is a pseudo-science, and most of its hypotheses have been long disproven. The people who push that stuff are almost never scientists, just cranks who believe that aliens came down and gave technology to ancient civilizations. They believe that the gods of mythology were actually aliens whom humans worshiped because of their technology. Can't you see I think that's all nonsense? The only thing I have in common with them is that I also believe that humanity is much older than we think. But not because I believe Homo Sapiens has been around that long. What I believe is that humans ruled this planet before."

"Then where did they all go?" Gould sounded like he was being open-minded, but Ron didn't believe he was genuine about it. Pretty much everybody found his ideas laughable, except for maybe the few students who had come out here with him looking for adventure.

"Well there might be any number of reasons. Maybe an M.E.E., or maybe they left the Earth by spaceship."

"M.E.E.?"

"Mass Extinction Event," Ron explained without looking up from what he was doing. "Mass die-off caused by a meteor impact, supervolcano eruption, earthquake-caused tsunami, etc., etc., etc."

"Well, that sounds more plausible than spaceships, at least."

"You think so? In just a couple of years, SpaceX will be flying to Mars. When you think that it was barely two hundred years ago that Thomas Edison switched on the first light bulb, that's a lot of progress in a short amount of time. If my theory is right, the Builders' civilization lasted a lot longer than ours has. Now, where do you think we'll be after, say, eight hundred years of electricity? Or when the inevitable AI singularity arrives? Spaceships are not illogical —in fact, they're inevitable," Ron explained, and then abruptly and uncharacteristically cursed when the threaded connector piece of the camera slipped out of its socket. Without a thought, he took off his gloves and tried to seat it properly with bare fingers, but they began trembling immediately, and after just a few seconds he had to put the gloves back on.

"Okay, then," Gould said. "So, do you think that 'ancient astronauts' is bullshit, or do you just interpret their story differently?"

"Both," Ron answered, and looked up at Gould as he finished preparing the drone. "For one thing, we do have documentable objects like the 'Wedge of Aiud,' which was found on a construction site in Romania in 1973. It's a chunk of finely milled aluminum, over two kilograms in weight, and covered in a thick oxide layer that indicates it's ancient, thousands of years, maybe even millions. But the first metallic aluminum was only produced in 1825. When we get out of here you can Google it. The 'ancient aliens' people claim it's a piece of the landing gear from an alien spacecraft. But I think it's a relic of the Builders—humans, who lived here in the early Paleozoic."

"But don't you think that if that were true we would have found many more traces of them, many more relics?" Gould asked hesitantly.

"No. That's one of the differences between my theory and that ancient astronauts' stuff. What I believe is that the Builders lived here about sixty million years ago, when

Earth was dominated by a climate that was very hospitable. We know from our science that, after *that* long a time, there would be basically no trace of us. Movements of tectonic plates, deposits, upheavals, would mean that nothing we ever built would ever be found—not steel, not plastic, not anything.

"The only thing that could still be detected would be atmospheric data like the high CO_2 content of the time. Now, we already know that there have been huge fluctuations in the level of atmospheric CO_2 over time. What we can't say for sure, however, is whether they were natural or industrial in origin."

Ron stood up and turned the drone around several times before holding it still in one hand. Next, he picked up the remote control with its wide display in his other hand. "Here, you hold this for a sec." He handed the drone off to Gould and began punching away at the buttons on the remote control. When the rotors started to hum, and then spin, he told Gould to release it.

"Of course, all of that assumes that they were stupid enough to wreck their climate, just like us," Ron continued as the drone rose virtually straight up to the apex of the ceiling. "Now *that* I have trouble believing. Nature generally doesn't give stupidity a second chance. It's not an evolutionary advantage."

"With you there," said Gould, craning his neck to follow the small aircraft. Now that it had risen above the light cast by the construction spotlights, it was only an occasional glimmer in the darkness. "Do you really believe we're going to find anything here?"

"I have to believe."

"That wasn't my question."

"Yes, I really believe we're going to find something here,"

Ron replied, without looking up from the display. He pushed a button and turned to look straight into Gould's eyes. "My instincts have never let me down."

"Did your instincts also tell you that some unknown group of people was going to come here?" Gould asked. He was grinning provocatively when he said it, but Ron could see the worry in his eyes.

"My instincts are more interested in stones than people."

"I thought you were also an anthropologist."

"Yeah, that's why I understand that grown people still act like children," Ron snorted.

"Let me guess. You don't like kids."

"Actually, I do like kids. But you have to lead them by the hand so they don't run out into traffic, don't cross the street against the light, and don't eat the poisonous berries along the roadside."

Gould returned Ron's gaze with a provocative sparkle in his eyes. "So in other words, you see yourself as the adult, and you want to take humanity by the hand," he said, and kept staring until Ron turned away, shaking his head, to look back at the display in his hands.

"I'm only trying to help."

"You think proving that people died out here once before is going to help?" Gould didn't sound very convinced.

"No. What I think will help is finding what they left behind, so I can *prove* that we've already wiped ourselves out once. Maybe then people will wake up and try to change something."

"You're too optimistic," the accountant said.

"You're not optimistic enough," Ron shot back. All of a sudden he hit the middle of the display with an outstretched finger, hard, as if he might punch right through it.

"What is it?"

"You see these markings?" Ron shoved the display into the other man's face.

"That looks like a long seam."

"Look there, the top, the bottom, and the sides."

"There are seams everywhere," Gould replied. He put a gloved hand over his mouth, so the steam of his breath wouldn't fog up the screen.

"Yeah, but exactly four of them are a little deeper. Maybe you're not practiced in seeing patterns like this, but try. Take a good look and concentrate," Ron challenged him, smiling so broadly that his near-frozen lips opened.

After a while, Gould said, "You're right. With a little imagination, you can clearly see four seams—straight lines, running at right angles towards the middle there. But they stop right before where they would meet at the midpoint."

"And that's exactly where we'll put the muon detector," Ron said. He pulled his radio from his belt. "This is Ron. I need the muon detector in Cavern One right away."

About ten minutes later, the two students who had been working on networking the camera feeds came in, rolling the machine with them. The detector was a collection of rack-mounted devices in a large, wheeled case. It looked like any other collection of rack units that you might find anywhere—certainly nothing like what it ought to look like when you considered its function, which involved detecting cosmic rays.

Ron, who was now standing with Gould next to the roughly one square meter of floor where the four deeper seams in the floor stopped, motioned the students towards him and rolled the box with them over the last few meters until the detector was placed as precisely as possible over the exact center of the spot.

"Did you find something, sir?" one of the students asked.

The hole in the center of his hood was more beard than face.

"I said call me Ron, okay?"

"Sorry, uh, Doctor, sorry."

Ron sighed and made a final adjustment on the muon detector. "We haven't found anything. Not yet. But I have a hunch that this is a good place to start looking. Is this data feed going to go straight into the network?"

"Yeah," said the other student with an eager nod.

"Good. That'll take a few hours. Get back to what you were doing. We've got time pressure here," Ron said, raising a hand in gratitude.

The pair hesitated briefly and then ran off, back down the passageway leading to Cavern Two and the living-quarters module. Ron almost felt sorry for them, and under normal circumstances he would have let them all stand here and wait for the results. But that was a luxury they didn't have anymore, not with a second, unknown expedition breathing down their necks, due to arrive in a few days and with intentions unknown.

"Now we wait," said Ron.

"How long?" Gould asked, giving the nearly two-meter-high wheeled metal case an up and down look-over as if it was some kind of circus curiosity.

"That depends on how deep it is. First, the instrument is going to perform some baseline measurements. I'm guessing that's going to take an hour or two."

"We'll have frozen to death by then," Gould protested, suddenly pulling his arms together over his chest similar to a prayer-posture and rubbing his hands together fiercely.

"Maybe so. You can head back if you want. I'll wait here that long." Ron rubbed his hands together, too, and then started walking around the spot he was standing on to try to generate at least a little internal heat.

"I'll go fill these up," Gould said, indicating the thermal containers, "and then I'll come back with some new heating elements for you."

"That would be great, thanks."

As Gould's footsteps faded off into the distance, Ron peered at the floor under the muon detector. It looked like it was smooth beneath the thin layer of ice crystals that covered everything here, which gave it a roughened appearance. He kept looking at the feed scrolling by on his tablet's display. They all looked like the same images, and soon his eyes began to glaze over. Then suddenly his device beeped, just once, and so quickly and unobtrusively that he almost didn't hear it. But in the dead silence of the cavern itself, with the distant hum of the generators the only sound, it jolted him out of his trance.

"Okay, lay it on me," he whispered, grabbing the tablet with both hands to hold it right in front of his face. Could these readings be right? The detector had only been at it for a few minutes and had already found something.

Ron stared in disbelief at what the image results showed —a roughly cubical cavity below measuring three meters in each direction. If the information was correct, he was standing on just a few centimeters of rock, with a hidden chamber below it.

Immediately going into action, he tossed his tablet aside and began scraping away the layer of ice with his hands, searching for pictograms, a mechanism, anything to indicate an opening. But he couldn't find anything. Next, he pushed the detector aside and did the same where the device had been standing. Again he used his tablet to check that nothing had changed.

Nothing had. Sitting at the spot where the seams pointed before they discontinued, he was directly above the cavity. Its dimensions were absolutely regular. It could not possibly be of natural origin.

"This is Ron Jackson," he called into his radio, his voice wild with excitement. "I'm in Cavern One and I've found something—"

His sentence cut off abruptly, and his voice changed to a surprised scream when the floor beneath him suddenly ceased to exist and he plunged into the darkness.

16

FILIO AMOROSA, 2042

Filio stood at the wheel of the *Ocean's Bitch,* crying. Her tears were so plentiful and hot that they burned her cheeks almost immediately. She had just thrown out another emergency lifeboat and had her hands over her ears, desperate to block out the sound of Thomas screaming from the water, begging her not to leave him and her comrades behind. She felt terrible, but at the same time knew she had no choice. In the crew of the *Bitch*, she had found a new family. But her old family needed her even more urgently now.

A framed copy of the scrapper manifesto hung on the wall directly behind her. She could feel it physically, as if the piece of paper had eyes that were boring into her back.

Item 6: All found objects will be liquidated and shared equally by all crew members, regardless of position, after the investor shares have been paid.

Item 7: The decision-making authority on the sale of found objects falls to the investor.

The worst thing about it was that she knew full well that her own signature was right there on it, next to Romain's,

Thomas's, Jane's and Alberto's. It was as if it was a family photo and she had just ripped herself out of it.

"I had no choice," she said, sobbing, and turned to Oscar, who was sitting next to her. He looked up at her attentively. "You understand that, don't you?"

Oscar barked affirmingly and panted.

"These samples can only go to one party—the one who can get me back on the Mars Project and assigned to the next mission... but our investor's an American, who's just going to sell it to NASA. And money's not going to get me there." She looked pointedly at the box that was lashed to the wall behind her by a heavy-duty strap.

Filio wiped the tears from her eyes and looked at the clock. She had been underway with her transponder signal turned off for half an hour, so it was time to radio the Maldivian Coast Guard. She took down the radio, tuned in the frequency, and began to speak: "Mayday! Mayday! This is the scrapper ship *Ocean's Bitch*. Request immediate assistance! Coordinates are..." Filio looked at the on-screen window she had prepared earlier and read out the GPS coordinates of the emergency lifeboat. "Repeat. Mayday! Mayday!"

"*Ocean's Bitch,* this is Captain Inaritu speaking on the *Gallasolé*. Message received. We are on our way to you. Estimated arrival time, three hours. Keep your lifeboat activated. Do you have any injuries?"

"Affirmative," she lied, and pressed the button for white noise before hanging up. That would make sure the Coast Guard didn't take their time.

"Three hours," she said out loud, looking at the clock. "That's good news. With their gear and the life raft, they'll make it that long."

Filio took a deep breath and set the autopilot for full

speed on a course north by northwest. Then she strode to the meeting room, Oscar following close behind, and picked up the satellite phone from the table.

"When you do this, there will be no going back," she cautioned herself, steeling her shoulders. Then she dialed a number and returned to the bridge with nervous steps.

A woman with a cheery, ringing voice answered. "General-Director Rietenbach's office, this is Spärling. Who's this?" She sounded half call center and half porn star.

"This is Filio Amorosa," she replied, with voice tense. She licked her lips. "I need to speak with Mr. Rietenbach."

The pause that followed was so long that Filio was afraid the satellite phone had dropped the connection, but then the secretary composed herself. "I'm sorry, Ms. Amorosa, Mr. Rietenbach has just left the building."

"Just tell him I have the thing he wants most, and that I will still have it for exactly five more minutes before someone else gets it." She cut the connection and then exhaled deeply.

If this Spärling had even two properly firing neurons, she would be calling her boss like her life depended on it. While she waited, Filio started looking up the number of her friend and lawyer, Martin Lücke, on her hand terminal. But the satellite phone was already ringing.

"Rietenbach?" she asked when she picked it up.

"Yes, Filio, it's me. I just arrived in Lake Geneva, but my secretary said that you have something for me. Something that I really want. You have my full attention."

Filio moved to the vacuum-sealed box and clicked some seals until it hissed and the lid released, moving upwards slightly. The box contained eight transparent test tubes, packed in close-fitting, shaped foam. Some contained stones that looked like amber, others were full of tiny shards, pale like ivory, while the others were full of a dark liquid.

"I've got the samples."

"What samples, Filio?"

"The samples taken from The Object."

There was a long silence on the line, long enough for her to check the display of the satellite phone carefully several times, making sure that the connection was still up.

Finally the director spoke again. "This better not be some kind of joke," he cautioned. His voice was measured, but not enough to hide an underlying note of excitement.

"You really think I'm the kind of person to joke about this? About *this*?"

"Where are you now? Where are the samples? Where have you been all these years? You know you've been gone so long you've been officially declared dead?"

"No, Director," Filio tutted, shaking her head. "I'm not stupid enough to fall for your tricks. Not this time. I know how to play the game now. So first of all, I want some guarantees. In one hour, my lawyer is going to walk into the Paris office with a contract. You're going to sign it, or you're going to get somebody to sign it. My lawyer will verify the signature and then send a copy of the signed document to three addresses that he's already prepared. Then you're going to get what you want, and I'm going to get what I want."

"And what exactly is that?"

"You know very well what *that* is."

"*Mars Two* is going up in less than two weeks." Filio couldn't see him, but she knew exactly how Rietenbach was shaking his head as he said it. She had always thought that he looked like a dachshund, with his droopy chin and thick, horn-rimmed glasses. "You haven't been trained up with the crew. You haven't even been trained at all! Not to mention the administrative nightmare we would be inviting down upon ourselves. No, Filio, it's impossible."

"Nothing is impossible, if you want the European Space Agency to get its hands on the most valuable artifacts humanity has ever possessed. That's going to be good not just for your career, but for the Mars Project. Anyway, I'm the most qualified astronaut for *Mars Two* there is, so don't try to tell me what's possible and what's not. And I just did something that everyone thought was impossible. Don't forget that either. As soon as I get a call from my lawyer, I'll give you the coordinates for an extraction. It needs to be quick, and you'll want to start out from southern India. Have your people ready."

Filio hung up and had to exhale deeply again before she pulled herself together and dialed Martin's number.

"Lücke."

"This is Filio."

"Ah. Did you make the call?" he asked. His youthful voice just could not be reconciled with the fifty-year-old veteran attorney she knew was on the other end of the line. He spoke the slightly lilting German of Alsace, which she liked so much and which had become so familiar to her over the decades they had known each other.

"Yes," she replied, her voice trembling.

"You already sound a lot better than before."

"But I don't feel better."

"I wouldn't worry about it. Your friends are all going to be rich men and women as soon as they get picked up. It's actually a good thing that the Coast Guard is coming to them, so they can get their claim officially registered and no other scrapper ship will be able to come in and steal anything."

"I hope you're right. But I still need you to do me a favor," she said.

"Isn't that what I'm doing? I just got in a taxi. I'm heading to the bureau right now."

"Please. You have to inform the investor that his crew hit the jackpot. And give him the GPS coordinates I'm going to send to your terminal. That should speed up the rescue and make sure that they get to salvage everything." There was pleading in her voice, and she was very careful to avoid looking at Romain's picture of her and the crew pinned over the captain's chair while she spoke

"I'll make it happen," Martin replied.

"Thank you. For everything."

"Well, I owed you a favor. When this is all over, we're even."

"Deal."

"I'll keep you posted."

The lawyer hung up and Filio closed the transport box immediately, as if the test tubes inside it might learn to walk and somehow escape before reaching their destination.

Oscar's dark eyes followed her movements, and when she tossed a treat at him, he caught it in midair.

"Well, my friend, we're almost there. Almost there," she repeated, and corrected her course to Thiruvanamthapuram. The *Ocean's Bitch* was running at the top speed it could sustain indefinitely, thirty-two knots, which meant it would cover the thousand kilometers in seventeen hours. India and the Maldives weren't on particularly friendly terms, so she wouldn't have any immediate problems if the crew decided to report her to the island nation's authorities. Of course, there was the possibility that Romain would call the investor the first chance he got, but since she had made sure that Martin would be calling him right now, he wouldn't be

The Fossil

doing himself any favors by doing that. Besides which, he had enough on his hands with rescuing his crew and their precious finds.

She liked materialistic people who prioritized money and worldly possessions. She liked them because they were predictable, like a dog at the track chasing the mechanical hare. In the end, if they came out ahead, it was almost guaranteed that they wouldn't complain. Their friendship could be bought, literally, and their actions and reactions were always oriented towards the same thing—money.

Politicians, up to the very highest ranks of public officials, suffered from a similar predictability. In the end, it was not the leaders of the democratic states who held the political strings, but rather the people at the controls of the public administration apparatus. Perhaps more in Europe than anywhere else, from the twentieth century on, bureaucracy had grown rampant to the point where new laws and decisions that the administrative officials did not like simply got bogged down in complex procedures, reviews, and revisions. They had created a bureaucratic monster, one that could no longer be controlled and that no one fully understood. Of course, that gave people like Manfred Rietenbach considerable power, even though the levers he was able to pull were much more obvious than, for example, the ones that heads of administrative districts or local authorities with connections to national ministries could reach.

Nonetheless, he was one of them, the broad class of politicians, whether elected or appointed, whose currency was power. Rietenbach would use what she had found to land himself an even more powerful position. Maybe he was angling for the position of Director-General for life—not an official position, obviously, but doors did open for the powerful—or perhaps he would go after the big money by maneuvering himself into a State Secretary position on a ministerial committee.

Whatever his plans were, Filio was sure that at that moment he was rubbing his hands with glee at the thought of it, and she could use that.

She hated that kind of thinking, but she knew how to use it. She couldn't understand, nor did she want to, how someone could look at what was arguably the most important find in human history—samples of organic material that did not come from Earth—and see an opportunity for personal enrichment.

Of course, the copies she had sent to the German and French governments and NASA would ensure that the most important institutions knew about all of it and that the find would ultimately benefit all mankind. When he saw them, Rietenbach's wrinkles would double in size. But she didn't care, because she knew that he would grit his teeth and sign on the dotted line. He didn't really have any choice. All he could do was make sure to tell all the right people that he had been grooming her and supporting her the whole time. And the fact that she had trusted him, and no one else, with the samples would be his proof.

She had set it all up this way, and Rietenbach was not going to disappoint—he was too predictable.

After about an hour of Filio biting her nails and staring nervously at the radar screen, the satellite phone finally rang.

"Yes?"

"It's Martin," her friend and attorney replied.

"And?"

"He just skimmed everything and signed. You're getting your spot on *Mars Two*," Martin assured her. As his words sank in, she almost fainted.

I did it, the thought echoed in her head. *I really did it, and I'm getting my second chance. The chance to understand why my friends died, and make sense of it all.*

After two years of working obsessively, and unimaginably hard, and living a lie through it all, she could hardly believe that this phone call was real. All the time spent zealously learning how to dive, so she would be believable as a treasure diver; all the long nights on the bridge, watching Romain to learn the basics of steering and navigating at sea; all the practice in parrying the advances of each of the men who made a move on her; all the charades it took to wrap them around her finger—but the hardest thing she had ever had to learn was putting her goal above all the people she had let into her heart.

"Just a few more days and they'll all be very, very rich," she said out loud, sighing. "So rich that they won't miss one little box. They're going to be too busy swimming in money to care. That's... that's..."

"It's wonderful, yes," Martin finished for her. "The faxes have been sent. That raised a few eyebrows, and some of them didn't even know if they still had a fax machine, but in the end my research paid off. In Europe, *old-fashioned* still means *official* and *water-tight*. Hold on, Rietenbach wants to speak to you."

There was a brief moment of static on the other end of the line, and then she heard the booming voice of the Director-General. "Filio, where are we supposed to pick you and... The Object up?"

"In the harbor at Thiruvanamthapuram. There's an international airport near there," she said without hesitation.

"I'll make sure you and The Object get to Darmstadt safe and sound."

"But I don't want to go to Darmstadt."

"That's not negotiable," Rietenbach insisted. "There are some people who want to talk to you before you fly to Nevada for training. The Americans aren't going to be happy at all when they find out what we snatched from under their noses, so we can use a few days' lead time before the shit hits the fan." Now he sounded like the inflexible public servant he was.

"All right, then," Filio acquiesced.

"But be warned that the crew of *Mars Two* is not going to be thrilled about this. We're going to have to find some excuse to take one of our best ESA astronauts off this mission, and he's not going to be happy. And neither is the crew," the Director-General cautioned.

"It'll work."

"It has to work. Okay, so, I'm initiating your extraction from Thiruvanamthapuram, wherever that is."

Wherever that is, Filio repeated in her mind, and frowned. That choice of words seemed to indicate that he had, or would have, a lot of resources at his disposal, and that might mean that he had already talked to members of the government or the BND.

All of a sudden, Filio realized that she would have to be very careful from here on out. Everybody was after this Object, literally *everybody*—at least anybody who knew it might actually exist. While that didn't include the general public, it did mean a whole series of powerful state actors, private sector organizations, and institutions. All with enough resources to exercise their power anywhere in the world.

Her eyes wandered to the dark box behind her, and it suddenly seemed cold and threatening, and the bridge felt too small. That city in South India seemed very far away, and Darmstadt, all the way on the other side of the world, seemed even further.

What if she hadn't prepared well enough for this moment? What if she had underestimated somebody out there, or overestimated herself, and overestimated ESA as an ally?

She hadn't won anything yet, and wasn't going to breathe a sigh of relief until she was physically standing in the Astronaut Training Center in Nevada, alongside her future team. That moment was still a long way off, something she became more and more aware of the longer she stared at the box.

17

AGATHA DEVENWORTH, 2042

"Ladies and Gentlemen, we will shortly be arriving at Cape Town International Airport. At this time please fasten your seatbelts, return your seats to the upright position, and stow your tray-tables. We would like to point out that for the rest of your flight, the use of the toilets is no longer permitted." It was the voice of one of the flight attendants, the attractive brunette, coming through the speakers.

Agatha exhaled a sigh of relief. She hated flying, because every time she boarded a plane she felt she was giving up control over her life. And what made it worse was that this was actually true, because she had no clue as to how to fly a plane, so could only sit there in the metal tube high above the clouds, racing through the air as thin as American coffee at twice the speed of sound.

"You seem tense," Pano said.

"Just excited."

"I understand."

Fortunately, he left it at that. She was already rolling her eyes internally every time he felt the need to comment on what he observed—or believed he observed, which he did all the time. Evidently he also knew when to keep his mouth shut, so as to not push it too far. She guessed that at some point in his life he had developed a feel for other people's moods, and he wanted to make sure he was interpreting them correctly. *That will be useful for our joint investigations,* she thought, *because it is something that I don't have the slightest idea how to do.*

The plane landed in beaming sunshine and brutal turbulence. The Cape of Good Hope was not only the city's namesake, but also one of the windiest places on earth, which made it all the more astonishing that the pilot set the Delta wing down with no more than a gentle bump.

As always, half of the passengers jumped up from their seats the moment they touched the ground, despite all announcements to the contrary. They were jostling into the aisle with their luggage, even as the plane continued to roll towards the gate. It was like a brilliant ballet of collective disobedience that was reflected in the eyes of every stratum of society. It was a symptom of human impatience and the belief that you could do anything you wanted to, the way you always did it, just so you could be that much faster and more efficient—even when it came to getting off an airplane.

Agatha recognized these small but important signs everywhere, all the time. There was a time when she wondered whether there might be something wrong with her because she only crossed the street when the light was green and only ever in the crosswalk, she had never once so much as cut in line, and certainly never disobeyed a flight crew's instruction to remain seated.

Somewhere along the line, however, she had concluded that huge swaths of the general population suffered from a fundamental disorder that she had not inherited. It was the understanding of being a detached subject, part of a collective and yet not. For most people, laws only applied when they were practical, like while driving a car. You knew that driving too fast would not only get you a ticket, but would increase the risk to other road users. But then you said *ah, nothing's going to happen, I'm really in a hurry*, or *it's just another 10 miles*. But if someone turned out to be responsible for the death of your friends or your family, because he had been driving too fast, well then, no penalty could be too severe. That was just the way people were.

Fortunately for the last ten years, the only vehicles on the road had been driven by AI. Virtually all cars were autonomous now, so they couldn't make the mistakes that humans did, because that type of blunder would be going against their algorithms. Agatha loved algorithms, and had really never understood why most people had major issues with AIs. Those human errors didn't happen in law anymore either, since the entire legal system had been automated. Algorithms were simply more objective than human judges, who by nature could only rely on their own interpretations and assumptions and reading of the law.

The air travel industry was next, and then hopefully soon, politics. In her eyes, an algorithm at the top of the social and political ladder would be a blessing for all. Then it would finally be possible to know the necessary and logical thing to do—and to actually do it, and enforce it, rather than trying to do what would ensure re-election for the sitting government.

She and Pano shuffled along in the line of about 400 passengers from the big Airbus, down the jetway and towards the desks at immigration control. They recognized the woman who had been sitting in front of them in first class, doing her best to make sure everyone on the flight knew she was in a bad mood. Now, she was falling down drunk and being dragged away by security officers, struggling all the way.

"Strange woman," Pano remarked, shaking his head.

They passed to the right of the throng waiting in line for regular immigration and proceeded to the checkpoint for diplomats and flight personnel. Agatha presented their passports and intelligence IDs to the dark-skinned officer at the counter, who dutifully scanned everything.

"Have a good stay," the official said, completely lackadaisically, and waved them through.

They approached a frosted glass wall, which parted down the middle, revealing two men in civilian clothing smiling at them.

"Welcome to South Africa, Special Agent Devenworth, Capitano Hofer," said the older of the two. He had a manly mustache, straw-colored hair, and the creased, leathery skin of a chain smoker. His partner, a stoic black African with chiseled features, also shook their hands.

"This is Agent Aluwi. I'm Agent Moosbech," the older man continued.

"Pleasure," Pano said, and they flashed their IDs at each other to confirm their identities.

"We'll be taking you to your hotel, and we can tell you a little about our city on the way if you like. That will help you get around, all right?"

We need a little time to question you and give the hotel room team a chance for one last sweep to make sure all the bugs are in place and out of sight, Agatha translated mentally. She nodded in agreement.

They already had everything—just two long aluminum cases each that they had taken as carry-on baggage so they would not need to go to the baggage claim carousels and could walk straight out of the airport with the agents. They escorted Agatha and Pano to a flashy black SUV with tinted windows. An airport security officer was waiting where it stood at the curb, ready to open the doors for them.

Agatha felt someone watching her, like eyes burning into the back of her neck, and she cast a glance over her shoulder. But there was only a teenager there, earbuds in, who seems to be looking right through her.

The drive through the city was uneventful, except that Agent Moosbech never stopped talking. He told them about anything and everything, while still managing to say nothing: the planting of the green spaces, Nelson Mandela, the post-apartheid years, the gentrification of the townships, Cape Town's renaissance and emergence as the 'best city in the world' thanks to the fame and wealth of Luther Karlhammer, and how much more beautiful and safe Cape Town was compared to sprawling Johannesburg.

When they arrived at their hotel, a five-star number right on the beach, she politely refused Moosbech's offer to help with the luggage—as well as his proposition to have a drink with him and Aluwi in an hour or two.

"Sorry, we're just plain exhausted from the flight and want to get to bed early and start our investigation first thing in the morning." Pano faked a yawn that couldn't possibly have been better timed.

"Well, if you change your minds, let us know."

With that, the two agents drove off.

"It's five in the afternoon. We're getting started right now, aren't we?" Pano asked obligingly.

"Obviously. I don't know about you, but I'm not interested in lying around a bug-infested room and giving them all the time in the world to put a tail on us before tomorrow morning. If we've got a little head start right now, we'd better use it. They can listen to us snoring tonight for all I care."

"Good. So what's your plan? You have one, no doubt?" Pano asked.

"Oh yeah. Those students whose files we found, they flew to Cape Town. The flight data shows that some of them landed late in the evening or at night. So what's the first thing that a student does?"

"Goes to a hostel," said the Italian, but then thought some more. "But if they worked for the Human Foundation, they could have afforded hotel rooms."

"You forget that in 2018 the Foundation was on the verge of bankruptcy, and was a very small player that only political prisoners and hippie activists supported. At that time it was a well-financed foundation at the end of its lifecycle, not the global mega-consortium it is today," Agatha reminded him. "No, I think you were right the first time. We'll start with the hostels."

"Let's see what hostels were in the city back in 2018, and see if we can get the booking data for the periods we need. We've got the names and the exact date so that part should be easy, especially because even back then South Africa required hotels to copy the passports of every guest." Pano seemed pleased with himself. "I'll bring the luggage up to the room. Why don't you take care of getting a car?"

There was a small desk for a rental car company in a corner of the hotel lobby. She went to it, and ten minutes later a Tesla Model X was driven up to the door for her, courtesy of her department credit card. It was the most significant charge she had ever put on the expense account.

She sat in the driver's seat and waited. Five minutes later Pano dropped into the passenger's seat and put on a pair of mirrored aviator shades. He looked at her with a smirk, and she saw that he was chewing gum. Rolling her eyes and shaking her head, she turned to the dashboard and said, "Downtown."

The large display in the center console came to life and displayed a route as the car silently sprang into motion.

Agatha reclined her seat as far down as it would go. "Tesla, show me a list of all the hostels and low-budget hotels in Cape Town today that were open in 2018."

The windshield turned into a huge heads-up display, and a long list of names, addresses and phone numbers appeared on it.

"Woah, that's a lot," Pano remarked, pushing his aviator shades so far down his nose that they almost fell off.

"It's an hour to downtown. By the time we get there we'll have called all of them."

It took a solid forty minutes, thirty-three phone calls, Filio acquiring a hot left ear from the hand terminal, and Pano a deafened right ear, also from being on the phone the whole time. But they got lucky. Not only did they find the hostels where the students had booked when they arrived in Cape Town, but it also turned that they had all booked the same hostel. Evidently they had networked before they traveled, quite possibly through the Human Foundation.

"This is our lucky day," Pano said. "Are we going there?"

"Obviously we're going there."

"Okay, but what are we hoping to find?" he asked skeptically. "It's been twenty-four years since they checked in and checked out. What could possibly still be there of interest to us?"

"Have you got a better place to start?" she asked, and shot him a sidelong look.

Pano sighed. "All right, then. Cape House Green Hostel."

The Cape House Green Hostel was near the beach at the northwestern edge of the city, down a narrow alleyway off the main road. Like most hostels, it looked either run-down or authentic, depending on how you looked at it. To Agatha, of course, it looked like they wanted to cultivate an image of drugs, HIV, herpes, hepatitis, rust, and decay. Pano, however, seemed drawn to the place and was particularly excited about some graffiti that depicted Nelson Mandela as a magician, complete with top hat.

"You find something interesting in this disfigurement of an old colonial building?" she asked, genuinely curious.

"It's art. I think that this kind of picture says more than a three-hundred-year-old wall, don't you?"

"No."

"Let's go in, shall we," Pano suggested, and gallantly held the door for her. "Milady?"

Agatha snorted and stepped into the lobby. It was dark and stuffy. To the left was a threadbare lounge suite, with a few listless young people staring at their hand terminals. To the right was the reception desk, staffed by a young man whose primary function seemed to be selling cans of cola to guests.

"Well, that guy can't have been here twenty years ago—unless maybe in his father's balls," Pano said.

Agatha rolled her eyes. "You're really disgusting, you know that?"

"Because I said balls?"

"Yeah, that too."

"You Americans really are prudish, you know that?" he shot back with a grin. "Have you ever actually seen any balls, by the way?"

Agatha returned a look that was somewhere between revulsion and a wordless warning, but it didn't kill his smile. On the contrary, it only seemed to increase his amusement.

"Hey, bub," Pano said, approaching the dark-skinned

The Fossil

young man at the reception. His hair was close-cropped, with jagged edges, and shaved around the ears.

"Hey," the receptionist replied, nodding first to Pano and then to Agatha before noticing her very unusual clothes. Something about Agatha and her pantsuit in particular seemed to irritate him. "What can I do for you?"

"My name is Pano, and this is my sister Agatha. I wonder if you can help me, see, we're trying to set up a surprise for our sister Dana's wedding."

"Oh, cool," the receptionist replied, barely feigning interest.

"See, Dana has lived a very exciting life and has traveled a lot, and that's why we're going around to all the places she's been to collect photos and videos for a little show at the wedding. We're trying to get everything, really everywhere she's ever visited—but show them as they look now, so she can see how different everything is since her traveling days. Now, it seems she stayed here twenty-four years ago. I know it's kind of crazy, but if there's any chance, we'd really like to take a photo with the person who checked her in all those years ago. Do you think, maybe, that might be possible?" Pano really did manage to sound like a brother who was very excited about his own surprise.

"Uhhhh," the young man behind the desk sighed, and ran the fingers of his hand through his hair. "See, I've only been here a year, and I have no idea who would have been here then."

Agatha didn't need much knowledge of human nature to figure out that the man she was looking at had very little interest in digging any deeper.

"I see you have a tip jar right there. Is that yours?" Pano asked, pointing to an old welded metal cup with a slit-shaped opening on top, and a label with the name 'Marcello.' When Marcello nodded, the Italian pulled out a fifty-dollar bill and put it halfway in the tip jar. "Let me make you a deal: You call your boss or whoever you need to call, and find out who would have been working this desk back then. Then you're going to call that person and get them in here so you can take our picture, okay? Whoever that turns out to be, I'll have a tip for them too."

The receptionist first looked at Hofer, then at the fifty-dollar bill, and then quickly produced his hand terminal.

"That's my boy," Pano replied, while the other man spoke to someone in Afrikaans on his hand terminal, then hung up and made another call. The second conversation took a little longer, and perhaps seemed a little more difficult, but after about five minutes Marcello put down his terminal and nodded.

"His name is Solly Shoke. He worked here until about ten years ago, and he'll be here in about half an hour. And if you don't have a tip for him, I think he'll be pissed," Marcello noted.

"Thanks very much, Marcello," Pano said cheerily, and let the banknote fall into the jar. "We'll wait over there."

The receptionist nodded, turning to help a few new arrivals who had just come in with exhausted expressions and ridiculously oversized backpacks, while he kept a greedy eye on the tip jar.

Agatha and Pano went to the lounge corner, and the European flopped onto the couch, satisfied. Preferring not to pick up a case of bedbugs herself, Agatha remained standing and went to study the bulletin board hanging above the long side of the couch. It was covered in hundreds, if not thousands, of photos and notes pinned up by former guests.

Almost reflexively, she took out her data glasses and put

them on. As she expected, the few guests hanging around on the couch didn't notice her at all, lost in their endless, languid scrolling on their terminals.

Using the camera menu in the edges of the headset frame, she activated facial recognition and ran a search for matches with the passport photos of the students they were looking for.

After a few seconds, a message lit up in red in the center of her field of vision, 'No matches found.'

"And?" Pano asked from somewhere below her.

"Nothing."

"Probably didn't want to leave any footprints."

"Apparently not. Let's hope this Mr. Shoke is a little more helpful," she replied.

It was a little more than forty minutes before a large, older man with gray hair and ebony skin burst in through the door. Under one arm, he was carrying an oxygen tank with a thin tube running to his nostrils to keep his lungs working.

He looked at Marcello, panting, and Marcello, without stopping his conversation with the new guests, pointed in Agatha and Pano's direction. Shoke waddled over to them.

"Hi. I'm Solly," the man introduced himself and extended a hand to Agatha with a friendly smile. She hesitated for a moment, then extended hers to shake his hand. Something about this old man brought to mind a good-natured donkey. His lips were full and his mouth was wide. His face looked like he smiled a lot, even though his eyes looked watery and sick. "What can I do for you?"

"Glad to meet you, Solly!" Pano jumped up from the sofa and shook the man's hand vigorously. "My name's Pano. This is Agatha. We wanted to talk to you because I think my sister came here on a backpacking trip, twenty-four years ago. Her name is Dana Pickert, from Germany."

"Hmm, could be," said the old man, rubbing his chin. "Do you have a picture?"

"Of course!" Pano whipped out his hand terminal and showed it to him.

Agatha watched Shoke very closely, and noticed immediately when his pupils widened and his eyelids twitched slightly. He didn't think, he *knew* right away.

"Ah, no, I don't remember, sorry. It was such a long time ago."

"Are you absolutely sure?" Pano seemed to not have noticed the recognition in the man's eyes. "Just take another look, please. She came with some friends, here, see..." With a finger, he scrolled down to pictures of the other students who had disappeared at the same time. Shoke's eyes became more and more agitated.

"Hmm, no. I'm sorry. You know, I saw so many faces in the twenty years that I worked here, and now that I'm sick," he said, pointing to the tank under his arm, "my memory hasn't gotten any better. Really sorry, I wish I could have helped you."

"Well, it was worth a try," Pano said, disappointed, and slipped the man a fifty. "That's for your trouble. Thanks anyway."

"Thanks. I'm sorry," Shoke said again, and shuffled back towards the door.

"I guess we were just being too optimistic," Pano said with a sigh. Agatha paid no attention to him, and followed the former receptionist into the rapidly descending darkness of the alley.

Shoke went left, where a turn down an even smaller alley led to the parking lot, and she followed him. Pano followed her, and when she looked over her shoulder and saw he was about to shout something to her, she put a finger to her lips. His mouth closed, and he followed her slowly.

When Shoke rounded the corner of the house, Agatha checked to see that nobody was walking in the alley, and then accelerated her steps.

In the parking lot there were three cars, an old Volkswagen E and two ugly Renaults. A quick glance along the buildings told her that there were no cameras, so she made a sudden move, came up behind Shoke, and put her hand over his mouth. She pulled him around and slammed him against the graffiti-covered wall, muffling his frightened stammering with her hand. She felt the hot dampness of his breath on her fingers immediately.

"I know you lied to us, and I know you'll do it again," she said without emotion.

Pano came around the corner. His eyes bulged in surprise. "What are you doing?" he asked.

Agatha ignored him and pinched Shoke's oxygen cable with two fingers as he struggled against her grip. The result was immediate. His eyes rolled, and he began to sweat.

"Whoever's threatening you, they're not here. Now look at me," she ordered, and transfixed him with a look that said she wasn't kidding. "If you're trying to cover up a crime, I'll let you die. So you'd better start talking."

Pano had now come up behind her, and casually put a hand on his hip where he kept his gun.

Agatha carefully removed her hand from Shoke's mouth and let the oxygen flow again. Her captive immediately nodded anxiously. Panting, the South African struggled for air and looked at her like a skittish deer staring straight down the barrel of a hunter's shotgun.

"You remembered every single one of those students,

didn't you? Even though it's been so long."

The old man tried to shake his head, but when Agatha's hand shot back to the transparent oxygen tube that led to his upper lip before splitting and disappearing into each side of his nose, he raised his sweaty hands submissively. "All right, all right, I remember them, yes," he admitted meekly, gasping for air.

"Somebody threatened you to make you act as if you didn't recognize them, isn't that right?"

"No," Shoke replied, and this time she didn't see any anxious expression in his eyes or on his face—at least nothing going beyond the anxiety and fear of death that he was obviously feeling right now.

"Did someone pay you off?" she asked, and Shoke nodded.

"Yes."

"Who?"

"It was... oh, man, they're gonna kill me for sure!" The old man was crying now, and really looked like he was sure someone was going to spring out of the shadows and shoot him.

"I can kill you faster than they can," Agatha threatened, ignoring Pano's sideways glance.

"It was somebody named Peter Gould, okay?"

"Peter Gould? The former CFO of the Human Foundation?"

"I don't know what he was. He came to the hostel around two weeks after the fourteen students had left and gave me five thousand dollars to never say anything about those kids staying there—never, to nobody," stammered Shoke. "You don't know how much power the Human Foundation has here in Cape Town! Goddamn it! They gonna kill me when they find out!"

The Fossil

"Hold on," Pano interjected from behind Agatha. "Did you say *fourteen* students?"

"Yeah, there's five you don't have no pictures of. It was a group of fourteen students, no question!" He nodded animatedly and shot a hopeful look at the exit to the parking lot.

Agatha grabbed his flabby chin and turned his head so he was looking at her.

"Now why do you remember that so precisely?"

"Because I had to organize drivers for them to take them to a private airstrip, out at Malmesbury. That's not the kind of request I get very often. It was two minivans with seven seats, so sure I remember that. It was like something out of James Bond," Shoke explained. "If Gould finds out I told you this, then…"

"I wouldn't worry too much about that," Agatha interrupted him. "Gould's been missing for over twenty years."

"But Karlhammer! He can find out, and then it's all over for me!"

"Well, Mr. Shoke. My partner and I won't say a word to anyone, and I can only suggest you do the same. Then we're good, right?" She took a hundred dollars from her wallet and put it in the chest pocket of his sweaty shirt. "Go buy yourself some lottery tickets," she advised him, looking pointedly at his oxygen tank.

With that, she gave Pano a nod and the pair calmly walked away down the alley.

"So Peter Gould pays this guy off to keep him quiet, but then disappears himself right afterwards?" Pano pondered out loud when they were back in their Tesla X. "That doesn't make any sense."

"It doesn't make any sense *yet*," Agatha corrected him, and instructed the navigation system to find the private airstrip near Malmesbury, to the north of Cape Town. Surprisingly, the system found it, and she saved it as a destination.

"You want to head out there today?"

"Obviously. Why not?" Agatha asked.

"You know it can be dangerous driving around in the countryside in South Africa at night, don't you? The rise of the Human Foundation didn't make all the problems of race and crime go away overnight," he answered. He looked at the route the navigation system had calculated. It was about eighty kilometers, mostly outside of the city.

"Well, you're a big boy with a nice gun, right? You just showed it off back there. I'm sure that trick will work on your basic small-time pickpocket, too," she replied.

"If it was just pickpockets, that would be one thing... but besides, remember, we're authorized to carry our guns but not use them. You know the rules."

"Don't you want to find out where those students were flying to, and why Gould was so keen on making sure nobody came after them?"

"Of course, but..."

"All right, then," Agatha said. "Drive," she ordered the Tesla. The car hummed to life.

She hadn't thought they would make this much progress on the first day, but she chalked it up to the fact that it was such an old case that no one was interested in it anymore, and it had been botched at the time. Besides, they had come well-prepared. And it was always an advantage when no one else knew what you were looking for.

Peter Gould, she thought, and recalled the picture of the innocuous pencil-pusher she had seen in his file. *How do you fit into this puzzle, eh? What was your game? And who were you playing for?*

18

RON JACKSON, 2018

Groaning, Ron first fought his way to his elbows and then raised his head. Everything around him was pitch dark, except for the circular zone of light where his flashlight shone on an area of rough stone wall. He looked up, but there was nothing but blackness above him.

"How the hell..." he muttered, groping for his flashlight. When his fingers finally found it he closed his hand around the weighty device, and he pointed at the ceiling and looked up.

Nothing. Just rock. Nothing that could explain his current predicament.

He had obviously fallen through... but where was the opening? Why were there no stone fragments around him? No light from the cavern above reached him.

"This cannot be!" He stood up hesitantly and stretched out his hands towards the seamless ceiling, but it appeared to be at least an arm's length beyond his reach.

Ron nervously licked his lips and pointed his flashlight left and right. The room was a perfect cube. The walls and floor had no seams, and no irregularities at all. Every inch was smooth and flawless.

Suddenly, he noticed movement to his left, and he spun around as if electrically shocked. "The tablet!" he cried, half relieved and still half panicked. He stooped down to the device, which was still showing the results from the muon detector, still switching back and forth between the several display modes.

He picked it up and looked it over. The screen was cracked in the upper right corner and some of the pixels were flashing in ugly colors, but it seemed otherwise intact. The battery meter read seventy-one percent.

Breathing heavily, he reached for his radio, only to discover that it was no longer attached to his belt.

"Well, that's just great." Nervous now, he pressed the home button on his tablet and opened the messenger app, only then to remember that it needed to be online to work.

"Dammit, I can't believe it!" he sighed, and felt his nervousness morphing into fear inside him. Creeping dread was growing inside him and extending it tendrils into his innards. He had a working flashlight, and a tablet with him, but no way of contacting the others. It was enough to make a man cry.

He took a few deep breaths, trying to push away the new scary thoughts crowding into his mind. He didn't even have water with him, and he would freeze to death within a few hours. He would find a solution. There had to be a solution.

He stuck the tablet into his hip pouch where he kept his notepads in the zippered journal-cover that he always carried with him, and went back to the wall with his flashlight. He just had to stay busy until, hopefully, Gould came back and saw his radio lying where it landed when the floor had opened.

But what if it was the same up there, with no evidence that there had ever been an opening to fall through? How had it even been possible for him to fall through to here, and yet the ceiling look like nothing had happened?

"Focus," he admonished himself. "Concentrate on what you see." He closed his eyes and then took three deep breaths, in and out. "You've been in this kind of situation before."

Of course he had—he would never forget the time in Palmyra when he had accidentally been buried, with three liters of water and a mayonnaise sandwich. But then, three of the local laborers had seen it happen, and he had known that they were digging for him, that every passing minute brought him closer to getting out... But now?

"Think, think, think," he told himself out loud, pulling the tablet back out of his pouch. He entered the passcode and opened the Connections tool where he could access the camera feeds.

"*Please*, tell me I have a Bluetooth connection."

He did.

"Yes!" he exclaimed, and began looking at the camera feeds from around the site. Cavern One was still empty. It seemed Gould had not come back yet.

Ron swiped through the cameras until he found Gould in the work module at the coffee machine, where he was immersed in conversation with the blonde student.

"Come back already! What could you be talking to her about all this time?" The other students were off taking soil samples in the West Quadrant, and that was going to take them the rest of the day. Patchuvi and Ross were in the work module supervising the analysis of the rock samples for iridium and other platinum group metals, and the two students who had brought Ron the detector were in the north quadrant working on two drones.

No one would be coming Ron's way any time soon.

It took a few moments to sink in. When it did, his shoulders tightened. He swiped back until he found the camera located next to the light switch for Cavern One, and zoomed in towards the spot where he had been standing.

The floor showed no change!

A small, dark object lay there. The resolution was so poor he couldn't tell for sure, but he guessed it was his radio. But, there was no sign of an opening, not even so much as a crack.

Suddenly something occurred to him. He went to the settings and checked under 'Bluetooth devices,' but there didn't seem to be any other devices in range.

"Shit." He would have to keep watching the cameras. When Gould came back, he might be able to send a connection request to his hand terminal, and get his attention that way if shouting didn't work. But to do that he would have to save his battery power, so he turned Bluetooth off and put the tablet into sleep mode.

He looked at the time display. He had to remember to check every five to ten minutes whether anything was happening up there. As if he could forget. And, he thought, he would probably hear it anyway, since the surface that he had fallen through—as if by magic—was only a few centimeters thick. At the same time, however, he had this nagging feeling that when one unbelievable thing happened, more were in store. If he had really fallen through solid matter, what else should he expect?

It was only now that he realized he had lost his gloves. When he looked down at his hands, it was like he was looking at a miracle—they were cold, but they were not frozen solid. Anywhere else in the compound he would have been showing the first signs of frostbite by now, but here they looked healthy and he still had feeling in them. He didn't feel chilled to the bone anymore, as he had up there in the cavern. In fact, now that he thought about it, he almost felt a little too warm.

"What the hell's going on here?" he asked out loud, and expelled a long breath. It came out of his mouth like steam, but it was a weak and pale cloud that dissipated as quickly as it had appeared. If he hadn't been looking for it, he might not have noticed it at all.

Once again he exchanged the tablet for the flashlight and shone it on the walls. There was something odd about what he saw. He took two steps forward until he was close enough to touch the wall at his left. The reflected light got brighter as he approached, and his eyes needed a moment to adjust, but then he saw it, clear as day—there were paintings!

"Well, I'll be damned," he whispered. His throat was dry, and he gulped before taking a step forward and wiping a thin layer of dust away with his hand. As the colors underneath became clearer and clearer, Ron rubbed faster and faster, like a madman, and he didn't stop until he had gone all the way around and returned to his starting point, sweating from the effort.

Then he took two steps back, putting himself in the middle of the chamber, and illuminated the walls with his flashlight, slowly turning to his right.

"It looks like early Oriental," he said out loud. He always spoke loudly when he was getting engaged with something, but now it probably also had to do with the fact that he was starting to feel a little nauseous. But his curiosity fought its way to the forefront, pushing aside his sense of danger and fear of the unknown.

"Sumerian? Is that Sumerian?"

He moved to the wall again and traced the inscription with his fingers, following the curved lines, wedges, rectangles, and other geometric shapes. The wall was cold, but none of the cold penetrated his excitement in seeing a long-dead written language.

"Yes, it's Sumerian! Let me see, let me see... This here says ADARU. Adaru means 'fear.' Wonderful." Ron's fingers kept wandering. "Hmm... That's MAHRU, yes, so 'absence.' No, 'presence.' Damn it, why didn't they write it in hieroglyphics?"

He sighed and looked around at the other symbols. For some, he had to blow some residual dust from the engraved lines before he could recognize them. "This is the symbol for BELU, 'extinction.' No, 'destruction.' Almost the same thing, but we can't get sloppy now!"

Ron took out his journal and hastily copied the Sumerian symbols he saw. He wasn't totally sure of all the symbols he saw, but even the experts in this, the oldest form of writing in the world, had only translated about nine hundred words with any degree of certainty. So really, he had nothing to be ashamed of. But many of the symbols carved here he had simply never seen before. Not that he was sure about all the Sumerian vocabulary, but at least he knew all the characters. Some of the ones he was looking at now were certainly not among them, that was for sure.

"All right, so... hmm... fear, absence, and destruction. 'Destroy the absent fear?' 'Absence of fear, though we be destroyed?' 'We're scared because someone's absent, while we're being destroyed?' I don't get it."

Deep in thought, he let the light of his flashlight wander

upwards, until it shone directly on the painting, which covered all the space between the writing and the ceiling. It reminded him of some of the cave paintings in ancient African cave dwellings, except that they looked so fresh here, as if they had just been made. But that was impossible. The image showed a scene with a tall person who seemed to be wearing three pearls on his neck, but was otherwise naked. Six other figures, drawn like stick men, thin and emaciated, knelt before him and offered sacrifices.

No, not ritual sacrifices, Ron thought, and closed his eyes. *They're tools!*

"They're offering their work. Their help, perhaps. But who is the giant they are supplicating themselves to? A Builder? Oh please, be a Builder, please tell me you're a Builder!"

Still shining his flashlight, Ron moved to his left. Here was another painting depicting the tall figure. With an outstretched finger, he was pointing to some kind of sarcophagus, alongside which a few amphorae were arranged. The sarcophagus stood upright against the wall in a small room, not much bigger than the one in which Ron was now. The smaller people were starting to carve things into the walls.

"Wait, wait a minute... is that *this* room?" he asked the drawing, as if it was going to answer his questions. "That's not the right place!"

Ron ran back, past the image of the presentation of the tools, to the left, and looked at the picture there. It showed the same sarcophagus on the wall, only this time the giant was in it. His eyes were open and the six people were kneeling before him. And as in the other image, they were presenting their tools.

He moved left again, where he saw that in the drawing

people were doing something to the wall, placing their hands on it. Part of the wall was already gone, and he could see the upper part of the sarcophagus.

"All right, I think I understand. You dug him up and awakened him. But who is it? A deity? What does all this represent? Why aren't you using the tools to free the sarcophagus... Laying hands?" Ron took a step back and a deep breath, and then a long look at the painting in front of him. After a while he saw, a little further to the left, six people standing in the middle of a fire, their arms raised and their mouths contorted in silent screams. In the background, he could see something that looked like a volcano.

"Wait a minute..." Ron ran back to the right, to the picture of the people offering their tools. "You weren't offering your labor, you were presenting your tools to the giant. You didn't want to work for him, he was supposed to work for you!"

He quickly took out his journal again. When the flashlight began to flicker, he put it in his mouth so he could see and write at the same time, and copied everything as fast as he could. The paintings were very primitive, so it wasn't that hard.

Then, he copied the symbols around the drawings. There always seemed to be one or two sentences that he didn't understand, except for a few individual words that together didn't make any sense. He needed his notes, and they were in the...

"The living quarters!" He cursed, dropped the journal, and frantically took his tablet out of the pouch. Obsessed with what he was discovering, he had completely forgotten to check whether anyone was looking for him yet. He had probably been down here for an hour, maybe more.

He hastily switched on Bluetooth and swiped through the camera feeds until he saw the feed from Cavern One.

"Yes!" he shouted when he saw four shapes standing near the muon detector, next to where Ron had been when he'd fallen through. It looked like they were having a big argument, because they were gesticulating wildly.

"I'm down here!" he shouted at the top of his lungs. "Down here! Help!"

As he shouted as loud as he could, he kept watching the feed from the camera, but he saw no reaction whatsoever from the people standing there.

"Hey! Can't you hear me? Hey!!!"

Still no reaction.

"Why can't you hear me?" Ron asked himself, giving up, watching helplessly as the four figures moved on. They spread out into four different passageways, switching their flashlights on and talking to each other through their radios.

He sank helplessly to his knees, and let his shoulders fall. "You're looking for me, but in all the wrong places. Why didn't you hear me? I was right below you!"

Ron took a deep breath, and then wondered if the air had become a little damper and warmer since he had fallen in here. He took off his jacket and peeled himself out of his thermal pants, until he was standing in nothing but his thick, thermal merino wool underwear, feeling surprisingly comfortable.

"Can't afford to sweat too much," he muttered to himself. "Stay awake and active, Ron."

Following his own advice, he shined his light on the other walls and looked at them. At first he thought they were all the same sequence of pictures. But when he looked closer, he kept finding slight differences. On the north wall, it was not a volcano, but a cloud spewing rain, while on the east wall it was a group of people killing each other. On the south wall it was a stone with a long tail, falling from the sky.

A meteor, he thought. *These are all Mass Extinction Events. Every drawing here is a mass extinction.*

"Wait a minute," he told himself, bringing an index finger to his lips. "If this really is a Builder, he must have lived after the dinosaurs. It was only after the dinosaurs that mammals could take over, because the reptilian predators were gone and the oxygen content in the atmosphere nearly doubled."

He brought the light of the flashlight to bear on one of the pictures showing the standing giant. "The increased oxygen content meant that mammals could grow much larger than they are today. There were five-ton sloths, bears the size of a bus, and... you." He touched the picture of the oversized man. "You're a human, who lived at that time, and who had the benefit of that oxygen content. You... are... a Builder!"

A little voice in the back of his mind warned against getting ahead of himself, but he couldn't help jumping from one conclusion to the next. Maybe they were premature, and maybe they weren't. His whole academic life, he had been a laughingstock. But now he was at the point of finding the evidence to prove it all—perhaps he already had.

"Could it be that I didn't fall through the stone, but some kind of hatch opened up?" he asked out loud, and looked up. "It's gotten warmer since I came in here, hasn't it? That's not possible, unless... something's responding to my presence."

Suddenly, a cold shiver slithered down his spine and the hair on the back of his neck stood on end.

"Easy, Ron, don't get jumpy." He looked over the drawings on the different walls again, and this time he noticed that the figures of the six people were also a little different on each wall, as if each had been done by a different artist trying to copy the same style.

To keep from getting lost in panicky thoughts, he picked up his journal again and started copying the rest of the Sumerian—or pre-Sumerian—symbols. It was only when he read back through his own handwritten scribbles that he saw an anomaly. At first he thought he had made a mistake, but then he compared his notebook to the originals again and discovered not only that there were unknown symbols, but that there were more of them the further left he went. On the western wall, he could only recognize a few individual characters. Turning right, there were a few more he could recognize on that wall. He recognized most of the characters on the third, and virtually all of them on the last as coming from the Sumerian dictionary known to him.

"That means..." he whispered, turning around full circle and shining the flashlight back on the western wall, "that means the paintings were made at different times. Of course!" Ron slapped himself on the forehead. "The makers of the drawings changed, obviously, and the script changed too. It's based on the basic characters, but some of these hooks and strokes are clearly placed differently. This one here," he pointed to the western wall, "this is the oldest. And that over there," he went on, turned to the south, "is the latest, maybe only ten thousand years old, who knows? We still don't know how long the Sumerian language as we know it existed."

Ron frowned and looked at the images in sequence again, beginning with a catastrophe, continuing with unearthing and then worshiping the God or Builder, and ending with him being entombed.

"What kind of story is this? You called upon your god, in the times of greatest need? That's what all cultures have done when they couldn't understand or prevent something," Ron concluded. He found it a little disappointing, and sighed. But something about the drawings still nagged at him. Depicting a god as something in the real world, unearthed and reburied, was quite unusual. Gods were always beings of the sky, the stars, the cosmos—never beings of the Earth, the depths, the underground.

"Except the bad guys," he whispered, and felt the chill skate down his spine again. He suddenly spun around with the flashlight, lighting the corners of the room a little too quickly, because he'd been overcome with the sudden feeling that he was being watched.

19

FILIO AMOROSA, 2042

The hours it took to sail to Thiruvanamthapuram passed like time spent in the waiting room of a dental clinic. Filio became more agitated by the minute. Very early on, she had prepared the small Zodiac that she would use to enter the harbor.

With six lashing straps, she had fixed the box to the front of the wooden partition that separated the motorboat from the two electric outboard motors. She'd checked everything, then shook and pushed and pulled, and checked once again, needing to make sure that no rogue wave or anything else could send her precious cargo overboard.

Oscar had watched her doing all this, and even at one point held one of the lines for her when she put it in his mouth.

The whole time, she kept interrupting her work on the Zodiac to run back to the bridge and check the radar and the radio.

She knew full well that she should try to sleep, because it was critical she stay focused and alert, but she couldn't even think of trying to sleep now, excitement and anticipation coursing through her like electricity. So she used the time to write each of her friends a letter, leaving one in each of their bunks. Maybe it was maudlin, perhaps they would tear up the letters without reading them, but it felt good, and it felt like the right thing to do, to tell them her reasons and her regrets. Maybe it would still mean something to them.

Then she tore through the ship to find everyone's stash of marijuana and threw it all into the sea, so customs would not confiscate the vessel in the Indian port.

Eventually, after wandering the *Ocean's Bitch* like a restless ghost and talking to Oscar, she was only an hour out of Thiruvanamthapuram. With the crane, she moved the bulbous, inflated shape of the Zodiac over the starboard railing and checked the swells one last time. Just before the *Bitch* passed the twelve-mile marker and entered Indian territorial waters, she lured Oscar into the Zodiac with a treat and lowered it into the light swell with the crane's remote control. The boat was still on autopilot—she couldn't afford to give customs the idea that they had stopped to let somebody off—so she had to concentrate. If a big wave came by at an inopportune moment and yanked the retaining rope, the Zodiac would go over the side and be forced under water by the bow wave. It was a pretty daring maneuver to try to pull off, but then, so was this whole business.

Oscar, barking, was crouched next to her bag behind the small steering console, while Filio, swaying with the waves, operated the crane with the remote control, waiting for a wave. When it came, she pushed the button and released the crane claw.

The Fossil

The Zodiac fell the last meter and landed with a splash on the waves.

Filio was knocked off her feet and fell, and her left ankle began to throb slightly. She ignored it, then jumped up and started the outboard motors, which gurgled to life and propelled them forward. She turned the wheel hard to the right to avoid the *Bitch*'s bow wave and the whirlpool effect of her own screws as quickly as possible, and throttled the engines to three-quarters forward.

In the pitch dark, she saw the *Ocean's Bitch*, the only home she had known for the last two years, as a noisy constellation of lights in the dark, gradually getting smaller and smaller among the dark waves. She felt like she had lost something forever, and it made her feel terrible.

Soon, she was skimming the waves, plowing through the smaller burst of spray, her attention fixed on the small screen displaying the radar and GPS data. It was vital that she not miss the coordinates that Rietenbach sent for the extraction. Approaching specific coordinates with the aid of satellite navigation sounded easy, but seeing something on a screen and then spotting a place to tie up, navigating by sight alone in complete darkness, was something else altogether.

The spray sloshed ever more wildly over the Zodiac's sides, and Filio was soon soaked through, but in the tropical heat she hardly noticed. Her whole being was focused on the box with the samples and the green LED telling her that the vacuum seal was still functioning.

Oscar, in the bow with his front legs hanging over the inflated hull, seemed to be enjoying the adventure to no end. He tried to catch every passing burst of ocean spray in his mouth, and his bushy tail was wagging wildly.

There were times when Filio wished she could have been born a cat or a dog. Pets always seemed to be able to be happy with themselves, the moment, and everything around them, while humans just stumbled from one problem to the next.

The coast was coming into view now. She first saw the wall of trees and mangrove plants as a strange shimmer, and then, when she got closer, as an interruption in the blobs of moonlight reflected on the surface of the water, which became calmer and calmer the closer she got.

"We're almost there, Oscar," she whispered, wiping the spray from her face so she could see more clearly. According to the GPS, there was supposed to be a small bay right in front of her, so she throttled back and came in slow, watching the sonar carefully to avoid hitting a sandbank. Luckily, her course was clear, and the Zodiac's displacement was so negligible that she had no trouble, even in the shallowest places.

Now, standing at the wheel with the engines whispering quietly behind her, she maneuvered the Zodiac between two small points into a sheltered bay that was curved like a circle. She scanned the bay with narrowed eyes, and when she was barely twenty meters from the beach she saw a tiny light blink three times in quick succession.

"Well, Oscar, I hope these are the right guys," she whispered nervously. Oscar let out a cheery bark in reply. "Shhhhhh!"

Not daring to breathe, she steered the Zodiac to the exact coordinates, accelerating a few meters before the pale sand of the beach. A meter or two in, the boat dug itself into the sand. She left the engines running low so their gentle thrust would keep the boat from being pulled back into the water on the tide.

The Fossil

The narrow strip of beach merged into the jungle after just a few meters. As she peered forward over the edge of the boat, she saw four dark shapes coming out of the blackness under the palms.

"Password!" she called out into the night.

"Assisi," came the reply. Only now that she heard the password she had arranged with Rietenbach did she start to breathe again.

With a few nimble moves, she loosened the lashing straps that had held the box and, with a groan, pulled it into the bow and told Oscar to jump ashore.

The four were already standing in front of her, men in civilian clothes, but their size and shape, and their close-cropped hair told her they normally wore uniforms. Two were slightly darker in hue than the other two. All four were middle-aged and eagle-eyed.

"I'm going to need you to identify yourselves, please," Filio said carefully, positioning herself behind the raised nose of the Zodiac, as if that could offer her any real protection.

"Of course," said the one on the left, in German, nodding to the others. They reached into their light windbreakers and each produced an ID. Two were from the German Federal Police, and the other two were apparently from some French authority or other, the name of which she could not make out. She handed their IDs back.

"Do you have the package?" asked the one on the left. The name on his ID had been Jakob Engels, although she didn't believe for a moment that it was his real name.

Filio pointed to her feet. "It's pretty heavy," she answered in German, noting his surprise that she knew the language.

Engels nodded to the others, and two of them climbed into the boat with her. Suddenly it became very crowded.

Engels extended his hand, but she shook her head and jumped lightly onto the beach.

"We have orders to take you to the airport and fly you to Frankfurt as soon as possible. There are already several cars waiting for you there," the tall agent said. He had obviously picked worn-out jeans and a thin windbreaker so as not to attract attention, but they didn't go at all with his cat-like stance. In fact, she thought, the outfit only made him stand out more.

"All right," she answered simply. Engels led them between two palm trees into the jungle. After about ten meters, they emerged onto a gravel road where two SUVs were waiting, engines running. Both driver's seats were occupied.

She looked over her shoulder and saw the other three agents schlepping the crate to the rear SUV, where they stowed it in the back and lashed it in place.

"Get in," Engels ordered, pointing to the back seat of the rear car. He held the door open for her and then moved to get into the free seat, Oscar bolting in after her. Engels got in and locked the door.

"Target and package extracted," he said quietly into a microphone that Filio couldn't see, and then patted the driver in front of them on the shoulder. "Extraction point B. Go."

"Can you make sure the dog gets taken care of?"

Engels looked at her for a moment with a raised eyebrow, and then nodded curtly.

Quietly, the car began to roll, following the SUV in front of it closely with just its parking lights on. They picked up the pace quickly, and soon were driving so fast that Filio was afraid if the car in front so much as tapped the brakes they would all be killed. But apparently these men knew what they were doing, and in fifteen minutes they had reached a paved rural road, which they turned onto at high speed, tires screeching. On the horizon, she could already see the coming dawn as a thin blue stripe over the lights of Thiruvanamthapuram off in the distance.

The closer they came to the city, passing into its fringes of corrugated metal shacks, industrial parks, and burning garbage patches, the heavier the traffic became. Amid rickshaws, old cars with combustion engines, newer electric cars, and scooters, there were also occasional cows, chickens, pigs, and horse-drawn carriages running around on the cracked asphalt.

By the time they reached the first outlying districts of the city, the isolated vehicles and occasional lines of traffic had become a steady stream that seemed to be bubbling over with honking horns and screaming people.

Filio had never been in India before, and the conditions she saw all around them shocked her. When the Human Foundation was established, one of its primary goals was turning the Third World into a leader in fighting climate change, but it seemed they still had a long way to go in India. Not that it was due to a lack of effort on the part of Karlhammer's foundation—on the contrary, it had made tremendous investments in the Land of Spirituality. The problem was in how the technologies were handled. Once installed, charging stations were regularly, illegally tapped, the autonomous cleaning robots were stripped for spare parts and precious metals, and CO_2 reservoirs were destroyed by natural disasters.

It was the same kind of thing that had taken place after the great Indian Ocean tsunami of 2004, when companies, including German ones, had installed tsunami early-warning buoys off the Thai coast. But only a few years later, virtually none of them were still working. The reason was that fishermen, trying to save fuel, had been mooring their ships to the buoys as they pulled in their nets. It was very tempting, from a position of Western arrogance, to blame the people who were doing these things, but that was too simplistic an explanation.

After her time as a soldier of fortune with the scrappers, after seeing parts of Africa, Asia, and some South Pacific island nations, she had come to see the inherent injustice of the economic system as the real source of the problems. In India, they were not demonstrating ingratitude when they destroyed the gifts of the Human Foundation—they were desperate. Vast segments of the population were still going hungry every day, and had to provide for their families. Protecting the environment was more of a luxury, an abstract problem, something that took a back seat to a starving child. Even though Karlhammer had quickly followed up with projects that promoted investment in education and food aid, with a population as large as that of the Indian subcontinent, this was a hundred-year undertaking, even with the vast resources of the Foundation.

Watching through the windows as they drove, Filio was amazed at how many signs were in Chinese. It gave some idea of how significant Chinese aid and investment here had become. As the United States had retreated into increasing isolation and irrelevance on the world stage, China had, after years of protectionism, risen to be not only the world's biggest economic power but, increasingly, a military rival to the USA. Their policy of noninterference, coupled with massive economic aid, had earned the Chinese respect on the world stage, despite their repressive political system.

The leadership in Beijing might not be democratic, but at least it was stable and reliable.

"Have you ever been in India before?" she asked Engels, who had been vigilantly looking out the windows the whole time as they drove, as tense as a watch spring. His gaze shifted to her briefly before wandering back out the window to search for whatever he was looking for.

"A few times," he said after a while, and his tone left no doubt to how little he was interested in making conversation. It was different for Filio, however, as she was looking for any possible distraction to keep her from thinking about the friends she had left behind.

"Who do you work for?" she blurted next.

"I am an agent of the Federal Police for... special missions."

"A statement that says nothing," Filio said, sighing. "You know, you don't really look like BND—you're a contractor, aren't you?" She took his silence for a yes. "Are we in danger?"

This time, the agent turned to her, and it seemed his expression softened a tiny bit. Filio decided he might have just gone from granite slab to block of hardwood.

"The threat level was classified as very high," he replied. "Most countries in the world, and all of the ones on the UN Security Council, are looking for what you have apparently found. But that is not the primary issue."

"What's the primary issue?"

"The Sons of Terra," Engels answered. At those words, he transformed back into granite. "They are mad extremists, with eyes and ears everywhere. And while they may not have access to the best equipment, they make up for it with the fanaticism of their people."

"But luckily no one knows that we found anything yet,"

Filio thought out loud, although she noticed that her words were more hope than actual conviction.

"Trust me, whenever anything relating to the *Mars One* crash happens, those terrorist bastards hear about it." Engels managed to shake his head in visible disgust without taking his eyes off of every passing car and person outside. "They are seriously convinced that an alien was responsible for the crash. And now they have infiltrated the highest levels of power in the world. You better believe that they're in a position to pick up any information on the subject. Don't underestimate how far their tentacles go, like all these politicians do. It's a real problem."

"I won't," she promised, and Engels gave a tiny nod in response.

By the time they reached the airport, the sun had risen over the city's few skyscrapers. They had not taken the same route as the other airport traffic, but instead turning off onto a gravel road that led them to a barrier gate at a guard post, where four uniformed men of the Indian Air Force were waiting for them. The driver of the car in front of them spoke to one of the men briefly, and the barrier went up and they were waved through.

"That was easy," Filio remarked.

"It was supposed to be, given what we paid for it."

"Who's 'we?'"

"Who do you think?" Engels asked.

"The Chancellor?"

A thin smile spread across his face.

Filio had expected that this would go straight to the top, but thinking rationally, she had expected that to happen one level at a time. The fact that Chancellor Greulich had intervened himself—maybe even been involved from the very beginning—showed the circles that her find had attracted.

It was especially telling that those at the top were willing to stick their own necks out by funneling a boatload of taxpayer money to get it—based solely on the word of a disgraced astronaut and the Director-General of ESA, who believed her.

Thiruvanamthapuram's international airport was divided into two parts. One side was for civil air travel, and the other was an Air Force base. Each had its own runways. They were now driving down a long dirt road at a breakneck pace. Finally they came to a halt, tires screeching, in front of six unassuming, green-painted hangars where Filio could see a few fighter jets. Next to a transport plane, there was a gleaming supersonic private jet, one of the latest electric aircraft from Airbus. A short staircase led from the tarmac up to an open door in the rear. At the foot of the stairs were two soldiers wearing a different camouflage pattern than the Indians wore. They had assault rifles in their hands and grim expressions on their faces.

This thing really did go straight to the top.

"No time to lose," said Engels, throwing his door open and placing himself protectively in front of Filio. His eyes seemed to be taking everything in at once, like a lurking predator waiting to strike.

Filio slid herself across the back seat into the humid heat of southern India and followed the two French agents, who were carrying the box up the stairs and into the jet. The gentle whirring of the electric engines reminded her a little of the sound of the sea, always in the background during her time on the *Ocean's Bitch*. The cabin of the small jet had twelve seats. In one of them, there was a man in a pinstriped suit, wearing data glasses and looking busy. Soldiers sat in two others. They looked up to give Filio a quick nod. One got up, moved to the cockpit door, knocked three times, and sat down again.

As she sat in a middle seat and Engels sat down next to her, she noticed the box being wrapped in foil and stowed inside another, larger box with a military identification number. The second BND agent disappeared into the cockpit, while the two French agents and the soldiers from outside locked their assault rifles and stowed them on wall brackets before taking seats farther back in the plane.

Filio hadn't even fastened her seat belt when the plane began rolling towards the runway. "When you said, 'no time to lose,' you meant it, huh?" she asked.

"If we lose time, we could lose everything," came Engels's grim reply. She made a mental note to not ask this guy any more questions.

She didn't know whether having all this muscle around her made her feel safer, because somebody had thought it was that important to protect her—or the box—or whether that made her more nervous because someone thought that this much muscle was going to be needed.

There was a short, almost mechanical announcement through the loudspeakers, a voice that said, "Brace for takeoff!" An instant later Filio was being pushed deep into her luxurious seat. She could see the terminals of the civilian airport zooming by on the other side of the parallel runway as she gazed through the window beside her. The city stretched around it in every direction, ensconced in a very visible canopy of thick smog blurring into a pastel soup in the morning light, but the jet's nose was already pulling up, and they shot into the sky like an arrow. A rumbling and a short clank told her that the landing gear had been retracted, and the plane banked left sharply, briefly following a narrow strip of beach before land suddenly gave way to the vast ocean. After the city had shrunk to the size of a dot behind them, the plane went into another burst of acceleration, and when the speed reached Mach 2 they veered off in a northwesterly direction.

Filio wondered how Romain, Thomas, Jane, and Alberto were doing right now. Had they salvaged everything already? She assumed so, since more than twenty hours had passed, but doubt still gnawed at her. Despite the care she had taken with her whole plan, so much could still have gone wrong. She knew that anything could happen out on the open sea, and the one thing you could count on was something that you hadn't counted on.

"Can I make a phone ca—?" she started to ask, but Engels was already shaking his head before she finished the question.

"Later," he cut her off.

About two hours later, she understood why. They landed at an airport in Sudan, outside of Mogadishu, where French soldiers with EU flags on their lapels were waiting. Engels motioned for Filio to get out.

"What's wrong?" she asked.

"You're flying straight to Nevada. The samples are getting split up and flown home."

"What? But..." So many questions that she wanted to ask all at once, but she knew she wouldn't get any answers. In fact she had expected this. For the powers-that-be, she was just extra baggage at this point. But she was still surprised at just how fast Rietenbach's arrangements had been changed. It seemed they wanted to get rid of her as quickly as possible and make sure she had nothing more to do with the samples. Of course, a part of her saw this as rejection and injustice. But as much as she would have liked to study the samples herself, and as much as it hurt her to realize she would probably never find out what they were, she also knew that she had a different path to follow. Her goal was Mars, because she knew with absolute certainty that the answers that she was searching for—no, that she needed—were there.

She just knew it.

20

FILIO AMOROSA, 2042

The plane change went very fast. Engels escorted her to a waiting SUV, while eight people in white HAZMAT suits stormed into the jet and quickly stormed out again, now each carrying a small box. Then each one of them, accompanied by a soldier or agent, jumped into a separate SUV, and then the entire column roared off.

When they were gone, the car Filio was in finally started moving. It seemed they were taking a long detour, down a fire access road, towards the civilian air terminal in Mogadishu.

"They split up the samples. Eight different airplanes?" she asked, still somewhat astonished. "Pretty paranoid."

Engels shrugged. "Safe is safe," he said.

"I guess now that the samples are on their way, no more private jet for me?"

"Uh-huh." The agent smiled for the first time since she had met him a few hours ago. Maybe no longer being responsible for the most hotly sought-after object on the planet had taken some stress off of him. "Now you get to fly first class and you get to take me along."

"Well, that makes me feel like a valued customer," she replied dryly.

"I can't imagine that you're going to get lauded as a hero at home. If you had just asked for money, they might have still given you the European Cross or something, but no, you had to go and set off a major bureaucratic and organizational earthquake. Let me tell you something. That didn't make you any friends in Berlin or Brussels, and definitely none at ESA in Paris, either."

"And what exactly do you know about ESA, huh?" she asked, more sharply than she had intended, but she knew that his words only hit her so hard because they were true.

Engels shrugged his shoulders again and his lips pursed slightly. "I know that the astronaut team has been in a media bubble for months, and has been giving interviews non-stop. After the *Mars One* disaster, the whole world is watching the *Mars Two* mission. Astronauts are the new superstars of the freshly minted global world, and ESA has only two seats on the flight. And there's only one launch window, and that's two weeks from now.

"So how do you think the crew is going to feel when one of those two Europeans, a guy who's on the cusp of achieving his lifelong dream and who had to work hard his whole life to reach it, gets the order to stand down because you wormed your way in? Well? How do you think the high-ranking ESA officials and higher-ups in the ministries are going to feel when one of their protégés, someone they've cultivated and protected and stuck their necks out for, gets the order from above to pack their things and go? One thing I'm sure of is this—while you're flying first class to Nevada, every one of them is going to be blowing a gasket."

Filio just stared at Engels after he said all this. He returned her gaze, coolly, but without hostility. It was more like he was trying to figure something out, or he wasn't sure what to think.

The SUV stopped right in front of one of the terminals. They were let out there and led up an airstair straight into an aerodynamic Airbus. A Lufthansa stewardess welcomed them aboard. They were the first ones there, as they could tell because the ground crew was still on board, clearing away all remaining traces of the previous passengers. They took their seats in the spacious first-class section.

"Well, they don't know what it's like," Filio, said continuing the conversation from before. "They don't know anything. I know full well that I'm taking someone's place on the *Mars Two* crew. And destroying a lifelong dream. But I'm the only one who's already been to the red planet. The only one. I lost my whole crew, my team, my friends. Without ever knowing why. All I know is that the reason is on Mars. I trained hard for my mission. And I flew there, and I came back.

"*Mars Two* absolutely cannot fail. If it ends like *Mars One*, that's the end of the international space program. And there's only one player big enough and with the resources to go up again—the Human Foundation. But Luther Karlhammer has made it absolutely clear that he is only interested in taking care of our 'bird in the hand,' the Earth. So don't tell me I don't know what's at stake. I'm not doing this despite how important the mission is, I'm doing it *because of* how important the mission is. I know that I can do something to make it succeed. And that I have to."

The agent watched her closely as she said all this, deep in thought. Now the first passengers were coming on board, chattering, boarding passes in hand, looking haplessly for their seat numbers.

"Pragmatic. I like that," Engels finally said, smiling

noncommittally. "I had already thought that if you wanted to give up your whole life, and spend two years poking around in the ocean while hiding out from half the key players in the world who mainly want to find you, stick you in a hole, and interrogate you, you've earned your place on that crew. Well, you have my blessing. Even if that doesn't mean much."

He leaned back, and his expression gave no hint of whether he was joking or stone-cold serious.

"Believe it or not, that means a lot to me right now."

"Glad to hear it."

"Can I make a call now?" she asked.

"Of course. You're a free woman now," he replied. "At least, you are again. Starting right now."

"Good to know," she said sardonically. She grabbed her terminal and scrolled through her contacts. When she found the contact she was looking for and saw the video avatar, she gasped. Her heart pounded, and she wanted to wipe him off her display, but instead she pressed the green call button.

There was some crackling, and some noise, and then the ring. Once, twice, three times.

"Yes?"

Just the sound of Romain's voice saying that one word hit her so hard that within a heartbeat her mouth went dry. Of course, he knew that it was her, and that meant that he hadn't rejected the call. But what was more important was that she had heard his voice, which meant that he was safe.

"Are you all okay?" she asked, voice trembling.

"Yes."

"Oh, thank God."

"I just want to know why, Filio. Why? Why did you betray us? Why did you steal the *Bitch*? Why didn't you talk to us about it? Was this your plan all along? Was your whole time with us just a lie?" the Frenchman asked, his voice taut with tension. His accent had intensified, which told her just how angry he really was.

"You know that I could only remember a few things that happened on the mission," she whispered into her hand terminal, turning the microphone up to maximum so he could really hear her—Engels and the other passengers blundering onto the plane be damned. "But one thing I remembered crystal clear was that I had prepared a case of samples for the flight. I remembered the ship's layout, and the routine protocols, so I knew exactly where the case would be."

"So that's why you said the stern was the most important part," Romain hissed, his frustration growing. *"Putain!"*

"Yes," she admitted, through gritted teeth. She wished she could lie to him, tell him it wasn't so, but after everything, the very least she could give Romain was her complete honesty.

"You're going to start seeing me on TV in the next few days and weeks, and I have to know that you understand why. I *need* to go back to Mars. It's... I can't talk about it. I'm not allowed to. But I owe it to my family, to all of you, to explain it. To explain what I alone can do there. I had to do it. Because there was no alternative."

"There's always an alternative."

"Not for me, Romain. Not for me."

"Why didn't you tell us?" he asked, voice straining. "You could have told us."

"Would you have abandoned the scrapper manifesto for me?" she asked back.

"No. If I had, the scrapper manifesto wouldn't be worth a damn."

"See? That's why."

"Is this what you planned? From the very beginning?"

Filio took a deep breath. When she did, she could feel how hard her heart was pounding against her solar plexus. "Yes," she said, finally admitting it. She was nodding, even though he couldn't see her. "Yes. It is, and I'm so sorry."

"And you wouldn't do it any differently, if you had it to do over, would you?"

"No."

"*Au revoir*, Filio."

"Wait!" she pleaded, so loud that she sank into her seat. And she repeated, quieter the second time, "Wait. Please. Just one more thing. Did it work? Are you all safe and... rich?"

"Yes, Filio, we are. But you made our hearts poorer, and took something from us that's sacred to us scrappers. You know what that is, don't you?"

"Trust," she whispered. The word hit her like a hammer.

"*Oui*. This is the last time we're going to speak. I want to thank you. Without your help, we wouldn't have made it. And I really wish you all the best."

"Tell the others I'm sorry. And take care of yourselves, okay?" she said. She was crying, and ignored Engels's sidelong glance.

Romain hung up.

Filio wept silently in her seat, and didn't notice or care that everyone boarding the plane stared at her as they passed.

The thought of never again hearing from Romain, Thomas, Jane, and Alberto, never again drinking beer with them again and laughing and talking about life—it simply crushed her. She was so distraught that it was only when

Engels spoke to her that she realized they were already in the air.

"Can you breathe again yet?" he asked, without a trace of empathy on his face. His expression was so emotionless that the contrast with what she was feeling on the inside nearly drove her mad.

"What the hell do you want?" she retorted, her anger bubbling over at him.

"It's not me," he replied, shaking his head. He reached into the small pouch he had been carrying, which in all the excitement she hadn't even noticed, and produced a transducer net and a pair of AR glasses.

"What the hell are you—" she started to ask with a frown.

"Someone wants to speak to you. Without anyone listening. There's a secure line via the cockpit, and with the transducer no one will hear you talking. This is not negotiable, by the way. So just take a deep breath, put it on, and see you on the other side," Engels growled. He was already putting the pads of the transducer net on her scalp. When he fastened the chin strap and tightened the drawstring, she felt the pads lock themselves down tightly against her head.

He tried to put the AR glasses on her, but she waved him off and put them on herself. She hated being treated like a child, and wouldn't allow herself to seem vulnerable, even with her eyes red from crying and tears streaming down her cheeks.

OK, Rietenbach, what do you want from me? she thought, and then muttered "Activate" under her breath to turn on the transducer system. The short triad of tones that she heard through the headphones of the AR system told her that the devices had paired successfully.

Then she was standing on the red sands of Mars, with

Olympus Mons towering in the distance. The brown-orange haze of the sky was so realistic that Filio was nearly overwhelmed with the sense of being on Mars again. So real, all the memories of landing there came rushing back—the first day, and how excited everyone had been. The first steps that humankind had ever taken on another planet.

"Well? Does it bring back memories?"

Filio spun around, and her jaw dropped when she saw who had spoken—it was German Chancellor Alexander Greulich. He was wearing his typical gray suit and orange shirt, his signature outfit. It had once earned him a nomination for best-dressed politician in Europe, in some magazine that she couldn't remember. He stood casually, with his hands in his pockets. Since he had taken his seat in the center of European power six years ago, the hair around his temples had turned gray, but his eyes still revealed the alertness racing within him, the alertness that enabled him to give such rousing speeches that his approval rating had remained virtually constant since he took office.

Greulich was not a particularly large man, but he exuded a kind of natural authority, and had that certain something that made people feel comfortable around him. Somewhere in the back of her mind, she marveled that she was able to notice all this in a simulation. Or perhaps, it was simply the gravity of his office, and the fact that he was one of the most powerful people in the world.

"Mr.—Mr. Chancellor," she stammered. "I didn't know..."

"What didn't you know? That your find would cause ripples that would spill over into my office? Really, now." Greulich smiled and came closer. When they were standing next to each other, he nodded towards Olympus Mons. "So you're going back there. Doesn't that scare you?"

"No," she said, shaking her head vehemently.

"Why not?"

That was his question? She had expected he would try to talk her out of it all—flying to Mars, and causing the federal government a massive headache. That maybe he would even offer her a payoff to drop the whole idea. But that he wanted to have a personal chat with her was the last thing she expected.

"Because I know I belong there. I know something happened there that we weren't prepared for," she explained, her voice resolute with determination. Now she could see that they were standing on the exact spot of the landing site she had been at, two years ago. They stood there for a moment, side-by-side, staring off into the reddish, shimmering landscape.

"And you're prepared now?"

"Yes." Filio raised her chin reflexively. "Yes, sir, I am prepared."

"I'd like to know why you think that. You see, I've gone over your case in great detail. And I was amazed to read your statements, and to hear them from you in your testimony before the UN committee. And I learned from multiple independent experts who checked you out, and found nothing mentally or physically wrong with you. And yet, you can't remember anything. Now, as a scientist yourself, what would you estimate the chances of that are, eh?"

"Essentially zero," she admitted.

"So, what conclusion can you draw from this?"

"That there's something responsible that I can't explain, and it's on Mars."

"Do you think the destruction of *Mars One* was an accident?" Greulich asked, turning to face her.

"I... I don't know."

"What does your gut tell you?"

"My gut?" she asked, confused. "I don't understand the question."

"Oscar Wilde once said, 'Intuition is a strange instinct that tells a woman she is right, whether she is or not.'" Greulich smiled a wise mile.

"I'm not sure if he was trying to be witty, or just misogynistic," she said, and immediately thought she had gone too far. After all, she was talking to *the* Chancellor Greulich here.

To her relief, he laughed a little. When he did, it accentuated the lines around his eyes that every statesman eventually got from bearing the worries of the world.

"I should talk to scientists more often. When you talk to politicians, you can never say what you want straight out. What I'm trying to find out is this—*is* it just your intuition that's telling you that you have an important contribution to make to the *Mars Two* mission, or is there something concrete that's telling you you're right?" he clarified his question, watching her closely as he did.

Filio suddenly felt uncomfortable, like she might be taking a lie detector test. "Sometimes I dream things. Things from the mission, things that I can remember, like the journey there and the landing. When that happens, sometimes I get shreds of new memories dropping in, and I know they come from the time after," she explained. Then she shook her head. "That probably sounds pretty weird."

"A little," the Chancellor acknowledged, and his eyes narrowed slightly, like an eagle that has just spotted its prey on the ground and is calculating when to strike.

"Those shreds were what helped me remember that I had taken samples from The Object, and what the case I had packed them in looked like," she continued, her voice becoming more clear and resolute with every word. "That's why I went after the samples, and that's how I was able to bring them to you."

Chancellor Greulich looked penetratingly at her, and Filio returned his gaze without flinching.

"That's pretty persuasive," he finally said, and smiled such a noncommittal smile that it would have even put Engels, who, she knew, was still sitting next to her on the plane, to shame. "Listen, you seem to appreciate honesty, so I'm going to be honest with you. Pulling one of our best astronauts off *Mars Two* and putting you in is giving me indigestion. Not to mention all the headaches that I would love to have spared myself in the next couple of weeks.

"And I still have doubts about whether you aren't suffering from some kind of undiscovered after-effects from your trauma. If you are, putting you on that crew is the worst thing we can do. But we've signed a contract that you and your lawyer have apparently worked out down to the finest details, and it's watertight. Well, that at least shows me that you're really determined about this. Now, when I sign a contract I stick to it. Apart from the fact that I couldn't get out of it if I tried, with all the work your friend in Paris put into it, and besides which he would go public about the whole thing with the samples the minute I did.

"But I still wanted to get a chance to see you personally, and appeal to your conscience. If you have even the tiniest doubt about whether you're completely all right, if you have even a glimmer of a feeling that there's any chance whatsoever that you might become a liability for the *Mars Two* mission—or even just a nuisance for the team—then I want you to step back now. I'm going to make sure you get what you want, but don't jeopardize mankind's dream of someday leaving Earth.

"The UN is putting a lot of money and more than a little

ambition into this project, and after the disaster in 2040 it almost didn't happen. If this mission to Mars fails, we've missed this once-every-two-years launch window, and we will have forfeited the financing for a third mission. That's not public information, but you should know it before you answer."

Greulich waited, maintaining eye contact with her the whole time. The virtual red sand of Mars billowed around her legs in the virtual wind, without touching her clothes.

"I'm aware of that, Mr. Chancellor," she finally said. The firmness and steadiness of her voice came naturally. She didn't have to make an effort to sound resolved, because she was speaking from her innermost conviction. "I have to go on this mission, because I know I'm the most qualified and best astronaut for this mission. You're not going to find a better one. I know for certain that the memories will come back as soon as I'm there. This phenomenon has been well-described, and I know I can save this second mission from suffering the same fate as the first. And if there is even a chance I'm right, then you want me on board."

The Chancellor nodded slowly and let out a long sigh. "All right, Doctor. Good luck to you, and good luck to us all." He extended his hand, and she shook it.

"Thank you, sir."

21

AGATHA DEVENWORTH, 2042

The trip to Malmesbury Airfield took nearly two hours, partly because they passed through two police checkpoints on the way. Both times, the officers couldn't hide their surprise when they shined their flashlights through the open windows of the Tesla onto Agatha's and Pano's IDs, but they didn't call it in, in the end, just waved them through.

So far, so good.

But they ran into a more significant obstacle when they turned onto the access road, passing the signs to the airfield, and the colorless light of their high beams hit a chain-link gate, locked with a heavy iron chain.

"Looks like this shop's only open for business during the day," Pano said, and pursed his lips. "Pretty standard for a private airfield."

"Hmm," Agatha growled, studying the gate and the razor wire through the Tesla's windshield. Out of the darkness, huge numbers of insects, some small and some shockingly large, swarmed to the light and began collecting around the car's headlights.

"You're not thinking of going in there, are you?" Pano asked.

"Yes... Yes, I am," she replied.

"That's illegal."

"I don't see a sign."

"I was kidding," he said with a snort, then sighed, and said, "All right, let's go. I brought the fission cutters."

When Agatha was sure her partner was on his way to the trunk, she turned to her terminal and began scrolling through the file she had prepared on South African criminal and civil law. When she had found the spot she was looking for, she tapped it briefly and then got out of the car, too.

"Everything all right?" Pano asked, approaching with a tool that looked like a small drill. He set to work on the chain, and she nodded.

"Just what are you hoping to find once we get inside?" he asked, as the barely visible laser beam from the fission cutter ate its way through the metal chain. A thin cloud of smoke rose, and then the chain fell to the ground with a loud clank.

"The destinations would be good enough for me," she replied. They each pushed one side of the gate open and went back to the car together.

"Private flights also have to file complete itineraries, right?" he asked, half optimistic, half worried.

"I think so, yeah. I'm pretty sure they don't have to keep passenger lists, just pilot information. And that's not even mentioning air freight."

They sat back in the front seats of their car and she switched the drive mode to manual. Then they followed a gravel road towards the large hangar building. It was corrugated metal, standing like a block of gray in the middle of the blackness of the surrounding steppe. The access road turned sharply and then headed straight for the hangar. Agatha had turned off the low beams and was now driving with only parking lights on, something the software was aware of and pointed out to her with flashing warning symbols. She ignored them.

Pulling up alongside the hangar, she parked the car, and they got out and started walking, bringing along their flashlights.

"Take the Maglocksmith with you," she instructed him, and while she was wondering if she hadn't been too commanding when she said it, he removed the metal suitcase from the trunk.

The hangar was at least thirty by thirty meters in size or perhaps slightly larger. Near the car there was a tiny door marked 'Private,' which they approached. When they got there, the Italian pulled out a device about the size of a wallet and attached it to the door. The device immediately started blinking frantically.

Agatha shined her flashlight around the paved area in front of the hangar, where two small propeller planes and three thrust-vectoring aircraft were lined up along the western edge. She watched as a cat came out from the shadow behind one of the wheels, stared at her briefly, looking directly into the cone of light, and then disappeared into the night.

A beep from over by the door made her turn around. Pano had just removed the locksmith, and winked at her as he opened the door. "After you, Agent Devenworth."

Agatha slid past him into the dark interior of the hangar and slowly directed her flashlight around the room. To her left was the open part of the hangar where four planes stood, hooked up to various hoses and cables. In front of her was a small office area that transitioned into a small lounge, the walls holding posters of naked women and a dartboard.

"Isn't it exciting to be doing something prohibited?" Pano asked, grinning with glee as he closed the door behind them. She shined the flashlight in his face, and he quickly covered his eyes with his hands in protest. "Hey!"

"Right now we're only committing an infraction, and not a crime. The minute we damage something or steal anything, it becomes a criminal offense and we're not going to get away with a fine," she countered, completely deadpan. She pointed the light back into the office where she saw an old desktop computer with a flat-screen monitor.

"If there was a pool here, we could go skinny-dipping, like back in high school," he suggested, still grinning. "That would still only be an infraction, right?"

Agatha rolled her eyes. "Oh yeah, baby, then I can finally see your whole magnificent manhood and finally accept that all I wanted all along is to give in to your manly charms. When at last the burden of unrequited lust finally falls from my shoulders," she whispered, then moaned, and then whispered again, going for the full-on porn star performance—or what she thought they must sound like, "then, I will finally be able to surrender to my true feelings!"

For the first time, Pano seemed really shocked. "Uh, could you please go back to being aloof and cold? Please?"

"Love to," she replied, and pointed to the computer. "Get over there and check out what the manifest says for the day that the students checked out of the hostel. I'm betting they flew the same day. While you do that, I'm going to make a list of excavation sites close to the flight. We might be able to figure out a logical destination if we correlate the students and their flight dates."

"On it," Pano said, and threw himself onto the plastic

chair at the computer, which creaked ominously. He was sure the blue plastic coating on it had already been old back when the students had disappeared.

Agatha entered a search string into her hand terminal and moved to the lounge, where she tried to ignore the pinups and instead focused on the second bulletin board she had seen. On the wall right next to the television was a map showing Africa in the center and, at the edges, the outlines of the neighboring continents. There were red pushpins all over the southern half of the Dark Continent.

"Interesting how men always have to mark where they've been, just like dogs," she mumbled, suddenly stopping, pricking up her ears. "Did you hear that?"

Pano's face was lit up by the glow of the monitor he was sitting at, and she saw him turn and look at her. "Huh? What?"

"I thought I heard a noise outside," she replied. Just as she was saying the words, she heard it again.

"Oh. That's the wind, blowing through this corrugated metal," Pano said, and turned back to the computer. "Corrugated metal starts to scale over time, and then you get these accretions that make noise in the wind. I used to have a garden shed in Ticino, and it sounded exactly like that."

"All right, then. Did you find anything?" she asked.

"No, the thing's password-protected," he replied. "So far I'm sure it's not *God*, or *123*, or *iloveairports* or *nelsonmandela*."

"You seriously don't have a hacking AI on your terminal?"

"Of course I do, but how am I supposed to connect my hand terminal to this museum piece? It doesn't even have a universal connector."

"There's no induction field?" she asked, surprised. He shook his head.

"Hmm." Agatha turned and shined her flashlight back on the bulletin board. She was just about to turn away from it again, when she squinted and moved the beam of her flashlight to the lower right of the world map.

"Well, hello there," she whispered, and stared at the lonely red pushpin that had been stuck near Hobart, Tasmania, at the southern tip of the Australian continent. She opened her mouth to call Pano over, but before she could, she heard sirens wailing in the distance.

"I think we need to be gone. Right now!"

22

THE KILLER

The man in the black suit walked at a moderate pace up the low hill. At the top, he had an excellent view over the tarmac and could see the hangar. The darkness didn't bother him and couldn't hide anything from him—not even the soldier, nestled in the knee-high grass, with a sniper rifle trained on the lonely building where the American and the Italian were poking around.

Far in the distance, he could hear the howl of police sirens gradually getting closer. He studied the soldier in front of him, and then looked around. On the other side of the tarmac he could make out another heat signature—possibly a second sniper.

He could hear the soldier breathing softly as he stepped up silently behind him and then said, "Good evening, sir."

The man jumped up and spun around to face him, pupils extremely dilated, attuned to catching the sparse moonbeams against the darkness of the night. The soldier pulled out a pistol, but the man in the black suit was already grasping his wrist and twisting. The gun fell to the ground.

The stroke with which he then dragged the razor blade

across the soldier's exposed forearm, underside pointing upwards, was short. The end came quickly, and yet with a curious sense of calm.

The soldier stared at the wound in disbelief as blood spurted from it, looking almost black in the darkness.

"It's all right," man in the black suit said reassuringly, smiling calmly at the dying man. "It's almost over."

When the soldier had fallen to the ground, eyes staring wildly, the man in the black suit pushed the body aside, deftly taking the sniper rifle from his shoulder as he fell. Then, as relaxed as anything, he spread out the blanket he had brought with him and lay down on it.

The .50-caliber rifle was over a meter and a half long, and the butt of it felt cold against his cheek. He did not enjoy the sensation.

He peered through the telescopic sight until he found the two police cars that were fast approaching the open gate that the two agents had already come through, three kilometers away.

"You're not invited," he said quietly as the first armor-piercing bullet left the barrel with a thunderclap. It seemed to take no time at all before it smashed into the first SUV, destroying the battery. The second bullet was already on its way, and it paralyzed the other vehicle in the same way before the first had even stopped rolling.

He calmly shifted the telescopic sight back to the hangar, where he saw Agatha Devenworth and Pano Hofer bursting from the small door. Right into his red crosshairs.

23

AGATHA DEVENWORTH, 2042

Pano opened the door, and they stumbled out into the night. In the distance, near the gate that they had broken open, Agatha could see the blue lights of two or perhaps three police cars—the distance made it hard to tell how many there were.

Then, suddenly, two thunderclaps pierced the night. Instinctively Agatha's head jerked back to look at Pano, but he didn't seem to be hit. He ran to take cover behind their car.

Agatha moved to follow him, but stopped abruptly when two figures came at Pano. They wore a wild mixture of camouflage clothing, and in an instant had pulled a black cloth sack over her partner's head. Pano kicked and struggled, but the second assailant, who was much bigger and heavier than Pano, held him in a tight grip.

The reflexes of her training kicked in, and Agatha threw herself aside as she reached for the pistol inside her jacket. But her thumb got caught and she couldn't get the gun out.

However, she had lunged at exactly the right moment,

because a man in a balaclava sailed past her in the same instant.

Off-balance, Agatha stumbled against the corrugated metal of the hangar wall, but used her downward momentum to deliver a kick to the side of her assailant's knee. He stumbled and sank against the wall.

She could hear Pano panting and someone falling to the ground, when a thunderclap sounded again, followed by the ugly squelch of a bullet tearing through tissue. Finally she had freed her hand, and revealed her pistol in her belt holster, when a shadow rose before her, eclipsing the pale moonlight.

Agatha drew the gun and pulled the trigger, but the figure she was facing knocked her arm aside so the shot went wide. As he lifted a black bag to put over her head, she spun with all her might.

She jerked his left hand hard, just as a thunderclap sounded again and blood and brains splattered against the gray metal wall where her head had just been. The shadowy figure in front of her, now headless, sank to the ground, just as the other man struggled to his feet.

Agatha raised her pistol and was about to shoot when she saw that the figure in camouflage clothes was not carrying a gun at all. He was holding a Taser wand in his right hand, and on the ground in front of him were the handcuffs that he had apparently dropped when he fell.

"Pano!" Agatha screamed, her voice breaking as the adrenaline pulsed through her veins. But he was already standing there, pointing his gun at his assailant, who was just now rising with one hand squeezed into his abdomen. Next to him, there were two figures on the ground, looking like crumpled camouflage rags—one missing his head, the other missing half of his torso.

"Sniper!" Pano shouted, and yanked her around the corner as another shot rang out and the remaining attacker was hit in the neck. Most of his head and upper body dissolved into a red cloud of mist that precipitated into metallic-smelling stains on Agatha's and Pano's clothes.

Pano had already thrown himself to the ground, and now Agatha did the same. Together they started crawling along the ground towards their Tesla.

"Did you see a muzzle flash?" she yelled, panting, even though it had already gone silent again.

"Yeah, northeast. We got cover here."

"That's anti-tank ordinance they're shooting, maybe M82," she speculated, as they both made it to the cover of the car, on the other side from where the shooter was. They crouched with their backs against the Tesla. "The hangar's not going to stop those bullets. Neither is the car. They're meant to go through tanks."

"Well, that's just fucking great!" Pano cursed, flung the door open, and climbed into the back seat. Agatha did the same through the door beside the driver's seat.

"Tesla, off-road mode!" she yelled at the selfdriving software, and counted three long seconds as the body of the car rose some twenty centimeters. Pano used the time to climb into the front and sit next to Agatha in the passenger seat. They both buckled up.

"Tesla!" she ordered again. "Full acceleration, off-road, direction southwest, deactivate collision system!"

The two-and-a-half-ton electric SUV peeled out over the tarmac with all of its twelve hundred horsepower, tires squealing. They accelerated to a hundred kph in two seconds. By the time they covered a long stretch of grass and dirt and broken through the chain-link fence, they had reached a hundred and forty. The self-driving software spun the car around while flashing a warning on the display, the red triangle for excessive G-force. It felt like the rear of the car was going to break off as the Tesla swerved to align itself with the road running perpendicular to the fence.

"Follow the road!" Agatha gasped, her seatbelt straining against the extreme forces. Finally, when they were driving straight ahead, and she had assured herself that no bullet had penetrated the car, she looked over at Pano. "Are you all right? Are you hit?"

Her partner looked at his gut, lifted his hand from where it had been pressed against it, and shook his head.

"Nope. That's just where I got tased," he grunted, making a face. "What the fuck just happened?"

"I don't know, except somebody was obviously trying to bag us, until somebody else decided to blow them away and shoot our way clear."

"Huh?"

"Anyone who blows four people away, that fast, from that distance, without missing once, would never have missed us or let us go unless he wanted to," she said, staring at the reflector posts lining the country road as they whizzed past.

"But who would do that?" he asked. "The South Africans?"

"No, I'm thinking they're the ones who wanted to kidnap us."

"What? The intelligence agency?"

"The attackers were unarmed and ready for us. And they certainly didn't seem like the run-of-the-mill kidnappers or criminals you were talking about," she said, and looked at her pantsuit, now completely ruined by the bloodstains. If they were stopped by the police now, for anything, their trip to South Africa was going to end, and not well.

"Damn it to hell!" Pano shouted, and looked between

their two seats towards the rear window. "How did they know where we were going to be? And to be honest, I'm not sure if whoever was doing the shooting did us any favors by getting us out of there."

"I'm sure," she said resolutely. "He didn't. They were probably looking to kidnap us and then drop us off somewhere, so we wouldn't be able to keep poking around in Karlhammer's backyard. Apparently, Solly Shoke talked after all."

"Even if he did, how did they get here so fast?"

"Maybe they had local assets, and all they had to do was make a call," Agatha speculated with a shrug. "Whatever. I'm calling Miller."

She grabbed her hand terminal and pressed the mailbox for her department, which redirected over several satellites until finally the director's line was ringing.

"Devenworth!" he growled when he answered. "You have any idea what time it is? I hope you're calling this emergency number with a very good—"

"No time, sir. Need immediate evacuation!"

"Where are you right now?"

Agatha was grateful that he recognized the seriousness of the situation and didn't ask questions. She typed something into her terminal.

"Sending data."

"Hold on," Miller said. There was a short pause. "Keep heading north, and leave the line open. The Navy's got a base in southern Namibia. I can get you out there."

"Thank you, sir. One other thing," she said, and took a deep breath. "If possible, we need to get routed to Australia."

"What? You're going to be lucky if you get out of there at all. Then you're going to have to give me a full report on—"

"Sir, you know me. We've got a lead. This case is bigger

than we thought. I'm asking you to trust me. You know me well enough to know that I take every case seriously and I don't waste resources."

"Wait, we have a lead?" Pano asked from next to her, raising an eyebrow.

Agatha ignored him and waited. She could hear Miller's breathing in her ear.

"All right. All right. I'll make sure you get a flight, but you better be after a real big fish. I'm going to have to clear this with the minister and call in a few favors with the Navy," Miller grumbled.

"Thank you sir, I—"

The director had already hung up.

"So?" Pano asked.

"We got a pickup. Soon."

"Thank God!"

They drove north for another hour, following the small back road towards the border with Namibia, and right before reaching the border they turned west. Driving down the dirt road with just their parking lights on, they were soon stopped by two Marine sergeants waving red lightsticks.

Agatha stopped the car. She and Pano collected their things and stepped out.

"I'm Sergeant Constantinos," one of the two soldiers said as they approached. He pointed behind him. "The helicopter's waiting right over there!"

She couldn't see it, but she had to shout over the sound of the rotors. "Where?"

"Just follow us!" The two soldiers hustled off, and she and Pano followed. It wasn't long before she saw a dark silhouette framed in a barely noticeable hazy green light.

It was a Navy Sea Hawk. When they reached it, the other

sergeant threw open the door and whisked them inside. Barely a minute later, she was strapped in, headset on, and the helicopter took off in a northerly direction, cruising just above the sparse trees that grew across the steppe.

The soldier's voice came over her headset. "We don't want to get picked up on anybody's radar, that's why we're flying so low," he said, pointing outside.

Agatha just nodded, because the flight didn't interest her very much, and her thoughts were slowing down as the adrenaline rush began to peter out.

Pano, sitting next to her, tried to catch her eye. "Hey, Agatha. You said something about Hobart?"

"Right. There was a bulletin board in the lounge back there, and I think the pilots pinned up their farthest destinations on it. They were all relatively close by, except for this one pin all the way over in Tasmania."

"Isn't that... in Australia?"

"Yeah. It made me think, because there are very few private jets that can carry fourteen people—except a Learjet. A Learjet would also have had been arranged to get from here to Tasmania, and back in 2018 there was only one person who would have been rich enough to afford a Learjet around here—Luther Karlhammer." She gulped a few times while she was speaking, trying to expel the nasty taste of someone else's blood from her mouth. It didn't go away. "I'll bet my career that's where our students went," she finished.

"Well," Pano replied. "I guess you did, bet your career, that is—when you called your boss."

"That's right," she answered succinctly. Of course she was very well aware that now everything that she loved and held dear, namely her job, depended on this hunch of hers leading somewhere. But it didn't worry her. After all, she saw no particular alternative. Breaking off an investigation based on political calculations was not something she did. She was going to finish this, like every other case in her career. Not for Miller, not for herself, but because it was the right thing to do. And it was her job.

"Tasmania..." Pano's voice crackled through the headset again. "I didn't know there was any kind of archaeology going on there."

"There isn't. There's basically none in Australia at all, except for maybe some aboriginal rock paintings."

"So they probably didn't fly to Tasmania at all."

"Probably not."

"Is there anything in Tasmania? Besides koala bears?"

"There are no koala bears there," she corrected him.

"No? Huh. So what is there, then?"

"I don't know," she admitted, and pulled out her hand terminal.

"Hmm. Tasmania is a popular destination for hikers and nature-lovers. A paradise for all kinds of outdoor activities. Aha. Hobart... Hobart is a major port stop for expeditions and supply ships traveling to Antarctica," she read from her terminal.

"Antarctica? Well, there's certainly nothing for archaeologists there," said Pano, peering at her device from the side, as if he was trying to find out if she was making this up.

"No. Weird. Does the Human Foundation have anything to do with Antarctica?"

"Does anyone have anything to do with Antarctica?" Pano replied sarcastically. "I've only ever seen one documentary about it, and that said that all the research installations were pulled out in the thirties because the melting ice was becoming a problem for all the stations. You Americans had a famous base there, didn't you?"

"I honestly don't know," she confessed, searching her

terminal again. "Here! The United States did have one apparently well-known base there. McMurdo Station. After a dispute broke out within the project and the funding fell apart, the Human Foundation bought the whole base in 2019. It seems the deal included sharing research data with the U.S. Environmental Protection Agency. What would the Human Foundation want with an Antarctic research station...?"

"That it picked up in the year after Jackson, Gould, and some students disappeared?" Pano added, finishing the question. Suddenly his face looked like it had aged a few years in the time his head had been swimming in this new information. "Is that base still in operation?"

"Yeah, according to the CIA database, there are four hundred Foundation employees living there in the summer. Sixty in winter," she replied.

"Don't tell me we're going from Tasmania to the last remaining ice area on the planet," Pano whined. When she just looked back at him with her deadpan stare, his shoulders fell. "You know, Special Agent Devenworth, I really hope that at some point you're finally going to succumb to my charms. Otherwise this is going to go down as the worst investigation of my life."

After about forty-five minutes of flying, they reached the Navy base in Namibia. It was an old port that once had a runway connected to it. An old concrete block house, a long and rustic wall, a few tents, and tangles of barbed wire everywhere made the image complete. It was the very picture of a remote outpost framed against the rugged appeal of the Dark Continent.

Instead of taking them into the base, the pilot set down on the old runway. The sergeant then ushered them from the helicopter directly onto the tarmac next to three C-220

Albatross transport planes. One of them had the lights on and its bay door open.

"I have orders to escort you straight onto the plane. The Major said a liaison officer from the Australian Armed Forces will be there to assist you on arrival. He'll be waiting for you in the military section of Hobart International Airport," the sergeant roared over the noise of the spinning props as they lowered their heads to get through the hatch.

"Sergeant," Agatha yelled back. "We have to change our destination!"

"What?" he and Pano shouted at the same time.

"We need to go to McMurdo in Antarctica," she explained, as they ran through the hatch into the cargo bay, empty save for the holding nets, lashing straps and various fixtures for hooks and ropes all over the walls.

"The pilot has orders to take you to Hobart—"

"We've got to change that order. Call this number!" Agatha held out her terminal to him with the direct dial of the Secretary of Defense on the display. She had never dialed that number before, but, like all lead agents of the CTD, she had it, and she was sure that Miller had cleared the whole thing with the Secretary of Defense. Otherwise they would never have been illegally evacuated out of a country that was a U.S. ally. It was a risk, but a calculated one, and she didn't want to give Karlhammer and the Human Foundation another chance to intercept and possibly succeed this time.

The sergeant seemed hesitant, but then he took the terminal and dialed the number. After a moment, his eyes grew as big as golf balls and he looked at Agatha with his eyebrows up somewhere under the brim of his uniform hat.

"Hello, sir, Sergeant Eversman, sir. I'm sorry, sir, sir! Uh, I've got a Special Agent Agatha Devenworth in front of me, from the Counter-Terrorist Directive, and she's telling me that instead of Hobart I'm supposed to send her to McMurdo in Antarctica... Yes, sir, the distance is about the same, but I have to point out that the new owners could refuse permission to land... No, sir... Yes, sir... Of course, sir."

Eversman handed the terminal back and, for a brief instant, shuddered. "That was—"

"The Secretary of Defense, I know," she said impatiently, throwing in a get-to-the-point gesture for good measure.

"You're getting your flight. But he also said if we don't get permission to land, you'll be doing the last part of your journey by parachute, because he's not going to risk a breach of international law without hard accusations."

"What he doesn't want to risk is losing his job," she muttered, but backed down, because her gamble had already paid off better than she had expected.

"Have you ever done a parachute jump?" Pano asked her as they found seats along the wall and clipped their three-point seatbelts.

"I have," she said evasively.

"When and where?"

"My ex-boyfriend gave me a tandem jump for my birthday one time. I hated it."

"Great," Pano sighed, leaning his head back against the wall behind him. He closed his eyes. It was about ten minutes before Eversman returned with a crate, strapped it and himself down, and the military plane finally started moving along the runway.

24

RON JACKSON, 2018

Ron rested for a while. He knew the excitement was taking its toll, because he felt exhausted. He had been checking his tablet over and over, trying to contact someone using Bluetooth, but without success, and now his device's battery was getting dangerously low.

At least the temperature in his tiny prison was pleasant, a balmy twenty degrees. But the humidity was getting a little much for him, and he was sweating more and more, which meant he was also losing water.

The thirst was not even the worst part. A pounding headache was spreading from the top of his skull and his temples to his neck, hammering his brain so hard he felt sick.

At first he had thought the headache and the fact that he was having moments of blurred vision were symptoms of his dehydration, but he had only been trapped down here for a few hours. Even with the temperature where it was, dehydration wasn't his problem yet. He knew that even without being a doctor.

Then he had realized that he was starting to behave

erratically without even noticing it. He had blamed that on the situation he was in, without realizing that he had been responding based on a peculiar anxiety, even given the excitement.

"It's the oxygen," he had decided after a while. "The partial pressure of the oxygen in the air has gone up. I'm getting hyperoxia."

Ron looked at his forearms, where he saw a slight rash was starting to emerge. "Oxygen acts quickly and produces free radicals, which is why I'm getting headaches and a skin rash and blurred vision."

And that wasn't all. In the longer term, he knew that excessively high oxygen levels in the air would lead to blood clots, seizures, and cardiac arrest.

But where are the oxygen and the heat coming from? he wondered as he struggled to his feet. He took the flashlight and looked at every transition between walls, at the ceiling joints, and along the floor, but couldn't find a single opening anywhere. Every inch was immaculate and seamless, without any gap, as if the whole room had been milled out of a single piece of metal.

Ron was just about to turn away when the light of his flashlight passed over the drawing of the giant and the characters below again. To orient himself, he took a look at the ballpoint pen he had placed in the middle of the room to mark the cardinal directions.

"Okay, so now I'm looking at the most recent drawing, if my theory is correct." He reread the text, and suddenly remembered two of the letters he had been busting his head over before. "Of course!"

He grabbed his journal and hastily completed his translation: "KATARU means 'pact,' or 'to make a pact.' Yes. The next word is UGGAE, that's 'God.' No, wait, 'God' is ILU.

The Fossil

UGGAE... UGGAE is 'God of the dead.' Or 'Death.' KALUM is a 'priest,' or someone who laments, who cries for the dead. A 'wailer.' SABATU means 'take away,' or maybe better to 'confiscate.' And the last one is TAPPUTU, 'help.' Or... is it? Wait, no, help is RESUSSUN, TAPPUTU is 'aids, resources.'"

Ron took a deep breath and read it all out loud again: "KATARU UGGAE KALUM SABATU TAPPATU, 'pact between God of the dead and priest of wailing to confiscate a resource.' Well, that doesn't make any sense."

He shook his head and hit the flashlight with the flat of his hand, because it was beginning to flicker at faster intervals.

He was done for if the batteries went dead now. But after all this time, he was so close. He was convinced that he was looking at something major, and though it was terrifying, considering the circumstances, he knew that he couldn't die right now, right here. This was too important.

With a sinking feeling in his stomach he moved the flashlight up to the picture that went with the sentence he had just read. With that sentence in mind, you could also interpret the image so that the god of the dead, the giant man, the Builder, was pointing to one of the six people.

"Is this the pact between the god of the dead and the priest of lamentation? What is this pact about? What does confiscating a resource mean? What kind of resource? Is he taking the tools away? Or did he take the tool to have an instrument in his hand to help people? But why would the god of the dead be helping people escape death in the form of mass extinction? Hmm..."

Ron looked at the depiction of the sarcophagus. "It might be that in this context, the word UGGAE also means 'dead god.' We know their vocabulary was limited, after all.

Whatever the case, it's clear that he didn't help them if they lived so long before *Homo erectus*, because they obviously died out without leaving a trace. Ahh, I just don't get it."

He went back and stared first at the characters, then at the drawing that went with them, and then repeated this at every section of the wall. His brain was on fire, but he just couldn't make sense of it.

Okay, Ron, just think straight, he told himself, and hit the head of the flashlight again, trying to do something about the flickering, even though he knew it was probably a dumb thing to do. But he absolutely needed the light, because he still hadn't figured out what he needed to understand. *What is this sentence supposed to mean? Try looking at it completely from the other direction. A dead god is awakened, to make a pact, in the form of some kind of confiscation. Confiscate what? The tool? No, the tool is some kind of performance—confiscating it doesn't make sense.*

Unless the confiscation isn't about the tool. What if the dead god is awakened to confiscate the priest of lamentation and use his body as a resource? If it is a dead god, maybe he didn't leave a body. Maybe he left something else... A text, perhaps? A manual? That could be what the confiscation is about. The priest reads the manual the dead god left, and the dead god confiscates the priest, indirectly, through his knowledge. And with that, he's supposed to be able to save the people from the catastrophe. Hmm.

"No, no," he said out loud. "How could the ancestors of the Sumerians use the ancient knowledge of the Builders to save the world from a mass extinction?"

He interrupted himself. "Wait, wait. Maybe it's not about saving the world at all... Maybe it's about some kind of ark! No one can stop the eruption of a supervolcano, or an earthquake, or a meteorite, although maybe the Builders could have. What if this place is a refuge, where

The Fossil

the people came in the direst emergencies, to survive a catastrophe? That would explain why there's always exactly six people. It's not about six people exactly, it just means there's a fixed number, like the eight passengers in the 'Noah's ark' story."

With his fingers, he traced the simple drawings of the human figures with their strange headgear. A sudden wave of headache and dizziness came over him. It hit him so hard he thought he would vomit, but he managed to stop himself at the last minute.

Gasping heavily, he forced himself to look up again. His eyesight was beginning to fail, and he had to come closer and closer to the wall to see anything at all.

"Damn oxygen," he murmured, and suppressed the thought that if the other expedition members didn't hurry up and find him, he wasn't going to make it out of this room. He forced those thoughts out of his mind by focusing on what was in front of him.

"Okay, one more time. A fixed number of people come here in times of greatest need to survive a mass extinction. Obviously, six is far too few to save civilization, so the six is probably a symbol for six hundred, or maybe even six thousand. That would also explain why technological development always starts over from zero. So they come here and ask the master of the house for his blessing and knowledge, and the priest in charge gets it somehow, and then they stuff the dead god back into his sarcophagus."

Ron looked again at the painting in which the Builder was pointing to the six people. At first he thought his vision was going again, but when he brought his eyes very close there was no mistaking it: he was touching the person in front, very lightly, with an outstretched finger. A small line of dust had made it look different, but when he had brushed it away, there was no mistaking it. The Builder was touching the first of the six people, very lightly, on the forehead.

"That is the confiscation. He possesses the priest." Ron's breath quickened. It didn't even register that the faster he breathed, the more harm he was doing himself. His pounding heart pushed him further along the wall, dragging his fingers over the Sumerian letters. "I think I understand. But where's the sarcophagus? Does it actually exist, or is it just a symbol?"

Not for the first time, he felt frustrated that the lost civilizations of antiquity preferred to express themselves in metaphors and riddles, never just spelling out what they had to say.

Kind of like today's academic authors, he thought with familiar indignation, and went on searching for clues. Any clues.

After a while, he did notice something new. In the image showing the people chiseling the images into the wall, there was one figure not actually taking part in the work. It was hard to spot, because at first glance it looked like he was doing something. On closer inspection, however, Ron was sure that he was only leaning with one hand on the wall of stone, or whatever the wall was supposed to be made of.

"So you're the priest who's meant to be taken over by the dead god, am I right? What are you doing with your hand?"

Ron studied the figure in as much detail as he could with his failing eyesight, but didn't see anything remarkable. He went around the other walls, but it was the same on the older drawings—he couldn't see any clues as to exactly where the priest's hands might have been.

"Somewhere, there has to be some kind of switch or handprint sensor," he said out loud, but then quickly shook his head. "You're hallucinating. Damn oxygen. Handprint

The Fossil

sensor!" Ron snorted contemptuously at himself and put his back against the wall, then slowly sank to the floor. He was now so exhausted that he really couldn't think straight anymore.

Then, suddenly, the flashlight went out.

Plunged into complete darkness, he normally would have screamed, but he was too weak, and his headache too powerful, to put up any kind of resistance.

Well, that's a fine ending, he thought, defeated, rubbing his temples so hard that the pain of the pressure almost masked his headache. *Just about to make the discovery that would probably prove my theories once and for all, and I die in this dark room, just inches away from rescue. If it weren't so tragic, I'd laugh myself silly.*

Suddenly, he was overcome with rage, and he began shouting out loud. "What kind of crap is this anyway?" He didn't know whether it was the oxygen or the knowledge that he was about to die, but the feeling rose up within him and he couldn't stop it. "You're one smart goddamn burial chamber, aren't you? You've got a hole in the ceiling that's sometimes there, and then all of a sudden not there. And then it's there again! I mean, what the hell? And then you pump the room full of oxygen and humidity until I die? It doesn't make any sense! It makes no goddamn sense! Why would you get me in here just so I can die?"

The chamber didn't answer, of course. The only thing he heard was the throbbing of his heartbeat in his ears, which almost drove him mad. It might have been simply the elevated oxygen that was pushing him over the edge.

At this point he had trouble concentrating on anything, but one thought stayed in his mind, in razor-sharp focus, even as the veil of madness descended on him. *How were the environmental conditions changing? Where was that coming from?* He was absolutely sure that the composition of the air, the temperature, and the humidity had changed since he had fallen in here. This room had to be connected to some kind of energy source, which in itself was proof that advanced technology had been used to build all this. But where was the heat coming from? True, the walls were relatively warm, but it was not like the kind of heat that came from a furnace. He had found no injectors or vents that could have been pumping air and humidity in here. So how was it possible that the conditions had changed anyway?

"What is it? Magic?"

Ron snorted. Sure, he believed in unproven theories about humanity and civilization long before the dawn of man, but he wasn't a complete nutjob. He had three PhDs, after all. One thing he was sure of. Magic had nothing to do with it.

"Any sufficiently advanced technology is indistinguishable from magic," he said, and then added, "Arthur C. Clarke. All right, so what kind of technology is behind this magic, eh?"

Ron thought for a while. In his current state, that took considerable effort, like trying to walk through waist-deep water.

But eventually he reached his conclusion. "Nanotechnology. It could be tiny pores in the walls, enough of them to feed oxygen and moisture into this room, but so small that they would not be visible to the naked eye."

Certainly not mine right now, he thought, rubbing fluid from the corners of his watering eyes.

"Perhaps," he went on, talking out loud to drive away the loneliness that had come flooding in with the darkness, "there's no switch at all, but it's a DNA reader that brings out the sarcophagus. No, no, not a sarcophagus. The sarcophagus is a symbol of death and the afterlife for gods and kings. But there is a mechanism somewhere. Unless... If the wall is covered with nanites, or something like that, then it doesn't matter—you don't need a reader mechanism, you can touch anywhere."

"But..." he was talking to himself now, and contradicting himself, "but I already touched the walls!"

But you only touched them with brushing, glancing movements, he thought. *Maybe that wasn't long enough to allow the reading to happen. Well, why the hell not?*

With tremendous effort, Ron turned around, but slumped to his side because he didn't have enough strength to stand. Then he raised his left palm and pressed it against the wall that he had just been leaning on, keeping it there with a dogged strength.

Nothing happened.

"Why not?" he cursed, and felt that strange anger, so unlike him, rising again like a toothy monster, fighting its way from the depths up into the daylight. Except there was no daylight here, nor light of any kind. "Why not, dammit, why not?"

But then something did happen.

The floor began to vibrate very slightly, so slightly that at first he thought it was the trembling of his own limbs. And then he saw a dim, hazy light. Yes, there. It was almost imperceptible, but it was definitely light! The vague silhouette of a rectangular object—or was that his eyes?

Ron heard a hissing, then, followed by a high-frequency beeping that hurt his ears, and then there was only light. In an instant, the rectangle was suddenly there, now composed of pure, blue light, and in the middle, an emerging silhouette of giant proportions.

"My God," Ron whispered.

25

FILIO AMOROSA, 2042

The trip to the astronaut training center in Nevada went by fast. Only six hours after she had boarded in Mogadishu, the plane landed in Reno. From there she was taken by taxi, with Engels as her escort, to the Space Exploration Training and Evaluation Facility, SETEF for short, about sixty kilometers north of Reno.

It was back in the 2020s that the United Nations adopted resolutions to spread the enormous costs of the planned missions to Mars and, later, to the moons of Jupiter and Saturn. Third World countries were exempt, and the emerging economies participated with financial grants in exchange for access to the scientific results. The winners, and the ones who bore the risks, were the big former industrial nations and the new big players: China, the European Union, the United States, India, Brazil, Canada, Australia, South Africa, Switzerland, and Norway.

The training center went to the USA, and the launch site for *Mars One* went to the EU, which meant that the launch site would be French Guiana. *Mars Two* was scheduled to be launched from Cape Canaveral, Florida. The SOL research center was opened in China, the launch site for the third mission was slated for Russia, and the mission control center was located in Darmstadt. Many smaller institutions and suppliers among the other member states had been assigned contracts with lower prestige value but high financial incentives.

Filio was glad enough that she would be spending the last two weeks before launch in the Nevada desert. It meant she would be far away from all the turmoil she had kicked up in Europe. Of course she still had some turmoil to face with this crew, but she had never expected this to be a walk in the park.

The center was simply 'sitting out there' in the middle of the desert, although they had to pass through a checkpoint with a significant barrier and NATO wire, and staffed by U.S. troops. Armed drones whizzed through the air, circling the center, and she was quite sure that there were some satellite weapons up there somewhere, locked on to this sensitive site. The actual buildings could not have been more unspectacular if they had tried, consisting of three gray cubes, with no windows or outbuildings, as if three concrete dice had fallen from the pockets of a passing family of giants—out here, in the middle of nowhere.

They stopped in front of the middle building. A tall woman was there to meet them, wearing a pantsuit and carrying an old-fashioned clipboard under her arm, shielding her eyes from the withering sun.

"Well then," Engels said, extending his hand. "This is as far as I go. I wish you all the best... Really."

"Thank you." Filio shook his hand, picked up her small bag, and stepped out of the silver GMC Falcon to shake the woman's hand.

"Greetings, Doctor. My name is Laura Morris. I'm the

assistant to Director Hugh Jones, who runs the facility." Her face stayed emotionless as she gestured toward a door in the middle concrete block. In the giant, featureless wall, the door looked ridiculously tiny.

"I know Jones," Filio replied, nodding. He was a Texan, a good man, very organized and quite rational and approachable, even under stress. Jones was the man who had set the tone, all those years ago, during their preparations for *Mars One*. Filio was relieved to hear that he still held the job, because they had always gotten along well.

"I see. I'm sure you still know your way around, Doctor, but I'd like to give you the tour of the facility anyway. There have been a few changes since you were last here."

"Of course," Filio agreed, and Jones's assistant escorted her through the entrance into the air-conditioned interior. Passing through the entirely undecorated entrance area, they walked down a corridor to the elevators, and ascended all the way up to the tenth floor. The cubes only contained offices and living space, as well as the lounge and dining areas. The actual training areas were underground, along with the massive water tanks containing the mockups of various rockets, stations and modules, the centrifuges, and the fitness equipment.

"The director wants to see you first, and then I'll show you the new additions, all right?" Morris asked.

Filio nodded, her exhaustion showing. The scattered moments of sleep she had managed to catch on her several flights to get here had not been particularly restful. Whenever she had tried to sleep, she had dreamed of the *Ocean's Bitch* and how she had left her friends underwater. Now that the heaviest part of the burden she was carrying—at least, of the things that she might not be carrying with her for the rest of her life—had fallen from her shoulders, her eyelids were getting heavier and heavier.

"Yes, of course." She tried to hide her yawn behind her hand, and had to wipe her tears from her eyes to see clearly as the elevator doors opened.

Morris led her straight to a lonely door which was labeled simply 'The Director.' The assistant knocked quickly and then opened it.

Filio walked in, and felt like she was walking into a wall. Director Jones was sitting behind a broad office desk, and he looked up when she came in. He wasn't alone. Seven people were sitting in front of him, all in blue one-piece suits, each with different badges and a different country's flag. She quickly scanned them and saw the EU, the United States, Canada, China, Russia, Brazil, and India.

Filio was shocked to be so suddenly confronted with the entire *Mars Two* crew, and was sure there had to be a reason for doing it like this. But she also realized that if there were seven sitting here, it meant that Jones had already sent the EU's second astronaut home. That could only mean that he didn't want to make this absolutely as difficult as possible on her, which she took as a win.

"Ah, Filio," the director said, standing up from his office chair to greet her. He pointed to the vacant eighth seat in front of the desk.

All eyes were on her, and the faces behind them were anything but friendly.

So far, exactly as expected.

As she sat, she nodded to Jones and looked around among the three female and four male astronauts she would be spending her next mission with. She felt like the new kid in the class who had skipped a grade and would now have to struggle to be accepted.

"I know this situation is hard on you," Jones said into the uncomfortable silence, and nodded, his gray halo of hair wobbling slightly. "But it's as hard for this team to swallow, so I thought it was only fair to start with a clean slate and get everything out in the open.

"These seven astronauts came to me to protest the removal of their teammate, Nicole Richter from ESA, who they've been training with for over a year for this mission, and who now, two weeks before launch, is being replaced. For these men and women, Nicole was not just a team member but a friend, and I have to be completely honest with you, Filio, not because I don't respect you as a person or as an astronaut, but because I do.

"I don't like this decision on the personnel change. Not one bit. You know how much a transparent organization and smooth processes mean to me. This kind of change at the last minute is an absolute nightmare and endangers the whole mission. Now that I've said my piece on this, I will never raise this issue again, because I see it as unprofessional to keep hammering on something that you can't change. This is the team we have, and we're going to make the best out of it. I expect nothing less from you and the rest of your team members.

"Anyone else have anything to say?" At this, Jones stopped to look every single astronaut straight in the eye, one by one.

No one moved, and no one looked at Filio. So she raised her hand.

"Yes, Filio?"

"I think I owe you all an explanation, and without expecting you to understand or accept me as one of you, I do want to explain exactly what my motives are," she said, and took a deep breath before continuing.

"The *Mars One* mission is still with me like it was yesterday. I remember the months it took getting there, the hours spent laughing and crying on board. I remember the cramped space that also made for a special kind of closeness—a chance to grow together as a team. I remember all the hard work that we put in trying not to go crazy. I remember the landing, that we had to make adjustments to the atmospheric controls. I remember what it feels like to stand on Mars. All these things are going to be a benefit to you and the mission, of that I am sure.

"I know what you're all thinking, that I've been traumatized, or I've lost my mind. But I hope that in the next two weeks you're going to find out that that's not the case. There's nothing wrong with me, and I want to tell you why I can be so sure. My last crew was my family. More than friends or colleagues. They were pioneers and adventurers, courageous scientists giving their all to broaden mankind's horizons.

"We found something on Mars that didn't belong there, something organic, and I believe that what we found had something to do with our crash. I am aware that we were violating orders when we aborted the mission and returned to Earth, but believe me, there must have been a reason. I need to find out what that was, and I'm sure my memories will come back as soon as I set foot on Mars. I know that being there will trigger them."

Filio looked around the room. The faces of her future comrades were still blank but at least they were a little less hostile—or maybe she only imagined that they were—and they were looking at her now, instead of the floor or the ceiling.

"One thing I promise is that I'm always going to be honest with you. To show you that these are not just empty words, or a ploy to deflect your anger, I want to tell you now what I've been doing for the past two years.

"After being kicked out of ESA, there was one kidnapping attempt before I was given police protection and three more after that, a murder attempt that left me with a scar from my left shoulder blade to my hip, and countless death threats. After that, I went into hiding in Africa. I joined a scrapper ship crew, the only one that didn't ask me for my passport or about my past. They were only interested in my future. We searched the entire Indian Ocean in the hope of finding something that would make the crew millionaires.

"But the only thing I was looking for was a crate that I knew had been in the stern of the ship before the crash. A crate containing samples of the organic material that we, evidently, had found on Mars, and which had been the reason for our premature return. I suddenly remembered that I had packed that crate, and knew where I must have stowed it. This is the type of insight that I know I'm going to have more of as soon as I'm back there.

"Throughout these past two years, I made detailed calculations of the probable location of the stern section, then refined my formulas and researched the system of currents in the Indian Ocean, and worked out the most likely mass of the stern section after the crash. All this was guesswork, because I only had recordings of the burning wreckage to go on. The fact that I found what I was looking for should be proof enough for you of how persistent and successful I am in pursuing my goals.

"I'm not trying to sound arrogant, I'm trying to sound valuable to you, and I want you to know one thing. There's something up there. Something disturbed us so much that we turned straight around, without reporting the find to Mission Control. Whatever it was, it's also what was responsible for me losing my memories. But I survived. Some called it a miracle. I call it an opportunity. An opportunity to return, but prepared this time. If you think that's bullshit, and just some mentally traumatized former astronaut talking crap, that's just one more reason why you should want me next to you when things start to go off the script—which they do all the time, by the way.

"I've sacrificed everything to be sitting next to you right now—not for my career, not for my ego, not to restore my reputation... No, I sacrificed everything so my former colleagues can be at peace. I want to make sure that they didn't die for nothing, and I want the Mars missions to go on, and to succeed. I was a part of a team of motivated, intelligent, and totally committed men and women like you.

"I know I'll never be able to replace your colleague, Nicole, but what I can do is make sure I give you everything I've got. And that's a lot."

When Filio had finished, there was silence for a while as the team looked at each other. Finally, the mission commander, Michel Longchamps, stood up. "If you don't mind, we'd like to be dismissed," he said to Jones.

"Of course," he said with a nod and a quick wave of his hand, and the seven all filed out.

Filio stayed in her seat. When they were alone, she looked at the director.

"Well, that certainly went way better than I expected," he said, and folded his hands on the top of his desk. "Ms. Morris will show you the rest of the facility now, and you have my word that will be the last of our difficult conversations. At least for today."

The tour lasted about an hour, and at the end of it Filio realized that virtually nothing had changed. The living quarters had been moved, but the training rooms were still the same. Apart from that, probably the only thing that had changed was the picture of the President of the United States.

Because the preparations were in the final phase, at this point the crew was only doing simulations, which meant the entire team was running through various disaster scenarios in a one-to-one replica of *Mars Two*. The real one was currently being transported to Cape Canaveral and undergoing its final assembly. They were expected to cope with a collision with micro-asteroids causing loss of pressure in all sections, medical emergencies with two different crew members simultaneously, several different types of fire, an outbreak of the flu, a team member going crazy, accidental radiation exposure, and so on, and so on, and so on.

The list was long, and Filio bore the full brunt of all of it. She was a physician and a physicist, a rare enough combination that put her in the dual role of a medical professional and the person who got questioned about more or less every type of problem. She had to give the crew credit for how professionally they conducted themselves. Nobody made pointed comments or tried to pick a fight with her, even though there was never a moment that it wasn't clear that they were all unhappy with the situation they were now in.

Michel Longchamps turned out to be a good commander who performed calmly and stayed focused at all times, almost like Jones. Filio found it reassuring to have such a competent and professional astronaut in charge of *Mars Two*. Audrey Burton, the engineer from Canada, seemed very introverted and focused, rarely smiled, didn't talk much, and followed instructions with grim precision. That, of course, couldn't be said for James Wittman, the only American on board. He cracked joke after joke the whole time, most of which were funny, but Filio was sure that this would be exhausting in the long run. Men like him were always acting in their own feelgood movie and, in her experience, were the first ones to lose it when the real problems started. After a week of disaster drills, she still had nothing with which to judge his competence as a geophysicist, because there were basically no emergencies that intersected with his field of expertise. But his performance as an astronaut was rock-solid. The same went for Marcelino Bordotta, the xenobiologist who was always smiling, except when he was looking at Filio, and Putram Revi, the Indian whose job on the flight was to germinate the first seeds of the genetically modified fruits and grains for the functioning greenhouse that would be his task to set up on Mars.

Doctor Hue Tao Xing seemed to live up to the stereotype of the dedicated and focused Chinese woman, but also turned out to be the only potential ally Filio could find in the group. She was the only one who actively sought contact with her and asked her questions about *Mars One*. Clearly, the doctor understood that the more knowledge they all had, the higher the chances of the mission's success. No doubt it also had something to do with the fact she hadn't beaten out a few hundred million people in her country for this position, like the rest of the crew, but 2 billion. Finally, there was the chemist, Tatyana Kalashnikova from Russia, who had apparently been close to Nicole Richter, the German woman who had been bumped from the mission for Filio. She never so much as looked at Filio, and never spoke a word to her outside the bare minimum of communication needed to complete the simulations.

Filio knew that the problems would go away over time, no later than the first moment that they had to depend on each other in a life-or-death situation. But still, the thought that in less than seven days she would be boarding a ship with this crew, and be locked in with them for four months, gave her stomach cramps. The first mission had been a cakewalk, because they knew each other, coordinated with each other, and liked each other. This time everything was under a black cloud, and that cloud was herself.

The fact that there was no alternative made things inevitable, but not any more comfortable.

On the evening of the seventh day, Filio was sitting alone at one of the tables in the small canteen, looking over at the other table where the rest of the crew was gathered. Until just then some of the staff had been sitting with her and keeping her company, but they had left for their last shift, and Filio hadn't eaten yet. As she poked around in her vegetables listlessly, separating her peas from her carrots, a voice next to her suddenly asked, "May I sit down?"

Startled, she turned and looked into the face of Michel Longchamps. He was still wearing his training jumpsuit, but looked astonishingly fresh.

"Ah... of course," she said quickly, gesturing to the seat opposite her.

"I've been wondering something, and I thought if I just asked you it would spare me from wracking my brain about it for days, or maybe weeks," he said. His English was startlingly polished for a Frenchman, almost accent-free.

"Well, you've got my full attention right now," Filio replied, and tried to muster a smile. It was perhaps a tiny sign of reconciliation, his simple presence at her table, but it helped her tremendously.

"There's this friend of mine, he was on a scrapper ship for a year, the *Concordia*. I don't know if you know the ship."

When Filio shook her head, he gave a brief nod of acknowledgment and continued. "He told me about his experiences out there, and I remember him telling me one time about the scrapper code of honor."

Filio felt an uncomfortable feeling beginning to rise in her as she began to suspect where this conversation was going, but she forced herself to keep listening.

"Well, Doctor, you assured us of your honesty, and I really genuinely want to know something from you. How is it that you managed to avoid the pooling of all your finds, that the code requires, after you and your crew found the stern of the ship? I'm referring to the crate here. Since you're sitting here in front of me, I can only assume that you traded the samples for a place onboard *Mars Two*. How did you manage to convince your crew to let you make such a trade? I mean, selling it would have made you all immeasurably rich."

Filio stopped playing with her food and dropped the fork onto the plate.

She looked at the Frenchman for a moment, but saw nothing other than curiosity and something like an eagerness in his expression, which she didn't know whether to interpret as positive or negative.

So she began to speak. About the day in Mombasa when she met Romain, about her first dives with Thomas, the evenings cooking with Jane, and the endless planning of the search areas with Alberto. She told him about her formulas and calculations, how she always had to start over from scratch, and how they had faced illegal confrontations with competing scrappers.

As she kept talking, one by one the other crew members came over, hesitantly at first, to listen to her story. In the end, only Kalashnikova remained sitting at the other table, but Filio barely noticed because everything around her disappeared as she told the story of her last two years. Finally, when she came to the story of her last dive and recovering the crate, she was crying openly, heavy tears that fell on her barely touched plate. She didn't even stop to think about it as she went on, and told them about her final telephone conversation with Romain. It took a while, because she was overcome with sobbing and had to stop more than once.

When Filio finished, everyone remained sitting in silence. At some point Filio looked up, because she thought she was alone. They were all still there, but they were not looking at her. All eyes were fixed on Longchamps, who she now saw was holding something in his closed hand. He looked at his team members, one by one, and each of them nodded—some immediately, and some after a moment of hesitation.

Finally the commander turned to Filio, looked her directly in the eye, and held out his closed hand to her. He opened his fist, and she saw he was holding the *Mars Two* mission badge, with the image of the elongated cylinder of the ship, and at the bottom, the word 'Crew.'

He put it down in front of her, nodded, and silently left the room. The others followed him, while Filio, half touched by the gesture and half distraught from reliving her own story, could only stare at the badge on the table.

At that moment, a great weight fell from her heart. She had no illusions that it would be clear sailing from here, but she knew that she had taken the first, most crucial step to being accepted by her fellow crew members.

26

AGATHA DEVENWORTH, 2042

The flight was loud and turbulent as they flew south, degree by degree. To Agatha, the plane they were in might well have been a museum piece. After all, why were there still any turboprops flying around in 2042? But Sergeant Eversman had explained to them that this type of plane could land on gravel and extremely short runways, was less damage-sensitive, didn't suck foreign objects into the engines, and could generally handle a lot more maneuvering at much lower speeds.

As they crossed 40° latitude, and entered what they called the 'Roaring Forties', the plane was rocked so violently that Pano dug his hand in tight to his seatbelts—and her right arm.

"You're hurting me," she said.

"Sorry. I... I'm not a big fan of flying."

Half an hour later, as they crossed the 50th parallel and forged ahead into the fierce winds of the Furious Fifties, he did it again.

"Have you made contact with McMurdo yet?" shouted

Agatha across the plane to the sergeant. He was sitting on the other side, strapped in all by his lonesome in a row of seats that would have typically had fifty to one hundred soldiers in it.

"I'll ask the pilots," Eversman replied, and began speaking inaudibly into his headset. His expression became expectant, and then he moved the mouthpiece of his headset closer to his mouth and spoke into it again. Watching his lips, Agatha decided that he was repeating what he had just said.

"What's wrong?" she asked.

"They're not answering," he replied. "I'm going up front. Maybe there's a malfunction in the radio." He began to unbuckle his seatbelt. Halfway through, he stopped cold, like he had just heard something, and strapped himself in again. "They talked to McMurdo and we have permission to land."

"That's a relief," she sighed, and let her shoulders relax a little. She hadn't even realized that they had been bunched up tight since... she didn't know when.

"So we don't have to jump?" Pano asked. He had been looking worse and worse as the turbulence went on, and was now quite pale around his nose.

"Doesn't look like it."

Pano gave her a sidelong look, trying to tell if she was telling the truth, and then leaned over and kissed her on the cheek.

"Hey, what the—"

"Don't! I don't want to hear a word," el Capitano said smugly. "It's just, where I come from, when you realize that you're going to live a little bit longer, you have to share your joy."

Agatha frowned, but when she saw the exuberance in his eyes she could only sigh humbly. She didn't understand people who could get that emotional, but right now he actually looked more alive than he had before—and that was a good thing.

"Fine, whatever. Go mark this date on the calendar, if you want," she suggested.

"Now that I think about it, I would have found a tandem jump with you quite erotic," Pano said, his cheeky grin back on his face. "Would you have preferred to be in the front or in the back?"

"Just don't go there," Agatha growled.

"Are you ever in a good mood?"

"Define good."

"Have you ever laughed?"

"Yes."

"When?"

"Last year. One of the guys from the FBI told me a joke," she replied.

"Last year, eh? Are you being serious?"

"Yes," she said, annoyed by now with this line of questioning. "You asked me if I'd ever laughed, and I told you."

Pano shook his head and cursed under his breath in German, possibly something about the Virgin Mary. Then he switched back to English. "Tell me the joke."

"The joke is... not for sophisticated company."

"Great, I'm not sophisticated company. Just tell it," he said again.

"All right, then. This macho guy in a Mustang is driving around in Las Vegas, and he pulls up to a stoplight next to a hot blonde in a convertible. He knows he has to make his move fast, so he shouts over at her, 'Hey babe, it's too bad the light's about to change, I was going to tell you a joke about my dick, but it's too long.' She looks at him and goes, 'Yeah, I'd tell you a joke about my pussy, but you'd never get it.'"

At first, Pano just chuckled, and then he burst out laughing. "That's funny!"

Agatha's face didn't move, and when Pano noticed it the smile vanished from his in a flash. "What? Why aren't you laughing?"

"I didn't laugh at it back then either. It's puerile and stupid." She shook her head. "But we were in this fancy cake shop at the time. After he told the joke, I raised my fist to make like I was going to hit him. And he was so intent on avoiding my blow that he jumped back and ended up with his head in this huge cake. Now *that* was funny."

Agatha was smiling now, just thinking back on it. Pano pulled out his hand terminal and held up to her face. Her eyes immediately narrowed and her smile vanished. "What are you doing?"

"I just wanted to get a picture of this historic moment when your mouth took on that unusual shape," he replied.

"You're annoying," she growled, and they looked at each other for a moment. Then suddenly Pano couldn't help laughing, and that made Agatha crack a smile, until she, too, was giggling.

"Fifteen minutes!" Eversman, still shouting over the propellers, had called to them from the other side of the plane. He pointed to the box he had carried on board before departure and said, "You should put those on!"

Agatha and Pano unbuckled themselves and released the crate from its transport straps. Opening it, they found three snow-camouflage suits for arctic conditions, each with a mask, and insulated helmet and boots.

The Fossil

"I had to guess your boot sizes. If they don't fit, try a bigger pair and wear two or three pairs of socks. But McMurdo's supposed to be pretty small, so you won't be doing too many long marches," said Eversman as he appeared next to them and squeezed himself into the third suit after removing his gear.

Ten minutes later they had strapped themselves back into their seats, despite each having doubled their body circumference, and were ready for landing.

Agatha's hood didn't fit well under her helmet, and it pressed against her uncomfortably in several places. She had pulled the ski goggles up to her forehead, and the face-mask, which could be clipped to the goggles to protect the mouth and nose from frostbite, hung from the side of her chin like a pilot's mouthpiece. In the hold of the transport plane, with its yellow wall covering and gray floor and ceiling plates, the white-and-gray snow camouflage pattern looked ridiculous.

"Prepare for landing," came the announcement from the cockpit over the speakers. By this time the plane was rocking and vibrating tremendously. More than once Agatha had the feeling that the massive plane was being buffeted like a toy in the wind, so she was all the more surprised when they touched down gently and braked quickly.

There was whistling and hissing as they rolled to a stop, at which point the lamp above the cargo bay door turned from magenta to green.

"All right, let's move," Eversman called, having an easier time shouting over the quieter propeller noise. "We leave the engines on so they don't get cold. The pilot says McMurdo told us to come out unarmed because this is a civilian facility." He looked at Agatha and Pano, who had both strapped on their guns. They looked at each other briefly, then undid them and refastened them under their snowsuits. Eversman smiled. "You got three hours, and then this bird is taking off, you got that?"

"Got it," Agatha and Pano replied at the same time. The sergeant pressed a button and the cargo bay door began lowering.

The blast of wind that screamed in through the opening was ice cold and so biting that Agatha's face began to hurt immediately. She put on her snow goggles and attached the mask.

Much better, she thought, and headed down the ramp with Pano and the sergeant. With his assault rifle at the low ready position, Eversman stopped halfway down the ramp and waved them out.

McMurdo was built at the foot of a cone-shaped mountain that was as free of snow and ice as the land surrounding it, as far as Agatha's eyes could see. Everything was the same dirty brown, pale and lifeless. There was no vegetation at all, only elongated, single-story houses painted red, green, and yellow, in a vague clump between the mountain and the Arctic Ocean. Among them were a few yurt-like structures, probably water tanks or storage silos. The runway on which Agatha and Pano were now standing, which doubled as takeoff and landing runway, was short and constructed from colorless concrete slabs. At the end of it was a hangar, with two ACVs stationed in front of it.

"I have to say that the welcome receptions in Antarctica leave something to be desired," Pano quipped through the radio integrated into his face mask.

"In this cold, I wouldn't be standing around just for the sake of shaking hands either," Agatha replied, trying to shake off a growing queasiness. The place was like a ghost town. It looked like at these temperatures, life didn't happen outside the buildings. And she had never felt so far away from everything as here, at the edge of humanity.

"Agatha? There's someone there!" Pano suddenly shouted. Something in his voice made hot adrenaline shoot into her veins. She jerked to the side and saw her partner, who had turned around. She did the same, to see what he was looking at.

And everything went black.

Agatha stood up on the tarmac, groggy and confused. Next to her, Pano was already standing, looking at his hands, which he kept turning over and back, over and back again.

"What happened?" she asked.

"I don't know. We... just got off the plane."

"Yeah, and then I said I wouldn't be standing out here waving in the cold."

"And then?"

"What 'and then?'"

"I feel like I'm missing some key piece somewhere," he murmured over the radio while looking around.

Everything looked as it had before—the houses, the silos and water tanks, the bare, rocky mountain, the plane behind them. Except that there was no Eversman.

"Where's the sergeant?" she asked.

"He was standing right there," Pano said. They looked at each other for a moment before sprinting the hundred meters to the waiting transport plane, propellers still turning. They ran up the ramp, but found no trace of the sergeant inside, either.

"Weird," she said, and headed for the narrow cockpit door. It was unlocked. Agatha knocked a few times, heard no response, and pulled it open.

In the two seats in front of the bank of controls and instruments, the pilot and co-pilot sat in their thermal-lined gray uniforms, headset on their heads.

She raised her goggles and mask. "Hey, where's Sergeant Eversman? He's not here and we can't reach him by radio," she said out loud, but there was no response.

She reached out a hand and tapped the man on the left on his shoulder. Nothing.

"What's the matter?" Pano called from behind.

"No idea," she said under her breath, and moved forward to squeeze herself between them. Their eyes were closed. She quickly reached out a finger to feel for a pulse in the carotid artery, one guy and then the other. It was very slow, but firm, as if they were both just asleep.

"They're asleep!"

"What?" Pano came into the cockpit, raised his goggles and took off his ski mask. When he saw the pilots, his eyes bulged.

Agatha shook the man on the left, and then the man on the right, but couldn't rouse them no matter how hard she tried.

"They're just not waking up," she said. She slapped them both across their faces, which proved to be as ineffective as the shaking.

"It's like they're in a coma," Pano said, and looked around nervously. "What's going on here?"

"I don't know," Agatha admitted, and scanned the many knobs and readouts. "Any idea which one is the radio?"

"No. But we won't get anything on the radio anyway. Down here we need a satellite linkup."

"Well, any idea which of these thousand gizmos might be the satellite phone?"

"No," said Pano shaking his head.

"Dammit! Come on, let's go look around in the station. Maybe the Foundation people in there will be able to tell us more," she proposed, and they pulled down their ski goggles and snow masks.

Once back outside the plane, they stayed to the right and approached the first building that they saw, a red building with solar roof tiles. It looked dull and forlorn in the watery light of the sun that filtered through the low clouds.

A short staircase of three metal steps led up to the door, which was unlocked. Agatha shot Pano a surprised look and then opened it.

The first thing they noticed was that it was significantly warmer inside. The whole interior was one large area with wood-paneled walls and the Human Foundation logo emblazoned on the ceiling. The space was filled with office desks, most of them with multiple screens of various kinds on them, including the latest display films.

Agatha and Pano walked among the desks and looked at the screens. They were all active, showing graphs, data plots, diagrams, weather information, and e-mail programs. Agatha even found an ashtray stuffed with extinguished cigarette butts, and one still glowing and giving off a thin, pale wisp of smoke.

"Weird," she observed, and pointed out the still-burning cigarette to Pano.

"Hmm. Assuming this room isn't full of invisible people, someone just left the building."

"Yeah. Hold on..." Agatha took a step to the right and reached for an old-fashioned walkie-talkie she spied under a stack of paper. She pushed the send button and then said into the microphone, "This is Special Agent Agatha Devenworth of Homeland Security, CTD. Is anyone reading me?"

She lowered the walkie-talkie and listened to the static that was her only reply. She repeated the process on a few other frequencies, with the same result.

"Hmm. Well, let's try the next building," Pano proposed, and Agatha nodded. An unpleasant feeling suddenly arose in her, and she felt it move through her veins like mercury—slow, cold, and relentless.

They left the red building and went to the next one, which was a little longer and painted yellow. There was no response to their knock and this door was not locked either, so they entered and found themselves in living quarters, all with sheets rumpled as if they had been slept in. On the floor, they could make out traces of muddy boot-prints leading to the door.

One bed had a hand terminal on it next to the pillow. Agatha picked up the transparent device and swiped on it. It flashed to life immediately, and displayed a background image of a man and a woman grinning into the camera. Below them, the familiar unlock frame showing the date, time, and request for DNA authorization appeared.

"Pano," she said quietly, without noticing that she had called him by his first name. "What time did we land here?"

"Fifteen hundred hours local time. Why?" he asked, the tone of her voice making him curious, and he stepped over to her.

Wordlessly she raised the hand terminal so he could see it, and his eyes bulged. "That's impossible!" was his terse reply.

"I'm really hoping that for some reason this thing wasn't setting the time automatically over the data network, and whoever it belongs to set the clock wrong," she said, but what she was about to say next gave her goosebumps. "Because otherwise, this means that we somehow lost over six hours."

Pano just looked nervously at the hand terminal with his lips twitching slightly. "I'm suddenly getting a hardcore sinking feeling."

"Six hours? We can't possibly have... what even? *Jumped?* Six hours?" Agatha's head spun as she looked around the room, which suddenly seemed cramped and claustrophobic, as if the nondescript plain walls were closing in on her. Slowly and carefully, she opened her down jacket and drew her pistol.

Pano saw her and did the same. "I don't know what's going on, but something is very wrong here." He stooped to one of the low windows and looked outside. "Looks like it's slowly getting dark."

"Oh, great. And I understand when it gets dark here, it's dark for a long time, right?" she asked.

"I think that, or it's perpetually light. Actually, to be honest, I have no idea."

Together they left this building and searched the others. There was no one to be found anywhere. In the workshop, they found machinery still running amid work gloves and safety goggles seemingly abandoned in haphazard fashion, and thermal coffee cups with their contents still warm. At the garage for snowmobiles and hovercraft, they found the roller gate open and the vehicle hall empty, charging cables carelessly tossed to the floor and abandoned.

In a water treatment station, there were several protein packs in a microwave oven, which had been heated so long they had burst open. Moving to an office building, they found the smoke alarm going off because the charred remains of a stuffed animal were smoldering on a heater. Along the way they returned to the plane to check on the pilots, who still seemed comatose. Of course, some part of Agatha and Pano wanted to return to the plane just to check that their only means of getting out of there had not vanished.

After about two hours of searching, it was pitch dark and there was only one building left, the biggest, in the center of the complex. Standing in front of it, they could see the small harbor behind it where a large ship was moored.

They went inside. It was clearly the main building of the complex, and in it they found multiple workstations, two AR cabins, a number of AR suits, and many desks.

All the devices were online. Like everywhere else, they found plenty of signs of the crew's sudden disappearance: half-eaten sandwiches, lukewarm tea, open bags of snacks, a TV that was on, and programs running on all the screens.

"What the devil is all this? Where did everybody go?" Pano asked as he squeezed himself next to Agatha at one of the workstations.

"Damned if I know," she answered, and in her thoughts added, *and that scares me. For the first time in my life, I am genuinely afraid.*

"If Jackson and the students really came here, they must have had a reason," Pano said, putting on the data glasses in front of the display they were looking at. He began making invisible entries with his fingers. "Whatever it is, it will be on the station's hard drives."

"But definitely encrypted. With all the secrecy around this whole thing, don't be expecting them to have left a big red dot on a map." She turned and poked through the things on the desk in front of her. Apparently it belonged to a chain-smoker, because there was an ashtray overflowing with cigarette butts right in front of the display.

"Well, the good news is that I can connect my hand terminal here, you know, the one with the hacking AI," Pano replied, putting his hand terminal on the rectangular induction field on the desk. "We'll see what kind of encrypted data there is to find."

Meanwhile, Agatha had begun looking over some logistics logs she had found and was trying to make sense of the routes that the supply aircraft and ships had taken. It looked like transports arrived from Australia once a month, bringing fresh food, medical supplies, and personnel. At six-month intervals, Human Foundation ships also docked here in what used to be the Antarctic Ocean to conduct climate change studies. But according to the logs, none of them had unloaded any cargo, which Agatha immediately found suspicious. A ship had a dramatically greater cargo capacity than a plane, and she didn't think those hovercraft she had seen arrived by airmail.

"Questions, questions," she murmured, and went to the window to look at the ship. It looked like it had seen better days, and those days had probably been in early antiquity. She was about to turn away when she thought she spied a dark figure on the railing above the bridge. Startled, she rubbed her eyes and looked again, but saw nothing except the flagpole that had stood there before.

Pano had taken off his glasses and had turned to Agatha. "What is it?" he asked.

"Nothing. Just getting tired, I guess. How's your AI doing?"

"Working. This system's defenses are solid."

"You really think your program's going to beat the

Human Foundation firewalls?" Agatha asked, and her tone left no doubt as to what she expected its chances were.

"Yes. Europol always gets the latest algorithms from Deep Sec. Unless someone's flown in here within the last two weeks and run an update, this little guy here will get through," Pano said, patting his device with a hand.

"Well, I hope you're right." Agatha returned to her display and made another try at activating the satellite uplink on the display she was looking at. Once again, the uplink program returned an error code. Sighing, she checked the equipment lists on the current inventory. She was startled to find a reconnaissance drone that was supposed to be in the small hangar at the end of the tarmac. She jumped up and ran to one of the AR cabins.

"What are you doing over there?" Pano asked, curious.

"I found a drone. Maybe I can get her up from here and get a signal to the outside world," she answered, already standing on the multidirectional treadmill and putting on the AR glasses. Then she put on her gloves. Immediately, an unobtrusive menu appeared, which told her that she actually had several autonomous vehicles to choose from, including the reconnaissance drone.

Agatha established a connection and then opened the hangar door by remote command. Next, she instructed the drone to roll out and position itself on the runway. Searching the options on the autopilot, she selected Hobart as the destination, which was just barely within range. She looked for a way to save a message, but didn't find one. Evidently this drone was always flown by a pilot, so had neither an inbox nor a selectable file system that went beyond maintenance functions or the actual piloting software. There was only one element she could edit—the drone's device name. It didn't take her much thought to decide what to change it to—the Secretary of Defense's phone number. That, in combination with the data in the black box, would give whoever found the drone enough to go on.

Agatha activated the autopilot and pulled the AR glasses from her head.

At the same moment, Pano announced, "I'm in." He was pointing to the curved display in front of him.

"And?" she asked, tossing the AR gloves aside and moving behind him to look over his shoulder.

"As far as I can tell, there have been three research projects conducted here. One of them was called 'Blue Hole,' and was all about the phenomenon of the last ice floes around the South Pole melting from the center outwards, which started happening around the early 2000s. Then there was 'Project Globe,' that looks like the satellite system for the Human Foundation, and 'Project Heritage,'" Pano read off the display, and scratched his unshaven chin.

"Heritage? That sounds like something Jackson might be working on. What was that about?"

"I don't know. All the files about that are empty," Pano answered, throwing up his hands helplessly.

"What about those other two?"

"Well, there's a ton of documents about Blue Hole, everything from logistics logs to staffing schedules, budgets, everything. Same with Project Globe. It looks like that was about trying to figure out how to pull off the Solar Genesis thing."

"Solar Genesis?"

"Yes, something the Human Foundation has had on the drawing board for quite a few years now —building a series of huge solar collectors in high Earth orbit, using them to generate power and then transmit it to earth with microwave technology," Pano explained. "Don't you watch the Science Channel or anything?"

"I don't generally watch any television at all."

"Of course you don't," Pano said with a sigh and a smile. He took a breath and then pointed to a map of Antarctica on the display. The continent was easy to see, with its brown edges around the white center, and there, in the middle, the blue ocean. "Well, it's clear that they tested the microwave reception technology there."

"So Project Heritage is the only one that there's nothing about in the system?" Agatha asked, digging deeper.

"Yeah, that's right. Just a list of releases for the project marked with an internal priority of Rank A-1, whatever that may mean."

"Well, then that's our target. Where was that project happening?"

"No idea. I've got eight supply routes leading inland from McMurdo. Two of them end at the Project Globe operations sites and two more end at Blue Hole. It looks like the other four go nowhere," Pano explained. He stifled a yawn.

"Bring up the most recent satellite data. Let's go through the supply routes manually, and check them out from above to see what's on them," she proposed.

"That's going to take forever."

"You got a better idea?"

Pano declined to answer, and instead made some gestures in front of the display. The screens switched to a satellite image of Antarctica. Agatha thought back to her childhood, remembering a picture in her encyclopedia that showed Antarctica as an entire continent covered with gleaming white ice. The satellite image she was now seeing only confirmed how far climate change had progressed before the Human Foundation intervened with a tremendous technology push. Luther Karlhammer had blanketed the market with truly astonishing ideas and products, but it remained to be seen whether the damage that had already been done could ever be reversed—even though there was intensive research going on right now into technologies that might bring the Earth's temperature back to normal.

Pano zoomed in on McMurdo until they could see the cluster of forty solar rooftops reflecting the weak sunlight in the latest satellite image.

"Okay, let's start with route number one." He swiped left on the image on the display, gradually at first, and then with larger and larger gestures as it became clear the smaller ones were barely changing the view at all. After a quarter of an hour, Agatha's eyes closed heavily for the first time, and she woke with a start after having dozed for a few moments.

"I need coffee," she said, and Pano looked at her imploringly. She stood up, went to the coffee machine, and placed two clean cups from the shelf above onto the machine's dispensing platform. After a few seconds of grinding and humming noises, she had two steaming cups in her hand. She offered one to Pano while sipping from the other. She had hoped it would help, but not even the warm caffeinated liquid running down her throat could dispel the sense of dread, or the feeling that they might be the last human beings on earth—and that they were far beyond the reach of any civilization or rescue.

After another fifteen minutes had passed, Pano was about to make another swiping gesture—perhaps his hundredth—when Agatha grabbed his hand and held him back.

"Wait, what's that?" she asked, pointing to something that looked like an X in the whiteness of the ice.

"Huh. Looks like a marker," he replied, and moved his face closer to the image.

"Can we see this in 3D?"

"No. When this image was taken, the satellite was directly over that area. We only have a bird's-eye view."

"What the hell is this? What's the scale of this image?"

"Let me see. This right here is about five hundred meters," Pano said, identifying a distance on the screen by spanning it with his thumb and forefinger. "That would make the X about three kilometers on a side. Roughly uniform, but not entirely."

"So the thing in the image is symmetrical?"

"Close to it. It seems that it's also raised, because the distance between the satellite and the tip is almost three kilometers less than the distance to the ice crust," Pano said, and traced the edges of the structure with his fingers.

"Nature abhors symmetry," Agatha said, at which Pano turned to her with a frown.

"Huh?"

"That's something Dr. Jackson wrote in one of his books. I read it on the flight," she explained curtly. "Does that look like a pyramid from above to you?"

"Sure it does, but there are no pyramids in Antarctica."

"And what if there are?" she replied.

"Then," Pano replied, and thought for a moment, continuing after a pause, "our Canadian doctor would certainly be the first to go there and disappear, with a few students he had managed to enlist to his cause to come here and dig around with their hammers and chisels."

"Exactly," Agatha whispered. "How far away is that?"

"One hundred and ninety-nine kilometers."

"Then what we should do is load up one of the hovercrafts and get out there."

"But that thing," Pano said, pointing to the gray X in the endless white of the display, "still doesn't explain where the several hundred people operating this station suddenly disappeared to, and certainly doesn't explain the six hours that the clock says we skipped."

"No, it does not," she agreed. "But this mysterious Project Heritage might have some answers for us."

27

RON JACKSON, 2018

Ron stared at the silhouette, powerless, unable to lift even a finger. When he regained some strength, he exerted all his might to drag his body to the opposite wall and lay there, staring.

The piercing light behind the shadowy figure, still nothing but a black outline, began to get weaker and weaker, like the sun slowly going down behind the horizon.

Please no. No! No, no, no, don't go out, he begged in his thoughts, and felt silent tears running down his cheeks. The light had hit him like a final glimmer of hope that might give him back a flash of sanity, a little control of his mind. Losing the light again was the worst thing he could imagine at that moment.

But the light stopped dimming at a low but visible level. It still shimmered in a bluish, artificial-looking color, enveloping the silhouette like a spectral wool blanket. Even in the fog of his mental state there was no mistaking that this was an artificial light source. There was, of course, the possibility that sunlight might be entering from outside through tiny shafts, as happened in the pyramids of Giza, but this light was far too intense to be that. And what he was looking at was blue-white light, in a form not found in nature.

Ron reached for his tablet and withdrew it from his bag, just as he remembered that the battery had long since died. He shook it in frustration, but the screen remained as dark as the walls around him.

Without taking his eyes off the figure, he crawled a little closer, like an insect drawn to a lamp. He didn't know if this light source was hot. It might be so hot that it would burn him to a crisp, but right now it looked like the only sign of life left in the room. His breathing was heavy, and the elevated oxygen content was ripping through his brain, but he struggled closer on his hands and knees, even though everything in him was screaming to run the other way. There was something here that wasn't right, that wasn't acting the way the world he knew should be functioning.

It was also a crazy thought.

All my life I've been trying to convince people to open their eyes to the possibilities they couldn't see, because they didn't dare to dream them, he thought. He could still recall the many long arguments he'd had with his fellow students during their studies, about the current state of science. Ron had always held the view that so many scientists limit their research horizon because they can't accept the possibility that something might function beyond the bounds of currently accepted laws. Anthroposophists and archaeologists around the world simply rejected the possibility that the history of the Earth might be very different than they assumed, even given that so much of it was still a mystery. Now, faced with the possible proof that he had been right all along, he could hardly believe it.

And no one will ever know I was right, he mourned

inwardly. *There's a technology in this pyramid that can generate artificial light. And there's a figure. A figure... what figure? Am I hallucinating because of the changed air composition?*

When he had crawled one or two steps forward—in the weird light and in his current state, it was hard to tell exactly how far—he looked up like a homeless beggar at a passer-by, and forced himself to look straight into the light despite the throbbing pain behind his eyeballs.

My pupils just need to adapt to the conditions, he said to himself through the viscous, toxic molasses into which his brain cells had transformed under the oxygen's relentless assault. By the time his eyes were registering images again, what he saw would have sent him running away screaming if his arms and legs had still been responding.

The silhouette he had thought he had seen was in reality not a figure, but a painting of a skeleton on a standing sarcophagus. The lid was illuminated, and it was embedded so precisely that its outline in the floor, walls, and ceiling was absolutely seamless. The painting of the skeleton was unnaturally large, and the gaze of the empty eye sockets had something unnerving about them, as if there was life behind them. Which, of course, couldn't have been possible.

Even though it was only painted there, the sight of the skeleton had a morbid quality about it that terrified Ron. He had never in his life been so closely confronted with his own death. Now, looking death in the eye, it hit him that everything he had done with his life so far had been a waste. So much was clear to him now. If everything was leading up to this final moment anyway, this moment when nothing you had done, experienced, or felt mattered at all, why was a human life so wrapped up in human travails and concerns? Just a few days ago he would have dismissed these thoughts as the bitter ravings of an angry old man, but at this moment it was entirely clear to him. In the face of death, nothing mattered except life and the realization that nothing else mattered.

Unwillingly, his thoughts wandered to Rachel, who had begged him more than once not to make this journey. Of course, she had been horrified at the thought that he would be gone for a few months again, so soon, and that she would have to keep so many secrets, but the last time was still fresh in her memory, when he had fallen into a crack in the earth and been trapped for a whole day. She had made him promise that he would never put himself in such danger again, and he had made that promise gladly. And he had meant it, he hadn't said it just to put her off. She was the love of his life, and had been since they had met in high school.

Fucking high school, he thought lamely. *It feels so far away, it's like I'm thinking of a past life.*

Now he would die, breaking his promise to her, and without her ever even knowing how or why he died—not even where. Rachel, the only person who had ever really cared about him, would never know that he had died trying to prove his theories. It was a tragedy, plain and simple, and his tears did not even begin to express the real grief that was wracking him at that moment.

I'm sorry, he thought, Rachel's image in his heart. She was smiling at him in that special way of hers, laughing at him, and yet giving him the most loving look with that little shake of her head.

Death was very close now, he could feel it like a tingling touch on his skin, a gnawing weakness in his limbs and in his mind, which began to wander more and more as his head became lighter and lighter. He knew it would be a relief to be freed of this unbearable pain, and he was almost ready.

"But not like this," he whispered hoarsely, gritting his teeth and putting his last strength into standing on his feet. His knees buckled and he almost lost his footing more than once, but in the end he managed to stand up and raise his chin. Something inside told him it was ridiculous to want to die with his head held high, like a hero in a movie putting all his remaining strength into one last, heroic act, but it somehow felt right. Ron looked the painted skull straight in its empty eye sockets and prepared to accept the sweet caress of death.

When the lid of the sarcophagus suddenly popped open, he was so close that he felt the air move. He would have fallen to the floor in shock if he had still possessed any control of his limbs.

Just as suddenly as the light had appeared, the scene changed. He was now looking into an open sarcophagus, and there was a person inside it staring back at him.

No, not a person, he corrected himself in his thoughts, staring at the giant figure in disbelief. The figure faced him like a statue. It was at least two-and-a-half meters tall, with long arms that were slightly disproportionate to its frame, and completely naked. Its limbs were covered in knots of muscles, and its skin shimmered in strangely caramel hues. Its face was also disproportionately long, and its eyes were completely black, with no visible iris or pupil. They radiated something deep and menacing. Looking at them, Ron felt the urge to submit to the creature's will immediately, even though there was no sign of life in it. The giant was completely hairless, and his nose was also noticeably longer than a human's would have been.

He couldn't shake the feeling that he had suddenly shrunk, like a comet that had flown too close to the sun and was now slowly burning away.

Like a mortal standing before a god.

Ron took a careful step forward, and fell as his overly weak legs gave out under him. He would have bashed his face on the floor of the chamber, but something caught him.

As he struggled to raise his eyes, he saw two imposing feet before his face, attached to muscular calves and broad thighs. Then he was being lifted by his right arm, and was suddenly staring into the pitch-black, almond-shaped eyes of the god, who had stepped out of the sarcophagus. Behind him, a mist flowed from the interior and a chemical smell filled the room.

Ron had not even noticed that the god had walked out of the sarcophagus.

The being then roared, "ADANNU?" in a bass voice so full, and so loud, that it made Ron want to simply scream.

When Ron gave no response, the god paused for a moment, tilting its head, and then fixed the black opals that were its eyes on him again. "ADANNU?"

"Adannu?" Ron repeated, panting. "Sumerian. Yes, that's Sumerian."

He thought feverishly, mustering all of the strength left in his moribund body to keep his eyes open, looking back into the god's face.

Sumerian, he speaks Sumerian. Of course. The last time he had contact with humans was at the time of the Old Sumerian civilization, Ron thought, and when the realization hit him he almost passed out. The thought of standing before a being who might be millions of years old, the ancient ancestor of his own race, an extraterrestrial, or maybe even a real god, was not something he could fit in his head. It was just too much, too much to get his mind around.

"ADANNU?"

"Time! Yes, yes, *time*. ADANNU means 'time.' It, ah... what time? It's 2018."

The god's mighty head bobbed briefly and he looked around before returning his gaze to Ron.

"You don't understand me," Ron thought out loud, trembling, and pulled out his notebook. He scribbled hastily, nearly dropping his pencil twice as he wrote down the number sixty-six million, and then added a cartoonish dinosaur next to it for good measure.

"GALA NABU."

"Gala nabu," Ron repeated thoughtfully, forcing the cotton wool in his head to act like a brain again. "Priest... Prophet... No! Oh, LA! Scientist, I'm a scientist. But there was no such thing back then, of course."

When the god, who looked somehow human despite the strangeness of his features, simply stared in reply, Ron licked his lips and continued, stammering, "LAMADU MEI. I'm a scholar. KIMAH? Is this your grave?"

With his free hand, the one not in the being's iron grip, he pointed to the sarcophagus. The being's touch on Ron's forearm felt like he had stuck his hand in an electrical socket, and the surface of the palm was surprisingly warm, even though he was already sweating in the heat of the room. It was only then he noticed that the hand that the being was using to hold Ron off the floor, which was so huge that it nearly enclosed Ron's entire forearm, had five fingers.

"LA KIMAH," the being replied in the thundering voice that shook Ron to his core. "EUNIR!"

"Eunir? I don't know that word. I..."

The alien look in the eyes of this being, who might well be one of the Builders that Ron had spent his entire career trying to convince the world had existed, was overwhelming, and dangling like a marionette in its powerful grip around his right arm, Ron had lost all feeling in his limbs. In the gaze of this powerful presence, he felt like a fragile butterfly. Just trying to imagine the age of the being looking at him through the impenetrable blackness of those eyes hit him with a crushing sense of his own insignificance.

"PETA BABKAMA LURUBA ANAKU," the giant bellowed, now casually lifting Ron higher by his arm until they were looking eye-to-eye. The grip around his arm had not tightened, but Ron felt that the other's patience was not infinite.

"What does that mean?" Ron whimpered. "I don't understand."

"PETA BABKAMA LURUBA ANAKU!" the ancient face repeated. The skin was smooth and poreless, like freshly oiled marble, but it was the eyes that projected an age and a depth that left Ron dumbstruck. He wanted to say something, but could not make a single word escape his trembling lips.

PETA means open, he thought, but the rest meant nothing to him. He had never been an expert in Sumerian, and what he did know was rusty at best, but he could not escape the impression that what this being was speaking was actually protoSumerian—an extremely simple language from a modern perspective. Trying to speak it was like using hand-held wedges to create a pictogram that had to serve as a meaningful, comprehensible image.

Here I am, at the most important moment of my life, and I just can't find the words, he thought, crushed, and his eyelids began to flutter. He almost lost consciousness, and although the feeling passed quickly, he was getting weaker by the minute. What he really wanted to do was shout at the top of his lungs, cursing the fate that brought him to the goal of his whole life up to now, the vindication of all his activities of

The Fossil

the last several decades, at the moment he was robbed of all his faculties—the great injustice of reaching the finish line and not being able to do anything.

"Ana simtim alaku," Ron blurted out, choking, because nothing else came to him. "I go now to meet my fate. My doom." With his left hand he pointed to his solar plexus, the place that the ancient Sumerians thought was the source of death. "Ana simtim alaku!"

The god now raised his other hand to take Ron's left arm. His powerful grip made Ron's arm feel as fragile as a rotten twig. Then he looked Ron up and down, finally staring penetratingly into his eyes. It was as if he was being pierced by a thousand stares at the same time, each one sucking out Ron's soul, piece by piece.

"Sak antu dabam, I've been looking for you," Ron managed to croak. Again the being paused, tilting its head in an all-too-human gesture.

"PETA BABKAMA LURUBA ANAKU," it repeated, and something in the infinite blackness of its eyes changed.

The god then turned his gaze away, seemingly looking around the room, while he shifted his grip to hold Ron under his chin, keeping him in the air in front of him with a playful lightness.

He raised his now-free giant hand to point to something. Out of the corner of his eye, Ron suddenly saw something floating in the air next to them. It was his tablet. It emitted a long, high-pitched beep before exploding into pieces, leaving its components floating in the air like a cloud in the dim light. The parts hung there, spinning slightly, until the being lowered his hand and it all tumbled to the floor in a clattering downpour of plastic and metal.

"IMBARATU!"

"Imbaratu?" Ron repeated. "That means... Surprise,

right? Yes, surprise. You haven't encountered humans with technology before."

The god studied him for a while, and Ron couldn't shake the feeling that a lot more was going on in this moment than he could see.

"PETA BABKAMA LURUBA ANAKU."

"You want something from me, but I can't understand you, and I'm dying. I'm sorry. I can hardly... can... hardly... hardly speak anymore."

"ADARU LA, PETA!" the penetrating bass voice sounded again as it rang from the being's pitch-black lips, rattling Ron's body as if a tremendous gong had struck. The being's breath had no odor at all, except perhaps a slight note of spices, something like cloves.

"ADARU LA, have no fear," Ron translated out loud for himself. Those words he understood. But PETA? "PETA means 'open.' The opening. Have no fear of the opening? What opening?"

The god tilted his head to one side and blinked, much to Ron's surprise with some kind of inner eyelid that flashed out from under the smooth outer eyelids and then disappeared again as quickly as they had appeared. There was something in the god's look now that passed straight through Ron like some kind of cold radiation, and the voice of this ancient being, this miracle that in the eyes of humanity simply could not exist, became ever so slightly quieter.

"ADARU LA, PETA. PUHRUM."

"Puhrum? Meeting? Yes, we are meeting." He could hardly get these words out of his mouth. He knew his last breath was near.

I never expected that you'd understand it right at the end.

"ADARU LA! PETA, PETA, PETA," the god said, in a new

tone of voice that Ron interpreted as being comforting, something like you would use on a house pet you had just brought to the vet for the last time. An odd last thought to have.

"PETA," Ron repeated with the last of his strength. As the caress of death finally enveloped Ron, the god's hands grasped him around the head and he felt something liquid forcing its way into his mouth. Something was being stolen from him in this last moment, something that he had never even known he'd had the whole time. It was gone before he could even try to understand what it was.

A heartbeat later, Ron's last, it no longer mattered.

28

FILIO AMOROSA, 2042

The entire last week before the launch of *Mars Two*, Filio hardly slept a wink. Seven days beforehand, she and the rest of the crew had been flown to Cape Canaveral.

Her days consisted of up to twelve hours of simulations. In the evenings, when the other team members had family visits, she immersed herself in her work, which she didn't mind because there was no one to visit her anyway. That work began with memorizing the changes made in the mission protocols since *Mars One*, with a particular focus on emergency routines. After that came three or four hours of sleep, before waking up to cram on specifications and updates to the ship before the next round of simulations began.

She harbored no illusions. Even though she had a lot of experience, and having already been on a Mars mission gave her a considerable edge, jumping in two weeks before the launch after having been out of it for two years proved to be extremely ambitious, even by the standards to which she held herself.

The atmosphere between her and the others had gotten

a bit better, but was still quite cold. They had felt some level of sympathy for the painful path that had brought her here, but that sympathy was starting to collide with sympathy for Nicole, and that was causing a conflict. Where the lines blurred, the fact that her predecessor had spent much more time with this crew tended to prevail, which meant that Filio still had to fight an uphill battle. But there had been a start, and things were getting better.

The new situation gave her all the more reason to focus her time as intensively as possible. She was always the first to arrive and the last to leave. She helped out everywhere she could, and always made herself available for just about anything.

She continued to scrutinize the mission commands down to the last detail, right up to the day before the launch, looking at every possible nuance and every special clause. A couple of the others had tried to persuade her to attend the farewell party that was being held at the nearby Air Force base, but that was the last thing she intended to do. For one thing, it hit her hard to see that the others all had someone who would miss them. Secondly, she knew that this would put her in contact with the news media, and whether that proved to be a good thing or a bad thing, she didn't want it.

Ever since her arrival, she had been receiving a steady stream of press inquiries in her e-mail—hundreds of them, asking for interviews and statements, always quite friendly at first and then increasingly insistent. Obviously, her participation in the mission had made a lot of waves, and it was clear that the media was covering this whole project a lot more intensely than they had covered the first Mars mission.

Hue, the Chinese team member, was continually telling her about the near-daily broadcasts about the mission, its impending launch, and its importance. Even Luther Karl-

The Fossil

hammer, probably the most in-demand celebrity on the planet, and basically a self-confessed space skeptic, had apparently been increasingly outspoken about the project. It seemed that he saw it as emphasizing an international dimension, with competing superpowers and blocs pulling together rather than competing against each other as they had in the past.

For Filio, this extensive coverage was an unwanted distraction from what she wanted to concentrate on—the mission—and did nothing but put her under even more pressure.

Of course, the day came when none of it mattered anymore. Early in the morning, she was awakened by the alarm on her hand terminal. The ascending triad ringtone was an assault on her ears, and for a moment she was completely disoriented, not knowing where she was or what day it was.

Looking at the display, which turned the transparent terminal into a black surface showing the time and date, fully jolted her from her restless sleep. *Launch day!* she realized. *Scheduled for fifteen hundred hours...* She swung her legs out of bed and focused on her hand terminal.

"Weather report," she ordered, and the display instantly showed current weather information. Slight southwesterly wind, up to six kilometers per hour. Clear skies across all of central Florida.

In short, perfect launch weather.

Standing in front of the bathroom mirror, brushing her teeth while staring suspiciously at the dark rings under her eyes, she rolled her shoulders backward and forward. Her back and neck were so tense and knotted from brooding over her display foil for so long that she needed pain pills to get any sleep at all.

After brushing her teeth, she ran to the canteen and forced a sandwich, two bananas, and an espresso down her throat, against her own will. She had just put her cleaned cup away when the others came in.

They greeted each other curtly, then all took their trays to the table and began eating in silence. The tension in the room was almost physically palpable. Filio knew only too well what was going on in all their heads at this moment, as they stared at their food, making as little noise as possible. They were thinking of their family and friends, everything they would be leaving behind, and wondering what awaited them. They were thinking of the rocket launch and the fact that they would be propelled through the atmosphere on top of a giant explosion. They were thinking of the docking maneuver in orbit, when they would connect their ship, once separated from the boosters and rocket stages, to the drive section that had been built in space. And then the four-month journey, during which so much could go wrong that even the nine hundred emergency scenarios in the protocols might not cover everything.

These were dimensions, parameters, figures that the human mind could not conceive of, so you abstracted. But that quickly became exhausting, because you had to constantly steer your thoughts into rational directions and convince yourself of so many things.

Filio had done all this three years ago. But for her, today was different. She was excited, yes, but in her case it was the excitement of finally shedding light on her past and the failed *Mars One* mission. She had never been closer to solving the mystery of the disaster that had become her life than right now. But rather than being excited or scared, she was simply anxious. She could not wait to finally have Martian soil under her feet again and understand what happened. She *knew* that she belonged there. At last, nothing would stand between her and learning the truth.

After breakfast they put on their pressure suits, which were designed to protect them against the extreme G-forces at takeoff. They were orange, just like the suits of the Apollo missions, only much less bulky and wide. A whole legion of assistants and technicians tested every single seal and the fit of each astronaut's suit before releasing them to watch the final launch preparations in the waiting room. The weather was still stable, with no indications of any imminent change.

Three hours before the scheduled liftoff, they were brought to the electric personnel carrier that was waiting in front of Mission Control. The distance from the glass doors, opened for them by soldiers, to the black vehicle with its dark windows was precisely one hundred meters. Their path was marked off on both sides by barriers and security personnel, behind which hundreds of news crews swarmed, waiting to greet them with a flurry of camera flashes the moment the door opened and the astronauts stepped out into the swampy heat of eastern Florida.

"Just smile," Longchamps shouted over the already-deafening clicking of cameras and yelling of the reporters drowning each other out with their shouts.

Filio, at the end of the small group of orange-clad astronauts, forced the corners of her mouth upwards, but she didn't wave, in contrast to some of her teammates who did not seem particularly averse to fame.

The hundred meters were extremely loud, tiring on her ears and eyes, and the walk seemed to take much longer than she thought a hundred meters should take.

"Doctor Amorosa!" most of them shouted as she passed, although virtually everything else was lost in the cacophony of screaming. Every so often she picked out a single question.

"Amorosa! Are you fit to fly?"

"Have you overcome your trauma, Doctor?"

"How did you get yourself on this mission?"

"Where have you been all this time?"

"Who was responsible for your deployment?"

"What is your response to the allegations against you?"

Filio swallowed hard and forced herself to look straight ahead. When at last she was able to climb into the personnel vehicle and disappear, she let out a great sigh of relief.

"Well, we made it through the hardest part for today," Longchamps announced with a grin, and the others giggled politely. But it was clear from the sound that their laughter was not really at the captain's joke. Rather, it was an outlet for the extreme nerves they all felt.

The drive to Launch Pad 1 took them past Launch Pads 2 and 3 and past an Air Force hangar.

Finally, *Mars Two* came into view and Filio felt like she was in a dream. It looked exactly like *Mars One*. The few minor improvements that had been made based on the black box data were virtually invisible.

There she stood, *Mars Two,* upright on the launch pad, cradled by the spider-like scaffolding of the tower next to the ship. Her slender bow towered one hundred and sixty-six meters above the launch pad. From their position down here, the windows looked minuscule. The top stage, with its interplanetary engines, was firmly connected to the second stage. What was essentially the main craft stood at the very top. It contained nine hundred square meters of pressurized cabin space with twenty rooms. Below these two, the smooth first stage, which was driven by thirty-four Rexum engines, made up half the length. Loaded up with enough methane-oxygen mixture to fill up a small lake, those engines were designed to deliver 7,300 tons of thrust to put the entire 5,000-ton hulk into orbit. It was another one of those dimensions of this miracle of human engineering that made the head spin.

"Isn't she a beautiful baby," Marcello asked in his lilting South American accent.

"Mm-hmm, that she is," Longchamps answered him, and they all stared out the side window as if they were seeing *Mars Two* for the first time. "She looks... sleek."

"Yes, except that she's not going to be flying nose-first," Audrey remarked, pointing towards *Mars Two* extending into the sky like a monolith, looming ever larger as they approached. "The whole flight, the nose will be facing the sun, not Mars, so the solar radiation doesn't heat up the supercooled fuel."

"I love space, where everything works just a little differently," James, the American geophysicist quipped.

"I love space because we're going to be far away from the earth," Audrey said. "Did you hear what happened the day before yesterday? The attack on Senator Brown?" She shook her head.

"Yeah, it's shocking..."

Filio was no longer listening to them. Instead, she was focusing on a flock of birds off in the distance, silhouetted against the sky. They must have been large migratory birds on their way to their summer habitat, passing along the coastline where, a few kilometers away, more than forty thousand spectators were sitting on grandstands waiting to watch the launch, as people had done since the moon missions.

"I hope they won't delay our launch." Filio had spoken her thought out loud. All eyes turned to her.

"Who?" asked Longchamps, and Filio pointed west towards the grandstands where the crowd could be seen as indistinct spots of color, a vast vague mass along the coast.

"Those migrating birds."

"It's not the time of year for migrating birds," Marcello objected, and at the same instant Filio noticed that the flock was not flying in a natural formation, looking instead more like a big swarm that was getting bigger.

"Those aren't birds," Longchamps said in alarm just as the howl of sirens sounded outside. They reminded Filio of the air raid sirens they used to test once a month in the town she grew up in.

Suddenly their vehicle stopped and moved back. The rest of the team began to shout excitedly as Filio continued to stare out the window. From somewhere, rockets were shooting into the sky, first a few, and then dozens, heading straight to the swarm of drones and leaving trails of smoke in their wakes. Through the open windows, she thought she could hear distant screaming, rising and falling like the waves of the ocean.

The dark objects, each only slightly larger than a large bird, had come a few kilometers closer, when explosions began blooming among them, turning many into columns of smoke falling from the sky.

"Drones! They're goddamn drones!" Putram shouted. Like the others, he had left his seat and was glued to the vehicle's sloping windows. He was wild-eyed and sweating.

"Oh, God!" someone cried. It was Audrey, as she sank back into her bucket seat. "It must be the Sons of Terra!"

Filio only watched, amazed, as fighter jets scrambled behind them to support the squadron that was already patrolling the airspace. They must have already been in the middle of their interception maneuvers, because more and more explosions were rending the sky and picking off the drones.

As far as the team could see from their vantage point, they were just normal rotor drones, the same that parcel services used or any private individual could buy. They continued to swarm and drew slowly but steadily closer.

On the patches of lawn about a kilometer away from the launching pad, soldiers were springing out of speedily arriving troop transports and jumping into crouching positions before opening fire. It was all happening so fast that Filio felt like she was in a nightmare.

She didn't know what she was seeing as she watched some soldiers in the long lines suddenly stand up, raise their arms, and simply explode, killing their nearest comrades. At that point absolute chaos broke out. The soldiers who remained then spread out and began firing at each other as more drones in the sky above were brought down, explosions crackling in the air as they fell.

"They're going after the rocket," she whispered pointlessly. No one could hear her over the panic-stricken screams.

What happened next, Filio saw as though it occurred in slow motion. At a height of about fifty meters, a single drone flew almost casually through the dying wisps of an explosion. To its left and right, ground-based artillery that Filio could not see brought down its comrades. But this one particular drone weaved right and then dove left before reaching the steam cloud coming from the vents of the cryogenic boosters for the oxygen and hydrogen tanks as the supercooled fuel boiled off from the heat.

Despite the ear-splitting sirens accompanying the apocalyptic fireworks show like a kind of doomsday soundtrack, everything happened oddly quietly, almost hesitantly, when the drone destroyed itself. The explosion blew a small hole in the outer shell of the first stage, which was enough to ignite the fuel.

In an inverse cascade of fire, *Mars Two* exploded from bottom to top, and the whole world seemed to be engulfed in flames. The entire horizon lit up in a red-gold hue, and every window of their transport shattered in the same instant. It was safety glass, but tiny shards still drilled into Filio's face, and she screamed in agony. The wave of heat was so overwhelming that she felt like her skin was boiling away and falling off her bones.

A second later, or perhaps it had been an eternity, she found herself on the floor between the rows of seats, propping herself up on her bleeding hands. The loudest sound in her ears was her own pulse, and then, distantly, she heard cries of anguish and screams of pain.

She saw, as if watching through hazy glass, the side door of the vehicle being thrown open, and a soldier with gun drawn jumped in. "Which one of you is it?" he screamed, eyes wide and lips trembling. "Who is it?"

No one answered, and Filio saw that most of the team was either dead or seriously injured anyway.

Then the soldier started shooting. She could only watch as he shot Longchamps in the head, even as he was lying across his chair and holding up his hands defensively, pleading. He then did the same to Audrey, who seemed to be unconscious.

Marcello, who was lying on the floor just like Filio, tried to crawl to the door when the soldier saw him and shot him through the neck with absolute precision and not a hint of hesitation.

Then, suddenly, more shots rang out, and the killer flinched, spasmed, spat blood and finally fell to the floor.

Filio was barely conscious, but was aware of more uniformed men storming in, pulling her out of the vehicle and placing her on a stretcher. The next thing she saw was a woman's face hovering above her, asking questions.

"Yes, I can breathe," she managed to stammer after a coughing fit.

"Name and date of birth?" came the woman's next question. She seemed distraught, and the whole stretcher was bouncing, as if they were moving very fast. Suddenly she was in an ambulance.

"Doctor Filio Amorosa, born March 4, 2001." Her reply was almost a whisper. "I'm thirsty. What happened?"

"You've been injured, Doctor, but not severely. I'm going to give you something for the pain now, and then I'm coming right back. Do you understand?"

"Yes... I... what happened?" she asked again. And again, and again, "What happened?" but no one seemed to be listening to her.

But she knew. She knew what had happened, and when it came to her, silent tears ran down her temples to her ears, and silent sobs wracked her body.

29

AGATHA DEVENWORTH, 2042

Agatha and Pano left the control room in the heart of McMurdo Station with pistols drawn and flashlights on. They'd been lucky enough to find a few compatible replacement batteries. The entire complex was bathed in an eerie light that struggled to drive away the darkness with dull beams that disappeared in the spaces between the buildings as if they'd been swallowed by hungry snakes. The darkness here was blacker and more absolute than any darkness Agatha had ever seen, and it was made all the blacker by the low-hanging cloud-cover that wasn't letting even a single moonbeam through.

"Are we taking a hovercraft or a snowcat?" Pano asked quietly, as if speaking at full volume might awaken the ghosts of this place that had seemed to be descending around them since their arrival.

"I don't know," she replied in just as low a voice, scanning the small islands of brightness between the buildings.

Out here, even the light seemed like a dead thing.

Where the hell is everybody? Agatha wasn't much for old-time TV, but she knew her classics, and she felt like she was in the creepiest X-Files episode ever. And she didn't like it one bit. She had seen her share of real-life violent crime scenes, with dismembered victims, strangled women, men who had lost a fight and had their intestines hanging out to show for it. Her job had required her to watch countless videos of terrorists beheading their hostages. But despite all she had seen, she had always slept securely because she knew that the probability of being killed in a violent crime was about the same as dying in a plane crash. She knew too much about statistics, and was too rational, to think anything else. But that was only because the world was predictable, and she could perceive the world as a system of cause and effect, governed by unbreakable laws.

But what she had experienced here had broken all the laws. The whole personnel contingent of an entire base had vanished in the blink of an eye, and either every clock had gone crazy or she and her partner had been comatose for over six hours. All in all, Agatha didn't even know what to be freaked out about anymore.

"Let's take the hovercraft," Pano proposed. "It should have the most range, and the route didn't look particularly rocky or uneven on the satellite image. And we should take some supplies."

They exchanged brief glances and then turned back to study the shadows between the buildings. Agatha knew right away that he would have preferred to split up to save time, and appreciated that he had rejected the idea. She had to admit to herself that she didn't want to be alone in this place for even a second, but couldn't admit it to him. Up to now, being alone was the only thing she had ever wanted. But right now, she wondered how this all would have played out if she had stuck to her guns with Miller and taken on this case alone.

Now they were moving stealthily between a water treatment system and a long building full of workshops. With their flashlights held atop their guns, they made sure to illuminate every dark corner along their way.

If she had been watching this as an outsider, she would have called herself crazy, gun drawn, hunting shadows out here at the literal end of the earth. But she wasn't an outsider.

"They were out there in front of the hangar, weren't they?" Pano whispered.

"Yeah," she whispered back, her words swallowed by the all-encompassing silence. Suddenly, every breath seemed as loud as the peal of a church bell. "We can swing by the plane on the way. There must be some rations on board."

"Good idea."

Ducking behind a small building containing living quarters, they turned onto the wide gravel path, which after about a hundred meters transitioned into the tarmac. Looming in the darkness in front of them was the slightly less dark silhouette of the triangular-looking mountain, threatening and powerful, and to the left of it their military transport with its cabin lights shooting a long corridor of yellow light onto the runway.

It would have been an inviting sight if she hadn't known that the two pilots were in there, in a mysterious coma-like state for which she had no explanation. And where was Sergeant Eversman?

Reaching the runway, they picked up their pace. It took all of Agatha's willpower to not let the adrenaline take over. She just couldn't shake the unpleasant feeling that she was being watched and followed. It was as if the darkness had eyes, tracking their every step from a thousand angles.

When her boots hit the ramp, Agatha turned and swept

the lighted area behind the plane with her flashlight and gun. Nothing.

Together she and Pano searched the compartments on the walls. Pano was right, there were about twenty packages of field rations, labeled 'U.S. NAVY.' They stuffed them in the crate that Eversman had brought their snowsuits in, maintaining complete silence, masked by the noise of the propellers that continued to spin in mournful circles.

"We should check on the pilots one more time," she suggested as they stood on the ramp, ready to leave the plane again. Setting the crate down, they turned around and entered the cockpit together. Both pilots were still there, in a deep, hard sleep. They simply could not be awakened.

"You weren't by any chance a doctor, were you?"

"Worse. A lawyer," Pano chuckled, but his eyes and mouth betrayed the tension that was affecting him, too.

"Okay then, let's go. Pulse is stable and strong for both of them, so they don't seem to be in any acute danger."

"And we can't do anything for them anyway," Pano agreed. After a moment's silence they turned and headed back out. When they reached the ramp, they bent at the knees to lift the crate with the food supplies and then headed towards the opposite side of the runway where the two hovercraft were.

"What do you think happened here?" Pano asked as soon they had stepped out of the patch of light coming from their plane.

"I have absolutely no clue," she confessed, and the admission sent a cold chill down her back.

"That doesn't happen to you very often, does it?"

At first Agatha thought it was another one of his barbs directed at her, but in his face she saw nothing but concern.

"No. I'm an expert on international terrorism, not X-Files. This here is... It's just not right."

"I feel it too," Pano agreed in a hoarse voice, looking left and right into the darkness on either side of the narrow cones of light coming from their flashlights. "Everything here just feels... wrong."

"I'd be lying if I said I didn't want to get out of here just as quick as possible."

"Are you sure that this area on the satellite image is the better option?"

"I'm not sure of anything anymore, not since we got here," she replied grimly.

Followed by the oppressive darkness, and a silence that was only broken occasionally by a gentle crash of surf coming from the harbor area, they hurried across the tarmac with the crate until finally the two hovercraft appeared within the beams of their flashlights. As they passed, the shadows they cast on the locked hangar door behind them danced to the beat of their footsteps, like delicate insects. Then they swelled, rose, and shot away to hide behind the bulbous vehicles with their fragile-looking sensor arrays.

Agatha pointed to the one on the left and they deposited the crate there. Pano then hastened to the driver's door, which, like every other door on McMurdo, was unlocked.

"What does the battery read?" she called as loudly as she dared, scanning around the area with her flashlight, piercing the darkness like a lighthouse.

"Eighty percent," came the answer from inside.

She looked over her shoulder as Pano activated the array of spotlights above the narrow windshield, and half the tarmac was immediately bathed in a frenzied flurry of photons.

"I'm going to look around the hangar to see if there's any extra batteries that we can..." she started to say, but the moment she moved to circumnavigate the hovercraft's bus-length diameter, she cut herself off.

There, less than two meters away from her, was Sergeant Eversman, staring at her with an empty look on his face and his assault rifle pointing at the ground. Agatha stopped in her tracks as if rooted to the spot, and observed the soldier. In the beam of her flashlight, his face looked like a glowing wax mask.

"Sergeant?" she said, her voice cautious and her expression skeptical. "Where were you? Is everything okay?"

Eversman looked at her for a moment with that vacant expression, until it seemed that a veil fell from him and he nodded. "Yes, ma'am. I..." He looked around, chewing his lips, which were chapped from exposure. "I don't know what's going on here. I was standing on the ramp and then all of a sudden I was in one of the buildings. When I went back to the plane, I found Lockwell and Marks asleep."

"Lockwell and Marks? Those are the two pilots?"

"Yes, ma'am. I couldn't wake either one of them up. Believe me, I tried. Then I tried to make contact by satellite, but only got an error message. And there doesn't seem to be anyone in radio range."

They were still standing at the same distance from each other, barely two meters apart. They hadn't moved—and they stayed put even when Pano came out of the door above them. "Well, then, where were you?" Agatha asked.

"Eversman," Pano said, surprised.

"Hello there, Capitano. Good that you're here. I was beginning to think that I... that I..."

"That you were all alone?" Pano finished for him. "Us, too, my friend. Good to see you."

The Fossil

"Thank you. Any idea what the hell is going on here?"

"There's nobody left here," Agatha said simply, nodding towards the lights of the station to their right. "Looks like they were all here one moment, and then just gone the next."

"Or fled," Pano added.

"Or maybe fled. But then where did everybody go? The ship's still moored at the jetty, and there were no planes here. And the airstrip is too small for a plane that could carry that many people anyway. And out there," she said, pointing off into the darkness on the other side of the tarmac, "there's just nothing."

"At least nothing within walking distance," Pano agreed.

"They got to be somewhere!" Eversman's voice was suddenly penetrating and forceful, which surprised Agatha. Back in Namibia and during their flight he had come across to her as more of a casual soldier, just doing a job and following orders. But now, suddenly he sounded not only engaged, but insistent. His tone of voice reminded her of Miller when he began one of his infamous interrogations of employees who were under the wings of one of his political rivals.

Probably just like me—when you lose six hours of your life, something changes in you, she thought grimly.

"That's what we're going to try to find out," she replied evasively, and exchanged a quick glance with Pano.

He raised his eyebrows slightly, seemingly trying to tell her wordlessly, with his expression: *You're too paranoid,* while she tried to signal him that they shouldn't trust this man, or anyone.

In the end, though, she knew he was probably right, and she nodded with a sigh. At any rate, they weren't about to leave an American soldier here alone—and even if he hadn't been an American soldier, they couldn't leave anyone behind. Not in this place. Even her worst enemy should know she wouldn't do that.

"We may have a clue. We just need to find a spare battery for the hovercraft to get us there," she explained, pointing first to the hangar behind Eversman and then to Pano.

"Check," said Eversman, and seemed reassured. "I'll help you. And once we find all those people, they might be able to tell us why the hell Lockwell and Marks are in a coma and our satellite uplink isn't working."

"Can you at least shut off the engines?" Agatha asked him. "If they keep running the whole time, we definitely won't have enough fuel to get us back."

Eversman thought briefly, then slowly nodded. "Yeah, I should be able to handle that. How long will it take... to get where you said we're going?"

"It's hard to say. It's about two hundred kilometers," Pano replied. "We've got basically no payload, so I'm thinking a couple of days, if we take turns driving."

"That thing doesn't have an autopilot?" asked the sergeant.

"Well I don't think there's any GPS satellite signal here, and certainly no street maps for this area in the system."

"Gotcha. I'm going to go take care of the plane. Don't leave without me, you hear?" Eversman said, and a brief expression of fear flashed across the soldier's face.

The question stung Agatha slightly, because she still felt a little guilty about what she had been thinking just a moment ago.

"Of course not," she assured him. "We've got to get those spare batteries first anyway if we're going to cover that distance."

"Roger!" Eversman nodded, pulling his ski goggles and

mask down over his face and then running off down the runway.

"So where did he come from all of a sudden?" Pano asked as they watched the path of the sergeant's gun light as it bobbed away.

"I don't know. He was suddenly just standing there. He probably saw us when we walked here from the plane," Agatha said. "To be honest, I'm glad that at least he turned up again. I think maybe I saw him before, when I was looking out the windows in the control center. I thought I saw someone on the ship."

"Besides which, he can handle a gun, and that gives me a little extra peace of mind." Despite saying this, Pano looked worried, his eyes darting around the darkness that assailed their tiny island of illumination.

"I'm going to go look for those batteries," she said. When he tried to follow, she shook her head. "Better if you stay here and start getting familiar with the controls and everything. No doubt we'll have to figure most of it out as we go, but a little head start can't hurt."

With that, Agatha ran off to the small side door of the hangar and raised it. On the inside was a small light switch next to the door. She flipped it before she took a single step further. It was like she had developed a pathological fear of the dark within the past few hours—not something she would have believed yesterday. In fact, she probably would have scoffed at the idea. But something about this place, and its absolute darkness just beyond the bounds of any human light source, shook her deeply. It might have been the fact that all the people here had vanished without a trace—or maybe she had just needed to fly to the end of the world to discover that she had a vulnerable side that was irrational and scared.

When the irrational becomes part of the rational, would anyone act any differently? she asked herself, quickly looking around the hangar as one LED tube after another flickered to life across the ceiling. Under their cold light, there was virtually no place for a shadow to hide between the two lonely-looking hovercraft, which were still attached to their charging cables.

Overcharging could potentially destroy the batteries—so why had they been in such a hurry to get out of here that they left the cables connected? There was also another small work area here with desks and computers, out in the open and not partitioned off from the rest of the hall. There were eight power stations, four charging cables extending from each of them like the tentacles of some kind of cyber-octopus. On the desks she found half-eaten sandwiches, unwrapped soy bars, and half-finished cups of coffee—just like in the other buildings.

"Okay, okay, spare batteries, spare batteries," Agatha murmured, and hurried to the gray heavy-duty storage shelves at the rear of the hangar, which had dozens of crates piled on them. Each was marked on the front by a strip of masking tape with the contents written in black marker.

"Tools, glue, tape, cables, cable ties, flashlights, relays..." she read the labels out loud as she scanned them, and then, "Aha. Bingo. Mobile batteries."

She pulled on one of the three crates labeled with that description and almost fell over as it dropped off the shelf, hit her in the chest, and crashed to the ground.

Grumbling, she righted herself and checked the surprisingly heavy, hard plastic crate for signs of damage, but didn't see any. She removed the lid and looked inside.

Two rechargeable batteries—each the size of a toddler—were nestled there, in form-fitting foam molding. They were

The Fossil

white, and had no buttons or labels, only a connection jack on one side.

"Looking good." She pushed the lid back down over the top and locked it with its simple clasp mechanism, and then dragged the crate behind her by one of the handles until she reached the door. Moving behind the crate now, she pushed it the rest of the way to the hovercraft, before running back to the hangar and returning with the crate marked 'Cables' dragging behind her.

With Pano's help, she schlepped both crates into the driver's cabin, where there was a bucket seat for the driver and another for the passenger, and a bench behind them. Everything in the cabin was cramped. The ceiling was low and looked solid, the windows were tiny, no bigger than the window of a commercial airplane seat, and there was practically no legroom at all. It was a vehicle that had been built for a purpose, and comfort was not part of that purpose.

Just above the small windshield, which was reminiscent of the viewport of an armored tank, there were a few blinking buttons of various colors of the rainbow, and in front of the driver's seat was a steering toggle, nothing more than two handles protruding from either side of an armature.

"You gonna be able to drive this thing?" she asked Pano skeptically.

"I'll manage. I've driven a Caterpillar in the Alps once or twice. How different can it be?"

"Well, to start with, Caterpillars drive on treads and this thing rides on an air cushion," she responded sardonically.

"It'll be like falling off a log."

"Logs are not what I'm worried about," Agatha said with a frown. She pointed through the front windshield at a lonely figure that was running into the light of their headlights. "He's back."

A moment later, Eversman was climbing up the short ladder on the passenger side. He tossed three carbines onto the back seat.

"You never know out here," he said, when they each shot him a sidelong look. He was probably right. Agatha did feel much more comfortable with a little firepower for the trip, even though what concerned her most—the dread lurking in the darkness—couldn't be fought off with guns.

She simply couldn't shake the feeling that there was something out there waiting for her, and that she was about to regret leaving the one place in Antarctica where they could hole up and survive for a while, or at least had a ghost of a chance of contacting the outside world. And there was an airplane as well as a ship here, although none of them could pilot either one.

She suddenly thought of something. McMurdo wasn't the only thing in Antarctica. Before climate change turned dramatic, starting around 2020, when each new impact seemed to trigger another, more significant, faster one in a kind of domino effect, dozens of nations had put research stations on the continent, as far as she remembered, anyway. Maybe the Human Foundation crew had moved on—or fled—to one of them? But even if that was the case, none of them were in the immediate vicinity and it made no sense to leave everything lying around out here, definitely not the vehicle, to try to reach one of them.

"All right then," Pano said after a pause, and flipped two toggles on the bank of switches above his head before pressing the START button. The cabin was instantly filled with a surprising amount of noise for an electric vehicle. Next, Pano moved the lever that was between himself and the passenger seat, where Agatha was sitting, to the halfway position, and they began to glide on the cushion of air across the tarmac, heading north.

Eversman, on the bench behind them, leaned forward between them and stared out through the front windshield as if spellbound, peering into the cone-shaped area of light their headlights cast into the darkness. To Agatha, it looked like a gleaming bow wave as they sailed into a sea of pure black.

The runway was at the north end of the base, so they floated straight off the concrete slabs onto the rocky terrain, which had looked browned and dirty in the daylight, but now seemed as colorless as a lunar landscape.

Pano had fed the satellite data from the control center into the onboard computer, and was now following the coordinates on a navigation grid overlaid onto the integrated map displayed on a wide screen on the front panel. Their goal, deep inside Antarctica, looked so far away that Agatha could not believe they would ever reach it.

For the first two hours the journey was monotonous, and all three of them stared silently straight ahead at the endless, homogenous, never-changing hundred meters of Antarctic terrain directly in front.

Suddenly, Agatha noticed something. "Stop!" she shouted, so loudly that it made Pano jump.

"What is it?" he said, clearly frightened.

"Do you see that?" She pointed ahead of them after he brought the hovercraft to a halt. Barely twenty meters ahead of them there was an elongated, shimmering object lying in their path.

"Yes."

"What... what's going on..." Eversman mumbled in a

sleepy stupor, scrambling upright on the bench. Apparently he had nodded off.

"There's something there. Or someone," Agatha told him, grabbing her gun. She checked the chamber and opened the passenger-side door.

"I'm not sure that this is such a..." The rest of Pano's words were lost as she slammed the door behind her.

She carefully climbed down the ladder and went around the short snout of the vehicle, keeping the headlights to her back so she wasn't blinded. Pano appeared next to her, with pistol drawn. Nervously, he looked into the darkness left and right and pulled his hood tighter around his face. Out here in the open, the wind was much stronger, and it hammered relentlessly against their clothes.

After exchanging a quick look and a nod, they slowly approached the figure lying on the ground in front of them. As they approached, they saw it had arms and legs—that, and the pale blue clothes that they could identify, possibly a down jacket, left no doubt that this was a human being.

For one last, tense moment, they looked around in the darkness and then traversed the final few meters to the figure on the ground.

Pano, gun raised, covered the scene, while Agatha knelt down and, with one outstretched arm, turned the body over.

She was looking into the frozen face of a young woman, perhaps thirty years old, her skin pale bluish and covered with a thin layer of ice crystals. Her eyes had probably been dark in life, but were now pale and broken. With her quick inspection, Agatha could see no signs of injury.

"Frozen," she determined, looking out into the wall of blackness beyond the headlights. With a quick hand motion, she turned down the collar of the unfortunate woman's down jacket and held it towards Pano. On the inside, the word 'McMurdo' was clearly visible.

"This shit just gets weirder and weirder," he growled, and nervously chewed his chapped and freezing lower lip.

"Yes. So why does she leave McMurdo to freeze to death out here?"

"I don't know."

"Uh, agents?" they heard Eversman call out from behind them. The soldier was standing in the open passenger door and waving at them from his position above. When they looked at him, he pointed to the left and shined his flashlight on the ground. Where the beam of light landed, they saw another body. Then it moved to another, and then another. There were dozens.

"My... God," Pano coughed, gagging, and crossed himself.

"I don't think your God comes out here much," Agatha said grimly. She rose, stiffened her shoulders, and fighting every instinct in her, walked into the darkness to where Eversman's flashlight was shining.

The other corpses she examined were, as far as she could tell, in the same state—either frozen to death or collapsed from exhaustion. Returning to the vehicle, she once again had the unpleasant feeling of the darkness following her, as if it had eyes. Suppressing the urge to run away in a panic, and forcing herself to return to the ladder without showing any signs of terror, took everything she had.

"Let's go," she said when she had returned to the passenger seat and taken a deep breath.

Over the next two hours they found two more bodies that they also examined, but there was nothing unusual about them—apart from the fact that like the rest, they had apparently run off with a complete disregard for their lives, to die outside in the remotest place on earth.

She and Pano didn't talk about it, so the journey passed mostly in silence. After all, what was there to say? Any worried look, any expression of confusion about what they had seen here, would have just been redundant, and would have only made things worse.

After a while, Eversman fell back to sleep, and eventually Pano was so tired that he, too, nodded off, and Agatha had to shake him awake.

"I'm going to take over," she said, in a tone of voice that left no room for discussion.

"I'm okay," he replied anyway. "It's just, this drive is so unbelievably monotonous, staring at the same terrain in front of us, never changing."

"And yet, unless we are completely focused, we could hit an obstacle that would rip our air cushion apart. It could happen at any moment," she said, and waved him over.

Pano sighed, finally giving in. He moved the lever to slow down so that she could switch places with him.

Agatha strapped herself into the driver's seat, looked back at Eversman, who seemed to still be asleep, and brought the hovercraft back up to speed.

After another hour, the terrain in their headlights changed, becoming increasingly icy, until finally they were riding on pure white snow and ice. In the rearview mirror, she could see a whirling red cloud of ice crystals kicked up by their passage.

"Oh, wow," Pano said sleepily, yawning and stretching as he rubbed his eyes. "We hit the snow line."

"Yeah, that means we're making good progress."

"Can you imagine how long it must have taken Jackson and the students to get all the way out here, back in 2018,

The Fossil

with tracked vehicles, when the whole way was covered in ice?" he asked, yawning so hard that his jaw popped.

"Well, I'm pretty sure that the path they took back then wasn't paved with the bodies of suicidal researchers."

"I wish we could've at least called for some backup," Pano sighed, and his face suddenly looked sad as he turned to look at her.

She glanced over at him. "What is it?"

"I... oh, it's nothing."

"Just tell me. It will keep me awake," Agatha insisted, checking the battery level. It still showed forty-five percent.

"Well... It's my sister's birthday today. She's got stage IV cancer. It's probably the last birthday I could have spent with her..." Pano trailed off and was silent for a moment, looking at his hands. Then he added, in a whisper:. "Should have spent with her."

Agatha didn't know what to say, because she never knew what to say in these kinds of moments. She used to think that she knew, but it had always gone wrong because social conventions generally didn't allow for her pragmatic and forward-looking arguments.

"Remember when I came up with an analysis of your background? Was I right?"

"Huh?"

"In the conference room in the CTD," she said.

"Oh. Well you weren't as wrong as I would like to wish, let's put it that way," he replied, and looked off into the distance. After a moment, he went on. "When I was six, my father tried to throw my mother out the window of our apartment. On the tenth floor. Know why?"

"No."

"Because they had been fighting, and he hit her so hard that her head slammed against a door frame so hard that she got a concussion. He had already been in jail once, and knew that he wasn't going back for anything, so he just figured he'd throw her out the window and say it was suicide." Pano snorted, and shook his head. "You can't ever know what goes on in the mind of an alcoholic."

"That's... I'm sorry," she said carefully, and he gave her a sidelong glance that she didn't reciprocate. She kept staring straight out the windshield, scanning the endless expanse of white ahead of them.

"I stopped him. I stopped him by screaming so loud that the neighbors got scared, and the police came before he could do it. All my life I've told myself that I saved my mother, but I think he was just too drunk to really do it."

Agatha saw her partner lift a hand to his temple, on the side facing her, and brush aside his curly hair so she could see a bulging scar running from his ear to his forehead. "This is my memento from that day. I got it because I jumped in front of my sister, when he thought that she was the one screaming."

"What became of him?"

"My father? He went back to prison."

"And you decided to study law, because you thought his sentence wasn't severe enough, right?" Agatha guessed.

Pano nodded. "Yeah. And after that I joined the police force, because I learned that's where I had better chances of fixing that."

"How did you end up in counterterrorism?"

"I didn't have a choice. They put me there, four years ago. And they told me that after six years I could choose whatever position I wanted."

"Well, I'm glad that they put you there," Agatha said, surprised by her own words.

Pano didn't answer at first, just looked at her for a while.

"Thanks," he finally said, and did the decent thing, not embarrassing her by saying anything more. "So what's your story?" he eventually asked.

"What you mean?"

"Well, how about you tell me how you grew up? If we're the only people on this continent, and we're driving through a sea of endless darkness, I'd like to know who I'm trusting my life to when the shit goes down," he said.

"I grew up in an orphanage in Maine. My parents put me up for adoption when I was a year old. I guess nobody wanted me," she told him.

Pano's eyes widened, and he seemed genuinely shocked. "My God. I really didn't think that you might have had it worse than I did. I'm sorry."

"Don't be." She made a dismissive gesture. "I got used to being unwanted, and made my peace with the fact that all my thoughts about that were only that—thoughts. I had no way of knowing what my parents' situation was. Were they in trouble? Did they have to keep my birth a secret because of the trouble it would have caused them? Spending nights in a dormitory with twenty other children, staring at the ceiling and going over every way that being rejected by your own parents is traumatic, that doesn't get you anything other than distraught and tired of life.

"Then there came a night that I was lying awake in that dorm and I asked myself, 'what do I really know for sure? What's really real, and what is just fiction?' What was real was that I lived in a big house, with other children, I always had playmates around me, and I probably had more contact with kids my age than the so-called normal kids on the outside. If you think about it, I had dozens of brothers and sisters and many mothers, all taking care of me.

"The caregivers at our orphanage really did take care of

all our needs. This pastor from Indonesia and his wife ran the place. They were really very warm and loving. Sure, they were strict, and conservative about things like television, what we ate, and the stupid shit that we did. But the truth of the matter was I was cared for, I was loved—maybe not the way real parents would have loved me, but it was real—and I never went hungry..

"The fiction was the story I had created in my head about parents who didn't want me. I didn't know one thing about them, and I would never find out anything about them, so why was I letting thoughts about them spin around and around in my head? In that one night, something changed in me, and I started automatically questioning every thought in my head. I'd ask myself, "What just happened?" What did I imagine happened, and what was a real fact that I could see in front of me and judge objectively? I thought about a bird."

"A bird?"

"Yeah, a bird. Here, look," Agatha extended her right arm towards him. "Pull up my sleeve."

Pano did as he was told. On the inside of her upper arm he saw a tattoo, a simple picture of a sparrow sitting on a branch. "Hmm. I have to say I'm not following you."

"A bird sitting on a branch doesn't ask itself, 'How do I know if this branch is still right for me? Should I fly away? Is there some other branch out there better than this one? What if I land on another branch and it can't support me, and it breaks off? Then what will all the other birds say about me?'"

Pano chuckled.

"There, see?" Agatha blurted out, chuckling and pointing to the man sitting next to her. "You think it's absurd, that a bird would be thinking things like this, don't you? You know why? Because it is absurd! But if the bird had what we call common sense, it would be thinking all those things! But a bird doesn't think those things. It just does what has to be done. What it sees in front of it. It sees the world, and it acts in harmony with what is. When I realized that, I decided to be a bird. For the rest of my life."

"So, you're not a robot after all," Pano said, and she instinctively scanned his face for signs of sarcasm, but she didn't find any. "You are enlightened."

"No, I'm just somebody who realized that psychological suffering requires two things—giving up control of your thoughts, and closing your eyes to the world. All that grief, all that stress, everything about negative emotions that goes beyond normal physical defense responses, are all just your own choices. Of that I'm convinced."

"You know, I have to admit that at first I thought that was all pretty weird," Pano said after a while. "But the more I think about it, the more it makes sense."

"I studied psychology at Harvard, you know. Somewhere in the third semester of clinical psychology, we learned that emotions are a physical, chemically-quantifiable response to thoughts. Your measurable emotions follow your thoughts. Isn't that an incredible realization? So many people I've worked with over the years have assumed I'm an emotionally cold person. But I'm not. I just stopped letting my thoughts control me. I prefer to keep control of my life.

"I'm sure that fits the profile of some kind of neurosis—but who doesn't have some kind of neurosis? *Nobody,* that's who. So I might as well admit to myself that when it comes to the circus of human emotional game-playing, I just don't want to play. 'Oh, what a nice dress you're wearing today, but really I'm just jealous that your hips don't look as fat as mine in it. I'm so happy for you that it's your birthday today, only I don't give a shit because it's just another day for me,'" Agatha twittered, in an exaggeratedly feminine voice. "No, thank you."

"Well, now I *really* want to get you into bed," Pano said drily, at which Agatha shot him a look. She could no longer hide her scorn, so she didn't even try.

When he just grinned and shrugged his shoulders, they both chuckled. It was a liberating sound coming from their throats, a small victory against the darkness ominously descending on them, and through which they were fighting their way by the scant light of their vehicle, thousands of miles from the nearest outpost of humanity.

30

FILIO AMOROSA, 2042

Filio was only in the infirmary at Cape Canaveral Air Force Base for one night. The Colonel had explained to her that she had apparently hit her head against the front seat, giving her a mild concussion. The glass shards in her forearms and right cheek had been removed, the wounds sealed with Plastigel. Putram and Tatyana were in the same room with her, but were not very talkative, as both had been put in artificial comas. Hue was also placed in the room, but had spent the first few hours after the incident in radiology and then surgery.

Filio was flown back to the training facility in Nevada the next morning because the Air Force wanted to get all the civilians off the base to give Homeland Security's CTD the widest possible berth for their investigation.

A small private plane carried her and around twenty others, all NASA and ESA personnel. During the flight she watched all the various news feeds on a pair of AR glasses. The terrorist attack on mankind's titanic project was the one and only thing that was being talked about on every station, everywhere—Filio's project, *Mars Two*. Images of the exploding rocket, of pieces flying in all directions, of soldiers shooting at each other, and the absolute chaos at Cape Canaveral were shown again and again, from every angle. Experts analyzed the tactic of using over 6,000 mini-drones to overwhelm the military defenses. It was an almost entirely new form of terrorism, one that no one had expected. It was reminiscent of Japan's kamikazes in WWII, when airplanes themselves were used as offensive weapons for the first time, and the terrorist attack on the Twin Towers in New York City on September 11, 2001. Before 1944, no one had even considered it as something anybody would try. Until then, no one had even considered it as something anybody would try.

Now, the mission was history. One hundred and fourteen dead, and the world in turmoil.

Very soon after it had happened a video began circulating on the news feeds, showing none other than the long-lost treasure hunter Workai Dalam, visibly aged, claiming responsibility for the attack. "They will excoriate me and my brothers in the Sons of Terra, but the day will come when they will thank me for stopping humanity from making a grave mistake. We cannot leave this planet, because that is what *The Enemy* wants! As we sit rooted to our displays and our AR devices, transfixed by the miracles of the human spirit of invention, we are too blind to see that *The Enemy* is the one driving all our destinies!" Dalam had proclaimed in the video, standing in front of the flag of the Sons of Terra.

"Your governments are playthings in his hands, your elected representatives nothing but marionettes in his puppet show that ends with the extinction of the human race! Today, many brave brothers and sisters gave their lives, members of the U.S. military who supported our struggle for humanity and who were forced to stand against their comrades for the cause. Their sacrifice will not be forgotten. We must never give up the resistance. Against *The Enemy*. For Terra, because we are not the rulers of this planet."

Listening to this man, who had been idolized on every scrapper ship, a literal icon of scrappers everywhere, Filio was too confused to really be shocked. The idea that he was the mastermind behind the most dangerous terrorist organization in the world was so absurd that convincing herself she had gone mad was easier to believe than that this was really happening.

Later during the flight, the news feeds started to report about military operations underway around the world, dismantling suspected terrorist training camps and hiding places. But Filio knew how little that would accomplish. When the public had watched their dream go up in fire and smoke before their eyes, live and in ultra-high definition, the powers that be had to resort to decisive action to reassure a scared and insecure world. That was just how things worked. In reality, the terrorists were almost certainly ready for this response.

Even so, airports were closed, border checks were intensified, and raids were carried out with impunity, all around the world, and would continue to be for a long time to come. Every spokesman for every security agency around the world promised, live on video, to locate and neutralize the Sons of Terra and make the results available when the time was right. That meant, in so many words, '*We* have no idea exactly what we should do, but we are working on a strategy.'

At a certain point Filio had heard enough and she yanked the AR glasses off her head, tossing them onto the seat next to her in frustration. She rubbed her eyes sleepily. Her eyelids were heavy, and her head felt hollow. She wished she could cry, but after spending the night with tears streaming down her face as she punched her mattress in frustration, she had no tears left.

The terrorists, with their fanaticism and tactics so simple no one expected them, had destroyed the dream of a whole generation—building a future in the solar system.

Even worse, it meant waiting at least two more years for a chance to achieve closure on the *Mars One* disaster—and the very thought drove her mad. She still had no answers as to why her friends died in 2040. She still didn't know what had happened on Mars. She still had no explanation for her amnesia.

Filio was back to square one. The torture she had put herself through, betraying her friends on the *Ocean's Bitch*, had been for nothing. Her second crew, with whom she had made her first tentative step towards creating a bond, were either dead—killed in cold blood before her eyes—or gravely injured. It was a disaster that she could never have prepared for. She had been so close, and then watched everything go up in flames.

A few hours later she disembarked from the plane as if in a trance. On the tarmac there were minibuses waiting for her and the other passengers. The faces of the NASA people who met them were gray, ashen masks. The shock of recent events was inscribed on those faces in the wrinkles that had appeared overnight and would probably never go away.

They passed the trip to the training complex in silence, everyone wholly absorbed in their own dark thoughts. Exiting the vehicles, they walked as if in a funeral procession to the middle of the three concrete cubes, where Jones's assistant Morris was waiting, just like the last time Filio had been here. But this time her shoulders drooped helplessly,

The Fossil

her hair was in no kind of style at all, and her eyes were ringed by dark circles.

"Welcome back," she said in a strained voice, with a tired nod to Filio.

"Hello," Filio answered simply, and pushed her way past Morris into the reception area. The others shuffled in around her and made their way to various elevators, apparently knowing where to go. Filio came to a stop in the middle of the room.

And which way should she go, now that *Mars Two* no longer existed? Which direction would now take her toward the goal of reaching Mars? She no longer saw any way toward it.

"Doctor?"

The voice belonged to Morris. She had appeared next to Filio and was looking at her with sympathy in her eyes. The woman's obvious compassion brought out the sadness in Filio that her rage and confusion had suppressed until now.

"Hmm?"

"I think it best if I show you to your quarters, all right?"

Filio turned her eyes away from the assistant so that she wouldn't reveal how much she was struggling to keep her composure. After a few breaths, she finally said, "I'd like to speak to Jones. Is he here?"

"Yes, but he's been on the phone all day and is about to be picked up by helicopter to go to Los Angeles," Morris replied apologetically. "I'm sorry."

"Could you possibly just do me the favor of asking him if he would take the time to see me anyway?"

The blonde looked at Filio and they read each other's faces for a moment. Finally, Morris sighed, took a step away, and began speaking. It wasn't long before she came back and nodded. "I'll take you to him. But you have to keep it short."

"Of course."

Feeling heaviness in her limbs, Filio dragged herself along behind the assistant and entered the elevator, which was as empty as she felt inside. The elevator stopped on the tenth floor with a gentle 'pling,' and the doors slid open. She stepped out of the elevator alone. Morris said goodbye and pushed the button to go down again.

Reaching the door to Jones's office, Filio knocked twice and entered.

Jones was sitting behind his desk and had just tossed his hand terminal onto a stack of papers. His eyes were red, his suit was in disarray, and when he looked up at her she saw that the cool composure that once emanated from him was gone. Instead she found herself looking at a man broken and old before his time, as if he had just heard that his grandchildren had died. And in a way, they had.

"Please sit down, Filio," he said, pointing to one of the three available chairs, all of which looked more functional than comfortable.

"Thank you, sir."

"I just want to say I'm thrilled you made it through the attack relatively unscathed. I've been told that some of the others came off much worse—the ones who survived at all." The director shook his head in sorrow. "It's unthinkable that something like this could happen. On a military complex, of all places, with the whole world watching."

"Yes... it was..." Filio tried to go on but couldn't draw a breath, so she only lowered her gaze to the floor. The feeling of being helpless, being at the mercy of the whims of a pitiless fate, shook her to her core. But as long as she had something to fight for, something to work for, there was still hope. And that hope was: *Mars Three*.

She knew it would take a long time to process what had happened, but there was that one thing that she could still focus on. Once again, she had walked away from a disaster, and she had to see that as a sign that she could not give up. She had already nearly convinced herself of this.

"You shouldn't be talking about that right now, Filio. I'm just about to fly to Los Angeles. Better if we talk the day after tomorrow, when I'm back." Jones reached for a terminal and was about to make an entry on it when he looked up at her again, raising his eyebrows as if he was surprised that she was still there.

"Is there any hope that *Mars Three* is going to get funded?" Filio asked straight out.

"I really don't know," Jones admitted, and folded his hands over the terminal.

Filio trembled slightly.

"At least the Minister is assuming that the community is going to come together behind it," Jones continued, "because they don't want it to look like they're giving in to terrorists. We'll only get a real answer to that question in the coming weeks and months. But I've had one foot in politics long enough to know that that's always the way it goes."

"That's good," Filio sighed, the dread wrapped around her suddenly somewhat lightened.

"But you're not going to be on it," Jones suddenly added, and Filio felt like she had just been punched in the gut. She was suddenly unable to make a sound, so she just looked at the director until their eyes locked. He didn't look like he was joking.

"But... I don't understand..." she stammered, stunned.

"The contract you signed," he said, calling up a document on his terminal and turning the ultra-thin device around to face her, "says you will be put on the next Mars mission. *The next Mars mission* was, in this case, *Mars Two*. And that's gone." Jones's lips seemed to harden to stone when he said that last sentence.

Filio didn't know how to reply, so she just stared at the director, feeling like someone had just thrown a switch and turned off the totality of her life energy. Weakly, she sank back into her chair.

"But the... I... there's no other way for me to get to Mars. I have to get to Mars!"

"Well, you had your chance. And I can guarantee you that for this mission there's not going to be a repeat of that stunt you pulled," Jones said calmly, and stood up. "I'm sorry, but I've got to go. Get some rest. In a few hours, a driver will be waiting to take you to the airport in Reno."

The director walked around the desk and extended his hand to her, but Filio didn't even register that he was there. He waited for a moment, and then left the office, walking out the door and leaving it open.

Some time later—Filio didn't even know how long it had been—Morris appeared in the doorway, looking at her with an expression of pity.

"Doctor?" she asked gently, before slowly entering the office and moving towards Filio, like she was approaching a lost dog that might be aggressive.

"Huh?" Filio could only make a bewildered sound and she raised her head with a resigned look.

So that was that. She had reached the point where she didn't know how to go on. There was no hurdle to overcome with her strength of will and her perseverance. Instead, there was just an end. Nothing but an ending, with no alternatives. It was a void in her head that scared her so much, it

The Fossil

pushed her to a place she didn't want to go—self-pity. She had no one to run to. No family, no friends. Here at the end of the road, she looked back and saw how she had sacrificed everything in her life for her dreams of Mars. The first victim had been her social life, which had still existed on some level during her studies, although she had accepted a steady stream of new jobs in new places to get where she was going.

Completely withdrawn from the world, she followed Morris from the office towards the living quarters, but all the while she was silently shaking her head. She didn't want to stay here one moment longer than necessary, because every inch of the place reminded her of the two failed Mars missions she had been on.

Finally, the assistant led her out of the complex into the sunshine of the Nevada desert. A car was waiting.

"Well, this gentleman will take you to the airport," Morris said, and her full lips pursed into a sympathetic pout. "I... I'm just so sorry."

"Yeah, me too," Filio said, and got in the car. Even before they had reached the fence that circled a wide radius around the site, she noticed she had forgotten her bag. But she didn't say anything. It didn't matter if she brought her few belongings with her or not.

Where am I supposed to go? she thought. The first thing that came to her mind was Romain and the crew of the *Ocean's Bitch*. But Romain had been crystal clear—he never wanted to speak to her again.

Did Thomas, Jane, and Alberto feel the same? She hadn't spoken to them directly. But she couldn't imagine that they felt any different.

The driver made a few attempts to break the oppressive silence of the electric vehicle with some small talk, but she didn't respond. Even under normal circumstances she hated small talk, because it didn't serve a purpose and was only about irrelevant things, but in this case it was mainly that she was lost in her thoughts and registered his questions too late.

In 2042, having a driver was still seen as a sign of luxury. Ever since cars had become fully self-driving there was really no purpose in having a man sitting behind the wheel other than to show everyone else that the passenger had money. But for Filio, it was nothing more than a distraction.

When they reached the airport in Reno an hour later, she left the car in silence and stumbled, as if drunk, through the automatic doors into the terminal.

Every face around her seemed unreal, as if they were all figures in a surrealist light opera that had no story and no meaning.

As she stopped to look at the short lines in front of the check-in desks, a sudden thought popped into her head. It petrified her. *It would have been better if I had been killed in the attack.*

It was not the thought itself that was so shocking, but that it clung to her like something sticky, and she knew it was how she really felt. She had never felt anything so painful as the knowledge that she had no place to go, no home, no contacts, no goal. Filio had become redundant and no longer served any purpose—she was just a drag on society, because there was nothing left for her to do.

She was so wrapped up in these thoughts that she didn't notice the two men approaching her from different sides—one from the nearby men's room and the other from the security checkpoint leading to the gates. They wore nondescript civilian clothes and stood out mainly due to their boots, which looked like heavy-duty hiking shoes or military boots.

She also failed to notice that the two policemen armed with automatic weapons, who just moments before had been patrolling the hall vigilantly, had disappeared.

Her sense of danger only kicked in when she was grabbed from both sides. She looked up in horror. Someone wrenched her around and forced her arms behind her back, hurting her shoulder.

"Hey! Let me go!" she shouted, half angry and half frightened, struggling to break free of the iron grip. But she couldn't!

Some passengers at the counters turned at the sound of her shouting, but she was already being hustled towards the exit. She struggled to look left and right to catch a glimpse of her abductors, only managing to catch a vague glimpse of two angular faces crowned with short hair, eyes hidden behind sunglasses. Their expressions were stone-cold serious as they dragged her out of the terminal.

Filio squirmed and kicked. Now she was screaming for help and for the police, but the officers had vanished without a trace. Passengers around the terminal were looking concerned and pulling out their hand terminals, but no one seemed prepared to interfere with the dangerous-looking men.

"What are you doing? Let me GO! HELP!" Filio screamed, just as she managed to hook her left foot in the back of one of the men's knees and make him stumble. At that, the man on the other side tightened his grip and dealt her a heavy blow on the back, knocking all the air out of her lungs.

"POLICE! HELP!" she screamed louder, as soon as she could breathe again. One of them hit her so hard that she saw stars as her head was knocked hard to the left. From the corner of her eye, she thought she saw two policewomen coming up the sidewalk in front of the terminal, weapons drawn.

They leveled them at Filio and her kidnappers.

"Freeze! Police!" one of them shouted, at which her abductors actually halted for a moment. But then one of the officers turned and shot her partner in the head. The fountain of blood splashed over a parked taxi, and in the next instant people were screaming in panic and running in all directions.

"No!" Filio gasped with all the breath she could muster, flashing back to the soldiers who had turned on each other at Cape Canaveral. It could only be the Sons of Terra. As soon as she realized that, she began to shriek inarticulately like a stuck pig, surprising herself with the strange, piercing sounds coming from her own mouth.

But what happened next threw Filio for an even bigger loop. The police officer who had just shot her partner in cold blood stopped, gave a slight shudder, and fell lifelessly to the ground. Behind her, two other people on the other side of the parked cars also collapsed like marionettes whose strings had been cut.

Her two abductors quickened their pace until they reached a black van standing at the curb. One threw the door open and the other pushed her in, hard.

Filio slammed into one of the front seats with her right shoulder, and would have bashed her forehead against the door on the other side if it had not suddenly opened. Hands reached in to grab her.

Before she knew what was happening, she was being pulled roughly out of the vehicle, with the staccato sound of gunshots cracking off in the breaking dawn. She just managed to catch a glimpse of one of the men who had dragged her out of the terminal. He was lying on the sidewalk, bleeding from a hole in his head, his dead eyes staring skyward. Then she felt a tiny jab in the side of her neck.

"What the—" she just managed to say before a black bag descended over her head and she lost consciousness.

31

AGATHA DEVENWORTH, 2042

Agatha kept staring ahead into the ice in front of them. It was pure white, but somehow looked dirty in their headlights. Pano had fallen asleep, like Eversman, and the snoring was driving her crazy. But being that this was her third shift at the wheel, at least the abominable noises from Pano's mouth were helping to keep her awake. The clock showed that they had been traveling for fourteen hours since leaving McMurdo when something on the console caught her eye. It looked like something on the camera feed from the right-side mirror.

Irritated, she pressed the zoom button and watched what she had first taken for a pinpoint bad pixel as it grew into a pinhead-sized glowing spot.

Instinctively, she brought the hovercraft to a halt and switched off the engine. Quiet. It seemed to go 'silent as the grave,' because Eversman rolled onto his side and Pano woke up.

In the all-encompassing silence that dominated Antarctica, they could have heard a snowflake fall.

"What is it?" Pano whispered, deep wrinkles burrowing

across his brow before he rubbed his cheeks and eyes and then stared out into the darkness.

"I saw something in the mirror feed," she replied, pointing to the screen. The point of light had now grown bigger—whatever it was, it was approaching. She now saw it wasn't a steady light at all, that it was blinking at a rapid frequency.

"I think that's a position light!" Pano said in surprise, leaning in close to the screen and squinting as if that might draw out the solution to the mystery. "A plane? Or a helicopter?"

"Maybe. It looks too high up for a ground vehicle, although it's hard to say in this darkness."

"But who could it be?"

"Maybe it's one of those UFOs the Sons of Terra keep warning everybody about," she said dryly, but Pano only looked back at her with a combination of worry and disbelief.

"That was supposed to be a joke," she clarified.

"Frankly, out here, nothing would surprise me. Want me to try the light meter in the outside camera, or use the radar, to see how far away it is?"

"No!" she replied quickly, shaking her head. "I'd rather not use any active sensors. Whatever it is might be able to pick them up. I have the feeling that it's better to stay undiscovered out here."

"You're probably right," he agreed, nodding. "Who would be flying around out here so far from the coast and so far from, well, anything?"

"Someone from McMurdo?"

Pano looked at her in disbelief. "You mean the turboprop pilots? They didn't really look flight-ready the last time I saw them."

Agatha shrugged. "Maybe somebody kissed those sleeping beauties. After everything I've seen out here, I'm not ruling anything out."

"You've already made that clear. Well, anything would be preferable to a goddamn UFO."

Agatha could see in Pano's eyes that, although he laughed off the possibility that there were aliens behind them, he couldn't laugh all the worry from his face.

By now the point of light on the screen had become significantly larger, and it was pulsing in a steady rhythm. They listened tensely, but heard nothing. Almost nothing.

She tried the window control, but it had no power, so she opened her door a crack. Ice-cold polar air whistled its way in, and the windows fogged up immediately. Above the whistle, she could now hear what before she had only guessed at—the sound of rotors. Still far off, but there was no doubt that the barely audible, cycling sound was the noise of spinning rotors.

"A helicopter!" Pano whispered. He seemed irritated, almost as if he would have preferred the UFO.

"Yes." Agatha closed the door again, and the battery in the floor of the vehicle strained to raise the cabin temperature back to where it had been.

Exactly four minutes later a long, two-rotor transport helicopter thundered right over them. In the otherwise absolute silence around them, the volume was so tremendous that they thought the hovercraft might shake itself apart.

As they both stared forward, hunching over to peer through the narrow windshield, they watched the position lights move away from them and slowly disappear.

"What's going on?" Eversman asked from the back seat, in a sleepy stupor.

"We've just been flown over by a helicopter," Pano explained. At these words, the sergeant immediately reached straight for his gun.

"Dammit! Did they see us?"

"'They?' We have no idea who *they* were, and no, I don't think *they* were looking for us. I didn't see any searchlights, and they were flying with passive illumination, just a single position light. Our engine was off, so we weren't radiating much heat, and from up there they wouldn't have seen anything in the darkness," Agatha explained confidently.

"It looked like someone flying past with a clear destination. They were in a pretty big hurry," Pano said, agreeing with her and pointing forward. "Yeah, and in the exact same direction that we're going."

"And that's good," Agatha said, starting up the engine again.

"Are you sure about that?" her partner asked with a frown.

"Well, that certainly makes it seem like a place worth visiting. And anybody who can get their own helicopter to Antarctica has got money, and resources."

"Yeah, that's what I'm worried about."

When they couldn't see the position light anymore, Agatha started driving again. Less than an hour later, they could see the feeble beginnings of a dark blue horizon line appearing, which soon turned a watery lapis lazuli. As the horizon became more evident, the darkness along it seemed to be slowly moving upwards as the ground became brighter and whiter. If Agatha had been a tourist and in the safety of some adventure travel group, she would have thought it beautiful, even breathtaking. As things were, it only added to the oppressive and unnerving sense of being at the end of the world.

The Fossil

But as otherworldly as it was—this strange slow sunrise, as if the sun didn't have the strength to detach itself from the horizon—there was something else disturbing ahead.

"Pano?" she asked, turning to look at him when she didn't get an answer. He had fallen asleep again. "Hey! Pano!" she repeated, putting a hand on his shoulder and shaking him.

"Hmm? What?" The Italian shook his head as he sat up in his seat. "Did I fall asleep again? Didn't notice."

"Are you seeing this too?" she asked, pointing to the triangular shape on the horizon, which she could only see because the sun was not really rising over the horizon. Rather, it was just following a shallow arc, and would soon be setting again. But because of its oblique angle, when the sun was behind that triangle it cast a long, dark shadow that stood out from the rest of the terrain.

"Yes, I am," Pano said in amazement, and turned to grab one of the guns that Eversman had brought. He closed his left eye and, with his right, looked through the scope. "It's a mountain."

"A mountain? Nature abhors symmetry, remember?" she said, alluding to what Jackson had written.

"Yeah, but it's either that or we're heading straight for a pyramid. A huge pyramid." Pano lowered the short rifle and stowed it back in the bag behind the seat. "As far as I know, if you want to see a pyramid you have to go to Egypt."

"Wrong. You should have paid more attention when you were reading Jackson. There are pyramids in Mesopotamia, South America, Europe, and Asia."

"But not in Antarctica."

Agatha didn't know what to reply. She had a real urge to agree with him, but at the same time had trouble believing that a natural rock formation could be as conspicuously triangular as what she was looking at.

"Maybe we're just not close enough yet," she finally said, and Pano just shrugged.

They kept driving for another half hour, until she had to stop because she was staring through the windshield in disbelief. Now there could be no doubt about it. In front of them was a gigantic pyramid jutting into the sky. It looked like a mountain, with rough edges and jagged angles that resembled the pyramids of Giza in overall shape, but had few similarities to their even surfaces. It looked like it had grown from stone just as it was, rather than being built, which was utterly impossible.

"This can't be real," she said in a whisper. Next to her, Pano couldn't seem to find any words at all as he sized up the structure, which was two thousand, maybe even three thousand meters high.

"I'm going crazy!" said a voice from behind them. It was Eversman, and the sudden sound of his voice startled Agatha because she had completely forgotten about him. "How far away is that thing?"

She looked at the display behind her steering control. "Three kilometers."

"Anything on the radar?"

"Nope, nothing. It's not showing the mountain, or anything else. According to these readouts, there shouldn't be anything here at all."

"But that can't be!" the sergeant exclaimed.

"Look for yourself if you want," she replied brusquely. "But my eyes are fine, and I can read, and there's nothing on the readouts."

"All right, all right," Eversman said, pulling back a little.

"Well, let's keep driving some and take a look around,"

Pano proposed. He squirmed for a moment as though uncomfortable, then bit his lip briefly and suddenly jerked his hand up to scratch his left ear.

"Is something wrong?" she asked as she hit the accelerator to get them moving over the endless ice again, towards the pyramid.

"Oh, it's nothing," said Pano with a dismissive gesture. "It's just my hearing aid is acting up a little... OUCH!" He tensed up suddenly and slammed the flat of his hand against his ear.

"What is it?" she asked more insistently this time, and looked over at him with genuine concern. His face was twisted in pain, and she could hear mechanical squeals and buzzing. It sounded like an old radio that wasn't locked into the right frequency.

"I don't know, this thing is just going crazy," he growled, then howled. He pulled a wire, and then he was holding a tiny molded earbud in his hand. He sighed, clearly relieved. "Wow, that hurt."

"Has that ever happened before?"

"No, never."

"That's weird, because I... Whoa! Hold on." Agatha was suddenly staring at the small screen above the steering control. All the readouts were going wild. Needles swept from one end of the dial to the other, the radar went down, and everything on the control panel began to flicker.

"What's happening?"

"The instruments are going crazy too," she said, and brought the hovercraft to a halt before letting go of the steering control and shaking her head.

"Maybe there's some kind of interference field here, like the magnetic shielding the military uses?" Pano suggested. "Strong magnets can have an effect on sensors."

"Those Chinese prototypes, you mean? Have you seen them? Gigantic containers. I don't think there's any of those out here," she countered.

"Maybe not, but the noises from my hearing aid got worse the closer we came."

"Maybe we can use your hearing aid to localize the source," she proposed. Pano thought for a moment and then nodded.

"If there really is a source of interference, it must be close, very close," he said, holding up the still squeaking device that was hanging from his index finger like an insect.

"You're probably right. We might as well get out, the instruments are useless anyway. Eversman, get yourself ready to... Eversman?" Agatha turned in her seat and saw the soldier lying down on the seats behind them. His eyes were closed. Apart from his chest rising and falling, it looked like he had just been turned off.

"What's wrong with him?" Pano asked. He reached over and tried to wake Eversman up. He didn't react, and simply wobbled where Pano touched him, like a slab of dead meat.

"I don't know about you, but to me that looks disturbingly familiar."

"The pilots," Pano hissed. "Maybe there was a similar interference field there, and some people are particularly sensitive to it. We know there are similar effects that you can achieve with electromagnetic pulses in certain spectra, which can make people nauseous, or dizzy, or even faint."

"I don't know either," Agatha admitted, a severe frown apparent as she took her jacket from the seat and put it on, drawing the hood over her head. Then she put on the helmet, goggles, and ski mask. "Let's go find your jamming transmitter."

They left the cabin and dropped onto the snow-covered

surface of the ice. Bone-dry ice crystals crackled beneath their heated boots. They came around the sides of the hovercraft and met at the front, Pano holding his hearing aid out in front of him like a scanner.

There was nothing to see in any direction, except for the pyramid mountain towering before them like a malevolent stone presence. Its shape was so surreal that Agatha felt like she was in a dream, and when she woke up it would all vanish in a puff of smoke. Apart from the pyramid, the terrain here was relatively flat. Far to the north loomed the gentle slopes of a somewhat imposing chain of mountains, and beyond them the rocky peaks jutted out from the snow cover like black crowns.

A biting wind blew all around them, tugging at their military snowsuits like an impatient child—if that annoying child were capable of not just annoying its mother but killing her after only a few minutes of exposure, even through her thermal clothing. Like everywhere else on Earth, climate change had come to this place, and its effects were not always what one might have expected. For example, even the experts did not yet have a good understanding of why, even though the Antarctic ice sheet had melted away from the inside out and the Antarctic Ocean had heated up, temperatures on the southern continent continued to drop.

"It's ironic," Pano shouted to Agatha over the howling of the wind, holding his hearing aid up in the air. "Without this outdated piece of technology, we might have thought the hovercraft's software was acting up and never even thought of a jamming transmitter."

"That's right," Agatha said and cracked a smile behind her mask, but immediately felt the pain of her frozen lips splitting. "I guess I have to admit that in this case your... stubbornness actually paid off."

"Now, you were actually about to say pig-headedness right there, weren't you?"

"Yes, but at this point I've gained some respect for you, so I can make an exception to my general approach here and there."

Pano grinned behind his mask.

They took a few steps forward and were embraced by the gray twilight, for it seemed that the feeble sun on the horizon had already reached its pathetic zenith, and even the dim light wouldn't last much longer. Even though Agatha's high-tech clothing was working to warm her, she could feel the cold creeping in through every extremity.

"It gets stronger over here," Pano observed, and his voice seems to rise and fall on the wind. After a few steps further he shook his head. "Weaker again."

Returning to the spot where the hearing aid squealed loudest, they tried right and left. It became more intense to the right, so they moved that way until it subsided again, and they returned back to the point where it was strongest. There they stopped.

The static screech from the tiny device was so extreme that Agatha could hear it well in spite of the wind, even though its minuscule speakers.

"It's got to be here," Pano announced, pointing vaguely downwards.

"But there's nothing here!"

"Maybe the source is under the ice and the interference field is pointed upwards," he suggested, shouting even though they were right next to each other. "That would make sense if you were trying to hide something."

"Hmm. Don't we have a shovel with us?" she shouted back, pointing to the gently humming hovercraft about twenty meters behind them. "Stay here, so we don't lose this spot. I'll go find that shovel!"

Agatha strode off at a good clip back to the hovercraft and rounded the boxy vehicle until she reached the flap of the service module at the rear. She turned the handle and lifted.

Behind it, in something like a wall-cupboard that was inset about a half meter deep into the back of the vehicle, were some heavy tools—a fission cutter, two shovels, a pickaxe, some smaller spades, a plasma torch, two carbon nanotube-reinforced ropes, and a hand drill. She took the fission cutter and the two shovels and locked the door before starting back.

As she passed the driver's cabin, she paused, put the tools down, and climbed up to rummage through Eversman's equipment bag. She found what she was looking for, climbed out again, collected the tools, and hurried over to Pano, who against the fading light looked like a dark statue on a sea of gray.

"What's that?" he asked, pointing to the belt in her left hand.

"Grenades!" she replied, gesturing behind her. "Borrowed them from Eversman. Might be easier than digging."

"Borrowed? Yeah, right!" Pano said with a laugh. "But they're also pretty noisy!"

"The wind's coming from that way," she said, pointing north. "The pyramid's down there. The wind ought to catch the noise. Besides, they'll be easy to bury."

"How about if we try digging first and only use the grenades if we don't get anywhere," he shouted, and Agatha nodded. She handed him one of the shovels and took the other one, pushing it into the ice at her feet.

The ground proved to be surprisingly hard and challenging to break up. After about fifteen minutes of strenuous digging, and about one meter down, her shovel's metal edge hit something even harder that didn't give. She knocked it several times with the shovel. She couldn't hear anything over the steady howling of the wind, but she imagined a resonating, metallic sound.

Pano noticed her movements, and they looked at each other for a few seconds that seemed longer before kneeling down inside the hollow and trying to scratch the outline of the object free with their gloves. It was tough going, and they had to use the fission cutter to really make any progress, but after a while they had uncovered a spherical object about the size of a child's head. It was smooth, made of dark metal, and attached on the bottom to a thick metal rod leading deeper.

"You ever see anything like this before?" Agatha asked. She didn't have to shout as loudly as before, because they were relatively sheltered from the wind in the hollow, although the hearing aid was shrieking louder than ever.

Pano shook his head. "No," he said. Then he pointed to the zippers on her suit. The zipper pulls were all pointing towards the ball, and seemed to be vibrating slightly.

Agatha's eyes widened, and she suddenly felt a headache rising in the back of her head.

"Let's take this thing out," Pano suggested over his hearing aid's objections.

"You really think that's a good idea?" Agatha asked skeptically. "We don't even know what it is. All we know is that someone thought it was important enough to put here. If it really is a magnetic jammer, it's extremely advanced. It's way beyond the Chinese prototype."

"In any case, it's meant to deter vehicles. Maybe even shut them down," he suggested. "So—"

"—so that makes you even more curious about what it's meant to hide," Agatha finished his sentence and looked up at the pyramid ahead of them. Behind it, the sun was just about to set again.

Pano nodded.

"Yeah, you're right," she said, and handed him one of the grenades.

"I think I'd rather try the fission cutter. I'm pretty sure a lot of the research stations had seismic equipment. I don't know how sensitive they all are, but they might pick up the vibrations. Better play it safe."

Agatha nodded again. Her ability to think clearly was obviously compromised by lack of sleep, and she didn't like that at all. She had to keep a cool head and stay sharp, because she had the feeling that this day was only going to get longer. Much longer.

32

FILIO AMOROSA, 2042

Filio awoke on a bed in the middle of a perfectly cubical room, perhaps five meters by five meters by five meters, exactly the same in every dimension. She could see nothing else in the room.

She felt tired, but not exhausted. It was more like she had slept too long and now needed some time to get her circulation going again.

Where am I? she thought, rubbing her eyes. She pushed the thin microfiber blanket off herself and swung her legs off the edge of the bed as she sat up. The walls around her looked as if they had been hewn out of stone, but they were extremely smooth. There were no windows, just a metal door in a large door frame. Above, in the middle of the ceiling, was a hole with a diameter of about an arm's length.

"Hello?" she inquired timidly, eyeing a pair of boots that had been placed on the floor next to the bed. They looked like diving boots, narrow and skintight. She noticed her feet were pretty cold so she put them on, and then noted the clothes she was wearing—a pair of tactical-fiber pants and matching long-sleeved top with reflector stripes down the sides.

Suddenly the memory of the airport, and of being abducted by strange men, came flooding back to her. The realization that she had been kidnapped hit her like a blow, and the room suddenly seemed much darker and smaller.

"Where the hell am I?"

"You're safe," a full-throated, resonant voice answered her immediately, and she jerked to face the door.

When she saw who was standing in the doorway, she recognized him, but reflexively rubbed her eyes in disbelief. It was Luther Karlhammer, smiling the smile that only a man who effectively owned the world could wear. He wore his black-streaked gray hair short, with close-cropped edges that had been razor trimmed with painstaking precision. His face was slightly round for his extremely slender body, and it was dominated by a long nose that hooked downward slightly. His size, or perhaps his charisma, which hovered around him like a cloud, seemed to work like a magnet, orienting everything his way—as, it seems, it did in life.

"You are safe here, Doctor Amorosa," reiterated the founder and CEO of the Human Foundation, moving towards the bed where she sat.

"Mr. Karlhammer…" Filio tried to begin, but could only stammer. "I…" She shook her head in a final attempt to determine whether she was dreaming or on some kind of drugs, but it was real. It was just so hard to believe.

"It's surprising how fast a life can take its twists and turns, isn't it?" he said, flashing that smile again.

"Yes. How did I get here?"

"Oh, a couple of assets friendly to my foundation brought you to me. This here," he made a curt gesture to all the space around her, "is our... well, let's call it our guest room."

"It looks more like an interrogation cell," she replied, eyeing her host suspiciously.

Karlhammer raised his hands defensively. "I don't want to interrogate you, Doctor, I want to interview you. But you never responded to our job offers. You see, I've actually been looking for an opportunity to get you in for an interview for quite some time. So when I learned that third parties were going to make an attempt to kidnap you, well, you can hardly blame me for seizing my chance, eh?"

"But it was you who kidnapped me," she said as she recalled what had happened, involuntarily touching the spot on her neck where the needle from the syringe had gone in. Her skin was a little tender around the injection site.

"Well, yes. I knew that they were going to try to kidnap you, so I had to beat them to it," Karlhammer replied almost apologetically, folding his hands. "And I am sorry we scared you. But I assure you that you are free to go at any time. That said, I'd much rather that you stay under my protection and listen to my job offer."

"Is it an offer that I have the option to refuse?" she asked, her eyes narrowing.

"We always have a choice," Karlhammer replied nebulously.

"Meaning that I could get up and walk out that door right now, and no one would stop me?"

"I'd quite honestly rather you listen to what I have to say, but... yes." He took one step aside and pointed to the door.

In an instant Filio had hopped off the bed and, in three great strides, reached the door and opened it. Beyond it was a long, dark hallway with very sparse lighting. She had expected to see a high-tech setting and security personnel, but it seemed more like she was being held in someone's creepy basement.

Thoughtful now, she turned back to Karlhammer. He was still standing next to the bed, looking at her with bemused interest. She couldn't shake the feeling that she was in some kind of experiment, and he was like the scientist monitoring the lab rat.

"Well, since you've already gone to the trouble of *saving* me," she said, deliberately putting an ironic emphasis on the word and gesturing to the less than hospitable surroundings, "I'll be *happy* to listen to what you have to say."

You're talking to the real Luther Karlhammer, she thought, and as her ability to think gradually came back, she felt a combination of excitement, irritation, and disbelief growing inside her. Everything in the last two days had happened so fast, and she hadn't had any time to process any of *what* had happened while it was happening.

Or project the consequences that all of it will have, she added, still verbalizing only to herself.

"Fantastic," Karlhammer said, and his smile grew a notch wider. It still didn't look forced, but every gesture and every facial expression did seem to be carefully managed and metered, as if he measured them on a very precise postal scale. "What I'd like to offer you is a place on a mission to Mars."

Filio froze. Speechless, unable to move even a finger, she just stared at Karlhammer.

"Well, now, I had hoped that you might be pleased."

"But I... I... I... don't understand," she managed to stammer, her brain overheating and her thoughts grinding to a smoking halt. Was the Human Foundation going to conjure up a mission to Mars like a rabbit out of a hat? Karlhammer had never taken any interest in space travel and had never funded any international research projects.

"Team lead, of course!" Karlhammer continued, and then he added, "Let me explain." He opened his brown jacket and moved it aside to reveal his T-shirt, emblazoned with the Human Foundation motto, 'Save The Planet, Save Yourself.' It was a slogan that had become one of the trademarks of the executive and inventor, and one worn by millions of people around the world to display their solidarity with the foundation. "You see, I've decided to save the world with a mission to Mars."

"But how? Are you going to build your own spaceship? Buy the International Space Agency's technology?" Filio shook her head in disbelief, and kept telling herself to proceed with caution. What he was offering her sounded far too much like what she had wished for, likely too good to be true. She had to stay alert if she was going to find the trap, or see through the illusion.

"You could say I already have my own ship. It's something I've been working on for over twenty years."

"You're trying to tell me that you've been working on your own interplanetary spacecraft, for twenty years, and no one in the world noticed?" Filio couldn't stop shaking her head. "You. Probably the most photographed person on earth. Care to tell me how you pulled that off?"

"Oh, deceptions, distractions, public appearances... You know, really, the secret is to just give people a believable picture. Then everything they see will be filtered through that image, and they won't even believe the other possibilities themselves," Karlhammer said with a shrug. "Besides, as you know, I do have my resources."

"And when is this momentous mission to Mars supposed to launch?" Filio asked, still cautious.

"This week."

"THIS *WEEK*?" All semblance of caution vanished. She slapped her hand over her open mouth as soon as she realized that she had yelled.

"Yes. That's another reason why I, unfortunately, didn't have the option to wait any longer for this interview," Karlhammer explained, his full baritone voice still relaxed. He turned his palms up.

"You wanted to use the same launch window for the trip to Mars, when our orbits around the sun are this close," she thought out loud, but Karlhammer shook his head almost imperceptibly.

"Yes and no. We do have a time window we need to meet, but it's not the one you think."

"Well, I can't say that makes it any clearer to me," she replied with a frown.

"It's quite complex. The technology that we've developed for this journey is a little different than what you know. But we have a local expert who developed it himself. Of course, it's a multi-billion-dollar project and I want to ensure that it's a complete success."

"Like everything else you do."

"Precisely," he said, without a trace of irony, and something in his eyes suddenly looked as if he was gazing proudly on a distant future that only he could see. "I might be only half the man the world sees or wants to see in me, but I try to live up to that apparent half as fully as possible—for our Earth. Even if that might sound melodramatic. But the goal of changing the world, of saving it, the goal that I've had since childhood, demands much more than vision and a few clever inventions. It demands surrounding yourself with only the best of the best, because any misstep on the way to the top can lead to a fatal crash—whether it's a market crash, a computer crash, a rocket crash, or an investment blowing up in your face. That's one of the reasons we established and funded the Foundation campuses all over the world. I want you, Doctor Amorosa, to lead the mission, because I think you are the top expert on Mars that humanity has."

"Well, thank you very much. I assume you're saying that because I'm the only one alive who has ever been there. Not a lot of competition for that title," she protested. She wasn't much for flattery, but she wasn't sure that he was trying to flatter her, either. Everything that came out of his mouth sounded so absolute, as if he was simply explaining how the world worked.

Karlhammer responded with another bemused smile, this time with something of a frown in it. Although in that T-shirt, jeans, and jacket—all of which had no doubt been specially tailored by leading designers to look as casual as possible—he might have been no more than a somewhat affluent student, it was like every one of his movements was made from a position of superiority, as if he was moving in loftier spheres. Filio was having a hard time resisting his magnetism. His voice, his eyes, his words—everything seemed to be whispering to her that she should relax and say 'yes' to whatever it was he was asking.

"You're right about that. But consider that I'm not going to put money on a horse that has never crossed the finish line. Contrary to what some books and films make out about me, I am no big fan of risk where risk can be avoided. Of course, some risks are necessary, but not nearly as often as people think. You've been to Mars before, so you should lead the mission. To me it's as simple as that. Not to mention your life story, which I must say also really impressed me!" Karlhammer added, nodding thoughtfully as if reviewing a memory.

Filio frowned. *How does he know my life story?*

"You, Doctor Amorosa, have shown that you have an indomitable will to succeed, and that there are no problems or obstacles that will deter you from achieving your goals," the South African went on. "This is a quality that we share, and it tells me that I will understand you better than the superiors you have had up to now. And I am one who very much wants to understand my employees."

"If this is a job interview, you certainly know how to make a workplace sound attractive, I'll say that," Filio remarked.

Karlhammer once again smiled his slightly distant, yet infectious smile. "I'm glad to hear that. I must warn you, though. If you take this job, there will be no turning back for you, and everything that you do will be out of the public eye. Officially, you will be listed as missing, having been kidnapped by terrorists." Suddenly he seemed very serious, looking at her gravely.

"You had me at 'mission to Mars,'" Filio finally confessed with a sigh. "If you're going to get me to Mars, you can set any conditions you want."

"Then it's agreed." Karlhammer clapped his tanned hands together and flashed another smile, revealing his white teeth. "Now all you have to do is sign the two-hundred-page contract."

When Filio's eyes bugged out in disbelief, he put his hand to his mouth and snickered. "I'm kidding."

"Can I see your ship?" she asked out of the blue, casting a longing glance into the hallway behind her.

"Soon," he assured her. "Before that I have a little information about your last mission that I would like to share with you. However, first I need you to assure me that when you see it, you will contain your distress."

"That makes it sound pretty distressing."

"I want to be completely honest. You won't like what I'm going to show you. You might even hate me for it. Not because I showed it to you, but because I should have shown it to you much sooner. But I would like you to understand why I couldn't do that."

"If you hadn't had my attention already, you would have it now," Filio said. "But I don't think that anything could be so bad that I would risk my chance to go to Mars."

"I wouldn't rush to that conclusion just yet," Karlhammer replied with an expression that was hard to read. He didn't seem uncertain—he didn't seem capable of that at all—but he might have been exhibiting signs of discomfort.

"I think before I show you what this is about, it's best that I give you a little background. Back in the twenties, when I started developing the lottery system that made the Human Foundation what it is today, I had a huge number of construction sites on my hands. And I needed a fresh injection of cash to take care of them all. That's what the lottery was for. But I wasn't just trying to fight climate change, I was also taking up the fight against the sins of humanity.

"Like factory farming. The first time you ever really see an industrial slaughterhouse with your own eyes, how the animals are kept, and killed, and dismembered, cold, mechanical, inhuman—I promise you, you'll feel sick. I'm not saying this as a militant vegan—actually, I gladly eat everything our planet has to offer—I'm saying this as a human being, which means I have a capacity for empathy and compassion.

"Everyone has this capacity, but these emotions are not being triggered when you're standing in the supermarket, looking at a package, with a label that features a jolly little pig smiling at you. The cruelty of factory farming was always too abstract. Around the table, everyone nods and says, 'Yes, something has to be done, this cannot go on, we cannot let animals be kept this way.' But hardly anyone turned the one screw that could have made a difference—their own consumer behavior.

"This, in a nutshell, is exactly how I see the human condition. 'Out of sight, out of mind,' or 'Somebody else's problem,' or 'Rome wasn't built in a day.' Pick your favorite aphorism, they are all perfectly apt. As long as a factory-farmed animal that had lived a brutal life and gone through an even more brutal death was cheaper than an animal treated with dignity, people would still line up to buy it. You see, our brains register the label and the price, but cannot truly perceive the entire chain behind it. I never blamed people for this, because I can understand it completely.

"The solution, like for so many other things, was the lottery system. It's so much easier for people to pay ten dollars a month, or even a week, forever, if they know something good is being done with it and they might even win something back for it. People are bad at math, and good at hope, and that brings me to a very important point—people are good by nature, but you just have to show them the ways to live right. Then they will take them. Egoism is always there, but if you channel it in the right direction, it can be a force for good."

"The lottery system," Filio nodded. "They have a chance to win something for themselves, something to set them apart from everybody else, and meanwhile they can justify their trying because they know they're supporting a good cause, which they wear like a badge of honor." It made sense. The system was so simple that it was ingenious.

"Right. It gives them the option to show that they are really concerned, even altruistic. Isn't that exciting? How simple it is, I mean, the way people really work? To me it seemed to be an elegant solution to the fundamental problem of the asociality of large communities. When human societies were still built around tribes, we didn't struggle with issues like egoism, the individuality delusion, self-actualization, all these things. We lived in communities of fifty to a hundred people, and we all depended on the social group. It was our life and it was our habitat.

"But ever since we have been crowded into cities by the millions upon millions, these mechanisms have ceased to function, and we seek to alienate ourselves from ourselves. The lottery was the solution, even though ironically it's also the biggest scam ever foisted on the human race."

Karlhammer paused for a moment, and seemed to be gauging the taste of his next words before continuing. "But it's a benevolent scam. I never tried to tell people, or show people, where their meat was coming from, because it would never have worked. The solution was all about coming up with the right idea at the right time."

Filio was getting confused. "But what does any of that have to do with what you need to show me?"

"Everything. I have withheld information from you, information that has been in my possession for two years and that I could not share with anyone. In fact, I still can't," he explained, watching Filio like a circling falcon watches its prey.

Filio's mind raced feverishly, wondering what he could possibly be about to tell her. For two years? Did it have something to do with the *Mars One* disaster? Did he know something about the crash that she didn't? That nobody did?

When Karlhammer saw that she wasn't going to say anything, he began to speak again in his rich baritone voice. "I know what happened on Mars, and I also know why you crashed."

Filio took a step back and warningly raised an index finger in his direction. Her lips began to tremble and she felt her knees buckling. "Be careful," she whispered weakly.

"I have satellite images of you and your former crew. I have images of what you found there, and I have all the transmissions you sent to Mission Control on the way," Karlhammer continued, undeterred.

"What? That's... not... possible..." Filio's head began shaking frantically. "Mission Control didn't receive any transmissions from us! The whole mission, the whole four-month return flight, we never got one reply because they never received anything in Darmstadt." She was shaking her head almost uncontrollably now. "There's no way you could have these transmissions. That's impossible."

"It's not impossible, because I'm the one who intercepted them," Karlhammer said. He refrained from saying more when Filio's knees buckled and she collapsed to the floor, as if struck by a blow, her hands grasping her head as if to stop the shaking, which had become frantic again.

"But how? And why?"

"I have my resources, and I installed them before the launch of *Mars One*, so I would be able to influence the mission," he said, completely unmoved, as if he was reading a dull, dry audit report.

Filio raised her head, shooting an incendiary look at him as rage boiled up inside her. Her next words came out of her mouth unerringly and direct, like a shot from a gun.

"Are you responsible for the crash?"

"No," Karlhammer said without hesitation, looking her

straight back in the eyes. "No, I am not. On the contrary, I installed surveillance to protect you and your crew, precisely for reasons of public interest. You found something on the Red Planet that you were never meant to find. I *tried* to shoot down your ship, because I *had* to prevent you from returning to Earth at any cost, but our missile was intercepted by the NATO Defense Shield, and as soon as that happened we had our hands full covering up our involvement. I'm afraid that you have only your pilot, Timothy Knowles, to thank for the crash."

"Are you trying to tell me that he deliberately crashed us?" she asked, finally sitting up. Her rage was white-hot now, and she was clenching her fists.

"Yes," he replied, and that steely gaze he had been giving her softened slightly. There might have been something like compassion in it now, but she could find no trace of sadness, or regret. "He was trying to save us—humanity—from being eradicated."

"What? What the hell are you talking about? You're starting to sound like the terrorists, like the Sons of Terra with all their talk about *The Enemy*." She was growling now, as the intense memories of Timothy and the others who had been incinerated in Earth's atmosphere sent her anger beyond the boiling point.

"Well, that's because they're right, and I'm financing them, in part. The Sons of Terra know about *The Enemy*, because Workai Dalam found him at the bottom of the sea. *The Enemy* is very real, Doctor Amorosa, I assure you. And you brought him here from Mars."

33

AGATHA DEVENWORTH, 2042

Pano held the metal ball in his hands and looked at Agatha with a quizzical head tilt. She responded with a shrug. He dropped the strange object and then held up his hearing aid and moved it around. It made no sound. "Well, whatever that thing is," he said, pointing to the cut end of the metal bar, which had a few cables peeking out of it, "it's not working anymore."

"Is it completely off? Or just weaker now?"

Pano loosened his hood enough to put the tiny device into his left ear and looked off into the distance. "I can still hear some noise, but it's not nearly as loud as it was."

"So there are more of those things, to the left and right of us," she observed, and stuck her head above the rim of the hollow to look around. "I wouldn't be surprised if there was a whole ring of them around that thing." She gestured to the pyramid.

"Mm-hmm. Why don't we see what the electronics have to say?" Pano climbed out of the hollow and extended a hand to Agatha, which after a moment of hesitation she accepted and let Pano help her out of the hole. As soon as they were back on the unsheltered ice, the wind assaulted them, whistling in tiny vortices around their helmets in a quietly screaming chorus.

Tucking their heads down, they ran back to the hovercraft, tossed the tools into the rear compartment where Agatha had found them, and climbed up into the driver's cabin, where they found an awake but confused Eversman.

"What's happening?" he asked. His eyes were bloodshot, and he looked like he'd had a big night on the town.

"You passed out," Agatha told him, as she strapped herself into the passenger seat. Pano, meanwhile, had taken off his gloves and was rubbing his hands together. Then he grabbed the control toggle and pushed the power lever forward.

"And?" she asked.

"All systems are functioning normally. And now I can see the mountain on the radar." With an outstretched index finger, he entered something on the display screen behind his control module and then gave a thumbs-up.

"Could one of you just tell me what's going on?" Eversman interjected, sounding disturbed.

"Well, you lost consciousness when we started getting close to this... *mountain*. We think it has something to do with a jamming transmitter that we found buried over there. We've rendered it inoperable," Agatha explained patiently.

"Thanks. So now I know just as much as I did before, or maybe less." The soldier frowned and sank back into his seat in visible confusion.

"We're in the same boat." Turning to the Italian, she asked, "Pano, can you make out any openings anywhere?"

"Not with the sensors. There's a pair of binoculars in the glove compartment. Maybe you'll be able to see something with residual light enhancement." He gestured vaguely at the dashboard in front of her.

She opened the hard plastic flap and pulled out the heavy electronic binoculars. Zooming in with digital magnification, she searched the base of the pyramid, which looked green-tinted and slightly pixelated from the residual light enhancement. She scanned up and down the rough surface for any telltale black dots. She found one, right in the middle of the pyramid at ground level blended into the whiteness of the ice. A hole, probably about the size of a small car.

"There," Agatha announced, pointing through the windshield straight ahead. "Right in the middle. Head straight for the center."

"On it. Just about two kilometers until—" Pano never finished his sentence, because he was interrupted by a loud rattling noise, and then the hovercraft abruptly stopped. The thrust cut off so suddenly that all three of them were only held back by their three-point seatbelts.

"Damn! What was that?" Agatha groaned, rubbing her collarbone in pain. "Did the engine go out?"

"It sure did. No juice at all anymore. All the displays are dead," Pano replied. He pressed the start button, then pushed it again a few more times, but the vehicle didn't make a sound, and the lights and screens showed no sign of life. "What the hell is this? Do we have a burnout?"

"Maybe we drove over something," Eversman suggested from the back seat.

Agatha snorted a little harder than she meant to. "It's a hovercraft. We're on top of a giant air cushion. If we were about to hit something, one of the collision sensors would have been triggered, and then if we had driven over it the cushion would've been ripped open."

She pulled her ski mask down again and put her helmet on. "Let's go take a look."

She opened her door and went down the ladder and onto the ice. She had to hold the collar of her thermal jacket tightly around her neck, hiding her mouth behind the fur. Then she walked around the side of the vehicle looking for... what? She wasn't even sure. On her side, everything was normal, and there was nothing to be seen at the rear either.

"Hey, Agatha!" she heard Pano's voice calling on the wind. "You'd better come look at this."

She turned quickly and ran to the other side of the hovercraft, where she saw her partner framed against the oncoming darkness, standing at the front of the hovercraft and pointing his flashlight at a fist-sized hole in the side of the vehicle, just above the bulging cushion that rested on the ice.

The metal around the hole had split and bent inwards. The light from the flashlight traveled a full meter into the body onto the battery, from which a bluish smoke was rising. There was a sharp smell of plastic and ozone.

"That's a goddamn bullet hole!" she spat out, touching the steaming metal of the outer hull with a gloved hand. She could feel that it was still warm, even through the thick gloves.

Slowly getting up, she turned and looked around uncomfortably across the endless ice landscape that was rapidly disappearing into the spreading darkness.

"Don't you think we should take cover?" Pano asked grimly, but Agatha didn't seem concerned.

"Wherever the shooter is, he's got us in his sights right now. If he had wanted to kill us, he'd have shot us through the windshield, to get it done fast. That right there," she said, pointing behind her without taking her eyes off the dark horizon, as if one false move might get her killed, "was a shot from a .50 caliber, armor-piercing round. You know, an anti-tank gun."

"So someone wants us to turn around?"

"And they seem pretty insistent about it. I guess we'd better hope they also understand we can't do that now because they've shot our only ride out from under us," she growled against the biting cold.

Picking up the binoculars again, Agatha scanned the dim horizon, clenching her teeth in frustration—then suddenly she paused and looked at Pano. "If we connect the spare battery, we might be able to power the radio."

"Well, when the lights come on, I'm sure we're going to get a second shot, and this time probably not just in the battery," Pano pointed out with a concerned look.

"You got any better ideas?"

"No."

"All right, then." She tossed him the binoculars, which he only caught at the last second, and climbed back up to the cabin, pulling herself up slowly on each rung.

"Hey, Eversman," she said, turning to the sergeant as she closed the door. "You know how to connect the spare battery?"

"Of course I do," the soldier assured her with a nod. "To do that, you gotta open up the front hood so you can get to the engine."

"You can't do that from in here?"

Eversman shook his head. "Nope. The driver's cabin is pretty insulated, on account of the cold and all."

"Crap. If the shooter sees me dragging a spare battery out there, he'll shoot a hole in that one too."

"Shooter?" the sergeant asked, suddenly alarmed and reaching instinctively for his carbine.

"Easy, easy," Agatha said, trying to calm him down. "There's a sniper out there somewhere, and he shot through the battery."

"I can go out there and try to get behind him. Did you see him?"

"No, and I bet if you jump out there with a gun, it'll be the last thing you do."

"We could try the radio. Sounds like he didn't want to kill us as his first option, just get us to stop," Eversman suggested, and Agatha smiled a cheerless smile.

"That's exactly what I was thinking. But we need some juice to power the radio."

"If he can see us anyway, maybe we can make it clear to him, or them if there's more than one of them out there, that we're trying to connect the battery to get on the radio."

Pano had come back in while they were talking and was sitting in the passenger seat staring out the windshield nervously. "But if they wanted to talk to us out here, why didn't they radio us instead of blowing our engine to hell?" he asked.

"Let's find out," Agatha said succinctly, opening the door and then descending the ladder again. When she reached the front of the hovercraft, she waved both her arms and then took off her right glove to make the international 'phone call' sign with her right hand against the side of her head. With her other hand, looking like a shapeless lump in the heavy glove, she pointed vaguely in front of her and then to her mouth.

"Come on down with the battery, Eversman, and hook it up," she screamed as loud as she could over the howling of the wind, the effort of shouting helping to push the thought out of her mind that at any moment she might feel a stabbing pain rip through her and crumple her to the ground.

How do we know that the shooter will want to talk? she asked herself. *Well, if he shoots the replacement battery we'll have our answer*, she thought, gritting her teeth as if that might brace her for the bullet that was no doubt trained on her right now. She could almost feel it tearing through her body already.

The sergeant was climbing through the door slowly, dragging one of the spare batteries with him. He tossed it down into the snow and then jumped after it. Hitting the ground, he looked around and then dragged the large, heavy, seat cushion-sized battery to the front where he opened the engine cover.

Agatha counted every second that passed without a punishing shot cracking through the night air, hoping that Eversman also knew how precious each second was and could get it done as fast as possible.

"Do it fast," she urged him loudly, without taking her eyes off the pyramid, its outline barely visible now. She didn't want to think about what it would be like out here in the dark without any light source. With no reference points, they wouldn't even find the pyramid, even though it was less than two kilometers away.

"Working as fast as I can," the sergeant complained behind her, and it sounded like he was. She heard a metallic screech that barely reached her ears before it was carried away on the wind.

Pano appeared next to her with his hands in the air, like he was surrendering. "Nothing quite as shitty as knowing there's someone out there pointing a tankbreaker at you," he grumbled.

"It could be worse."

"Oh really? How?"

"It could be more than one sniper."

Pano turned to her and smiled a tortured smile. "I liked you better when you didn't make jokes."

"Wasn't a joke," she assured him. She nodded towards the darkness. "Anybody who can bury an advanced remote jamming system out here, and is getting visits from personnel transport helicopters, is not going to have a welcoming committee of one. They're going to have a whole team."

"So what? Looks like one's enough to pin us down right here."

"Mm-hmm. For a minute I thought we could wait until dark, but I'm sure they're using infrared or ultrasound, which we don't have."

"Finished!" Eversman shouted, an instant before floodlights lit up their backs and spread out ahead of them like a carpet rolling out.

"So, what are you going to say?" Pano asked, arms still raised.

"I'm going to start with 'please don't shoot.'" Agatha turned and, with slow and deliberate steps, walked around to the ladder. Before she touched the ladder's short grip bars, she made the phone call sign again and pointed to the cabin. Then she climbed up and dropped into the driver's seat. She grabbed the radio from above her head and waited until Pano and the sergeant had followed her, gotten in, and closed the doors behind them.

"All right, here goes," she said, and pushed the button for the automatic frequency scan, which sent out an automated request for contact until someone or something jumped on it.

Nothing happened except for static filling the cabin. In the enclosed space, it sounded louder and more ominous than it was.

Agatha scoffed, then pressed the *Transmit* button as she raised the fist-sized microphone to her mouth. "This is Special Agent Agatha Devenworth of the United States Department of Homeland Security, Counter-Terrorist Directive. My superiors have been informed of my location. If I do not report in within the next thirty minutes, it's going to get a lot more crowded out here. I would therefore suggest you talk to me."

"A bluff?" Pano asked in surprise when she had taken her thumb off the transmit button.

Agatha's face was grim as she awaited a response. "It's worth a try. I mean, I've got nothing to work with here."

"Look!" the sergeant interrupted them, sticking his arm between them and pointing ahead. The last glimmers of daylight disappeared beyond the horizon, and the world went pitch dark in an instant.

"Great," Pano muttered. Simultaneously, the loudspeaker roared with static and then went still.

"Come out of the vehicle, leave all items inside, and get face-down on the ground. Then put your hands behind your head and wait until we pick you up," a monotonous voice ordered through the radio, speaking so emotionlessly and precisely that Agatha shivered. From the sound of it, the man on the radio was ready to end them—and would do so without hesitation and without remorse.

"Who am I speaking to?" Agatha said back into the radio.

"Come out of the vehicle, leave all items inside, and get face-down on the ground. Then put your hands behind your head and wait until we pick you up," the voice repeated. "This is your last warning."

Then a burst of static, and then the frequency went dead.

Agatha and Pano looked at each other and nodded.

"Looks like we don't have a choice," Pano said.

"Mm-hmm," Agatha grumbled, and then sighed, puffing out her cheeks. "I hate being backed into a corner. All right, what are we waiting for? Let's get out."

"I thought we were supposed to be solving a disappearance, not disappearing ourselves."

"What about our guns? We're taking them, right?" Eversman asked.

"No!" Agatha and Pano answered at the same time, and then looked at each other again.

Without another word, they removed their handguns from their holsters under the snowsuits and put them, moving pointedly slowly, on the control panel where they could be seen from outside. Then they opened the doors, climbed down, and shuffled over to where they were in the light of the hovercraft's headlights, where the small reserve battery was still lying attached to a cable that disappeared into the hole in the engine.

When all three of them were in the light and had gotten to their knees, a single shot whizzed through the darkness, there was a bang, and the lights went out again. Instant pitch black.

"Anyone hit?" Agatha asked as she lay down on her stomach, tensing her neck so her nose would not touch the ice.

"Negative," Eversman's voice replied.

"No," said Pano's. They both sounded far away, even though she knew they had to be right next to her. *Must be the wind*, she thought, and waited.

For some time nothing happened, and it was terrifyingly quiet. Every sound that was not swallowed up by the ravenous darkness was torn away and carried off by the howling wind sweeping mercilessly over them and driving the cold deeper and deeper into their clothes.

When she was suddenly grabbed by several hands, it happened so fast that she screamed in terror before someone put something over her head and pulled her roughly to her feet.

"Hey!" she protested loudly, struggling to resist the powerful hands. They gripped so hard that she felt the fingers all but drilling into her bones.

No one spoke as she was dragged off in some unknown direction.

"Pano? Can you hear me?"

He answered in a muffled groan: "Yes, I'm here." It sounded like he'd had a sack put over his helmet and head as well, but he sounded close. Her air was rapidly becoming unpleasantly stuffy from her own breathing.

"Quiet," said an emotionless voice, and Agatha thought it was the same one that had spoken on the radio.

Frantically, she tried to estimate how much time it had been between the shot to the reserve battery and the moment they were grabbed. One minute? Maybe two?

Either way, it was so damn fast that she had to wonder how the shooter—and the team evidently backing him up—could have been so close without her or Pano seeing them.

"Who are you? Do you know what the penalty is for... AAAH!" she screamed as she took a violent blow to the kidney area. It was so hard, and the pain so jarring, that it took all her willpower to keep from pissing herself.

"I said, *'Quiet!'*" the dead voice repeated, and Agatha obeyed.

She felt the urge to whimper and curl into a ball as wave upon wave of searing pain emanated from her lower back and rolled uncontrollably through her whole body. But she couldn't even do that, because she was still being relentlessly dragged on as the wind tugged violently at the sack over her head. A few times the fine fabric of it caught between her cracked lips and became damp. She figured she might be drooling, but didn't really notice because her whole world was nothing but pain.

She took a breath and tried without success to concentrate on hiding how badly she hurt. After what felt like an eternity, she realized the wind had stopped and then the cold suddenly vanished as if a switch had been flipped. It was quiet except for the echoing clacks of booted feet. She heard machinery humming somewhere, and it smelled of mold and ozone, a strange combination.

So, where have I ended up now?

34

FILIO AMOROSA, 2042

Filio followed Karlhammer in shocked silence through the claustrophobia-inducing darkness of the hallways of the building they were in. She could not muster a single word as she struggled to digest what had just been revealed to her. It was all simply too unbelievable to be true. The Sons of Terror were right, and their conspiracy theory about an alien pulling the strings of mankind was correct? And Karlhammer was financing them? Meaning that he was indirectly, or maybe even very directly, responsible for the attack on *Mars Two*. And that would mean that he had sent the men and women who had wiped out her new team, and very nearly killed her, in cold blood. That would mean she had just signed on with the most dangerous, murderous man on the planet.

And he already told me that there was no turning back, she recalled, rubbing her sweating hands as these thoughts spun around in her head.

A murderer and terrorist... except... except the thing is... he's right. But how could he be? How could we have brought an alien to Earth? Filio could only shake her head as they walked into a room where men and women in unadorned red uniforms were working on wall displays, all of them wearing state-of-the-art data glasses, fully engrossed in their silent gestures. On the displays she saw endless rows of numbers and diagrams scrolling by in a mad, bewildering riot. She could make absolutely no sense of them, and could only imagine they were meaningful in combination with what was being displayed in the augmented reality space of the data glasses.

As they turned right to go down another hallway, Karlhammer stopped so abruptly that she almost crashed into him.

"What is it?" Filio asked.

"Possibly nothing," he said after a short pause, and then moved on without turning around.

Since he clearly didn't want to talk about it, she remained silent and followed him as he picked up speed, turned left twice, and finally burst into a vast room. It was gigantic, perhaps as large as a football field, and the roof was an arched shell high above them. The walls were covered in transparent paneling, which gave her the feeling of being in a greenhouse.

The floor was also covered in transparent paneling, and out in the middle of it were four separate areas filled with desks, workbenches, and various kinds of machinery. Perhaps a hundred men and women in the same red uniforms she had seen before were scurrying around working here. The air was clear, almost sterile, and buzzing with murmured conversations and equipment noise.

"What is this place?" she asked in amazement. Karlhammer, who had kept walking, only stopped and turned around when he noticed she had stopped.

"Research and development," he replied casually, and then, "Oh... right."

The Fossil

Filio's gaze wandered to four people in the back of the enormous room. They were just carrying a large, coffin-like object out of sight. Karlhammer, meanwhile, had moved further toward the center of the room and was standing in an empty space between four towering metal grilles from which a maze of sensors and cables were hung. In front of him were six figures wearing snow-white bodysuits covered in dangling white threads. They all had long guns over their shoulders, and in pairs they were holding three other people who seemed to have their hands tied behind their backs. Their heads were covered by black bags, but from their clothing, it looked like they were soldiers, too.

Filio was both curious and alarmed. She hurried to catch up to Karlhammer.

"Who are these people?" she asked.

"That's something I'd like very much like to know myself," he said, as much to himself as anyone else. "Well, then, Captain, who are they?"

One of the men in snow camouflage pulled his white balaclava down around his chin, revealing a hard, weathered face with a hooked nose and narrow lips. "It seems this here is Special Agent Agatha Devenworth of the Counter-Terrorist Division," he answered coolly.

"Counter-Terrorist *Directive*," a female voice corrected from beneath the black bag. The soldier drew a Taser wand and was about to use it.

Karlhammer stopped him with a wave of his hand. "Take those things off their heads!" he ordered.

The man Karlhammer had just addressed as 'Captain' shrugged and gestured to his men. They removed the black bags from the heads of the three kneeling figures, revealing two men and a woman.

She had long, blonde hair that was stringy and matted

where it showed below the helmet. Her face was attractive but steely, and there was a fighting spirit behind her eyes.

Kneeling next to her was a man with three-day stubble and a chiseled lower jaw. As soon as the bag was removed, he looked around the room trying to take it all in, and when he saw Karlhammer his eyes bulged. He seemed to be about forty years old, like the woman next to him.

The third figure, a man, was noticeably younger and looked pale, as if he had not slept for a long time. His eyes went first to Filio and then to Karlhammer, but if he was surprised he didn't let it show.

"No... this can't be real," Pano sputtered, staring at the South African as if he were the Eighth Wonder of the World.

"Oh, I can assure you, I am very real, and I am very truly here," he said, flashing a cold smile. "But unfortunately, you have me at a disadvantage. Perhaps you could help an old man out and tell me who you are?"

"I'm Special Agent Agatha Devenworth, of the United States Counter-Terrorist Directive," she said, throwing an angry look at the man who a moment ago was just about to tase her, and then turned back to Karlhammer. "This is Capitano Pano Hofer, and that's Sergeant Eversman of the United States Marine Corps."

"Hmm," the older man mused, rubbing his chin thoughtfully, and then said again, "Hmm."

"What are you doing here?" Agatha asked bluntly

"That is exactly what I was just about to ask you," Karlhammer countered, pausing in his movements to cross his arms over his chest. "After all, it is you who broke into my house. Captain, where is it you found our guests?"

"Right at the edge of the security perimeter. They came in a hovercraft. One of McMurdo's," the emotionless-looking man answered.

"Ah," Karlhammer said, and looked back at Agatha. "So, then, what is it you are doing here?"

"Wouldn't you like to know."

"Why yes, I would."

"Well, I'll tell you," Agatha replied. She took a deep breath before going on. "I'll tell you, when you've explained to me what the hell you're doing in a pyramid in Antarctica and where Ron Jackson is," she retorted. She breathed deeply again. "Then, maybe, I'll tell you."

His arms still crossed, Karlhammer tapped his right temple with an index finger in a steady rhythm, and smiled at the three new arrivals. "Did you search them?" he asked the captain, who nodded.

"No weapons, no virus."

"Virus?" Pano and Agatha asked at the same time.

Karlhammer didn't pay any attention to them, and instead looked at Sergeant Eversman. "This one is a soldier." His gaze moved back to the two agents. "These two are intelligence officers. Explain that to me."

"Basically, he flew us here."

"I see. Captain, please escort the young Marine to one of our... guest rooms." As Eversman was being hoisted up and dragged out, Karlhammer looked intensely at Agatha and Pano, as if trying to gauge their reaction. But they only looked back at him, returning his gaze flatly. After this staring contest had gone on for a while, Karlhammer nodded, as if he had just understood something.

"So, you were at McMurdo," he suddenly started speaking. "What happened there? We haven't had any radio contact with them since yesterday, and the helicopter I sent hasn't returned yet. Are they having another power problem?"

"You tell us what we want to know, then we'll tell you

what you want to know," Agatha replied in a cool, measured tone.

That ominous smile again, with something twisted at the corners of Karlhammer's mouth. "Very well. Unfortunately, I must inform you that you cannot leave this place for at least a week, maybe more, and I must fit you with tracking devices."

When Agatha opened her mouth to reply, he silenced her with a raised hand. "I'm afraid this is not negotiable. Consider it your first gesture to make amends for breaking into my home."

"Ouch!" Pano yelled angrily, as one of the soldiers held a gun-like device to his neck and pulled the trigger. There was a brief hissing sound. The same was done to Agatha, but she only grimaced and shot Karlhammer a withering look.

"Now then," Karlhammer said, seemingly satisfied. With a wave of his hand, he gave his armed men a signal and they moved behind the two agents. A moment later, their hands were free. They both rubbed their wrists as they stood up.

"All right, your turn to give us some answers," Pano said. "What are you doing here?" Filio couldn't place his unusual accent. His English sounded a little German, but he rolled his Rs in a way that was somehow more Spanish.

"To explain that, I will have to take you directly to Ron Jackson," Karlhammer replied, pointing to the far end of the vast cavern. The red-uniformed personnel swarming around the cavern seemed wholly engrossed in their work, ignoring them. "He's why you're here, am I right?"

"That's right," Agatha answered bluntly.

"If I may ask, why is it that, after twenty-four years, they finally send someone looking for my old friend?" Karlhammer was now looking at the female agent eagerly, and when he said the word 'friend' his eyes flashed with a strange glimmer that Filio did not know how to interpret. Perhaps a twinge of regret?

"Take me to him, and I'll tell you. That was the deal, wasn't it?"

Karlhammer responded with a quick nod, and gestured for them to follow him.

They passed several workstations separated by man-high partitions. As she passed, Filio could only just see the heads of the people working in them, and would have loved to peer over the walls and see what they were doing. But she needed answers, so she forced herself to keep walking without causing trouble. The two agents apparently felt the same. The American, in particular, Filio thought, seemed extremely focused, even obsessed. If there was anyone who could squeeze answers out of the most powerful man in the world, she was probably the one.

"So how is it that you're actually here, Doctor?" Agatha suddenly asked. "Shouldn't you be on the way to Mars right now?" Filio had not at all been expecting to be addressed by the agent, so she didn't even register it at first. When she saw the woman looking at her, she jerked in surprise and looked back at her in confusion.

"You recognize me?"

"Of course. You were all over the media in the week before the launch. That was the day before yesterday, wasn't it? I'm shocked to see you here."

Filio scrutinized the agent's smooth face for an indication that she might be making some kind of sick joke, but saw nothing other than genuine curiosity. "It must have taken you a while to get here, am I right?"

"Yes," Agatha nodded. "Why do you ask?"

"There was a terrorist attack on *Mars Two*," Filio explained, and realized that her voice was trembling when she said it. The memories of it came flooding back, and she struggled to not let it show, but they were still so fresh and intense that she didn't really succeed.

"What?" Agatha and Pano asked at the same instant, both in shock.

"Yes. The Sons of Terra attacked the launch site with thousands of drones, and they had moles among the soldiers who were supposed to protect us."

"Those damn swine," Pano growled, and followed this with a torrent of swearing in German that, if Filio hadn't spent two years of her life at sea, would have made her blush.

Agatha didn't speak, but looked equally affected and could only stare back in confusion.

"Yes. I—" Filio started to say something.

Karlhammer interrupted her loudly. "We're almost there!" He pointed to a brightly lit passageway that, like the rest of the vast chamber, was clad in transparent plates, but behind them the walls seemed to be smoothly hewn stone. "After you."

Agatha didn't trust him, and the look she gave Karlhammer showed it. But she went ahead anyway, and Pano followed her. He stood there a moment longer, and then gestured to Filio. It seemed that she, too, was meant to go in. He shrugged and went in after the two agents, leaving Filio behind. But the two soldiers in the snow camouflage suits made it clear with short movements of their machine guns that there was no going back for Filio, only forward.

35

AGATHA DEVENWORTH, 2042

Agatha stood, still in acute pain but refusing to acknowledge it, before a giant metal door. She'd been peeing blood ever since the kidney punch. The door looked like the gateway to a serious bank vault. In the exact center was a keypad, obviously intended for a code input, and above it was some kind of microphone-like nozzle protruding a few centimeters from the surface of the door. Above that, there was a thumbnail-sized LED shining in red.

"Allow me," Karlhammer said from behind them. He stepped forward, typed in a short sequence of numbers, and placed his mouth above the nozzle to exhale into it. The LED switched to green, and the door swung ponderously inwards.

Karlhammer took a step to one side and motioned for them to proceed. Agatha and Pano exchanged looks, and then walked through the doorway into a large room with a high ceiling, clad in transparent paneling like the first chamber they'd seen. On the left wall were two AR cabins in which uniformed personnel were busily processing invisible data with rapid gestures. Agatha looked around the room, but when she saw what was in the middle, she froze. Inside a glass cube—she estimated a five-meter edge-length—she saw a giant figure with caramel-colored skin. It was wearing red tactical pants and a form-fitting T-shirt.

At first glance, Agatha thought it might be the world's biggest man, but almost immediately she noticed a few differences—caramel-colored skin, arms that looked a little too long, like a chimpanzee's, and an impossibly long face with a nose angled downwards. And then there were the wide, jet-black eyes, which were focused on her, even though she was a good ten meters from the middle of the glass box in which the figure stood. She had the feeling that she was being X-rayed.

"What... what is that..." Pano stammered, while next to him Filio, the astronaut, gasped and put her hand to her mouth.

"This, my friends, is a Builder," Karlhammer explained. "Although he refers to himself as Xinth."

"'A Builder?'" Agatha asked. She was having trouble sorting out her thoughts, and as she did, she took a few hesitant steps forward. The figure didn't move, but its eyes followed her every movement. It was simply standing there, observing them. "The Builders were the civilization that Jackson hypothesized in his work. They were supposed to have lived millions of years before our era."

"That's correct."

"Is that... is this the alien you were talking about?" Filio asked. Karlhammer shook his head.

"No. *The Enemy* is not under our control. At least, not yet. Technically, Xinth here is not an alien, because he was born on Earth, like you and me. Only, he was born more than 60 million years before you and me."

"But how can that be?" Agatha whispered, unable to take her eyes off the muscular giant in the glass box.

"It seems that Ron found him in a kind of stasis chamber that some ancient advanced civilizations were able to access. They woke him up whenever they needed his help."

"'His help?'"

"Yes. He fulfills more or less all the criteria of a god, except that you can see him and touch him."

"Why is he in this glass box? Is he your prisoner?" Pano asked. He looked like he had seen a ghost, and it had scared all the color right out of his face.

"Oh no, he's not a prisoner," Karlhammer replied, shaking his head definitively. "The glass walls are for his protection. When he walked the Earth, atmospheric conditions were quite different. For example, the oxygen content of the air was much higher, so high it would kill us. And our conditions today would kill him."

"I can't believe what I'm seeing," Agatha confessed. "This is... I don't know what I'm supposed to say."

"Ron Jackson was right all along," Karlhammer said in a low voice, as if he was talking to himself.

"Where is he?" she asked. In response, the South African pointed to the Builder.

"Ron is now a part of Xinth."

"Wait, what?"

"The contact with Xinth was a most curious process," a third voice said, and Agatha turned around to see the person who'd spoken coming towards them from some kind of switchboard set up off to the right. Agatha narrowed her eyes. She felt like she knew this person from somewhere, but couldn't say exactly where. His hair was completely silvered, but immaculately styled, and he wore a sleek pinstripe suit that somehow seemed out of place in these surroundings.

"I believe you know Peter Gould?" Karlhammer asked, and for the third time that day Agatha gasped and held her breath.

That's why he looked familiar. He's so much older than in the photos from the files, she thought. Then she asked in disbelief, "You're Peter Gould?"

"Yes," he answered simply, holding out his hand. She shook it as if she was meeting someone in a dream. Gould also shook hands politely with Pano and Filio.

"I have to confess, we thought that you had staged Jackson's kidnapping."

Gould raised an eyebrow. "Well, I'm pleased to be able to inform you that that is not the case. We only had to take certain precautions to keep this place secret. Initially, for financial reasons relating to the Foundation, of course, and later for... obvious reasons." He gestured towards the Builder, who was still watching, waiting, motionless.

"What happened?" Pano asked.

Gould looked at Karlhammer, who gave a small, barely perceptible nod.

"Jackson was suddenly gone, as if he had disappeared off the face of the earth. We searched for him for nearly two full days, but found nothing, only his radio, just lying there in the main cavern, the one you just came through," Gould explained. "Then on the third day, *he* appeared before us," he said, with a nod of his head towards Xinth. After they all looked, he went on. "One of the students panicked and attacked him with a plasma cutter. Well, that did not end well for the student, I can tell you, but it nearly went far worse for us all."

"What do you mean?"

"Xinth killed the student instantly. He simply looked at him, and the student turned into a kind of... well, all his biological components dissolved into a sort of cloud, that hung there for a few moments, almost like you had taken the parts of a model ship and flung them into the air, and they just hovered there, spinning. It was quite terrifying, I can tell you. And I dare say we owe our survival to my... well let's call it my not-particularly-combative nature, as far as that goes. Another student named Dana and I were there and saw it happen, and we immediately knelt down in surrender, and raised our arms, when suddenly he spoke to us. He knew our names and everything about the expedition."

"And what about Jackson?"

"Well, it seems that Jackson was the one who found Xinth. But he had fallen into the antechamber, and lay dying. His body was destroyed by oxygen saturation, and Xinth... well, as he described it, *assimilated* him." Gould didn't seem particularly comfortable with the word.

"All your technological miracles," Agatha said, without taking her eyes off the Builder, "You got them from him, didn't you?"

"Yes," Karlhammer admitted straightforwardly.

She still couldn't believe that this was all real. It just seemed too fantastic. An ancient ancestor of mankind, in a pyramid in Antarctica, handing down new technologies to Earth's most powerful technocrat? How could it possibly be true?

"Now, Agent Devenworth," Karlhammer said, adopting a more serious tone as he addressed her, "I have kept my word, and brought you to Ron Jackson—such as he is. Now it's time for you to uphold your end of the bargain. Tell me how you found us, and why you came to McMurdo."

"Just one more thing," she replied, and took two steps forward until she was standing right in front of the glass and looking up at the towering Builder, who also took a step forward. If not for the glass wall between them, he could have reached out his long arms and touched her. In front of him, she felt tiny and fragile.

"Can I talk to him?"

Gould spoke before Karlhammer could reply. "Of course you can. There's a speaker and microphone connection between us. He's heard everything we've said this whole time."

Agatha licked her dry and chapped lips before she spoke. "Hello," she said, not knowing what else to say, and feeling pretty stupid as soon as she'd said it.

"I greet you, Agent Devenworth," a deep bass voice spoke, and the words seemed to reverberate into infinity. The Builder's dark lips barely moved at all, but there was no doubt that the words came from him.

"You know me?"

"You introduced yourself in Cavern One, and I am connected to all the monitoring systems in this facility."

"Your name is Xinth?"

"It is my first name."

"Your first?"

"Over the ages, mankind has given me many names. Once, the people of your belief system called me Cain," the being's voice boomed. It was so powerful that Agatha felt smaller with every word.

"Cain? You mean, the Cain who slew his brother Abel?" she asked, shooting a nervous look over her shoulder at Pano, who was standing next to Filio. Both were watching what was happening in front of them with open mouths.

"Yes. I did not slay my brother, I banished him. But the historical record of the new mankind is... imperfect."

"Why are you helping us? All the technologies to protect the Earth's climate, all the advancements in medicine, they're coming from you, aren't they?" she asked.

"Because you are worthy."

"The lottery system," Karlhammer added, walking up next to her. "That's how I proved to him that we humans can, with certain means, compensate for our weaknesses with the good in us. When I did that, he showed us the most fantastic technological solutions."

"And Ron Jackson? What have you done with him?" Agatha asked Xinth, turning back to look at him. She could not interpret his jet-black eyes without visible iris or pupil.

"You are not capable of fully understanding the process," he boomed, and for the first time he moved, opening his right hand. The movement was fluid, almost meditative. Agatha could not escape the feeling that the way the Builder spoke to her was gentle, yet distinctly condescending, like a father talking to a child in deliberately childish terms.

"It is truth that his... *being* was absorbed into me. His physical body, however, no longer exists."

"All right, then," Karlhammer said. "Heard enough? Because I really must know what—"

Agatha raised a hand. "Why did you pick this place for your base?" she asked the South African. "And what exactly is it you're doing here? Why didn't you take him somewhere else?"

"With Xinth's help, we are developing a transport system that will take us to Mars. That's happening a few levels down from this one. It's nearly ready, and as soon as it is, Doctor Amorosa here," he said, pointing to Filio, who was transfixed by the Builder, "will lead the team that's going to make the journey."

"To do what, exactly?"

"To recover the evidence of the existence of *The Enemy*, and destroy the Obelisk."

"The Obelisk?" Filio suddenly shouted, and hurried over to stand next to Karlhammer. "You mean the Mars monolith?"

"Yes. You were there yourself," he explained, and Filio's face suddenly turned ashen.

"You brought him here. You released him from his banishment," the Builder boomed. The penetrating voice gave no sign of whether there was any emotion behind this pronouncement.

"But... I... I don't remember it," Filio said. She seemed confused, and her eyes looked like they were focusing on something very far away.

"That is because he is making you forget. He is a master of deception."

"Who are we talking about here?" Agatha asked. "You two aren't talking about *The Enemy* that the Sons of Terra are always going on about, are you?"

"Yes, Agent Devenworth," the Builder replied, looking down on her. "Your ancestors knew him as Abel from the records I left behind, but they got the story wrong. It was I who banished him to his eternal grave on the sister planet, and thus I who brought death upon him. Under my eternal watch, he would never again be a danger to Tsanth."

"Tsanth?"

"The Earth," Karlhammer translated. Then he grabbed Agatha by both shoulders to turn her to face him, and looked her straight in the eyes with an insistent stare. "Listen. I need you to tell me right now how you got here, and what happened at McMurdo, do you understand?"

Agatha took a deep breath and nodded. "We were following the trail from a small private airstrip in South Africa..."

"Malmesbury?" Karlhammer interrupted her with a frown. "Why did they let you get that far?"

"Well, if you're referring to the police and intelligence operatives who tried to kidnap us, on your behalf I take it—they were eliminated. By an unknown. A sniper."

Karlhammer's frown turned into a wide-eyed look, and there was a new expression on his face that Agatha could not immediately interpret.

"Then we flew straight to McMurdo because we learned that Jackson had apparently traveled to Hobart. And there's nothing of interest there except transport ships for Antarctic expeditions," she continued. "When we landed in McMurdo..." She exchanged a glance with Pano. "Well, I don't know how to explain it. Suddenly there was nobody there. Later, a couple of hours out from the station, we found a lot of bodies. We assume they were the personnel."

"They're dead?" Karlhammer asked, alarmed. She realized that the flashing she saw in his eyes was expressing concern, perhaps even fear, and that made her very nervous.

"Yes. I'm sorry."

"Were you followed?"

"From South Africa?"

Karlhammer nodded.

"No." Agatha shook her head. "We were on a military plane, with just the two pilots, me, my partner, and Sergeant Eversman."

"Are you sure?"

"Well, I didn't check the cockpit or the cargo hold, but—"

"Did anything else happen on the flight or at McMurdo?" Karlhammer pressed her, and exchanged a look with the Builder, who was still looking down on them impassively from above. "Anything strange?"

"Well, since you ask, there was a moment during the flight when we lost radio contact with the cockpit, but it was just some temporary interference. What was weird, though, was that after we got out on the tarmac at McMurdo, we apparently had some kind of blackout. Hofer and I figured out that we had lost about six hours that we just couldn't remember."

Karlhammer was agitated now, and he looked at her insistently. "When you got here, what else happened?"

"We ran into your jamming field. We kind of got lucky that we noticed what it was, and didn't just assume the hovercraft had failed. It just so happens that Pano here wears an old-fashioned hearing aid because he's deaf in his left ear."

"Thank God," Karlhammer sighed. "The field is still intact."

"Well, about that... I'm afraid we knocked out one of your jamming nodes," Agatha confessed.

Karlhammer immediately stiffened. "What... did... you... say...?" All the color vanished from his face. It was the first time she had seen him fearful and not in control.

"Well, we couldn't go any further, because the field also seemed to take Sergeant Eversman out of action, just like the two pilots. They—"

Karlhammer was no longer listening. "Rogers," he called out to one of the soldiers that had escorted them. "Red alert.

Lock down the whole facility and make sure nothing gets inside."

The soldier nodded, but before he could move the ground beneath their feet shook slightly, and a painfully loud alarm began wailing throughout the installation. Lights dimmed automatically, and emergency lights bathed the entire area in a threatening red.

"Too late," Gould gasped. "*He* is already here."

36

THE INTRUDER, 2042

The man in the black suit still had a mild headache. The breach in the jamming field that the two agents had made had enabled him to enter, but had not left him completely unharmed.

Standing before the entrance to the pyramid, he closed his eyes and saw in his mind how Sergeant Eversman was killing the two guards escorting him, and then running through the facility.

With precise impulses, the man in the black suit guided him down two corridors. Along the way he had to kill a woman in a red uniform who blocked his way, staring at him in shock. Then he had made it to the long access shaft, which was manned by four other soldiers who were sitting around a table playing cards.

The man in the black suit waited for the exact right moment to push his finger against the massive steel composite door that was keeping him locked out in the cold. He couldn't get through it, but the material buckled against the strength of his will, and groaned so loudly that the men below all looked up. It was at that exact moment that

Eversman was in position to grab one of the automatic rifles from the clamps along the wall and mowed all four men down with a long burst of fire. He then grabbed a grenade belt, got on the heavy freight elevator that ran diagonally upwards, and set off to the top of the shaft.

It took half a minute, and then Eversman had arrived at the door separating them. Now the man in the black suit took a few steps to one side. On the inside of the door, Eversman pulled the pins from all the grenades and blew himself up.

The ground trembled slightly, and rocks came crashing down onto the ice around him. Amazingly, the door had held—rather than being blown off its hinges, it had just been bent outwards, more than enough for the man in the black suit to grab it and pull it completely free with a violent jerk.

"Well then, let's do this, shall we?" he said to himself with a grin, and set off down into the shaft, over the piles of rubble and the scattered remnants of Sergeant Eversman.

37

FILIO AMOROSA, 2042

Filio heard the crackle of gunfire and the screams of the dying, and none of it sounded as far away as she would have liked.

"This is Karlhammer," the head of the Human Foundation said, speaking loudly into a small device on his wrist. "Evacuation Plan Delta. Repeat. Evacuation Plan Delta! All civilian personnel to the lower levels immediately. Security personnel to the throne room!"

"*The Enemy* is here?" Peter Gould was still stammering, and looking around in panic as if the walls themselves might swallow him up at any moment.

"I sense his presence," Xinth's voice droned, and the giant figure of the Builder tilted his head a little, as if he was just noticing something terribly interesting. "It is... strange."

"Take your positions," Karlhammer ordered the two soldiers, and they ran to the sides of the glass case, then knelt and trained their submachine guns on the armored doors through which Filio and the others had come.

"We wouldn't mind some guns," Pano remarked. Karlhammer rolled his eyes and made an impatient gesture to his security officers, who produced pistols and tossed them to the two agents.

"What should we be expecting?" Agatha asked.

Filio thought that the female agent seemed amazingly calm, although her eyes were looking everywhere and nowhere at all times.

"Anything. *The Enemy* has exactly one goal—to kill Xinth, because he is the only one standing between him and his plan."

"What's his plan?"

"We don't know. Not even Xinth knows for sure. What we do know is that he created some kind of virus that mutates brain cells," Karlhammer summarized. He kept licking his lips as he spoke. "The Sons of Terra were able to isolate the virus after they killed some of his agents."

"Is there any other way out of here?" Filio asked, as the sounds of the fighting grew louder.

"No," he said, shaking his head. "Only through his chamber."

Karlhammer waved towards the glass box in which the Builder was standing and looking at them, seemingly interested and calm, as if nothing much was happening. "Underneath it. In the middle of the chamber, there's a passageway going down."

"Unfortunate," the Builder's voice boomed, and now it sounded very echoey and drawn out. "It seems he has already attacked the power network. The passageway no longer opens."

He was pointing to the center of his glass chamber when the lights went out. The screaming alarm signal died in an instant, replaced by a sudden, deafening silence underscored by the rising sounds of shouting and screaming, coming all too close now.

"Shit," Pano cursed. An instant later, a number of ceiling spotlights and a pale emergency lighting system switched on, bathing the room in a diffuse twilight glow.

The security door was shaken by a tremendous blow, and then another. The soldiers' flashlights gleamed off the cold metal, which was now significantly distorted in the middle.

Karlhammer and Gould moved back towards the wall, cautiously, step by cautious step. Agatha and Pano followed them, guns trained on the door.

Filio moved quickly after them, her heart pounding violently in her chest and her breaths becoming ever shorter.

At that moment, the door flew off its hinges into the room, crashing against the glass box and cracking it. The Builder stiffened slightly, but otherwise remained motionless. At first Filio saw nothing but smoke in the opening where the door had been, and then muzzle flashes from the machine guns of the security guards lit up the doorway. As they changed clips, she saw two perforated bodies squashed against the transparent plates in front of the door, crumpled in rapidly growing pools of blood.

Then, through the smoke, a man in a flawless black suit stepped into the room and looked around, smiling. His hair was short, black, and trimmed to ludicrous precision, and his features were smooth and nondescript. If not for the unspeakable malice that emanated from his eyes, he would have looked like an insurance agent. He looked from one of the armed men to the next. Just when they were about to fire again, they simply stopped.

"Uh-uh-uh," the intruder admonished, his smile becoming almost disappointed, as if he was scolding a pet and it made him feel guilty. Then the two soldiers began to turn, slowly, towards each other, and at the very moment someone shouted "NO!" they pulled their triggers simultaneously, and both collapsed to the floor.

His next words were uttered towards Filio and the others, who were holding each other back against the far wall. "You won't be shooting me," he ordered. Agatha and Pano aimed their guns at the intruder, but the triggers didn't get pulled.

"Shoot, dammit!" Filio howled, but nothing happened. Their hands trembled violently, and beads of sweat broke out on their brows.

"Well, look who we have here," the man in the black suit said, moving towards Xinth. "So this is where you've been hiding. The old homestead. I must say, I'd never have thought of that. To me it seems so..."

"Obvious?" the Builder's voice boomed. "Then it seems I made a correct choice for this location. What is this form you are in?"

"Oh, sadly, I was unable to come in person. This here is merely a vessel. Small, constricting... but useful."

"It is wrong."

"This? It's not wrong any more than it's wrong for a human to eat an animal. It serves a purpose. There's nothing evil about it."

"Where are you?" Xinth asked, unmoved.

"Nuh-uh-uh," snorted the man in the black suit, waving a raised index finger scoldingly. "I'm not here to tell you where my body is, the body you damned to death."

The intruder walked slowly to the body of the soldier on the right and bent down to pick up his machine gun.

"No!" Gould shouted, and ran from his position on the wall next to Filio, throwing himself at the intruder.

Completely unperturbed by this, the man in the black suit looked up and said calmly, "Stay right there."

As if someone had flipped a switch, Gould froze on the spot. Only his eyes continued to move, staring at his opponent in disbelief.

"I don't like being interrupted." The intruder pointed the submachine gun straight at Gould and fired. Gould's head rocked back, and he fell to the ground lifeless. The man then raised the weapon towards Xinth.

"I remember very well your final words before you banished me," he said to the Builder. "I remember them exactly. You told me, 'There is no more place for you in the Old World as there is in the New.' These are words that I choose to return to you, now."

A little smile, then he pulled the trigger, unloading a volley of shots into the exact spot in the glass where the huge steel door had cracked it.

Glass splinters and shards flew everywhere, but the structure of the glass still held. Barely. Filio was sure it wouldn't hold up to much more.

While she was still thinking this, and watching the spectacle unfolding before her in shock, Karlhammer screamed and ran at the murderous intruder. He even almost made it to him, but just before they met, the man in the black suit casually swung his weapon around and hit Karlhammer in the head with the butt of the rifle, so hard that he spun several meters to the side, where he fell, bleeding, to the ground and remaining motionless.

"I... I can't shoot him," Agatha croaked hoarsely, raising a hand to rub herself in the temple. Her face was twisted and clenched in pain.

"I know," Pano answered her, struggling. "I think he's controlling us somehow."

"The security officer," Filio heard Agatha whisper. "There's a knife on his belt. Maybe I can get to it."

"No, let me try it. I've got an idea," Pano answered her, as the stranger emptied the rest of his clip into the glass and loaded a new one. The Builder still stood, as motionless as ever, stoically looking his death in the eye from within the glass box that had become his undoing.

"Hey!" Agatha shouted at the intruder, firing a bullet into the transparent plate under his feet. Unable to penetrate it, the bullet ricocheted helplessly off.

"Do you know where your spleen is, Agent Devenworth?" the man in the black suit asked with a malevolent smile.

Agatha nodded, although it looked like she was struggling to not do so.

The intruder was aiming his gun directly at Xinth through the hole in the glass he had just created. "I want you to hold your gun there and pull the trigger, so you'll see what it feels like to interrupt me," he said tersely.

Pano screamed in rage as Agatha held the gun to her own torso and pulled the trigger. Screaming, she fell to the floor, dropping her gun and clutching her side. Filio leapt to her and reflexively pressed her hands against the bleeding wound.

Then a lot of things happened very fast. Pano raised his gun and held it very close to his right ear, pointed skyward. He squeezed the trigger, and screamed at the moment the shot sounded. A thin film of blood ran down his earlobe. At the same moment, the intruder fired the machine gun again. Three bullets passed through the glass and struck Xinth in the chest, the Builder flinching with each one.

A wailing sound arose, so penetrating and profound that it shook Filio to the core.

Pano ran forward, and the intruder's gaze hit him.

"Stop!" he ordered, but the Capitano did not stop. He made a running dive to the body of the security officer and drew the combat knife from his belt.

The man in the black suit spun around with his gun and fired but missed Pano, who in the same moment extended his arm and threw the knife at the stranger. A bullet then tore through Pano's right leg and he fell, screaming in surprise, but the knife sailed through the air like a gleaming flash and hit the intruder in his left eye.

For a long moment nothing happened, and the man just stood there, as if paralyzed. Then, finally, his machine gun lowered and slipped from his grip and he fell backward.

Pano stood up, his face twisted in pain, and limped over to Filio and Agatha, whose mouth was flung wide open in a silent scream of agony.

Filio was looking back and forth between Agatha and the Builder, who was sinking to his knees like a felled tree, dark-red blood running from his chest.

"Take care of her," she told the agent, but he didn't respond, as if he didn't hear her. Instead, he knelt down next to Agatha and told Filio to let him take over.

"I'LL DO IT," he said, extremely loudly, and she suddenly understood.

He can't hear.

With two quick gestures, she showed him how to keep pressure on the wound, and then ran to Karlhammer who was either unconscious or dead. Without thinking, she looked at his right wrist, where he had spoken his commands, and tried to recall his last announcement.

"Intruder neutralized," she shouted into the small band around Karlhammer's wrist. "Paramedics to the... to the throne room. Immediately!" She then stood and ran to the glass box, where the Builder was still hunched over on the floor and seemed to be gasping for air.

Filio grabbed the gun from the now-dead man in the black suit and began frantically pounding the hole in the glass with it, to make a passage big enough for her to get through. It took much too long, but she didn't stop until she heard voices shouting behind her. Looking over her shoulder, she saw two stretchers being rolled in. As they entered the room, paramedics in their red-and-white uniforms looked around in shock, and then spread out among the people lying on the ground. Two came to Filio and began helping her with the glass. Working together, the three of them created an opening they could slip through.

"We have to save him," she cried, gasping, and the paramedics, two brunette women with pale eyes, nodded. "Let us do our jobs," one told her.

"I'm a doctor," Filio replied, helping them get the Builder onto his back. He was incredibly heavy and they almost dropped him, but in the end they succeeded in getting him into a reclining position, more or less gently. His eyes were wide open, as was his mouth, looking like a fish on land gasping for air.

"He's suffocating, get him some oxygen!" Filio said, but one of the paramedics had already stepped away and come back with an oxygen device. She pressed the much too small mouthpiece over the being's mouth and nose as best she could and then pressed a few keys to start the flow of oxygen.

"Do you have an operating room?" Filio asked.

"Yes," one of the women replied, blowing a strand of hair that had fallen across her face. "But how are we supposed to operate on him? We don't even know if his anatomy is anything like our own."

"Well, we have to try. Get the OR set up. Call every doctor you've got. We have to move fast. Same goes for the agent there," Filio said, pushing the paramedic aside and tearing off her own shirt to press against the heavily bleeding wounds in the Builder's mighty chest.

His head turned in her direction. His eyelids were fluttering slightly, and he raised a hand towards her head. She wanted to pull back, but something told her to just let it happen. It was hard to turn away from the eyes, like black opals, staring hypnotically at her.

When the touch happened, Filio felt a slight tingling in her skin and then, in an instant, she was gone.

EPILOGUE

Filio was once again standing on a rocky cliff. Next to her, Xinth towered like a colossus. He was uninjured and dressed in some strange kind of raiment. It was skintight and bright, and seemed to be glowing from within, like illuminated reflector strips.

Below them stretched a broad valley full of lush green grasslands, bounded by three distant pyramids, one at each of three compass points on the horizon. Turning around, she saw another pyramid directly behind her.

Dotting the grassy landscape were several dozen flat, gray shapes like the concrete landing pads for helicopters she knew from Cape Canaveral and the Guyana Space Center. The ones furthest from them were tiny, barely perceptible gray dots in the distance.

Dozens of giant ships were lifting off from the smooth gray pads. They were slightly flattened spheres that reminded her of scarab beetles. As they rose majestically, as if untouched by gravity, their landing gear retracted and then they each disappeared, one by one.

After a few seconds' delay, Filio was assailed by a series

of booming sounds so loud she had to put her hands over her ears for fear of passing out.

"What was that?" she asked, once the ships were all gone—as if they had never been there—and the loud booms had stopped reverberating.

"This is the dawn of our civilization, over sixty million solar cycles ago," Xinth announced, his booming bass voice making it sound like some kind of proclamation. There was something sad in him, an impression that not even his mighty figure could hide.

"When we unlocked the secrets of the threefold four dimensions, we discovered our way to the stars. And after a virus nearly wiped us out, many decided to leave the Earth," he explained, looking down at the now idyllic grasslands dotted with gray launch sites below.

"The... threefold four dimensions?" Filio asked, confused.

"Yes. The four dimensions of space-time your species has focused on are just the beginning. But this is not why I brought you here." Xinth gestured, and everything in front of them changed.

A new landscape arose. The green on the hills had a slightly yellow tint and the sun in the sky above was somehow smaller.

"Where are we?"

"On Mars."

"On Mars?"

"Yes. In our time we called it Goldan, which means something like 'Little Brother.' This was our sister planet, which we had to abandon because of a nuclear disaster. Abandoned for Earth," the Builder told her, and as he said it a slurping sound escaped from his throat.

"That... so that means we're not originally from Earth,

but from Mars? Are we even descended from you?" Her mind raced from this thought to a thousand different possibilities, and they all began swarming around in her head in an impenetrable tangle.

"Yes, and no. You arose from the same amino acids, but not directly from our evolutionary gene pool. But we also went through the same cycle of development, from primate to the humanoids that we ultimately became."

"I think I need time to take this all in. If I even can. Why did you bring me here?"

"Because you need to understand, before I die."

"But we can save you," she protested, and wondered what was happening in reality at that moment. Was time passing differently in this... *vision?* Or was she still huddled over his body, and had the others just tried to separate them?

"I do not think so. So understand."

In the sky above ancient Mars, a glowing point appeared and began to get larger and larger, until she could see it was one of the spaceships she had just watched rise up from Earth and disappear. It landed in front of a long mountain ridge, and in the same moment, as the landing appendages touched the grass, its rear section, where its large, plate-shaped nacelles were, exploded. The ship tilted backward and stayed there, a smoking wreck in the sunlight. Small fires caught in the grass and began spreading.

"I don't understand."

"Some of my people decided against the Exodus, because they did not trust the propulsion system that leads through the Dodecasphere. We were never again able to contact our fleet, and so we felt vindicated in our choice. But the day came when one of the ships came back. It was the ship of a captain named Hortat, who told of the miracles of the Dodecasphere. Many of those who have stayed followed him like helpless creatures and I, as their leader, sensed that something was wrong. It is a very long tale, but I succeeded in placing an explosive charge on his ship, and I manipulated his ship's AI to fly it to Mars. I knew that Hortat would never be able to leave there without a functioning drive and the radiation there would destroy him."

Xinth made that slurping sound again, which came across to Filio as something like a sigh. "But it was too late. He had left behind some kind of virus, and soon it was ravaging our civilization. In his final transmission, he revealed to me that the cure for the death of the mind, as he called it, would be found in the Dodecasphere, and he would take me to it if I brought him back from his tomb on Mars. I believed he was bluffing, and I did not take his bait."

The Builder's figure seemed to flicker for an instant, like a faulty hologram, but stabilized again and he turned to face her.

"I still don't understand," she reiterated. It had all gone so fast. What was the being trying to tell her?

"I do not have much more time. You will find the wreck of the ship at the location of the monolith, where you recovered the fossil remains of Hortat."

Filio wanted to reply, but Xinth raised a mighty hand and silenced her. "Hortat, whom you call *The Enemy*, has somehow managed to survive and to assume other bodies. If there is an answer to the question of how he has done this and how it can be stopped, it is there."

The Builder pointed to the wreckage of the ship.

"You do not have much time. He has already brought many of the most powerful of your world under his control, as I feared. Whatever his game is, he is not the same as the Hortat I knew, before his jump through the Dodecasphere."

The Fossil

"Dodecasphere? I don't understand," Filio said, and shook her head nervously. "What does this all mean?" She had the inescapable feeling that she was staring at something that she had to understand at any cost, and she was helpless, not understanding anything at all—not what she was seeing, and not what she was hearing.

"Search the ship. In my chamber beneath the glass box, there is a data globe that contains the fleet key. That key will give you access to the AI on Hortat's ship, if you can connect it to a power source. If there is any information about what he intends to do here and what really happened on your mission, you will find it there. But you have to get there before he does, no matter what. Otherwise it will be too late."

Before Filio could reply, the vision dissolved, and she was staring again into the Builder's face, but his real, physical face, his huge body beneath her. But the face had gone pale, and the eyes were now covered by mighty eyelids.

"Doctor? DOCTOR!" a man she hadn't even noticed was there was screaming at her. It was as if they had come from different worlds. She turned to him, stunned.

"You have to let him go, so we can get him onto the stretcher!"

Filio let him go and fell, staggering, to one side, landing with her back against the glass plate. Her mind was racing as if she had gone mad, the images that the Builder had shown her swimming before her eyes as she tried to make sense of them.

Mars had been her goal all along, but not in the way she had thought. The Red Planet was a tomb—the tomb of *The Enemy*, who at that moment was trying to take over the Earth.

Out of the corner of her eye, she saw Xinth being lifted

by six paramedics through the hole in the glass and onto a stretcher. Behind them, she saw Agatha and Karlhammer being hurriedly rolled out of the room. Pano was holding Agatha's hand and running next to her as they disappeared into the corridor door.

It's not too late, not yet, Filio told herself. It took all her strength to struggle her way to her feet. Her work was not done yet.

AFTERWORD

The *Fossil*-Trilogy will be continued with the second volume *The Fossil 2*, expected to be published in May 2021.

Visit www.joshuatcalvert.com to subscribe to my newsletter, to be informed of all upcoming releases and receive exclusive epilogues and advance information about my projects. Subscribers can also take part in anonymous surveys about my books and even vote on what story I will write next!

If you liked this book, please consider leaving a review on Amazon. This is the best way to support me as an independent author.

. . .

JOSHUA T. CALVERT

Did you notice any errors or plot holes? Would you like to contact me with criticism or feedback—positive or negative? I am happy to answer every single e-mail! Please write to me at joshua@joshuatcalvert.com

Yours sincerely, Joshua T. Calvert

February 2021, La Palma

CHARACTER INDEX
LISTED BY COMMON FORM OF REFERENCE

Alberto (Angulo Camacho): Treasure diver and engineer on the *Ocean's Bitch*.

Aluwi, Tombatu: Agent of the South African intelligence service.

Audrey (Burton): Member of the *Mars Two* mission, engineer.

Brown, Barbara: Wife of Bob Brown.

Brown, Bob: Republican U.S. Senator.

Dana (Pickert): Student at LMU Munich.

Degeunes, Liza: Secretary to Jenning Miller.

Devenworth, Agatha: Special agent at the Counter-Terrorist Directive (CTD), United States citizen.

Enemy, The: Alien entity hypothesized by the Sons of Terra terrorist organization to be secretly pulling the strings of world affairs, and who has infiltrated national institutions worldwide.

Engels, Jakob: Hired bodyguard for Filio Amorosa.

Filio Amorosa: Member and sole survivor of the first Mars mission, *Mars One*, and crewmember on the *Ocean's Bitch*.

Gould, Peter: Former CFO of the Human Foundation.

Greulich, Alexander: Chancellor of the Federal Republic of Germany.

Hortat: Captain who became *The Enemy*.

Hue Tao Xing: Member of the *Mars Two* mission, medical doctor.

Jackson, Ron: Professor of Archaeology, Anthropology and Linguistics.

Jane Sarandon: Treasure diver and first officer on the *Ocean's Bitch*.

Johnson, Betty: Secretary to Jenning Miller.

Jones, Hugh: Director of SETEF (Space Exploration Training and Evaluation Facility) in Nevada.

Karlhammer, Luther: South African engineer, inventor and technocrat, head of the Human Foundation.

Knowles, Timothy: Pilot of the *Mars One* mission. Died in the *Mars One* disaster of 2040.

Longchamps, Michel: Commander of the *Mars Two* mission.

Marcello (Bonimba): Receptionist at Cape House Green Hostel in Cape Town.

Marcello (Bordotta): Member of the *Mars Two* mission, xenobiologist.

Marks, Heinrich: Geophysicist on the first Mars mission, *Mars One*. Deceased.

Miller, Jenning: Director of the Counter-Terrorist Directive (CTD).

Mombatu, Mitchu: Secretary-General of the United Nations.

Moosbech, Petr: Agent of the South African intelligence service.

Morris, Laura: Assistant to Hugh Jones, Director of SETEF.

Nikitu, Mayuka: Japanese envoy to the United Nations.

Pano Hofer: Italian police officer with the rank of Captain (*Capitano*), seconded to Europol. From the (German-speaking) South Tyrol region.

Patchuvi, Mitra: Indian archaeologist and professor at the University of Delhi.

Phelps, Montgomery: President of the United States of America.

Revi, Putram: Member of the *Mars Two* mission, botanist.

Richter, Nicole: Former member of *Mars Two*, removed from the mission.

Rietenbach, Manfred: Director-General of ESA (the European Space Agency).

Romain (Alhy): Captain of the *Ocean's Bitch*.

Ross, James: Doctor of Archaeology, assistant to Prof. Patchuvi.

Shapiro, Warren: Deputy director of the CTD (Counter-Terrorist Directive).

Solly Shoke: Former receptionist at Cape House Green Hostel in Cape Town.

Spärling, Regina: Secretary to ESA Director-General Manfred Rietenbach.

Tatyana Kalashnikova: Member of the *Mars Two* mission, chemist.

Thomas (Bergensen): Treasure diver on the *Ocean's Bitch*.

Vlachenko, Dimitry: Commander of the first Mars mission, *Mars One*. Deceased.

Wittman, James: Member of the *Mars Two* mission, geophysicist.

Workai Dalam: Legendary treasure diver, disappeared.

Xinth: Builder.

GLOSSARY

Accelerator mass spectrometry: Technique used to date fossils and archaeological finds using a particle accelerator.

ACV: Air-cushion vehicle.

Andesite: Form of igneous volcanic rock.

Antarctic Treaty: An international agreement that establishes that uninhabited Antarctica between 60 and 90° S shall remain reserved exclusively for peaceful use and specifically for scientific research.

AR cabin: Enclosed area equipped with Augmented Reality glasses, haptic suit with feedback sensors and multidimensional treadmill for a completely immersive virtual reality experience.

AR glasses: Augmented Reality glasses.

AR harness: Exoskeleton that, in combination with Augmented Reality, can be used to perform work on an object remotely through a robot receiving the signals from the harness.

Basalt: Form of igneous volcanic rock.

BCD: Buoyancy Control Device. Wearable buoyancy compensator, i.e. a vest that a diver can inflate or deflate with buoyant gas at the touch of a button.

BND: *Bundesnachrichtendienst*, the German foreign intelligence service.

Breathing Earth One: System of algae "carpets" constructed by the Human Foundation and located in the Pacific Ocean to filter CO_2 out of the atmosphere and convert it into oxygen.

Breathing Earth Two: System of algae "carpets" constructed by the Human Foundation and located in the Atlantic Ocean to filter CO_2 out of the atmosphere and convert it into oxygen.

C-220 Albatross: Military turboprop transport aircraft designed for heavy cargo or moving large troop contingents.

Cape House Green: Hostel in Cape Town.

Cleaning robot: Autonomous robot that performs cleaning processes both indoors and outdoors.

Clean Ocean Project: Human Foundation project designed to remove plastic waste from the oceans.

CTD: Counter-Terrorist Directive. Intelligence unit falling under the authority of the United States Department of Homeland Security.

Data glasses: Augmented Reality glasses with audio earbuds and a completely enclosed visual area.

Desertec: Solar project in the northwestern Sahara operated under a collaboration between the EU and the Maghreb states.

Drone ship: Autonomous transport craft that automatically collects algae from sweeper ships and adds them to the algae carpets in the Pacific and the Atlantic.

Earthling: Colloquial name for a supporter of the Human Foundation and participant in the lottery system.

EDI: Ship's AI on *Mars One*.

ESA: European Space Agency, the space agency of the European Union.

Fission cutter: Mono-bonded blade made of a single-molecule layer, capable of cutting even the hardest materials.

Flettner Rotor: A rotating cylinder exposed to an airflow that generates propulsive force perpendicular to the airflow utilizing the Magnus effect. It is the basis of a zero-emissions propulsion system first patented and used as a ship propulsion system by Anton Flettner.

Furious Fifties: Region of the Antarctic Circumpolar Current (West Wind Drift) between 50 and 60° S latitude. Characterized by violent storms.

Gloucester: British-registered scrapper ship.

GMC E-Falcon: Electric SUV made by U.S. car manufacturer GMC.

Iridium: A chemical element, precious metal and a metal belonging to the platinum group. Known to be the most corrosion-resistant element.

Jet: A handheld device with a propeller system used by divers to move more quickly through the water.

Maglock: Locking system that uses polarized magnets for closing and opening.

Maglocksmith: Device for used for picking maglocks.

McMurdo: Antarctic research station first operated by the United States (and later the Human Foundation).

M.E.E.: Mass Extinction Event.

MMR 3: Mars Mission Reconnaissance 3. The third robotic mission to Mars sent to prepare for the human-crewed landing.

Muon detector: Detector system that uses cosmic rays to detect and locate subterranean cavities.

Muon tomography: A method for three-dimensional imaging of large-volume objects using muons found in cosmic rays.

NASA: National Aeronautics and Space Administration, the space agency of the United States of America.

National Intelligence Service: The South African domestic intelligence service.

Ocean's Bitch: Old scrapper ship under the command of Romain Alhy.

Okamalé: A ship belonging to the Coast Guard of the Maldive Islands.

Paleocene: Geological epoch of the Earth that began around 66 million years ago and ended about 56 million years ago.

Paleogene: A geological epoch of the Earth, lasting from approximately 66 million years ago until the start of the Neogene approximately 23.03 million years ago.

Pleistocene: Geological epoch of the Earth that began around 2.588 million years ago and ended about 12,000 years ago with the dawn of the modern era.

Project Blue Hole: Research project exploring the mysterious "blue hole" in Antarctica, the location where the

Antarctic ice sheet exhibited the phenomenon of melting from the inside out.

Project Globe: Human Foundation project to use microwaves to transmit energy from space-based solar power systems to earth.

Project Heritage: A top-secret Human Foundation project.

Pyramid Mountain: A 2,800-meter-high mountain in Antarctica, roughly pyramid-shaped.

Regolith: Covering layer of loose material on top of an underlying source material, which formed on rocky planets in the solar system as the result of various geological processes.

Roaring Forties: Region of the Antarctic Circumpolar Current (West Wind Drift) between 40° and 50° S latitude. Characterized by violent storms.

Roskosmos: Space Agency of the Russian Federation.

Scrapper: Term denoting a treasure hunter searching for wreckage from *Mars One* in the Indian Ocean.

Self-driving software: Artificial intelligence responsible for the control and safety of a vehicle, and capable of autonomous action.

SETEF: Space Exploration Training and Evaluation Facility. Astronaut training center located north of Reno, Nevada, in the United States.

Sharkskin: Skintight neoprene suit worn to protect divers from minor injuries.

Solar Genesis: Human Foundation project in its planning phase to use giant solar sails in near-Earth orbit to supply the Earth with clean energy.

Sons of Terra: A terrorist organization the goals of which include warning humanity against an alien presence known as *The Enemy,* which they claim has taken control of the world powers.

Space Dream: Lottery operated by the Human Foundation promising the winner a place on a future Mars mission.

Sweeper: Huge autonomous ship sweeping the world's oceans to collect plastic waste, which it then breaks down into carbon dioxide and hydrogen.

Thiruvanamthapuram: A metropolitan city in Southern India.

Transducer net: A mesh of electrodes that can be worn on the head and which measures and interprets brain waves to produce speech output through a computer system.

TSA: Transportation Security Administration. The American federal agency tasked with the security of the transportation sector.

Universal connector: The universal interface architecture that replaced the USB system.

Volkswagen E: The best-selling electric car in the world.

X-ray fluorescence analysis: A materials analysis method based on X-ray fluorescence. It is one of the most commonly used methods for qualitative and quantitative analysis of the elemental composition of a sample.

COPYRIGHT

Editing: Steven and Marcia Kwiecinski
English translation: Kyle Wohlmut
Cover: Cakamura Designs

First edition: 2021
© Joshua Tree Ltd. all rights reserved.
Joshua Tree Limited
Skoutari 25, App. 73
8560 Peyia
Cyprus

www.joshuatcalvert.com
joshua@joshuatcalvert.com

Printed in Great Britain
by Amazon

The Waking Worlds
- BOOK I -

A CLATTER OF CHAINS

by A. van Wyck

The Waking Worlds Series Copyright © 2016 by André van Wyck
First edition: A Clatter of Chains Copyright © 2016 by André van Wyck
Second edition: A Clatter of Chains Copyright © 2021 by André van Wyck

All rights reserved.

No part of this book may be reproduced in any form or by any electronic or mechanical means including information storage and retrieval systems, without permission in writing from the author. The only exception is by a reviewer, who may quote short excerpts in a review.

Cover designed by Cherie Foxley

This book is a work of fiction. Names, characters, places and incidents either are products of the author's imagination or are used fictitiously. Any resemblance to actual persons, living or deceased, events, or locales is entirely coincidental.

ACKNOWLEDGMENTS

To my wife, Lindie, for getting me this far. I know it wasn't easy. You're a better hero than I ever could have written.

To my mother, Annie, who believed even when I didn't, thank you.

And to my poor proof readers, who suffered through selflessly. Thanks to Jandré, Thys, Sanet and Mia.

Special thanks goes to Kevin, for his notes and insights on this second edition.

ALSO BY ANDRÉ VAN WYCK

The Waking Worlds Series
A Clatter of Chains
A Fray of Furies

The Patchwork Prince Series
Stumbling Stoned

visit:
---www.andrevanwyck.com---